HOMICIDE—OR COSMIC CATASTROPHE?

Detective Vernon Moody is a modern cop who likes to catch killers the modern way—with computer webs, databases, and common sense.

So he's not happy when his latest case revolves around the supposedly mystical properties of a lost Navaho sandpainting. Or when the painting leads him to suspect an alien presence in his modern world.

Now Moody's getting scared, and what started out as a routine murder investigation may uncover the very nature of reality—or destroy it forever!

CYBER WAY

The newest and boldest science fiction thriller from Alan Dean Foster!

CYBER WAY

ALAN DEAN FOSTER

ACE BOOKS, NEW YORK

This book is an Ace original edition,
and has never been previously published.

CYBER WAY

An Ace Book / published by arrangement with
the author

PRINTING HISTORY
Ace edition / May 1990

ISBN: 0-441-13245-6

Ace Books are published by The Berkley Publishing Group,
200 Madison Avenue, New York, New York 10016.
The name "ACE" and the "A" logo
are trademarks belonging to Charter Communications, Inc.

PRINTED IN THE UNITED STATES OF AMERICA

10 9 8 7 6 5 4 3 2 1

This book is dedicated to the young Dineh I have met, in the hope that they may enjoy seeing a little of their past through the future.

This book is dedicated to the Elder Dineh, With respect.

Prescott, Arizona
May, 1989

If you would be a real seeker after truth, it is necessary that at least once in your life you doubt, as far as possible, all things.

—Rene Descartes
Principles of Philosophy, 1644

CYBER WAY

CHAPTER
1

THE POLARIZED BUBBLE glass in the window turned Greater Tampa into a fish bowl. It was a view which never failed to please Kettrick, and why not? He'd worked hard to earn it.

By rights he shouldn't be where he was. For years engineers had insisted anything over thirty-five stories high built within a half mile of the beach would eventually begin to sink into the saline muck that was coastal Florida. The bubble glass that lined his office was on the fiftieth floor. So much for engineering. There was sufficient solid ground here, just as there were always solid business opportunities. That had been one of his father's many mottoes. Nobody was better than the old man when it came to digging up business. The actual construction work he left to his son.

Whenever Kettrick thought of his father it was always with fondness. The old man had fought bravely against the weak heart which had killed him early, leaving the company to his son. Kettrick had built on that, just as he'd built this impossible structure on this inadequate land.

From the fiftieth floor you could see far out into the Gulf. Like a sheet of pressed sky, the lazy blue water stretched westward until it melted into a pale white horizon. Inland lay the industrial corridor that crawled northeast to Orlando, framed and constrained by the greenbelts which offered sanctuary to wildlife, recreation to workers, and salve for the consciences of those who had built the plants. Southward somewhere lay the eternal Glades, still surviving in spite of the pollution. Nature could be a tough old bitch.

Kettrick had seen pictures of early Florida. Flat two-dimensional images recorded on paper, old videotapes reconstructed for mollystorage. Cypress and pine, swamp and mud. Funny how the wildlife had adapted. Blue herons, snowy egrets, gators, and manatees thrived in the city parks as lushly as in the Glades themselves. The three gators who made their home in the indoor garden of this very building had never expressed any desire to move on.

Man adapts to the world, and the world adapts to man. The only thing man couldn't seem to adapt to was himself, which was why Kettrick had pushed the security switch the instant his unannounced visitor had appeared. He appraised, then relaxed, seeing no weapon, sensing no threat. Security personnel would arrive momentarily. Had he been truly concerned, he would have thumbed the red button instead of the orange one disguised as an inlay in his desk. Concealed nozzles would have buried the intruder in a shell of quick-drying immobilizing foam.

Kettrick knew there was no need to employ such measures. No need, because he recognized the intruder. Silently he vowed that this would be the last time he would indulge this particular individual. Even the traditional Kettrick courtesy had its limits, and these had now been exceeded.

No need to be nervous. His visitor was not psychotic. Merely obsessed.

The man gazed at the door through which he'd entered, as if aware his time was limited. Then, before speaking, he turned to nod at the sweeping panorama visible through the bubble glass behind the desk.

"I can see that you are an admirer of the natural order.

It causes me to wonder anew why you will not sell me the picture.''

"My love of beauty is what attracted me to the picture in the first place," Kettrick replied. "Why would I want to turn it over to you? We've been through this before. I thought I'd made it perfectly clear that I never sell anything from my collection. I told you that the last time."

"I needed to hear it from you again. There is always a first time. I must have the painting."

Since he had not invited him to come in, Kettrick did not invite him to sit down. He left him standing, convinced that the man posed no immediate threat. Kettrick chuckled to himself. Now, his son-in-law, the gargantuan white boy his daughter had married, *that* was a threatening personality. Cody had to be, since by profession he played backup nose-guard for the Bucs. This irritation who had burst into his office was only a little more than average height and of slim build. Hardly an imposing physicality. Kettrick thought that the man's straight black hair was exceptionally dark even for an Amerindian. The industrialist found himself wondering if Indians could tan. The intruder's clothing was simple and utilitarian.

All you really noticed were the obsidian eyes. You noticed them because they didn't notice you. They seemed to be focused on something behind Kettrick even though the man was gazing directly at him. Odd. Nor was his visitor out-grabed. He was much too coherent for that. There was no telltale clouding of the corneas, no nervous trembling in the fingers. Though come to think of it, this fellow did hold his hands in a strange fashion, with the fingers curved back and up like hooks. Or like paws.

He could be wrong, and although he wasn't an expert, Kettrick knew an addict when he saw one. Friends of his son-in-law were always hinting that it would be nice if he could obtain the latest designer steroids for them. All because a small chain of drugstores was included among his diverse holdings.

Of course he refused all such requests, no matter how oblique. Should it come out in the media, a single such story could harm the business, not to mention his social standing in the community, in which he took considerable pride. He had no intention of risking any of that simply to do a favor for some of his son-in-law's buddies or even to improve the team, on whose behalf he annually expended far too much money for season tickets. Of course the company paid for those, but still . . .

Strange face it was, and not only because of those eyes. It was sharp of side, like a piece of dark marble whose rough edges had been hacked off but not yet polished smooth. High cheekbones, nothing anywhere soft or rounded, the result a perpetually questioning expression. Lines ran from the base of his nose up into his forehead, which was itself unlined. The crow's-feet at the corners of the eyes seemed transplanted from someone far older. What might appear to some as arrogance was in truth only preoccupation. It was as if this stranger were too busy with his thoughts to pay much attention even to the conversation he had begun.

A single earring of silver and blue, as pure as the Gulf outside the window, called attention to one ear. He had yet to smile. Kettrick studied the strange visage and decided it was an expression foreign to this face. In contrast to the dark hair, his eyebrows were astonishingly light—almost not there. The few wispy hairs seemed to grow flush with the skin. He stood with a slight slouch, as though suffering from curvature of the spine. After a while Kettrick realized there was nothing physically wrong with his visitor. It was simply his natural stance.

And all the while, he kept the fingers of both hands curved up and backward. At any moment Kettrick half expected him to drop to all fours and approach on his knuckles. Distant he was, yet intense.

Well, if he was wrong about him, there was always the red button in case the visitor made a sudden move toward his host. Kettrick's fingers tapped on the desk close to the false inlay.

What might he be besides a truly odd duck? A collector like himself? Collectors could be fanatics.

Where the hell was Security, anyway?

"You've gone to a lot of trouble to force your way in here just to hear the same thing I've been telling you over the phone. So one more time: the picture is not for sale."

"You won't even discuss price with me?"

Kettrick gestured expansively at his surroundings. "I presume that by now you have some idea of who I am. Whatever you might offer me, I've no need of it, and I must add you don't look like you could offer much. If it's any consolation to you, the amount wouldn't matter. I don't sell anything out of my collection."

For a long moment the visitor did not reply, just stood there staring at Kettrick with those obsidian eyes. It made the industrialist uneasy, though he was careful not to show it.

"Suppose that I was the richest man in the world," the visitor said suddenly. "Suppose that I could offer you anything and everything you ever dreamed of."

Kettrick smiled condescendingly. "But I already have everything I ever wanted. A fine family, grandchildren, even a moderately famous son-in-law. I live out in the Gulf in a grand house that's half above and half below crystal clear waters. Business is good, the economic climate for the next year even better. I head one of the few corporations in Florida that has no tariff war with the EEC and we're free reciprocals with the West African Economic Union. I even like my work. So why should I part with something I love just for money?"

Kettrick saw the fingers of his visitor's right hand flexing. So, he could move more than his mouth and legs.

"I understand. I will bother you no longer about buying the picture. It is clear I cannot persuade you. I will manage without the painting itself if you will let me have one copy of it. Holo, vid, still flat color: anything will do."

Kettrick's patience was running out. He had work to do. "If you're anything of a collector yourself, you must know I can't allow that. If it was just up to me, I'd say sure, go ahead. But it would cost me my insurance. Regulations forbid reproductions. Nothing to do with you personally, but once you let reproductions of items you own out in public, potential thieves have a way of finding out what you own that's worth stealing. It lets them steal to order. It's an annual problem at museums. My collection stays private and out of the public eye." He leaned forward curiously. "In fact, I'd give a lot to know how you found out about this particular piece.

"It does not matter," said the visitor quietly.

"It matters to me."

"If I tell you, will you let me make a copy of the painting?"

Kettrick shook his head. Pity. The fellow seemed intelligent enough. He just had one big blind spot where the painting was concerned.

He wasn't through. "It belongs with me. It is a part of my heritage, not yours. You don't know what you have."

"Yes, I do. I have a beautiful, special, and according to you yourself, a most unique piece of primitive art. It fits in very nicely with the rest of my collection. As for it not being a part of my particular ethnic heritage, my collection contains primitive art from all over the world. I have my share of African and early Black American art, yes, but also work from China, Tibet, and most of the South Pacific. I'm sure there must be hundreds, thousands of reproductions of this particular type of art widely available in public collections for your perusal. Why not content yourself with some of them?''

"There is no other like this one."

"So *you* say. I've only your word for that. Again, it doesn't matter. The painting stays in my collection, and my collection stays private until I decide to donate it or tour it some day. At that time, and only at that time, you can take all the pictures you want—along with everyone else.''

"That is no help to me. I need the image now."

"I can't help what you need."

"I have told you that it has to do with my religion."

"Again, I've only your word for that. Even so, you're not part of some official delegation seeking its recovery. You're an individual acting on his own with motives of his own. For all I know, you're just another collector who wants a copy of my painting for your own personal use. Who do you think you're dealing with here, friend? This isn't downtown. We're not dealers swapping formula on the street.''

The visitor shifted his weight but not his stare. "This is the fourth time I have made this request of you. You cannot refuse me a fourth time.''

Kettrick couldn't keep from chuckling aloud. "That's one of your customs, not one of mine. I'm not bound by it. You can make all the requests you want. It won't do you any good. Is four a special number for you?" It was not necessary for the visitor to reply.

"Well, in this case it's a special number for me too, because this is the last time I'm going to talk to you.''

The three men from Security had entered so silently that Kettrick hardly noticed their arrival. If the visitor had, he did not acknowledge their presence.

"Now I happen to be a very busy man," Kettrick explained, "and you'll excuse the cliché, because in my case it happens to be true. So I'll only say this once more. I've given you rather more of my time than I intended to. You've used it all up, both on the phone and in person. It's clear you've come a long way and so I'm going to give you the benefit of the doubt and assume that you're a collector or lover of primitive art like myself, and not a thief.

"If you bust in here again like you did a little while ago, I'll have you arrested. The jails here in the Bay are as modern as you'll find anywhere—but sometimes the air treatment systems do break down, and even though it's almost spring, I still think you'd find that kind of environment unpleasant. Also, Florida is kind of a seine for the East coast, a net that stretches from St. Pete to Miami, and we catch all kinds of Caribbean sludge in it. A lot of crazyboys high on abbreviations that represent chemical combinations you don't want anything to do with. Pupapapas peddling Brazilian and Peruvian babies. Snuff-film importers. Great guys to share a holding cell with.

"You take my advice and go back where you came from. Concentrate your energies on a different piece of art."

"I cannot do that," the visitor said softly. "The enterprise I am engaged in requires precision and timing. I need this particular piece, or a copy, and I cannot wait any longer."

"That's too bad." Kettrick gestured slightly and two of the security guards moved forward until they were flanking the visitor. One of them put a big hand on the man's shoulder. He ignored it.

"Then I suppose I will have to find some way to work around your intransigence."

"That sounds like the sensible thing to do," agreed the industrialist, nodding and smiling.

The security team escorted the stranger out of Kettrick's office. From the rear the visitor looked like a splinter of black oak embedded in a mass of white flesh. Kettrick felt sorry for the guy. Under different circumstances the two of them might have spent an enjoyable evening together discussing early American art. Not that he'd been especially friendly. Distant without actually being impolite.

No, his attitude would have ruled out dinner. Sarah

wouldn't have liked him. She preferred people whose eyes met your own. Kettrick knew she wouldn't cotton to someone who daydreamed while you were trying to hold a conversation with them.

That business about not being able to refuse a fourth request would probably mean something to an anthropologist. It meant nothing to Kettrick. That was one of the pleasures of being a wealthy collector. You could affect an attitude of great knowledge without having to go to the trouble of actually acquiring it, because all of your friends knew infinitely less about the subject than you did.

CHAPTER 2

MOODY DIDN'T LIKE leaving his car. In the patrol cruiser he felt safe and protected from an uncompromisingly hostile world, encased in armored flexan and carbonate, coddled by air conditioning, lunch, the drink dispenser, and as many other creature comforts as the department could pry out of the taxpayers by claiming they were vital to ongoing police operations. It was unfortunate, but every now and then he had to leave his office and get in the car, and less frequently, abandon the car to work in the real world. There were two real worlds as far as Moody was concerned: the one he worked in and the one he fled to as often as possible. All they had in common was that both were located on the same planet.

You had to leave the car to net outgrabed crazyboys, or interview witnesses, or check the backbays for waterstriders trying to run pharmecuties up from Koobah or Whackaragua. At least the waterstriders made life exciting, though things had quieted down some since Haiti had become a U.S. Territory, providing the DEA with an ideal base from which to monitor flights out of SudAm. There was a rumor the striders were using trained porpoises to bring the stuff right into the bay. The bastards never gave up. You could almost admire their persistence and ingenuity, until the first time you saw some eleven-year-old outgrabed on sizzle, standing over his dead six-year-old sister with a bloody kitchen knife in his hand, the familiar feral glaze in his eyes and that horrid unknowing grin on his face. A couple of encounters like that would kill any admiration for the striders.

Moody had suffered through more than a couple.

Nobody, including the Interdiction Corps, had actually found a porp running drugs. That didn't mean they didn't exist. Only that they hadn't been caught. The detective wondered if you could hook a porp on pharmacuties. He wouldn't put anything past a damn strider.

It was so very different from Mississippi. In many ways the Sip was much nicer than Flo-ree-dah: quieter, friendlier, laid-back and relaxed. Less need to flinch when someone approaching you on the street reached into his coat. It was also a helluva lot duller, he reminded himself. Which was why after graduating from the Academy he'd moved to the Greater Tampa area with his first wife. His appraisal of his prospects in West Florida had been borne out by quick advancement. He'd also lost his wife, married a second time, and lost her as well, along with the physical conditioning he'd acquired at the Academy.

Every year when the regular examinations came round he always managed to shed just enough poundage to scrape by, subsequent to which profuse ingestion of beer rapidly returned him to the rotund form to which his colleagues had become accustomed.

Another reason for his early move to Florida had been a misplaced desire for excitement and sophistication. What a letdown to discover that in a highly charged urban environment those were only euphemisms for more degenerate forms of crime. He stayed anyway.

He could have joined a Mississippi department but without ever enjoying the prospect of rapid and regular promotion, simply because there weren't as many people to police. Nevertheless, he was surprised when he'd made detective. His background and lack of personality worked against him, not to mention the fact that he was no ass-kisser like half the kids in the department.

What he did have was a dogged, pit-bull persistence that insisted no case was unsolvable, no mystery too convoluted to crack. When others gave up, he persevered. Turn out to be right a few times in such matters and even disinterested higher-ups take notice. Apparently one or two had done just that. His was an attitude that would have been a hindrance on a SWAT team but which in a detective was a positive attribute.

Even after his unexpected promotion they rarely threw any of the glamour jobs his way. That suited Moody just fine. He didn't like seeing his picture on the vid, because he took a lousy picture. If someone stuck a vocup in his face he became helplessly inarticulate. When not assigned to the street he actually enjoyed being stuck at a desk, accessing the mollys with his desk spinner, doing the tedious, boring, dirty bits of police work that never made the evening news. He abhorred publicity. If a vidwit showed up at the station asking questions about a case he happened to be involved with, Moody always managed to find a colleague willing to usurp his place in the spotlight. No wonder his fellow officers loved him.

An officer who actually *enjoyed* mollywork was an invaluable component of whatever police department happened to be fortunate enough to have the use of his services. Moody knew he could have hooked on with any department in the country. Maybe that was why he'd received the unexpected promotion. No matter. He was comfortable enough in Greater Tampa, just a good ol' Southern boy with maybe a few more brains than his buddies back home and a few less than some of the men and women he worked with daily.

Whatever they thought of him privately, none of them

ever called him out in public. Because if you were caught making fun of Vernon Moody, why then when you needed his services he might decline to sit down and do the weeks of tedious research vital to your case. Moody's work had probably been responsible for more promotions than any other single factor in the department. So if any of his fellow cops laughed at his background or his girth, they did so well behind his back.

Only the insecure were guilty of that. The majority respected Moody and his abilities. He socialized readily if quietly, and had made a few casual friends—easygoing types like himself. He wasn't the only one in the department content to parlay his off-time into a few beers, a ball game, fishing trips to the Glades, or the company of women not too much younger than himself. In a department aswarm with ambitious hares, the presence of a happy tortoise or two was more than welcome.

It helped too that Moody's appearance was not threatening. He looked fat, slow, and stupid. Striders and ninlocos had discovered to their dismay that in the detective's case, appearances were more than slightly deceiving.

Despite his usefulness on the street, he much preferred spending his time at his desk, sieving the departmental mollyspheres, researching and preparing reports. You didn't have to be smart to use a spinner. Just persistent and good at following directions. The ability to follow directions had extracted him from a dirt-poor existence in Mississippi, had made him a detective on the largest police force in Florida. He enjoyed the respect of his peers, the admiration of the folks back home, a decent income, and the prospect of a comfortable retirement if some nameless crazyboy didn't someday expunge his guts on a filthy downtown back street.

None of that could help him now. No vehicles were allowed on Steel Key, not even those representing municipal authorities. The call which had come in demanded that he leave his office. Now he was forced to abandon his beloved cruiser as well.

Was a time when there'd been no barrier islands between Honeymoon Key and the Anclote Refuge. Then the gulf waters had been forced to make way for Steel, Steadman, Briarwood, and Cypress Keys. Artificial islets all, built of fill dredged from the gulf bottom and fortified with vitamins and minerals. Not to mention polycrete and titanium. Rich imported soil from the mainland provided regular employment for a small army of gardeners, and Bahamanian sand fringed each island like vanilla cream on a wedding cake.

There were no bridges to the artificial keys. Instead they were connected to the mainland and to one another by a tube which ran from Steel to just south of Tarpon Springs. Though fragile in appearance, the tube was in fact far more stable and secure than any roadway. Come a hurricane, Moody would much rather be trapped on artificial Briarwood than organic Caladesi. The latter was composed solely of natural materials, and no matter what the ecoengineers said, he'd take titanium over pulverized coral any day.

It was unusually hot and humid for March and Moody was sweating as soon as he stepped out of the cruiser. One of the pleasures of being a detective was that he was allowed to wear plainclothes on the job, but the special light fabrics he wore could evaporate only so much of a body's moisture. Bad enough to be doomed to a physique like the Graf Zeppelin's but why did the Good Lord have to add to the tribulations of the plump by making them sweat three times as much as everyone else?

He knew he was luckier than some. Beer gut aside, he didn't look obese, just big. He'd been told that if he gave up beer he could lose the gut. But giving up beer would've meant giving up a large chunk of whatever it was that comprised Vernon Moody. Shoot, he'd even miss being the butt of familiar jokes around the station. Besides which, it

would mean an end to his fishing. A man could sooner fish
without tackle than without beer.

He controlled his irritation while he waited for the tube
system's web to process his police ID. From a security
standpoint it was far from perfect—anyone could still land
a boat on one of the perfect, groomed key beaches. But it
kept the small-time thieves from having easy access to the
respected, wealthy ones.

He stepped up into the air-conditioned tube car gratefully,
punched in the address, and settled back in the padded seat
as the maglide accelerated over the intracoastal waterway.
As it neared Steel Key it began to slow, shunting onto an
alley lane, to finally deposit him outside one of the contemporary mansions that faced the sea. Since none of the artificial keys was more than two lots wide, builders had the
choice of facing the Gulf or the mainland. Of course "lot"
was a relative term when speaking of property on the artificial islets.

The tube shunt and a quaint, meandering walkway ran
down the center of the key. There was also a paved, lightly
banked road for the use of those who might want to bicycle
or powerskate. No motorized vehicles allowed, lest they
disturb the tranquillity of those who had paid immense sums
to leave such noises behind on the mainland.

Gonna be a hot summer, he thought to himself as he
stepped clear of the maglide car and headed for the gate
opposite, resenting even brief exposure to the climate of
Central Florida.

Though cars were absent, there was no dearth of activity.
Scavengers from the Coroner's office were working the
vine-scribed walls and flower beds. One was intently scru-
tinizing the trunk of a transplanted coconut palm which grew
hard by the opaque blue-green glass barrier that surrounded
the Kettrick compound. They were looking for heel marks,
or indications of forced entry. Likely was a forced entry,
he mused. Usually was, when murder was involved, though

you could never be certain. Perhaps the killer had arrived by parachute or hanglider, or had scubaed onto the beach. Or burrowed through the soil like a gopher.

They must be pretty sure it was homicide, though, or they wouldn't have called him in.

The patrolman on duty at the gate recognized him and let him through. He found himself walking through an immaculately maintained tropical garden, following a crushed coral path toward the house. An airborne mist-maker drifted past on its appointed rounds, moistening a dense clump of bright purple orchids and pungent bougainvillea. Moody was unimpressed. Downtown Tampa stank of the tropics. The unique, self-propelled aerial spray was present only because of the existence of expensive, private desalinization facilities.

As he walked he studied the scroll-up on his pocket spinner. It was standard department issue, gunmetal-gray with a four-inch-square screen, the controls well-worn and slick with skin oil. There was plenty of background on Kettrick, and Moody hadn't been given enough time to peruse all of it back at the office. So far, the most interesting piece of information to come up on the screen was the fact that Kettrick's son-in-law played for the Bucs. The team was cool and dry in the Northwest this week, getting ready to play the Portland Axe. The instrument informed him that Kettrick's daughter was with her husband. No doubt she'd already been notified of her father's demise.

There was nothing in the hastily compiled domestic dossier to suggest that this might be a family affair, something for which Moody was grateful. He was a big Bucs fan and they were short of good defensive linemen as it was.

Though the web was full of info on Kettrick, it had little to say about the killing beyond an estimated time of death. The coroner team was still plaiting. Moody knew that in the not too distant past cops had been forced to wait hours, even days for updated information. That was back before

police weavers had learned how to build good webs, before
the advent of pocket spinners able to access them. Wonderful devices. Not only could they keep your information
up to the minute, but if you got bored with the daily grind
you could surreptitiously switch over to a network or ESPN.

The house was full of professionals, a few of whom
recognized Moody and paused in their endeavors long
enough to acknowledge his presence with a glance or grunt.
Their number was a reflection of the dead man's importance,
not the department's desire for thoroughness. Off to his
right several were orbiting a crying woman. Moody angled
in their direction.

There was something about very rich people which enabled them to bawl like the Flood without disrupting their
poise. Mrs. Leona Kettrick was having a composed breakdown, mopping regularly at her eyes with an absorbent yet
exquisitely crafted handkerchief. She was in her mid to late
forties, well-dressed, handsome rather than pretty. No doubt
she was more attractive when she wasn't crying. She had
the look of someone who'd been teetering on the verge of
collapse for too many hours and was keeping herself going
on dignity and pills.

Moody stood quietly, able to see over everyone's head,
letting Berkowitz ask the questions. The other detective was
much better at interviews of this type than his colleague.
Asking no questions of his own while sorting substance
from sobs, Moody determined that Mrs. Kettrick had been
participating in some social function at Jekyll Island up on
the south Georgia coast and had returned only this morning
to discover her husband's body, whereupon she had immediately called the police.

From the tone of Berkowitz's questions Moody surmised
that at this point she was no more than a secondary suspect
as far as the department was concerned. If that supposition
turned out upon further investigation to be wrong and she
was in some way responsible for what had happened, then

she was doing a superb job of feigning grief. She was having a difficult time controlling herself long enough to supply coherent answers to the detective's queries. In his nearly twenty years of police work Moody had actually run across a few marrieds who'd stayed in love with their original partners. Hers might be no more than a good performance. He hoped not.

The two techs from the Coroner's office didn't have to make room for Moody. He made his own room. Big as he was, it was easy for him to nudge his way into the circle surrounding the distraught widow. It allowed him to study her close up, take note of the details. Moody was very good with details. It was a hallmark of his work.

He noted them mentally for later inclusion in a formal file: expensive faux jewelry, designer travel-wear, no overt evidence of pharmacutie use, telltale signs of collagen injections at the neck and forehead. She must have been a very attractive young woman and she was fighting middle age with all the tenacity of a last-place team making a goal-line stand against the Superbowl bound. Why was it, he wondered not for the first time, that it was the genetically blessed who chose to employ cosmetic surgery so extensively? Having been recognized as beautiful in their youth, perhaps they felt its loss more keenly than those who had never been subject to the admiring stares of the herd.

Moody now, having never been much for looks, didn't particularly care how he aged. He observed the good-looking guys on the force, the handsome ones with the sculpted faces and athletic bodies, as they fought losing battles with receding hairlines and sagging waists, and he found he didn't envy them. It was not a bad thing to be content within oneself, he'd decided.

He adopted his most compassionate expression, a half-moon smile that gave him the look of a tranquil Buddha, or a beardless Santa Claus. It made him resemble a big, sloppy, overgrown hound dog and took away from his bulk, which he knew some people found intimidating. Mrs. Kettrick took notice of him but did not cease her crying.

The coroner techs melted away. Berkowitz gave him a standard cop "Hope-you-have-better-luck-than-I-did" grimace and went off to put the make on a pretty worker from forensics.

"I'm sorry about your husband, Mrs. Kettrick."

She didn't try to reply.

"I'm Detective Moody. I know y'all have been through hell this morning, but I have to ask you some questions. It ain't quite the way I'm supposed to work it, but if y'all don't feel you can manage any more right now we can do this later. I'm sure you understand, though, that the more information we have and the sooner we can stick it into the web for analysis, the faster we can start following up potential leads."

Still not looking up at him, she nodded, blew her nose softly. Moody watched in fascination. It was the first time he'd ever seen anyone blow their nose in sixty-dollar-a-foot linen.

"You've been away from home for how long?"

"Two weeks. Some family friends—their daughter was getting married at the Jekyll Island Club. I was helping with the arrangements. I'm supposed—I was supposed to go back next week for the ceremony." As she spoke she waved the handkerchief around indifferently.

She was keeping herself under control. Enough control to have hired a husband killer? The speculation on his part was as inevitable as it was premature.

Motive? None visible yet. Certainly not money. Why kill to obtain what she already possessed? Still, people could weave webs as complex as anything the spingeneers could imagine.

"Mrs. Kettrick, would you know of any reason why someone might want to kill your husband?"

"Kill him?" She chose a fresh handkerchief from the

endless supply in her purse. "I know of a few dozen competitors who probably wished he'd drop dead, but not who'd have him murdered. Of course, you can't tell about people anymore, can you?"

No you couldn't, he thought silently. Aloud he was consoling. "I expect someone in your husband's position must have made his share of enemies. What we need to know is if you're aware of anyone threatening him overtly."

"If so, he never mentioned it to me. Elroy didn't bring his business home with him. He was very good about that. I know it was hard for him, and I always respected and admired him for it. He let us have a real family life. He was such a *good* man, detective. He worked hard and he took care of his people. Do you know that last Christmas he called in every one of his district managers and their wives? They thought it was for business." Her expression was tight as she fought the emotions within.

"He'd chartered a plane. He flew all of them down to Havana. For a week, in the best hotel, at company expense. In addition to their regular vacations."

Moody smiled gently. "Sounds like a man I wouldn't have minded working for myself."

"Elroy was no saint, mind. That man could be hard. But he was honest and fair. What I'm tryin' to say, I guess, is that I don't think he had any more or less enemies than any other man in his position."

"What about outside the business?"

As he listened to her replies he would glance occasionally at his spinner. Not to make sure it was recording: that function was practically fail-safe. He was studying the shifting readout on the voice analyzer. The little telltale stayed solid cool green, indicating she was continuing to tell the truth. Though not admissible in a court of law, it was a useful little tool for on-site analysis. There were times when a little ambivalence on the part of a suspect could be highly informative.

Moody wasn't one of those old-fashioned cops who relied on instinct and personal observation. He was a ready convert to whatever new equipment police R&D managed to churn out. Anything that made his job easier made life easier, and God knew he was all for easy. Experienced cops claimed to have a sixth sense about crime. Moody preferred to use the web.

His spinner told him that he was talking to a truly agonized, distraught widow and not some West Florida version of Lady Mac. It confirmed his initial impressions. Despite that, he would not rule her out as a suspect. Moody never ruled anyone out as a suspect until a case was declared closed. And even then, there were times when he was reluctant.

He questioned her a little longer before excusing himself. Follow-up interviews would provide more information, which he could study at leisure back at the office. When the initial shock wore off some, she might be able to recall useful details presently submerged in her sea of emotional distress.

First you had to assemble the parts of the puzzle. Only then could you start putting them together. He wandered off in search of additional pieces.

"Hi, Nance," he said to the slight figure working the far side of the living room. She turned to grin at him.

"Hi, good lookin'. Wonderin' when you'd show."

He didn't know why he felt so comfortable with Nancy Welles. Maybe because of all the women he knew on the force, she was the only one who shared his love of fishing. Or maybe it was her sense of humor. Most cops had one, but it was usually not gentle in nature. Nancy's was.

"You just got here," she said.

"How'd you know that?"

She gestured past him. "Saw you talking to the widow. That'd be the first thing you'd do. I know your style."

"Is that a fact?"

" 'Tis."

"So what've we got?" Time enough for gentle banter back at the office.

"Not a whole lot."

"Motive?"

"Preliminary psych suggests something personal. Not necessarily involving the missus. Maybe a disgruntled employee. All pure spec at this point."

I'll bet it wasn't a district manager, Moody reflected silently. Aloud he said, "I just did my own voice scan."

The sergeant nodded, looking past him. "Everybody's been running her specs. She seems clean. If she's covering, she's a champ at it. As for the Jekyll alibi, it checks out too. Couple hundred witnesses."

"But she found the body and called in."

"Kettrick's been dead approximately thirty hours this morning. She only got in a couple hours ago. Air shuttle, everything checks out."

"Did Kettrick play around?"

"He was a man, wasn't he?"

"You're mean-spirited, Nance."

"Like hell. I just know men. But they're no dead mistresses lyin' around, if that's what you mean. No evidence of any live ones somewhere else, neither. Just the housekeeper."

Yes, the housekeeper, Moody thought. Whoever had killed Kettrick had also taken the time to eliminate the only witness.

"So we're back to the disgruntled employee theory."

"It's as good a one to start with as any," she responded. "Maybe some subsidiary owned by one of Kettrick's companies up in North Dakota fired some guy ten years ago and he's spent the last decade plotting his revenge. Happens. Kettrick might not even have known the guy who deleted him, though the evidence so far suggests otherwise."

"How so?"

"No sign of forced entry and not much of a struggle."

"What about the housekeeper?"

"In the same room as Kettrick." The sergeant accessed her own pocket spinner. "Anna Hernandez, fifty-eight, single, been with the family six years seven months. Had combinations to every lock in the place, used the maglide tube to do the shopping, lived in room downstairs in front. Trusted family employee. Too bad for her."

"How was she killed? Same as Kettrick?"

"Looks that way."

"Coroner done a determination on that yet?"

"Not that I've heard." Welles frowned slightly. "Wonder what's takin' 'em so long? They're talking gun, but without real assurance."

"What kind?"

"Ask 'em yourself. Me, I'm just a lowly sergeant. They don't tell me nuthin'."

She led him down a hallway, past other members of the department intent on their work.

"I just got a quick look at the body before the boys from forensics descended and shooed out everybody who didn't know the secret handshake. If a gun was used, it was a weird little sucker."

"Why do you think that?"

"No blood. I got an early call, got here fast. There's no blood anywhere, Vernon. He's just lying dead in the middle of the floor and the old gal's nearby on some steps, and both of 'em as clean as an embalmer's sample pack."

"Then why do they think it's a shooting?"

"Because each of the poor dears has two holes in 'em. Kettrick in his neck, the housekeeper in the middle of her back. And no blood. Holes aren't real helpful, either. No vital organs punctured, appears to be complete cauterization at point-of-entry, but they're still both dead."

"The main veins and arteries are intact?"

"Yup. Coroner's been talkin' trauma. Hell, what trauma?

No signs of battery, use of a blunt instrument, no other marks of any kind on either of 'em.''

Moody glanced up the long hallway. "Where y'all taking me?''

"My secret orgy room. Where'd you think?'' She let out a derisive snort. "Apparently this guy Kettrick was a world-class collector of primitive art. To me it all looks like the kind of junk you find out on lawns at Labor Day garage sales over in Clearwater, but it must be worth something to somebody, because it's housed in a room all to its lonesome. Place is built like a vault. Hurricane-flood-proof walls, its own climate control system: you name it. Then there's the security setup. First class. I wouldn't give you squat for the best of the collection, but Nickerson from your office— yeah, he's here too—he says it's museum quality. All that tells me is that it's the kind of stuff rich people buy for investment purposes. You can judge for yourself.''

The big room was suffused with bright, soft light that spilled from unobtrusive sources set high in the ceiling. Bolted to the neutral gray walls were cases and cabinets of tempered glass. Sculptures of wood and bone and clay were mounted on pedestals welded to the floor. Some of the pieces in the room were oddly appealing in appearance. A few were pretty. Moody thought many downright ugly.

Welles pointed out Nickerson, pinched Moody on the butt, and left him with a wink. Moody watched her go, then turned and entered the vault.

He knew Nickerson well enough. They'd teamed together on several cases, even though Moody kept mostly to head-quarters while his younger counterpart worked the glamour districts along the coast. Moody didn't envy the younger detective his rapid advancement or notoriety. Every cat to its ashcan. In a beachfront pit the sly, slim Nickerson would blend in effectively while Moody would stand out like a beached baleen. Maybe the guy got laid more often, but he didn't make any more money than Moody and he didn't command any more respect.

In his own defense, Nickerson wasn't responsible for his good looks. Nor was he a poseur. Every cop in the Greater Tampa Bay area knew Moody's reputation, and Nickerson was no exception. He valued the big man's advice and opinions and didn't make fun of him.

"What d'you think of this stuff, Vernon?" he said by way of greeting.

Moody looked round the museum. That was the only way to think of it, as a museum.

"Not my taste. Y'all know how it is with art. You got this here stuff at one end and black velvet paintings of St. Elvis at the other." He held up a big hand and wiggled his fingers. "The kind of stuff I like's somewheres in the middle."

"Yeah, I know what you mean. Want to see the latest exhibit?"

Near the back of the room someone from forensics was running a scanner over Kettrick's body. The industrialist had been a big man, older than Moody and packing a lot less excess avoirdupois. Six-three or -four, the detective estimated. About two-ten, two-twenty. Someone who could manhandle an attacker, middle-aged or not. It hadn't saved him, just as age hadn't protected the unlucky housekeeper. Moody decided Mrs. Kettrick was damn lucky she'd been in Georgia this past Tuesday. Otherwise this room would be serving as morgue for three bodies instead of two.

He didn't linger. The coroner's report would tell him everything useful.

What caught his interest was the wall behind the body. Bright art lights illuminated every square inch of it. Something had been displayed there quite recently. Now there was nothing except four chromed bolts from which hung jagged shards of shattered plexan.

At the base of the wall was a pile of debris composed of

more transparent fragments mixed with broken bits of wood and colored sand. Kneeling, Moody picked up a handful and let the brightly dyed grains trickle through his fingers. That's all it was: sand and sawdust. It smelled dry and musty. He glanced up at Nickerson.

"What the hell's this stuff?"

"You mean, what was it." The younger detective eyed the pile bemusedly. "A big picture of some kind. We checked with the widow."

Moody rose. "She had enough sense to tell you what was missing and what wasn't?"

"Nope, but she did know where her husband stored the catalog for his collection. Easy enough to access." He waved at the rest of the room. "There's nothing else missing, and this isn't really missing either. Just vandalized."

Moody grunted, studying the pile. "Pulverized is more like it. Y'all said it was a picture. What's with the sand?"

"It was a sandpainting."

"You mean, a painting on sand?"

"That's what I thought." Nickerson brushed self-consciously at his hair. "The sand itself is colored first, then applied to a background. In this case, a wooden one. Cheap wood at that."

"Great. So we're looking for a homicidal critic."

"Doesn't this look like more than just vandalism to you, Vernon? I mean, whoever busted up this piece of work wanted to make sure nobody could put it back together again."

"Okay, so we're looking for a *serious* homicidal critic." The detective shook his head slowly. "Somebody slips in here, murders Kettrick, kills his housekeeper 'cause she's a witness, takes nothing. All he or she does is waste one piece of primitive art, which if it was as gruesome as the rest of the stuff in here, hardly seems worth the price of a cheap arson job, much less a double murder."

Nickerson was nodding. "That's about what we've got. You make anything off that?"

"Off the top of my head?" Moody responded without hesitation.

"Off the top of your head."

"A nut, but a nut with a purpose."

"Why purposeful?"

"Because he only went after this one item. A total psycho would've trashed more than this. Since he only wasted one piece, it stands to reason his purpose in coming here was to do just that. He knew what he wanted to do before he got here, knew what he was after." Moody studied the pile of debris thoughtfully. "Whoever did this took their time making sure. Not much of a motive to work with."

"You're telling me," said Nickerson.

"Mrs. Kettrick have anything to say about sandpainting phobics?"

Nickerson shook his head. "It doesn't make any sense to her either." He was staring at the body, watching forensics work.

Moody knew that the younger detective didn't like psycho cases. Drug deals were more to his liking. They made sense. Buyers and sellers and users, everything fitted together nice and neat. Something like this, that made less sense the longer you looked at it, unsettled him. That meant he would leave all the legwork to Moody, which suited the senior detective just fine. Psycho cases didn't bother him. Logic was always present. It was just twisted.

Nickerson was talking again. "The missus said she hardly ever came in here. She didn't care much for this stuff. It was her husband's passion. He'd show her a new piece when he had it delivered and she'd smile and forget about it. Not her style."

"Something we can all agree on." Moody gestured at the empty wall. "So she couldn't tell us anything about this one?"

"Just that it was a big picture composed of lots of smaller pictures; very organized, very geometric."

"Swell. Our motive, and we don't even know what it looked like. All this stuff must be insured."

"Already checked with the local rep for the company. Everything's heavily insured, all right, but they couldn't find Kettrick's file when we asked about it. Seems it's been wiped recently. Isn't that interesting?"

Moody's eyebrows lifted. "Definitely not a nut," he asserted slowly. "Nuts don't know how to penetrate insurance company security."

"Yeah, but they don't kill people who own art they don't like, either." Nickerson smiled. "Fortunately, we *do* know what the damn thing looked like."

The detective regarded his colleague in surprise. "How?"

"Kettrick had an old-fashioned still camera. You remember those; the kind that printed two-D images on paper? He kept his own little file locked away, a snapshot of everything." He reached into his jacket pocket and extracted a small square of hard paper.

Moody examined the image. It showed a painting some six feet square composed of brightly colored, intricately rendered symbols and designs. Some resembled highly stylized human beings, others looked like plants; much of it was like nothing he'd ever seen before. It was tremendously complicated and as tightly organized as if it had been laid out with a cadcam program. Colored sand on wood. Aesthetically it meant nothing to Moody, whose idea of fine art was a well-crafted beer can, but he could appreciate the amount of time and effort that had gone into the composition.

It certainly didn't look like anything worth killing two people over. But after twenty years as a cop Moody hadn't found anything that was.

"Sandpainting, huh?"

"Yeah." Nickerson nudged the photo. "There's a little

descriptive info on the back. Got it out of Kettrick's catalog. It isn't much.''

Moody turned the photo over. His eyes moved, not his lips. ''Navaho, it says. Out West somewhere, aren't they?''

Nickerson shrugged. ''Thought you'd want to be the one to dig into it.'' In other words, Moody mused, the younger man saw no vid opportunities here and was washing his hands of the whole business unless some arose.

''Phone?''

Nickerson jerked a thumb over his shoulder. ''Back up the hall.''

Moody nodded once and turned to leave, pausing only long enough to study the corpse of the unfortunate housekeeper. She lay face-down near the entrance, dropped by the killer as she'd tried to flee. The detective's expression hardened. He had no sympathy or understanding for those responsible for the deaths of innocent people whose sole crime was being in the wrong place at the wrong time. It took a real first-class cold-blooded bastard to shoot an old lady in the back. If she had been shot.

Lean close and the holes above her heart were clearly visible. Two of them, three inches apart. No sign of bleeding, just as Welles had said. Death by trauma induced by some kind of invasive presence. But what kind of presence if not metal slugs?

Coroner would let him know. He couldn't do everybody's job.

He found the phone, unclipped his spinner from his belt and jacked in. Department mollyserve found the Museum of the American Indian in New York, the Museum of the Southwest in Albuquerque, the Heard Museum in Phoenix, Museum of, Museum of . . .

He settled on the Museum of Native American Art in Fort Worth, waited for clearance, then entered his queries. Two minutes later replies began a slow scroll on his screen. When he found what he was looking for, he thumbed RE-

CORD, waited another two minutes, then hung up.

The department was beginning to pull out. Forensic techs had scoured every room in the house for hair, dandruff, fingerprints, loose skin, blood, sweat, tears, and anything else that might help them eventually identify the murderer. Moody found Nickerson waiting to use the john.

"Arizona," he told the younger man. "Also parts of New Mexico, Colorado, and Utah. That's where you find sandpainting Navahos."

Nickerson tried to sound interested. "So what does that give us, Vernon? A Navaho with a grudge?"

"We don't know that it was a Navaho. We just know that this involves a piece of Navaho art."

More often than most people think, the obvious pans out in police work. From starting with nothing, they went to having a prime suspect in no time at all, as soon as they began taking depositions from Kettrick's office staff. Someone who consistently bypassed Security to telephone Kettrick and then broke into his office to confront him directly made a pretty good suspect in Moody's eyes. The fact that several eyewitnesses described him as unmistakably Amerindian in appearance was conclusive as far as the department was concerned. It did not require a great leap of faith to assume for the purposes of additional investigation that he might well be Navaho.

They acquired a motive simultaneously with their suspect, because Kettrick's secretary had heard the two men arguing about the sandpainting. What the detective still didn't understand was what about it was worth killing for.

The first thing Moody did on returning to his desk was make several copies of the precious photograph. A couple went into the evidence vault beneath police headquarters, incongruous among tagged heavy weapons and ampules of self-injecting pharmacuties. A third he shoved under the mattress of his bed when he got home that night. Only then did he allow himself to relax.

As far as the murder suspect was concerned, no copies of the sandpainting existed. He'd wiped the insurance company's file and destroyed the original. With luck it might make him overconfident.

What didn't make any sense to Moody and what puzzled him all through the night was why a murderer would go to elaborate lengths to conceal a painting's identity rather than his own.

CHAPTER
3

BY THE FOLLOWING morning a preliminary determination had been rendered as to the cause of death in the Kettrick case. Nancy Welles told him about it before he had a chance to read it for himself.

They were in the commissary and she spotted him at one of the vending machines.

"Hi, Nance."

"Vernon. They think they found out how Kettrick and his housekeeper died. But not what caused it." Moody waited while she drew coffee from a nearby machine.

"Electrocution," she said.

"Gimme a break, Nance. They know how but not what?"

She nodded as she stirred artificial creamer and artificial sweetener into the suspect coffee. "Remember the marks? Like bullet holes, only no bullets? Coroner's report comes up and says they've both been corn-fried, but they don't know how. You shoulda seen some of the faces in the room."

"I'll bet. Any theories abounding?"

"Theories, sure. I dunno about the abounding. The prevailing wisdom is that they were shot with some kind of charged organic particles, maybe a gelatin that hit the body hard enough to penetrate. The holes weren't real deep, remember. High voltage would explain the instant cauterization and lack of bleeding. But it doesn't explain why two shots, and the same distance apart on both bodies. Unless some kind of double-barreled weapon was involved.''

Moody cracked his box of cookies. ''Maybe one capsule carried a positive charge and the other a negative, and they only reacted lethally on contact.''

Welles's expression brightened. ''That's one I haven't heard yet. I bet Coroners hasn't even thought of it.'' She eyed him admiringly.

''Just an idea,'' he mumbled deferentially. ''Preventing a discharge until contact seems the sensible way to design a weapon like that.''

''Why wouldn't the charge jump within the gun?''

''Insulated barrels, maybe. Hell, I don't know. I don't know anybody who'd kill two folks for the privilege of destroying a piece of art, either.''

''People are saying maybe it was some kind of fanatical collector,'' Welles informed him softly. ''The kind of person who wants exclusive possession of something, who wants to be able to say he has the only one of its kind in existence. Even if it's a copy. A painting mounted on a chunk of wood six feet square would be pretty hard to wrestle out on a maglide car. A holo wouldn't. Think about it. I gotta get back to my desk.''

Moody did think about it, without satisfaction. The hypothetical weapon made more sense than the hypothetical motive. No bullets to trace to a certain caliber gun, no poisons to track to a pharmacologist, no messy sharp blades. An electric charge left no calling card.

He didn't care much for the Chief. While Moody liked working with machines, he also enjoyed the company of other human beings. Feldstein didn't. If given a choice, there was no doubt in Moody's mind that the Chief would much prefer to run his department without any people at all. Just wall screens and mollyboards and memos and directives.

The science of law enforcement having yet to advance to that point, however, he was still compelled to make use of human beings. That included the likes of Vernon Moody, with whom the New York-educated Feldstein had little in common. Moody was sure the man had never handled a red wriggler or a nightcrawler in his life.

It didn't help that he was the shortest member of the department, with the exception of two of the female officers. In spite of his handicap he had risen to become chief of the largest police department in the state of Florida. The detectives often wondered how that had come about. Accidents of nature were frequently invoked.

Moody didn't think about it as much as some of his friends, because he had next to no contact with the Chief's office. Nor did Feldstein actively seek the company of his officers, preferring the seclusion of his office with its mollyboards and vorec circuits. They responded promptly and obediently to his requests and commands, unlike his often obstreperous subordinates.

Not that Feldstein was hostile. He was friendly enough when encountered in the hall or the commissary. Had he been unwilling to work with others, he never would have lived through his years as a patrolman and detective. He knew what it was like to work a beat, knew how to joke and bullshit on the street. It wasn't that he was incapable of sharing with others. It was just that he chose not to do so.

Moody turned a corner on his way to the Chief's sanctum. Maybe Feldstein thought it wasn't a good idea to get too close to people who might be found floating in the Bay the next morning. That Moody could understand. If he were Chief, maybe he'd feel similarly. Not that he ever would be. It didn't bother him. He was quite comfortable with the level he had achieved.

Security passed him through an admin checkpoint and on to Feldstein's office. It was not spacious, though it did command a nice view of the Bay. Molly and chip storage lined all the walls, warring with Feldstein for living space. Feldstein's intellect was all that kept the mutating files at bay, like a napalm-armed skier caught in a Colorado avalanche. Each time the files were reduced, western Florida's antisocial population inevitably restored them to their former dimensions. Try as he might, Feldstein would never be able to shrink them down to manageable size, nor would they overwhelm him. It was a perpetual stalemate.

Moody did his best to pay attention. It wasn't easy, because the silvery sheen of the Bay was clearly visible through the big window at the back of the office. It made him think of fishing, and that made it difficult to concentrate on his job. Don't eye the Bay, went the conventional office wisdom, and don't eye Corporal Laney in Processing, and a man might could get his work done.

Feldstein was working at his desk when Moody entered. The detective had never seen him not working. He was a small dark man, son of a small dark man, grandson of a small dark man, continuing a lineage of successful small dark men who had arrived in Florida by way of New York, East Europe, and the Middle East, the end product of several thousand years' worth of small dark men arising originally in Samaria, where—Moody did not doubt—Feldstein's ancestor many dozen times removed had served as faithful policeman or tax collector or accountant in the service of Solomon—or some lesser light.

"Morning, Chief."

Feldstein reluctantly looked up from one of the three screens that sprouted from his desk like flat-faced mushrooms.

"Vernon." That was his one concession to familiarity. The Chief knew everyone in the building, maybe everyone on the whole force, by their first name. Maybe the janitors who worked the night shift, too. "How long have you been on the Kettrick case?"

"About three weeks now, sir."

"Got anything yet?"

"As in 'results'?" The Chief hadn't invited him to sit down, which suited Moody fine. It meant this was going to be a short interview. "No more than what we had by the second day. We got a modus, a possible motive, and a good description of the prime suspect, but we haven't been able to run him down yet. We will. APB's are out all over the country, heightened in the Southwest."

Feldstein folded his hands on the desk. That was a bad sign. It meant the Chief had been thinking. "Having had to do it myself once or twice, I know how frustrating it is to try running an investigation twenty-five hundred miles from the likely territory of your prime suspect. That's why I'm sending you to Arizona to work on it from there. We need someone on the scene."

An image congealed like stale milk in Moody's head. A vision of endless horizons devoid of growth, of dry, enervating heat; of dust and cactus spines and venomous reptiles and insects. Not that Florida didn't boast its share of the latter, but they stayed down in the Glades where they belonged.

"If you don't mind, sir, I'd rather not go."

Feldstein turned to one of his monitors, his tone as coolly correct as the information being displayed on the screen.

"The local police will be doing most of the work. You're going to serve as backup, information source, and to keep us up-to-date." He glanced up from the glass. "Also because the media and city fathers are all over me to show some progress on this one. You can record five murders a day down in the harbor and nobody sneezes, but somebody like Kettrick gets deleted and important people get the shakes. You know the drill. Don't look so glum. Think of it as a working vacation."

"Chief, I don't like the desert. I like lowlands and open water. Lots of open water. There's nothing out there but sand."

"Get used to the idea. Think of it as a wide beach if it helps, but you're going."

"Why not send somebody else?" The thought leapt unbidden to his lips. "Why not send that tall, good-looking young detective who's so good at PR? What's his name? Nackerman? Nickerson? He was on the scene before I was."

"We're talking interjurisdictional cooperation, Vernon. Nickerson's a little too aggressive for an assignment like this, a little too involved in promoting himself instead of tending to business. You have a way of working with people without threatening them."

Moody knew he had no chance of extricating himself unless he produced a much more substantial reason for not going, but try as he would, he couldn't come up with one. Personal dislike was insufficient. Despite his distaste, he was flattered. Feldstein was sending him because he was the best man for the job. Or else because he thought the big detective wouldn't be missed.

"Isn't there anyone else who can go, sir?" It was a lame last effort but he had to try.

"Oh, there are other people I could send. There just aren't others I *want* to send. You're going, Vernon, because I know you'll get along out there, and because I know you won't miss anything, and because I know you won't waste the department's time and money gallivanting around at night."

That's me, he thought resignedly. *Good ol' boy Moody, the quintessential dull cop*. Not necessarily the most brilliant, nor the most obvious, but ever the safest.

"It won't be so bad, Vernon." Feldstein was trying to

be sympathetic. "Everyone needs a change of scenery from time to time."

But I like this scenery, dammit. What he said was, "If y'all have made up your mind, sir, then I'm just killing time for the both of us by standing here." He turned to go, hesitated at the door. "I get travel pay?"

Feldstein smiled broadly. He had bright white teeth. On the rare occasions when he revealed them, they added an uncharacteristic glow to his usually dour expression. As if conscious of the atypical display, his lips abruptly tightened.

"Full travel pay and time, but I want you out there pronto. No maglide connections. Take a shuttle."

"Fine with me, sir." And it was. Moody had no desire to spend hours in a transcontinental maglide car. "What about a place to stay?"

"Set up a per diem with Accounting and make your own arrangements. You've never been on assignment outside the Bay area before, have you?"

"Shoot, I've never been out of the South before, sir. No reason to. I like it here. I'm not one of those guys who yearns for faraway places."

"It'll be good for you," Feldstein insisted unconvincingly. "Broaden your horizons."

Moody didn't want his horizons broadened, but with the Chief exerting an unusual effort to be understanding, it would have been undiplomatic to say so.

"Arizona, huh? Maybe there's a lake somewhere."

"Not near where you're going. And properly speaking, you're not going to Arizona. You're being assigned to the Navaho Department of Public Safety, of the Navaho Nation. Those are the people you'll be working with. Not the Arizona police."

Shoot, Moody mused as he left the Chief's office; cops were cops. Whether from the Hindu Kush or the Great Rift Valley, he'd manage to get along with any new colleagues

so long as he could find one or two to share a beer with.
If they followed the NFL scores, so much the better. His
thoughts left him feeling slightly more sanguine about
things, but not much.

CHAPTER 4

BY THE TIME the shuttle crossed the Texas-New Mexico border, the air had become impossibly transparent, the views absurdly extensive. It remained thus as the shuttle commenced its descent from seventy thousand feet, falling like an amputated arrowhead toward the red-brown frying pan that was Northern Arizona.

Finally pausing in his reading long enough to glance out a window, Moody was appalled by what he saw. Gone was the fertile landscape of Florida, the reassuring tracts of homes and condos, the pale opalescent blue of the Gulf. Below lay earthtone gone amuck, reds and umbers and dirty pink and brown, sprawled from horizon to horizon like a Calcutta whore. In vain he searched for the signatory slash of the Grand Canyon, before realizing sheepishly it must lie too far to the northwest to be visible from his present position and altitude.

The barren emptiness of the terrain compared to that of population-swollen Central Florida was numbing. Like a drowning man nearing land, he began to breathe a little easier only when the support structures surrounding Klagetoh International Airport came into view. Fastech and light-industry manufacturing facilities clung to both sides of Interstate-40 like aphids to a rose stem.

It was a relief to leave the plane for the comforting bustle of the terminal, which was gratifyingly spacious and modern and full of color and life. Men and women from around the world swarmed like corpuscles through the corridors, bumping into each other while venturing apologetic phrases in half a dozen tongues.

They were drawn to this formerly isolated chunk of North America by the explosion of hi-tech manufacturing which in the past hundred years had radically transformed the Navahopi Reservations. The Koreans had arrived first, looking to steal a march on the Japanese, who hadn't been far behind in their never-ending quest for skilled labor and benign tax structures. After them had come, in a rush, the Taiwanese, the Malaysians, the Thais, and the Indians and the Brazilians and the South American Community. Slow to recognize the potential of the Rez, the EEC was now trying hard to catch up. The shuttle had been full of Germans, Italians, and Turks.

"If you think this is bad, you should see Phoenix. They have needed a new airport for fifty years."

Moody found himself eyeing a softly smiling man ten years his junior. He wore a long-sleeved cotton shirt and neatly pressed brown jeans. And cowboy boots, as if Moody needed any further proof he was no longer in Central Florida. Though probably in his thirties, he looked considerably younger. Slightly less than average height and slimly built, he tended to disappear alongside Moody. A lot of people did. His skin was as smooth and unblemished as that of a fashion model. The little half-smile—the corners of his mouth turned slightly upward, making the cheekbones even more prominent than they were naturally—seemed to be the only expression he had. He extended a hand.

"*Ya-tah-hey*. I'm Sergeant Paul Ooljee, NDPS."

Moody shook the proffered hand. "Vernon Moody, Detective, Greater Tampa PD."

The sergeant held the handshake a long time. His small fingers were like steel and Moody was conscious of the pressure of the thumb against the back of his own wrist. No doubt that meant something. Moody hoped he wouldn't have to hang around here long enough to learn the local customs.

"I'll tell you my theory if you'll tell me yours." The grin did not fade.

"Haven't got one yet." Moody walked beside the smaller man, letting him lead. "Title aside, what do I call you?"

"Paul will do fine. I would give you my other name but I do not think you could pronounce it. If you have trouble with Ooljee, you can call me Moon, which is what it means. Or you can call me crazy, which is what some of my friends call me. Especially my mother-in-law. You can also say 'my friend.' That is what I will be calling you."

"We've just met." Ooljee turned a corner and Moody lengthened his stride to keep pace. They were in a restricted corridor now, having left the airport crowds behind.

"It is only proper. If you don't tell someone your name and where you and your clan are from right away, then you mark yourself as a suspicious person. In Navaho it is more correct to ask, 'What is this person?' instead of 'Who is this person?' But since I can tell from the look on your face that everything I am saying is only confusing you, we can just call each other Ooljee and Moody for a while. If you do not object to the formality, my friend." He looked thoughtful.

"Of course, if you prefer the translation, that could be fun. People would be able to look at us and say, "There goes Moon and Moody.""

"I can manage Ooljee all right." Here he'd expected the local yokels to be quiet, even taciturn, and the first one he met wouldn't shut up.

They passed under the blower from a vid ad and his nostrils were awash for an instant in the tantalizing aroma of frangipani. He walked through it without taking the bait and turning to check out the ad.

An elevator took them to ground level.

"You know why I'm here or did y'all just come to pick me up and run me into town?"

"I know why you are here. We will be working together. I have been on this case for several weeks and in daily contact with your office, though not with you personally. Tampa and Ganado have been mollydancing for many days and I am quite familiar with the unfortunate details of the murder."

"What were you working on before they put you on the Kettrick?"

"A local killing. And I was not 'put on' the Kettrick case. I volunteered to work on it. Fascinating business." The elevator slowed. "Here we are."

Moody followed him out into a covered parking structure. That's when it hit him. The air. There was something not right about it. The lack of oxygen he'd expected and was prepared for. Klagetoh was nearly six thousand feet above sea level. But the dryness came as a shock. He was inhaling something cool and utterly devoid of moisture; oxynitro as pure as the symbology of a periodic table. Dizzy, he paused and tried to recover, convinced the potted plants lining the walkway were leaning hungrily toward him, about to puncture his moisture-rich form with hypodermic air-roots capable of sucking the water from his body.

"Hey, Moody; you okay?" Ooljee eyed him with concern.

"Just gimme a minute." The detective straightened, breathing deeply. The dizziness went away.

He picked up his luggage and resumed walking. Ooljee said nothing about the delay, but did slow his relentless pace.

"I'm glad somebody finds the case interesting," Moody wheezed. "Got everyone jittery back home. We haven't made a whole helluva lot of progress lately."

"I hope we can be helpful."

"Yeah. Say, why do your friends call you crazy?"

"Everyone in my clan thinks I would be a plant manager by now if I had gone into commerce instead of police work. It does not matter to them that I happen to like police work. It suits my nature. What do you know about Navaho sandpaintings?"

"I know one guy got himself killed over one. That's about it. In my department you don't have to take anthropology to make detective."

"Different departments. Why don't we rest here a moment? Sometimes it helps, when you have just come up from sea level."

Moody hesitated, checked with his heart and lungs, and gave in to their reply. He set his luggage down next to a bench and then gratefully let the hardwood slats cradle his weight. Ooljee remained standing.

"You will be seeing sandpaintings all over town, especially in the hotels and gift shops. It is a big business. Some are still done using colored sand, while others are just painted on canvas or board." There was a twinkle in his eye. "The first thing you should know is that every one of them is wrong."

"Wrong? Wrong how?"

"The colors, the tilt of a figure, the way it faces, the arrangement of plants or designs; one or all are incorrect. No one would make an accurate sandpainting to sell to a tourist, because the magic might get loose."

So now I know why they call you crazy, Moody thought amusedly, suspecting he was being skillfully put on. "You're not telling me anybody out here actually believes in stuff like that anymore?"

"Oh *no*," replied Ooljee with exaggerated concern. "To

do so would mark that person as an unrepentant primitive, a throwback, an apologist for ancient superstition.''

"Then why bother to change the paintings that are sold to tourists?''

"Many of the people here, especially the older ones, tend to adopt an unspoken agnostic-like position. They can be ninety-nine per cent sure there is no magic, but the remaining one per cent might make life unnecessarily complex. So those who manufacture the sandpaintings for mass distribution will tell you it is all old nonsense at the same time as they are making sure at least one small part of each painting they turn out is inaccurate.

"It's easy for them, because only a trained *hatathli*, a medicine man, knows how to make an accurate medicine painting, and they do not make things to sell to tourists. So you need not worry if you buy one. There will be no real magic in it.''

"That's a great relief,'' said Moody. "Now I can embark on a life without fear.''

"Hold to the comfort of your skepticism. We may need it later. Do not forget that someone, and I concur with your department that he is most likely Navaho, has murdered two people and violated the security of a major multinational insurance firm because of a sandpainting.''

"But no specific suspects yet?''

"I regret not. It will come. Your cadcam portrait was very distinctive, and we have more to go on than that. There is, for example, the fact that the victim's secretary heard the perpetrator make his request to acquire the sandpainting a fourth time. In our culture a request made a fourth time must be honored. I think it an unlikely ploy for a non-Navaho to try.''

"Any idea why he destroyed the painting after making such an effort to acquire it? The theory out my way goes that maybe he wanted to be the only possessor of the design, or something like that.''

Ooljee nodded. "A possibility. When we find him we will ask him."

"Damn right we will."

"There is a chance he could be Sioux or Kiowa or someone from another tribe masquerading as Navaho to conceal his true motives, but I tend to think not. I do not see someone from another tribe being so interested in a sandpainting."

For the first time, Ooljee appeared to hesitate before speaking. "Tell me, my friend, if you don't mind: why are you here?"

"My department wanted one of its own on the scene. Lucky me got elected when he wasn't looking."

"I see. I was not told, and I was curious."

"Shoot, who wouldn't be? Look, I don't want to step on anybody's ego. It's not that we don't have complete confidence in you people out here. This wasn't *my* idea. I'll try to stay out of the way."

"That would be nice. Are you feeling a little better?"

"Yeah." Moody rose. The initial lightheadedness had left him. "Let's go. But keep it slow, okay?" He bent to recover his luggage.

ON VEHICLES THAT had been left in the parking structure
for more than a couple of days he noticed a fine coating of
what looked like rust but which on closer inspection turned
out to be russet-colored dust. He wiped some off the nearest
car and rubbed the grit between his fingers, suspecting this
too was something he might become unwillingly intimate
with in the days to come.

Ooljee led him to a stocky, non-aerodynamic vehicle
mounted on oversized tires. The normally exposed back end
was covered with an extended accordion cabover. The sergeant unsecured it electronically, popped the back door so
his companion could dump his luggage in the rear. Then
they climbed into the passenger compartment.

Moody watched as Ooljee entered the ignition combination and waited for the control LCD to light. Without
waiting for the engine to warm up, he backed them out of
the official parking space and headed for the exit. Map lights
winked on the navigation screen. Moody recognized the
uncertainty pattern and queried his companion.

"I'm not set up to patrol in Klagetoh," Ooljee explained,
"so they don't issue me road software."

The exit gate flashed them through. Ooljee deftly negotiated the maze leading out of the airport, avoiding the town as he headed for the Interstate.

Once clear of commercial traffic he entered their destination into the dash. The onboard navigation unit confirmed the entry and they began to accelerate. Ooljee let go of the wheel and relaxed. Beneath their feet, the ROM laser tracked the guide strip laminated to the pavement, coordinating speed and direction with all vehicles ahead and behind. Unless Ooljee altered the entry manually, they would travel the rest of the way into Ganado on automatic.

"You always work out of a pickup truck?" Moody asked conversationally.

"Old traditions die hard. This is standard issue transportation for plainclothes work. A department road cruiser would look more familiar to you, except that it would also come with four-wheel drive and steering. The roads on the Rez are much improved over the last hundred years, but there are still plenty of places that will destroy a normal vehicle. That is tradition too. Like the sandpainting." He looked to his right as they passed a private vehicle stuck by the side of the road.

"Family breakdown. Help will arrive soon. Tradition is why I was able to get into this Kettrick business. For a lot of the people who work in the department, tradition is who won the league title two years ago. Now me, I have always been interested in the old ways."

At a touch, a locked compartment in the dash dropped open. He fumbled through a disorganized, highly compacted mass of papers, opdisks, and mollyboxes until he found a color fax. Moody recognized the Kettrick painting.

"I have been working with this a lot since your department contacted ours asking for information. I've already run it through the files at the Museum of Northern Arizona, the Navaho Museum in Window Rock, and the University of New Mexico at Gallup. My friend, there are hundreds of sandpaintings, each distinctively different, and this one does not match up with any of them. There are individual elements which do, but they are drawn oddly and make no historical sense in the context in which they appear. It is very peculiar. I have talked to specialists in all three places about it and they agree they have never seen anything quite like it.

"Of course, I am only a policeman and they are only academics. We all agree that only a hatathli with much experience and a very active imagination could make anything out of this. His interpretation might not be accurate, but it would certainly be entertaining."

Moody shifted in the seat. It was worn but comfortable. "So what you're telling me is that nobody has any idea what it means."

"That is what I am being told." The engine hummed as they began to climb. He ran his finger over the fax. "There are figures and shapes and designs in this painting that some say are wholly nontraditional in origin. Other experts are not so certain. That is not to say the designs are meaningless; only that I have been unable so far to find anyone able to tell me what they mean."

Moody stuck out his lower lip. "We assumed that it sure as hell meant something to the son of a bitch who murdered Kettrick and his housekeeper."

"I tend to agree. I do not subscribe to the theory that we are dealing with a crazed collector."

"Why not?"

"Because I do not see a collector, even an insane one, destroying what he has gone to so much trouble to collect. I think it was the substance of the sandpainting the killer wanted, more than the original itself." He looked thoughtful. "When we catch him I will be very anxious to ask him about that."

"Ask all y'all want. I'll settle for catching him."

Ooljee glanced at his colleague. "Your interests parallel but do not always duplicate mine. That is understandable."

He turned forward again, lost in his own thoughts.

It gave Moody time to study the countryside through which they were passing. Paralleling the Interstate to the south were the four major east-west maglide tubes, shooting cargo and the occasional passenger car between Los Angeles and Albuquerque or the Montezuma Strip.

They hadn't spent five minutes on the Interstate before the truck ducked down an off-ramp and crossed onto highway 191 running north. A glowing sign flashed past.

METROPOLITAN GANADO—40 MILES

"That's where you're based?" Moody inquired.

The sergeant nodded. "Window Rock's still the capital, but Ganado's the commercial center of the Rez. Has been for over a century. You'll be seeing high-rises pretty soon."

They were already in among sprawling assembly and manufacturing plants, Moody noted. "Nothing personal," he said as they passed mile after mile of faceless industrial facilities interspersed with residential dormitories and service structures, "but surely you folks don't own all of these?"

"No, but we are in most of them. There are not enough of us to fill the demand for skilled techs, let alone the unskilled positions. A lot of Hispanics and Filipinos live and work on the Rez. Plus Anglos, of course. And Nicarags, ever since the big eruption that wiped out Managua back in sixty-five. Asians mostly in the administrative posts." With a wave of his hand he encompassed the teeming industrial landscape.

"Most of the businesses here are tripartite joint ventures between Navahopis, Anglos, and Orientals. Isn't it the same where you come from?"

Moody shook his head. "Greater Tampa's still primarily a retirement and recreation city. Oh, there's plenty of industry, but not a lot of high-tech. Humidity's not good for electronics."

"That is a problem we do not have here."

They drove in silence interrupted only by Ooljee's occasional checks with his office. Only much later did he venture to ask, "I don't suppose any neighbors reported hearing any singing from the victim's house around the time of the murder?"

Moody was taken aback. "Singing? Why? You think our nut's the kind who celebrates over a kill?"

"Not exactly that. It is only that we are operating on the premise that our suspect is Navaho, or at least someone with detailed knowledge of Navaho custom. A hatathli always chants when destroying a sandpainting. I would give a lot to know if our killer is a hatathli. It would narrow the list of potential suspects considerably."

Moody could not keep the irritation out of his reply. "No, as far as I know, nobody heard any singing."

This sandpainting business was beginning to get to him. He'd been in the Southwest less than an hour and already he wanted out. Medicine men and chants! If any of this ever made it back to Tampa he'd have to deal with the jokes for years.

He tried to concentrate on the terrain. It was spectacular, but far too sweeping and barren for his taste. He preferred calmer horizons softened by the irregular green of tropical trees and framed by the glint of sunlight on still waters, not endless mesas that ran like veins of rust through a harsh blue sky. It was beautiful, sure, but to him, lifeless. And the lack of moisture in the air was making him itch.

He was only here to serve as a liaison, he reminded himself; to offer what aid he could while reporting back to Tampa on any local progress, which according to Ooljee was practically nil. He could back off from this hatathli nonsense and stick to standard police procedure.

If, he told himself suddenly, Ooljee wasn't simply having

some fun at his expense and setting him up for a few good
gags with his buddies at the station. Sure, that made plenty
of sense! He could envision it clearly: the paleface sucker
from Florida somberly questioning other Navahos about
sandpaintings and medicine men. He smiled to himself.
Ooljee was good, and his guest had nearly bought it. Nearly.

Well, two could play. Moody would smile and nod and
appear to take it all seriously, and when the time came,
he'd be the one to deliver the punch lines. Ooljee was a
good guy and a good cop. He was only having a little fun.

Just as Moody had it all figured, the sergeant threw him
a big, fat, sweeping curve.

"I have been devoting some time and thought to the
matter of a motive."

"You ain't been the only one, brother."

"The sandpainting is the obvious solution. What we do
not know is the question. I think whoever wanted it, or a
copy of it, needed it for a particular reason, and not to
complete a collection. It may be that this particular sandpainting was used against the murderer in the past, or against
his family, or a close friend. Or it may have been employed
against a stranger who hired the murderer.

"By destroying it according to tradition he may have
been removing the threat it presented to someone. You
would call it an exorcism."

Lordy, mused Moody. Just when common sense had been
reasserting its good ol' self.

"If this guy can electrocute people by an as yet unde-
termined method, why the hell would he need to trash a
bunch of colored sand? You ain't trying to tell me we're
dealing with something like voodoo, are you?"

"It provides a rationale for a seemingly irrational act,"
Ooljee argued. "The underlying principle is the same. To
affect another, they need only believe they can be affected."

"This is starting to affect me," Moody grumbled.

"It does offer us a motive."

Moody eyed him sharply. "You don't *really* believe in any of this scrim, do you?"

The sergeant sidestepped the question. "What matters is that someone else may. People who *believe* are people capable of anything."

"So we're back where we started," Moody murmured. "The guy's a nut."

"People have killed for stranger reasons: because their god or their devil told them to, or simply because they didn't like the cast of another man's eyes, or the tone of his voice."

Moody couldn't argue with that. He'd seen it happen too often on Tampa's mean streets.

"It does not matter," Ooljee went on, "that we are dealing only with a pile of colored sand and pulverized masonite. What is significant is that whoever did the damage may believe that the sandpainting had real power. It gives us a new line to pursue. There are ways of checking such things. Not as thoroughly or efficiently as I would like, but we can make a beginning."

"Right." Moody relaxed a little. It was a relief to find out that Ooljee had had a serious goal from the start.

Beyond the fact that Ganado served as the commercial center of a major high-tech manufacturing area, Moody knew nothing about the city. As they drew within sight of the first towers, however, he knew he was going to have to discard many of his preconceptions.

Fanciful spires rose from massive office blocks that had seemingly been integrated elsewhere and then laid down intact atop the high desert plateau. Not one of the buildings could properly be called old, every one of them having been erected within the last century. Patterned after the rugged buttes and monuments he'd seen from the air, the structures appeared a part of the landscape, as though escarpments and mesas had been hollowed out and overlaid with glass and plexan and composites. Climate-controlled pedways connected the major buildings above street level, soaring arteries of spun composite and metallic glass.

Downtown, the tall buildings shut out the sun. New construction was going up everywhere. Moody was assaulted by advertisements in a dozen languages. He might as well have been in Manhattan. Only the buildings themselves hewed to a smaller scale.

The peculiar squiggles and curves on many signs which he thought comprised some unknown Middle Eastern language were in fact, according to Ooljee, components of written Navaho.

"Until the early part of the twentieth century there was no such thing as written Navaho." The sergeant eased their truck around a slow delivery van. "It may look confusing, but writing it is nothing compared to trying to learn the grammar. And you should see what Hopi looks like!" He uttered a nasal mélange of consonants and gutturals.

"For something so difficult to write, it sounds beautiful. It is much like singing. The Chinese understand."

As he tried to make sense of his companion's linguistic discourse, Moody studied the hovering, acrobatic laser ads. Downtown Ganado was a stroboscopic maze of holos and cold neon, of plasma sculptures that beckoned and danced and teased tired travelers. They alternately tickled and battered the senses not only in English, Hopi, Navaho, and Zuni, but also in Japanese, Mandarin, Thai, Bahasa Indonesia, Malay, Tagalog, and the inescapable Spanish of the South American community.

"How much of this can you understand?" Moody inquired dazedly, more than a little overwhelmed by his unexpectedly cosmopolitan surroundings.

"Some Spanish. A little Japanese and Thai. A few words of Malay, plus my English and Navaho. Not as much Hopi as I should. You should hear the patter of some of the local street gangs. In the old days they used spray cans on the walls. Procter and Gamble's graffiti-out took care of that.

Now they mark their territories in other ways.

"You can't walk through certain parts of town without triggering a playback voc stuck to a ledge. It does not bother the standup citizens, because what comes out sounds like gibberish to them, but I have seen such messages drive other gang members to distraction.

"You take all those languages I just listed for you and mix them all up with street slang as a catalyst and the result is something we have to use a Cribm molly to decipher. It does not make street work easy."

"How's ya'll's gang problem here?"

"No worse than that of a city of similar size, though when you have so much new money and excitement concentrated all in one place you are always going to have trouble. There are many wealthy local people and, as always, many poor ones as well. Some of the young poor join gangs, as they always have everywhere. They run pharmacuties, weapons, industrial stats and information, the same way gangs have supported themselves since the beginning of time. I am told it is a little more intense here than some other places. We have unique problems of cultural as well as fiscal disenfranchisement.

"It helps that every major high-tech corporation in the world would like to do work here. It took them a while to discover that the people of the Four Corners region are the best high-tech workers on the planet. There are plants here that literally turn out zero-defect product. Combine those human resources with the unique tax advantages available to multinationals on the Rez and you have a combination irresistible to many companies. Our street people and our problems reflect this influx of outside influence and money."

So did the ethnic mix that swarmed the walkways, Moody noted. Between the Indians and Asians and Hispanics, Anglos were a distinct minority here, just as they were in parts of Tampa. It did not bother him. He'd been in the minority

all his life. Fat people were an unrecognized minority all
their own.

He had to agree that this would be a tough town to police.
You'd need specialists in a whole range of languages and
cultures. Tampa's ethnic mix of Anglo, Black, and Hispanic
was much more straightforward, whereas Ganado was a
seething southwestern bouillabaisse.

"Your people aren't restricted to assembly work,
though?"

"Oh, no. We own our share, individually and through
the Council Enterprises. You can always tell if a building
is Navaho-owned. Whether it is an apartment building, office complex, shopping tower or private home, the entrance
will always face east." He hesitated. "I am sorry. This is
a lot for you to absorb all at once, and you just got off the
plane."

"No problem."

"Well, you won't meet many Hopis, so don't worry about
that. They have their own commercial center over at Seba
Delkai. The Zunis stick mostly to New Mexico. But if you
have trouble with any Navaho, just smile and say '*doo
ahashyaa da*.'"

"Do a hashee duh," Moody essayed. Ooljee repeated
the phrase slowly and carefully until he was sure Moody
had it reasonably correct.

"What am I saying?" Moody asked him.

"It will tell people that you are a stranger here, not to
be feared, and in need of assistance. I assure you they will
be instantly sympathetic. Few Anglos make any attempt to
learn Navaho. This will endear you to anyone you meet. It
is a useful greeting phrase, though not readily translatable.
Just like *yatahey* is Navaho for shalom."

"Say what?"

"Never mind. Just stick with *doo ahashyaa da* and you
will be okay no matter who you meet."

"Except for the guy we're after."

"Yes. I do not think he will be instantly sympathetic to anyone. I would give a great deal to know if we are dealing with someone medically certifiable."

"I doubt it. A nut wouldn't be able to hide his tracks this well."

"Not necessarily. A sane person is somewhat predictable. A crazy one is not. He could be more difficult to locate because of that."

"Unless some other sandpainting collector gets himself blown away." Moody nodded out the window. "I've seen some paintings in a few storefronts, haven't I?"

Ooljee nodded. "Downtown is the center of the important tourist and shopping areas. It would be unusual if you had not seen any sandpaintings by now."

"Nobody uses the patterns for anything else? Advertising, maybe?"

"Oh, no. That would be like making underwear out of the American flag. Eye-catching but unsettling. It is interesting that even those who insist they are completely modern and do not believe in the old ways would never do such a thing. It might make your business go bust or your building fall down. The one per cent uncertainty factor, remember?

"Here is something else you might find of interest."

Ooljee switched off the laser pickup and resumed manual control of the truck, turning left and heading down an incline into a natural basin in the plateau. Ancient trees lined a stream through which water ran lazily. The land had been turned into a park, preserving the old trees and a cluster of aged buildings. Rocks had been sculpted into pleasing shapes or benches on which old people and young couples relaxed.

"This is what remains of old Ganado. This is what all this country used to look like. The only silicon and gallium arsenide at this spot is in the ground. Not that anybody uses that stuff much anymore anyway. The park idealizes things a little but I have seen old two-D pictures of the area. The simulation is accurate.'' He pointed to his left, at a hill fringed with gleaming towers.

"They even saved the old Hubbell Trading Post. It occupies the lobby of the new one on Betatkin Boulevard.'' He sat staring at the unhurried stream, the couples wandering along its modest banks. "Have you got a place to stay?''

Moody shook his head. "My department told me to check in anywhere comfortable.''

"I see. Then you will of course stay with me.''

"Hey, no chance! First off you probably don't have a bed that'll fit me.''

"I think we can manage something, if you don't mind sleeping a little on the diagonal.''

"And second of all, there's no way I'm gonna put you and your wife out on my behalf.''

"Are you a noisy person?''

"I'm not likely to play shuntbuzz all night, if that's what you mean. But that's not the point. The point is . . .''

"The point, my friend, is that it would be rude of you to refuse my hospitality. Perhaps I can convince you another way. How are you to pay for your accommodations here? Are you using a department card?''

"Card, but . . .''

"Restricted?''

"Of course.''

"Then you are functioning on a per diem designed to cover your daily expenses while you are working with us. A per diem you receive as a supplement to your salary regardless of how you spend it. If you choose to stay in an expensive place, you have to cover the difference out of your own pocket. But if you choose to live cheaply, you have a balance you can spend at your own discretion. That is how we operate here.''

"It's the same in Tampa,'' Moody admitted.

"Which means that if you stay with us, the money which would otherwise go toward your room and board will be yours to pocket. Would that not help to compensate some-what for being sent to a part of the country you dislike so intensely?''

"Hey, I never said I didn't like it here. Hell, I just got here."

"Your expression speaks eloquently even when your mouth is closed."

"What's that?" Moody was angry at having been so transparent. "An old Navaho saying?"

"No. Actually I got it from an Italian variety show that was on the RAI transponder last week. What do you say?''

Moody didn't want to start the week by insulting the guy he was going to be working with. By the same token, the thought of spending time in a cramped little apartment with kids underfoot—hadn't Ooljee said something earlier about kids?—struck him as less than appealing. But he didn't see how he could turn down the offer.

"I'll give it a try," he said reluctantly, "but none of this 'board' business. I'll pay for my own food or you'll be broke inside a week."

"All right." Ooljee grinned. "But I warn you. My wife loves to cook. She is an experimental gourmet and will be delighted to have a new vict—guest, to try out her latest recipes on. As to what you do with your money, that is up to you. The pleasures of full-time police work are few, and should be indulged in whenever possible."

They enjoyed the park for a while longer. Then Ooljee rolled up the windows and reprogrammed the onboard. The engine revved softly as the laser pickup exchanged infor-mation with the nav strip embedded in the pavement of the parking lot. The truck backed, turned itself around, and departed.

Now that his plans were settled, Moody was able to devote his time to examining the exotica of urban Ganado. He was especially intrigued by the kids' attire, an eclectic and inventive combination of all that Asia and America had to offer. It would have looked out of place back in Tampa. Here it all belonged.

He made Ooljee slow down so he could study an exceptionally attractive young woman. Her black hair was crested by a pair of dyed-blond aerodynamic curls that swept up, around, and out from the sides of her head. Silver wire shimmered among the obsidian strands. The rest of her outfit consisted of red leather jacket and skirt dripping with buttons and carved fetishes, bits and fragments of salvaged componentry, reflective plastic boots, and a false tail built up out of twisted silver.

Ooljee watched his colleague watching. "The hairdo is traditional Hopi. The decorations are not."

"How do they keep it up like that?" Moody marveled at the gravity-defying array.

"It's an old technique, though the girl is probably Navaho. There has been a lot of intermixing the last fifty years. Would have been more, but old enmities die hard."

"You don't have to tell me that. I'm from the South."

As they turned westward they left the city center with its glitz and flash behind, entering an area crowded with individual homes, apartment buildings, and service structures. Cedar and stunted pine grew densely on uncleared land.

"You do not have much of what I would call a Southern accent, my friend."

"Accents disappear fast in Metropolitan Florida." Moody shifted in his seat. "It ain't like living out in the country, on the family place. You find accents in Georgia and Sip, but Florida's full of folks from all over everywhere. In that respect it's a lot like L.A. I know Cubanos who sound like they're from Chicago, not Havana."

"Traditions are stronger here and down in the Strip," Ooljee replied. "You've probably heard about the Strip. Imagine a whole cluster of Ganados strung out along the Border. A good place for a man to lose himself. So we are concentrating our search here and there. Our suspect has a real dilemma. He could go to Portland, say, where he would stand out but where the search is not as intense, or he can stay here where he blends in naturally and try to hide. Me, I think he is around here somewhere." High beams from an oncoming truck dimmed tardily, highlighting the sergeant's face.

"You are not married?"

"Been there." Moody stared out the window as they rushed past a gleaming all-night market. "Twice. It ain't easy being married to a cop."

"My wife and I seem to have no trouble. I try not to bring my work home, and I think that helps. You look healthy. No serious on-the-job injuries?"

"I've been shot at a few times. Lucky so far. I do a lot of research for the rest of the department. After a while, you find out what you're good at and stick to that. Neither my mental, physical or work profile suits me for chasing outgrabed crazyboys down dark alleys."

"I know you must be good at what you do or your department would not have chosen you to come here. You are probably an expert at observation and at putting disparate elements together. Like sandpainting."

"Nothing personal," said Moody sharply, "and while it's central to the case, I'd appreciate it if you wouldn't keep bringing that up."

Ooljee glanced at him in surprise. "Why not?"

"Because I'm not a superstitious guy and I'm getting tired of it. I can't tell when you're putting me on and when y'all are being serious, and it's making me uncomfortable, okay? I'm a rational empiricist, or whatever the hell it is they're calling folks who believe in common sense these days. So gimme a break, okay?"

"Okay," Ooljee replied as he added very softly, "but it is central to the understanding of our suspect as well as everything else about this business."

CHAPTER
6

OOLJEE LIVED FAR out on the west side of the city, in a hexacluster of thirty-story multisided towers. Parks and service facilities separated the cluster from its nearest neighbor half a mile to the south. The parks were full of trees and sculpted sandstone, all of it alien to Moody. Trees and bushes wore their desiccated greenery defiantly. Each tower entrance, he noted, faced east.

A telltale on the truck's dash beeped as the building recognized vehicle and driver. A heavy garage door swung upward, granting them access to the subterranean garage.

"Don't you think," Moody said as the sergeant drove down the ramp and the door closed behind them, "you ought to call your wife and let her know you're bringing company home?"

"She knew someone was coming. She would be surprised only if you were not staying with us."

The elevator lifted them nine-tenths of the way up the tower, where they exited into a circular hall. Ooljee crossed to a door that was already opening. A short, stocky woman with a smile like an upside-down rainbow stepped aside to let them enter.

Her name was Lisa. The names of the four-armed, four-legged ball of fury occupying the center of the living room, when separated into its component halves, were Blue and Sun. The boys remained motionless only long enough to embrace their father before fleeing to the sanctum of their bedroom.

The floor was covered with a fabric that felt like carpet but resembled packed earth, a tour-de-force of manufacturing akin to dyeing a rabbit coat to look like mink. There were couches and chairs of rough-cut real wood, blankets and prints on the walls, pots and shelves full of holomage picture books. The kitchen was contrasting technoshock: all gleaming black plastic and brass.

When Ooljee told him he would have the boys' room, Moody was immediately concerned.

"Where are they supposed to sleep?" He indicated the long couch in the living room. "Hide-a-bed?"

"No." Ooljee turned toward the curved transparent doors that fronted the back of the living room. "Out on the porch. It will be a treat for them."

Moody walked over to the doors. The small size of the apartment was somewhat compensated for by the spacious terrace. It was shielded from the elements by the terrace immediately above it, the semicircular polycrete porches resembling giant poker chips stuck in the side of the building. Ooljee's provided a breathtaking vantage point from which to view the distant line of red which marked the escarpment of the Salahkai Mesa and the even more distant mountains beyond. Spectacular scenery, but not impressive enough to make Moody forget the pale blue of the Gulf.

One of the boys was tugging at his trousers. He was all black eyes, straight black hair, and youthful energy. Not knowing what else to say and figuring it was a safe place to try out what he'd learned, Moody smiled down at the kid and said, "*Doo ahashyaa da.*"

The boy covered his mouth and giggled, gazing wide-eyed at the massive visitor. His older brother broke out laughing. Chattering among themselves, they retreated to their bedroom.

Moody was pleased. He'd now mastered two Navaho phrases: *yatahey* and the one he'd just employed.

Ooljee was talking to his wife. Left to his own devices, Moody walked out onto the porch. Since he was standing on the west side of the westernmost tower in the condo complex, none of the other structures was visible. There was nothing to interrupt the view. Off to the south stood a second complex of glittering spires; electric necklaces stuck in the earth.

It was getting late. Lights were coming on in other apartments. Perhaps their murderer was sitting in one, quietly contemplating the results of his work. He wandered back into the living room, listening to the domestic chatter emanating from the kitchen, a mellifluous melange of English and Navaho. Some of the furniture looked old, but modern manufacturing could duplicate anything, including age. The blankets that were hung on the walls intrigued him. The patterns were not remarkably intricate nor were the colors especially bright, but there was a heft, a solidity to the designs, he had never encountered elsewhere. Gazing at them was like unexpectedly encountering an old friend.

The apartment was not large and he eventually found himself back out on the balcony, staring at the setting sun. If he squinted hard he could pretend he was looking at the sea. A voice startled him. He hadn't heard Ooljee approach.

"You should be here in the summer for the sunsets, after a monsoon thunderstorm. You would not believe how many shades of gold one sky can contain."

Moody leaned on the thin, inflexible banister that ringed the porch. "I didn't know Indians still practiced stealth."

"I don't know about that, but good cops do." He nodded at the sunset. "What do you think?"

"It's different from where I come from."

"And not really to your taste. I understand. The land

here takes time to appreciate. All the bright colors are in the sky.''

''I guess it's all what you grow up with.''

''Mostly I think it is the emptiness that gets to people, especially people from back East.''

''Yeah. The only empty land left in Florida is in parks.''

''As much of the Rez as possible has been allowed to remain in its natural state. Modern civilization is peculiar that way, don't you think? As soon as it achieves a certain level of creature comforts, it begins to spend huge sums on restoring what remains of the original habitat. In that respect we have been fortunate. Development in places like Kayenta and Klagetoh and Ganado has been intense, but if you go west from here, or north, you will find that the land looks much as it did to the Anasazi who settled here thousands of years ago.

''Peripheral development in places like Flagstaff and Gallup has not been nearly as well controlled. I do not think you would find those cities as attractive as Ganado, for all its typical urban troubles.'' He gestured at the sweep of distant land.

''One can still go out there and wander through the hills and know that there is the chance he may be the first man to set foot on that particular piece of earth. Or you might find things; a bit of pottery, an old arrowhead, a section of necklace, beads, maybe even a small overlooked cliff dwelling. The park service has been all over this country as have thousands of amateur archaeologists, but there are still places where no man has set foot in a thousand years and more.''

''I'm only interested in finding one thing.'' Moody was beginning to feel the strain of the cross-country hop and was not in the least interested in waxing poetic. ''Our murderer.''

Ooljee sighed. ''You are as persistent as you are direct, Vernon. With luck, we will run him to ground soon. Then you can fly back to your beloved Florida. I hope I am not asked to accompany you.''

''You don't like open water?''

''Not when it is full of salt. Fresh water, now—I wish I had the time to take you up to Powell.''

''I'm not on vacation.'' Moody tapped the spinner attached to his belt. Then, as if aware he might not be behaving as the most gracious of guests, he added, ''Helluva view you got from up here.''

''We like the place,'' Ooljee said simply. ''I would like also to have a vacation hogan, but there always seem to be other priorities. The boys, they eat up a lot of money, and I don't just mean that literally.''

''I'll bet.'' Screams and yelps reached them from the vicinity of the bedroom. ''Don't they ever slow down?''

''Never. I think they play in their sleep. As for you, I imagine you must be ready to eat.''

''I was ready to eat when I got off the shuttle.''

''We may not manage to fill you up, but I do not think you will go away from our table hungry. Do you like Chinese?''

''As long as it's not all vegetables and stuff.''

''I appreciate your honesty. Lisa would too. Then she would hit you with a spatula. Don't worry. We always have pasta or potatoes, and there'll be frybread for dessert.''

''Bread for dessert?''

Ooljee smiled. ''With honey and whipped cream. I don't think you will be disappointed. Ice cream, too. Ever had piñon nut ice cream?''

''Can't say as I have.'' Moody was beginning to salivate.

''Also made with honey. It will stick to your ribs. It certainly sticks to everything else. Every time Lisa makes some we have to watch the boys very closely, and we still end up having to dump them in the tub to dissolve them apart.''

The food was rich and wonderful, and despite his resolve,

he overate. The result was initial contentment followed by roiling dreams.

Kettrick was there, and his housekeeper. They orbited each other too closely, an obscenely entwined absurdity to anyone who knew anything about Kettrick's habits. If they were consistently rational, however, dreams would not be dreams.

Their place was taken by the grim, leering visages that populated the dead industrialist's private museum of the primitive, ghosts and spirits drawn from those parts of the world where the past still lingered and myths retained their ancient powers. In their midst drifted a figure without a face, whose arms were flexible bars of steel ending in fingers like tines. Sparks flew from them, and whatever they touched burst into flame.

Sepik River sculptures shriveled and burned. Masks from Southeast Asia exploded in showers of fiery cinders. African fetishes turned into blazing torches. The conflagration consumed half-remembered stories and unexplained mysteries. Dreams burned like crepe paper, flame giving way to ash, ash to smoke, smoke to a faint aroma of hot carbon where once there had been intimations of reality.

Kettrick too shriveled and burned, as did the housekeeper. Only when all had become ash and charcoal did the faceless figure stride forward to embrace the sandpainting which stood like an icon, untouched and immutable, in the very center of the destruction. When his finger touched the drawing, the shapes on the board sprang to horrid life. Symbols, stick figures of men and women, highly stylized creatures alive with flat, bright color leaped clear of the wood. They were accompanied by lightning and rain and rainbows, lots of rainbows, twisting and contorting like snakes.

They engulfed the faceless figure, melting together into a tornado that wore the garb of a double helix, contracting, tightening until the figure exploded, leaving behind only wisps of itself that drifted aimlessly away in every direction.

Moody awoke drenched in his own sticky sweat despite the fact that it was cool and comfortable in the apartment. Fading images clung tenaciously to his retinas: a hyperatmospheric shuttle, a dark shape rising high above a basket, an eagle inspecting a single spire of towering sandstone. All soaring, as children dream of soaring.

He rolled out of bed and sought his pants, not bothering with a shirt. Belly hanging over his belt, he tiptoed into the living room. It was silent and empty, the earthtones asleep in the moonlight that entered through the terrace doors.

He examined a pot, a piece of sculpture: cool, reassuring fragments of Mother Earth carried thirty stories into the air to remind the sky dwellers of the real world that existed beneath their feet.

Out on the porch Ooljee's boys lay still in slumber, secure in their sleeping bags, their internal springs finally at rest. It took him a moment to realize they really were motionless. Lying in the soft glow of moonlight they looked like utterly different beings, the darting black eyes shut tight, tiny fists curled tight against half-parted lips. Under his gaze they slowly metamorphosed into the young men they would someday become.

"I can't sleep either."

Moody glanced backwards. Ooljee stood in the shadows clad only in his briefs, gazing at his offspring.

"That's twice you've snuck up on me," Moody whispered. "I don't like it."

"You are pretty quiet for a big ol' Southern boy yourself. I didn't hear you get up."

"Then why'd you come out?"

"Like I said, I could not sleep either. Too much frybread, maybe. Too many thoughts, maybe."

Moody decided to say nothing about his unsettling dreams. His host might only be talking to help his guest relax. For lack of anything better to say, he repeated the phrase he'd been taught.

"*Doo ahashyaa da.*"

"That's for sure." Ooljee looked back into the living room, where muted colors and traditional designs held back the intrusions of a homogenizing technology. "Look, maybe something has come in since the last time I checked. Want to take a drive? Check out the office?"

"I don't like to bother night staff," Moody protested. "They might be busy with something."

"Like what? A floating card game? Ganado's big and busy, but this is not Tampa. If you would rather go back to bed, that is okay too."

Moody didn't have to think long. "As a matter of fact, I'd rather not. Once I'm up, I'm up. Lemme get a shirt and throw some water on my face."

"Good. We will take a roundabout. There is plenty of town you have not seen."

They ended up in one of those neighborhoods common to every large city; a place where cheap residential housing, manufacturing, commercial offices, and lowlife entertainment facilities came together. Not surprisingly, the focus of all this activity was a major university.

"Actual campus is up Keet Seel Street about a mile." Ooljee pointed out his window. "Lot of rich kids up there, plenty of poor ones hanging around the fringes looking to activate some action. Real interesting mix."

Ooljee was overstating. There was much here that was kin to similar parts of Tampa and St. Pete, though the ethnic soup was far more exotic. Moody recognized the same youth hangouts, noted the same furtive whisperings as ideas, concepts, goods, drugs, and information were exchanged. Much of the Hispanic insignia and posturing was familiar to him. The Amerind and Asian influences he found utterly foreign.

For example, you would not see in Tampa someone wearing a headband and fringed blue jacket decorated with rainbow figures called *Na'a-tse-elit* (according to Ooljee). The characters dripped blood, a most untraditional representation. The jacket was belted with silver and turquoise above cream-colored pantaloons tucked into water-buffalo-hide boots inscribed with indecipherable Asian symbols.

What struck Moody strongest was the realization that the locals—be they Navaho, Hopi, Zuni, Hualapai, or Apache—blended in better with the Asians than they did with the Anglos or Hispanics.

Ooljee slowed the truck as they cruised past a nondescript building. Twin doors fashioned of black composite gleamed in a small setback below street level. Glowing rainbow symbols, red and blue split by a thin strip of yellow, guarded both sides of the entrance as well as the lintel above the doorway. At each upper corner of the portal were a pair of heavily stylized neon birds.

"Golden eagle and black hawk," Ooljee informed his companion. "Guardian symbols borrowed from sandpainting, just like the rainbows. You do not usually see eagles and hawks used as guardians. That is what happens when people try to adapt old traditions to modern uses. Also, in a sandpainting you do not see eagles copulating."

The neon over the entrance writhed in confirmation of Ooljee's observation.

"Shima Club. A *shima* is any woman old enough to be your mother. There are worse hangouts around. This is the kind of place where upscale locals and kids from out of town can meet the children of underclass assembly workers and janitorial staff. Usually a couple of fights a night, but it rarely gets serious unless pharmacuties are involved. I had to break up an altercation right out here on the street a few months ago. It was over a really fine woman. My partner and I, we lingered just to look at her for a while. As she was thanking us for our help and saying goodbye, a half-pound packet of self-injecting *frisson* ampules fell out of her dress. They had been clipped to her bra. That sizzle is from the Ivory Coast and it will fry your brain. So she was not so fine after all.

"I thought you worked in Homicide."

"I do, but our department requires that everyone do time on the street once a month. To keep us in touch, the regulations say. I don't mind." He rolled up his window, shutting out the blast of weirding music which emanated from the club when one of the twin doors parted to allow a clutch of customers egress. Musicians inside hammered out notes like a bevy of blacksmiths forging knives.

"I am grateful your people sent someone with experience. I was afraid they'd send some young hotshot anxious to make a name for himself who I would have to wet nurse if things got awkward."

Moody remembered the young detective he'd spoken with at Kettrick's house. The one he'd tried to have sent here in his place. Nickerson.

"No, this assignment was mine all the way."

"I never doubted it for a moment," was Ooljee's cryptic reply.

IT WAS SLOW at the station, whose entrance, Moody noticed immediately, faced the proper direction. A steady but wieldy stream of drunks, addicts, burglars, and assorted ripoff artists flowed through the front office, though most had been safely tucked away for the night. It was slow time, the night shift winding its work down, the morning crew having not yet arrived.

The people Ooljee exchanged greetings with were variously tired, relieved, or uncommunicative, depending on how their night had gone. There had been times when Moody'd considered requesting a late-night shift himself. The pace was slower, the atmosphere less frenetic than during the day, the heat not as oppressive. From three until five A.M. the action inside the station varied from lethargic to moribund, because most nocturnal lawbreakers had concluded their activities, and those who worked during the day usually slept late.

But he liked the sunlight.

The building and what facilities he could identify were far more up-to-date than those he was used to. That was understandable, since Ganado was a young boom town and Tampa an elderly eastern city. With interest he noted that although this was an NDPS office, not all the personnel were Amerind. There were Anglos and Blacks, and a few Hispanics. Still, the feel was far different from any station he'd ever been inside before.

Ooljee led him to one of many cubicles and secured a privaflex screen behind them. The little office was neat and clean. Holos of his wife and boys were everywhere. Moody's practiced eye automatically scanned his surroundings, storing information. It was good to know everything about a man you were working with, he knew, especially if there was any chance of being shot at while in his company.

In addition to the family pictures, there were some mounted awards, a few small athletic trophies, and some expanded holos of spectacular canyon scenery. On the desk were several piles of papers, a notepad, the usual office paraphernalia, and a slick Fordmatsu office spinner. A pair of tall cacti gave the office some color. Only on closer inspection did he realize they were clever fakes. The small pink pincushion of a plant on the desk was real. A couple of chairs were well padded and of recent manufacture, not like standard office issue back in Tampa. The ubiquitous Zenat monitor hung on the wall behind the desk, a compact three-by-two model.

"Now we'll see if anything new has come in." Ooljee sat down behind the desk and activated the spinner board. The zenat sprang to life, displaying a fixed geometric ready pattern. Moody settled into the empty chair.

He watched without comment as Ooljee called out the Kettrick file and began weaving around inside. It was easy to pick out information the Tampa bureau had forwarded.

Ten minutes passed before Ooljee remembered the dispenser located above the single storage cabinet. No words passed between them, but Moody understood what his fellow officer wanted. He did have to inquire if the sergeant wanted his black or with cream and sugar.

"Nucane, one packet." Ooljee spoke without looking up from his work.

Moody added the artificial sweetener to the cup he'd siphoned for his colleague. "Howcum the faux? You're not overweight. That's my department."

"Some hypertension. Runs in the family. Sometimes just hyper without the tension."

"I could've guessed that from watching your kids." Moody returned his attention to the monitor as he sipped his own coffee. It was wonderfully aromatic and fresh. In Tampa you had to leave your desk and make do with whatever the central dispenser offered. This business of having one in your own office was something he could bring up at the next Union meeting. Moody enjoyed his perks as much as the next guy.

When the cup was half drained, Ooljee put his hands behind his head and leaned back in his chair. "Same old shit. Not that I expected otherwise."

"Hope springs." Moody eyed his partner. "I would've expected a lead or two by now."

"Oh, we've had more than that," Ooljee responded quickly. "The composite cadcam portrait of the suspect generated many calls. But none of them led to anything. Either nobody recognizes our man, or they do and they are not talking. Or else he is hiding somewhere down in the Strip."

"Shoot, he could've had cosmetic surgery by now. Chemically changed his color to white."

Ooljee smiled. "Not even a murderer would sink that low. But there is something else I've been wanting to try.

"My lieutenant insists I spend my time looking for someone to fit the composite. Well, we have been doing that for weeks without any results and I am sick of it."

Moody rolled his eyes. "Let me guess: you want to work with the sandpainting."

"You get credit for perception, but not much, because I

have been talking about it ever since you got here. Since they insist I concentrate on finding an individual while I am on the payroll, I thought I might try to combine that directive with my own interests. Especially since I now have an unprejudiced witness to confirm that I am following my orders.''

"Hey, keep me out of it.''

"Don't be so paranoid. I would not put you in a difficult position.''

"Yeah, sure.''

"It will be good for you.'' Ooljee was persistent. "Much more interesting to go into museums and gift shops and trading posts than talking to unpleasant people on the street.''

"You still have trading posts?''

"Sure. We passed one on the way in. The fifty-story tower just outside the park downtown. I pointed it out to you, remember?'' He glanced toward a window. The spring sun was beginning to wake up the city. "I have some lists we can work with. If a match is made with the composite, we will be notified. Besides, there is no reason to sit here and monitor the department web when we could be outside enjoying this fine weather.''

"You call this dry icebox fine weather? Anytime the temperature drops below seventy-five, I get twitchy and my skin starts to crawl. And it's too dry.''

"Despite what you may think, it does rain here. I will see to arranging a Blessing Way ceremony to call up some precipitation for you.''

"Do that. And while you're at it, how about arranging a ceremony to catch our killer?''

"Perhaps later.'' Ooljee said it with a straight face as they left his office, but this time Moody wasn't buying.

The streets were filling up fast as morning rush hour began to flood downtown Ganado. Pedestrians appeared magically on sidewalks and overhead walkways, their already harried expressions lit by first light. The police truck slid efficiently past the creeping commuters, making good use of the lane reserved for municipal vehicles. With ease born of long experience, Ooljee ignored the envious glares of travelers trapped in unmoving traffic.

"You think this guy might kill again?"

Ooljee considered the question. "It is anybody's guess, because we know nothing about him. I have run an extensive cross-country check and there are no records of a murder utilizing a similar modus, so we may be in luck. The Kettrick sandpainting may be all he was after.

"As to researching that, many of my colleagues think I am a little mad myself. Others say I have concocted a clever excuse for avoiding real work, like following leads on potential suspects."

"But your lieutenant gave you permission to follow this up."

"Lieutenant Yazzie is a good man for hunches. He has patience. But he also has his limits. He will not let me pursue this line of inquiry forever unless I start showing him some results."

They spent all that day and all the next talking to owners and managers of gift shops and retail stores and art galleries, from fancy ones in the lobbies of towering hotels—where a working stiff like Moody couldn't have afforded the frames, much less the paintings—to the tiny pawnshops and secondhand stores that pitted the fronts of ancient commercial buildings on the industrial end of town.

Moody saw more silver and turquoise than he formerly believed existed. Some of the men wore as much jewelry as their women, a sight that took some getting used to. In Tampa the only males likely to strut about so bedecked were pimps.

Nor was all the metal in the familiar form of bracelets and rings and necklaces. There were decorated belts and hatbands, headbands and boot tips and collar tabs, pins and insignia. Yet the more he saw of it, the more natural it seemed.

Ooljee tried to talk him into buying a silver watchband set with coral, turquoise, and synthetic bear claws, to replace the mundane ABSK he currently wore. Though tempted, Moody declined. The band was beautifully made and reasonably priced, but the detective could too readily envision the reaction it would produce back at Tampa HQ.

Not everything was fashioned of skystone and silver. Gold and platinum were also used, as were more exotic metals and stones. Even the smallest shop seemed to be overflowing with inventory.

"Who buys all this stuff?" Moody finally asked his colleague.

"Tourists, business travelers looking for something truly American to take back home. We also buy and sell among ourselves. The really expensive goods are called Old Pawn. Some of it was actually banged out of old coins; dimes and nickels preferred. Good, genuine Old Pawn is always hard to find. People do not have to hock their family treasures to pay the bills the way they used to. Although there is nothing wrong in doing that. It was a perfectly respectable way to raise cash or pay for goods.

"Have you been studying the sandpaintings?"

Moody replied dourly. "I'm trying, but they all look the same to me."

"I can't believe that." Ooljee did not try to hide his disappointment. "You have too good an eye not to have noticed differences."

Moody hesitated. "Well, maybe some of the overall patterns—gimme a break, Paul. It's like learning another language."

One more storefront, one more stop. Like innumerable others, the face it presented to the street was nondescript. There was the standard fluorescent BUY-SELL TRADE sign out front. The skystone and silver clutter in the windows that flanked the narrow entrance was more neatly arrayed than in most. Whoever had arranged the display had made some attempt to highlight quality instead of trying to cram as many cheap rings and bracelets into the available space as possible.

Inside the store the lighting was as subdued as the atmosphere. There were drums and pottery for sale, along with sculptures and rugs. The latter might be genuine, since unlike hundreds Moody had seen these past two days, these did not display attached cards declaring in superfine print that while they were Indian-made, they were only Navaho *inspired*. Which meant, according to Ooljee, that they were not woven on the Rez but down in Mexico, on mechanical looms operated by industrious Zapotecs.

The store owner was short, white, and active. He advanced smoothly toward them as if on maglide skates.

The wall behind him was full of paintings. Well, prints, anyway. Scenes of Ganado modern and ancient, of Canyon de Chelley and Monument Valley, of the Grand Canyon and San Francisco Peaks, of various cliff dwellings and Indian ceremonials. There were also more rugs, most of them small, some of them tattered. All colored with handmade vegetable dye, according to Ooljee. This was a store for the serious trader and collector, not for the casual tourist looking for bright trinkets to take home. The farther back into its depths one walked, the higher the quality of the goods became.

Ooljee methodically flashed his ID, embedded in its slice of softly glowing Lexan. The owner blinked at it, glanced somewhat apprehensively in Moody's direction, eyed Ooljee the way he might a box of jewelry of uncertain parentage someone was trying to sell him.

"I don't do *scav*, sergeant."

"Everyone in this town parks stolen goods sooner or later," Ooljee replied pleasantly, "but that is not what we are here about."

The owner relaxed visibly, though his tone still betrayed some unease. "Shopping? Birthday present, perhaps, or something for a lady?"

"It would be a real present if you could help us." Digging into a jacket pocket, Ooljee extracted the by now well-wrinkled eight-by-ten fax of the Kettrick sandpainting and shoved it toward the shopkeeper, who peered at it curiously.

"Any idea what Way this is from?"

"Oh, you want advice? Why ask me? Why not try a museum?"

"We have traveled that road." Ooljee tapped the fax. "The people I have talked with say they have never seen anything like this."

"Really?" The man brightened, thoroughly at ease now. He squinted at the fax, the implant in his right eye giving him some trouble. After a moment he excused himself. His visitors waited impatiently while he removed the offending implant and replaced it with a jeweler's lens.

"That's better," he murmured, as much to himself as to his guests. He examined the fax closely.

"Do you know anything about it at all?" Ooljee prompted him. "If not the Way it is from, then the style, or how old it might be? What it signifies? Any suggestions will be welcomed."

The proprietor looked up from the picture. "I was kind of hoping you might tell me. I've never seen anything like it either." He bent again over the image, his left eye closed, working with the jeweler's loupe installed in his right. "This is not a very good reproduction."

"Sorry," said Moody. "The original was pretty big. A full-size repro would be kind of hard to lug around."

"These designs here," the shopkeeper muttered as he traced part of the image with a finger, "and this up here; I don't recognize any of it."

"Do not feel bad," Ooljee said. "You are in good company. Nobody else does either." He reached for the fax.

The old man waved him back. "Wait a minute, wait a minute. Don't be in such a rush. You cops are always in such a rush."

He's having fun now, Moody mused. *We've set him a challenge.*

While the shopkeeper examined and compared and mumbled to himself under his breath, the detective passed the time studying the prints and paintings that filled the walls, trying hard to relate to the colossal landscapes, the abyssal canyons and immense skies. Everything in this part of the world seemed constructed on a grander, rougher scale, as if nature had set aside her fine-pointed tools and little brushes and had gone to work with the heavy machinery. This was country with spaces vast enough to give easy birth to mysteries and legends. There was little verdure in any of the pictures. Green was not an important color in this corner of the universe.

The old man finally paused in his inspection. "Where did you find this?"

"You do not need to know that, unless you can convince me it would make a difference in what you can tell us."

The shopkeeper hesitated, chewing his lower lip as he examined the fax from a greater height. "It's very strange. There is so much in here that is familiar but peculiarly arranged, and so much more that I've never seen before." Again he tapped the picture.

"This sequence here is Red Ant Way, but all changed around. And this up here, this is definitely Nightway. But everything is all mixed up. It makes no sense. Not only are there pieces from Ways that shouldn't appear together in the same painting, there are designs and figures and symbols that don't mean anything at all. At least, they don't to me, and I've been forty years in this business." He ran a finger around the edge of the fax.

"Take something simple, like the enclosing guardian design. I don't understand this interpretation of crooked lightning, and the specific guardians at the east opening I don't recognize at all. It's too aberrant to be traditional, yet too well rendered to be nonsensical. But this part here''—his finger moved to the upper lefthand portion of the fax—''I think I may have seen something like it before. It's not part of any ceremony currently in use, but you can see how distinctive it is. That's why I remember it. Because the pattern is so distinctive.''

Ooljee straightened slightly. Moody ambled back from the other side of the store.

''You don't see much stuff like this up here,'' the proprietor was saying. ''Most of the experimentation with traditional forms is done down in Scottsdale and Tucson, where the radical artists like to live. Ganado's too stolid, too old-fashioned a place for them. I don't usually deal in modern work, but you can't avoid seeing some of it. Occasionally you'll come across something that will stick in your mind.''

''You're talking artists.'' Moody leaned up against the counter. ''Are you saying you know who did this sand-painting?''

''I'm just guessing.'' He bent and rummaged through a drawer, produced a ten-inch square spinner which he placed atop the counter. It was an old model, beat-up and not molly-compatible. His fingers worked the keys with maddening slowness.

An eternity later hardcopy emerged from the single printer slot. He tore it free. ''Here's an address—of sorts.'' Moody started to reach for it. ''No, wait.'' More paper chugged out of the slot. ''Directions, as I jotted them down. I was on a buying trip, quite a while ago. I don't carry much in the way of sandpainting anymore. A lot of the newer stuff is junk and too much of the good old work is in museums and private collections. It's not worth my time to keep up. But this I remember. It was so different.'' He indicated the fax.

"It's not all of what you're looking for, but maybe it will lead you to something."

"*Y adil*. We could use some kind of a lead." Ooljee scanned the printout before pocketing it. "Rez local," he informed Moody, then turned back to the shopkeeper. "Thanks a lot."

"Sure, sure." The proprietor saw them to the door. "Do something for me, will you, if I've been of some help?"

The sergeant hesitated. "My budget does not allow for . . ."

"No, not that, I don't want that." The old man was still eyeing the fax that dangled from Ooljee's fingers. "All my life I've been in this business, and I've never seen anything like that picture of yours. If you find out what it is, what it means, what Way it's from, would you maybe stop back in and tell me? I thought I knew all the Ways still in use, or at least all those that are still represented in fixed sand-paintings. Those I don't recognize from memory, I've always been able to look up. But that one, it's not just somebody experimenting, not just an artist playing around with old themes and new ideas. It's too coherent. It hangs together, if you know what I mean. Whoever did that had an overall scheme in mind, and I'd sure like to know what he was getting at."

"So would we," said Moody.

"If we find anything out," Ooljee assured him, "I'll make it a point to let you know."

"Thanks." The old man smiled, rubbing his chin. "I'd appreciate it."

He was still staring after them, intrigued, thoughtful, somehow younger-looking, as they climbed into the police truck and headed westward into traffic.

They checked in at the station, where Ooljee and his superior engaged in a brief ritualistic argument over the validity of the sergeant's assumptions. Moody passed the time watching the more attractive spinner operators at their desks, until Ooljee emerged and solemnly beckoned for his partner to join him. A short drive returned them to the residential cluster, where Ooljee made his excuses to his wife and kids, explaining he would be away on work for a couple of days. Moody politely ignored the ensuing domestic scene and spent the time packing his travel bag.

Back on the road, they skirted the main arterials, which meant Ooljee had to do some real driving until they were clear of city traffic. Only then did he let the truck's autodrive resume control. Gradually the spires and industrial blocks of Ganado fell behind. Moody noted they were traveling almost due north.

"We're heading up to Chinle," Ooljee explained. "It is still pretty much a small town, a tourist town. To check out the name the shopkeeper came up with." He lapsed into silence, swimming a sea of inner contemplation.

"Tell me something." Moody spoke to take his mind off the barren immensity of the landscape. "What exactly are these 'Ways' you keep talking about?"

"Ways are ceremonies." Ooljee swiveled his seat to face his companion. "According to the Navaho way of thinking, the universe is in a perpetual, precarious state of balance between the forces of good and the forces of evil. Or if you'd prefer a more scientific description, between the forces of regularity and the forces of chaos. The similarities to General Relativity are quite fascinating. For example . . ."

Moody interrupted him. "Spare me. I get the idea."

Ooljee pursed his lips. "The Ways are used to help people deal with sickness, with personal problems, with any sort of difficulty or trouble. Even today, many people, particularly the older ones, will go to a doctor or hospital for treatment but will follow up with a visit to a hatathli."

"No offense, but it sounds like plain old witchcraft to me."

"We don't go around sticking pins in dolls. To me, real

witchcraft is practiced by people who make a living predicting the rise and fall of the Nasdaq index. Stuff like that. Or trying to figure out why the new guy gets the promotion and you do not.''

Chinle was not that many miles from Ganado on the map, but very far away in time. The town itself was modern enough. Foremost among the buildings of recent construction was the local NDPS office where Ooljee checked in, a free-form one-story structure of polycrete and bronze glass. It hugged the side of a wide, shallow canyon like some prehistoric herbivore, a thick coat of antennae sprouting from its back.

Moody waited while his companion engaged in small talk with his colleagues. Away from the commercial/industrial center of Ganado there were far fewer non-Navahos around, and he felt more conspicuous than ever.

Just outside Chinle the modern world seemed to vanish.

''The people we're looking for have a place inside the Park, down in the canyon. Now you will see why the four-wheel drive, four-wheel steer truck is and always has been the preferred mode of transportation on the Rez.''

They were traveling east out of town, when Ooljee turned off the main road, following a sandy path that paralleled a broad, lazy creek. Very soon the ridges on either side of the road began reaching for the clouds. The walls of the canyon they'd entered rose so rapidly that after only a few miles of driving, the crests of the smooth, rust-red ramparts were scraping the belly of Heaven itself.

Moody craned his neck to see. They were traveling between sheer rock escarpments a thousand feet high, the truck bouncing along a road that clearly owed its continued existence to Nature's whim. One swift, wild flash-flood down the deceptively somnolent stream would carry away anyone unlucky enough to be present at the time.

He felt as if he were threading the labyrinthine corridors of some immense antediluvian fortress, impregnable and unapproachable save for those who knew its secret passages and passwords.

"Canyon de Chelley." Ooljee was concentrating on his driving. No laser control strip buried in the sand and gravel here. "You pronounce it *deh shay*. That is a story in itself. It's a National Monument, but people still live back in here. Old land claims, old ways. Their impact on the environment is minimal, just as it's always been. No sizzle here, no slash music." He grinned. "These people get high on mutton."

Moody continued to gape at the unreal parapets towering overhead, glad he was down by the river and not up on the rim. He did not like high places. At least there was vegetation here; green life. The trees were pale and conservative compared to those back home, but they were real trees, not clever mimics like ocotillo and paloverde.

They crossed the river, the truck splashing and grinding its way through as Ooljee headed up a side canyon, narrower but no less impressive than the central chasm. Proof of his earlier words brought them to a halt as an avalanche of sheep tumbled across the sandy track in front of them.

It was directed by a medium-sized, impressively confident canine who barely took his eyes off his charges long enough to acknowledge the presence of the idling truck nearby. Moody observed the dog admiringly. It did better work than some of those who'd graduated from the Academy's course in crowd control.

"Each of the sheep has a small transmitter embedded in its flank," Ooljee informed him. "It tells the herder or owner how much that particular sheep currently weighs, what its body temperature is, how its internal systems are functioning, whether or not it is pregnant, and many other things. It also functions as a receiver.

"Notice the dog." Moody tried to keep track of the tireless black and white streak among the forest of legs. "He will be wearing a transmitter collar that tells his master where he is at all times. The herder can direct his animal via the built-in receiver, which also broadcasts a steady frequency at very low power. The frequency is irritating to sheep. This makes it very easy for the dog to turn and guide the herd. He doesn't have to bark or rely on his original predatory reputation. All he has to do is move close to a sheep and it will react by turning away. It is very efficient. Since the herder can communicate with his dog via the collar, he no longer has to shout to it.''

When the woolly mob was almost past, a boy on a silenced motorbike appeared. As he waved to them, Moody noted the two-inch antenna that protruded from his headband. A control unit was strapped to his right wrist. He followed the boy's progress until he and his herd had vanished into the brush on the far side of the canyon. The truck resumed its advance.

''Wouldn't it be easier to use some kind of remote tracking vehicle?''

''Perhaps, but nothing works as well in a confined space as does a good dog,'' Ooljee told him. ''It is also much better company. And there is something else. Not everyone on the Rez is into computers, or assembly, or debugging and repair. Some families prefer to hew to the old ways. Women still weave rugs on hand looms, though many will use cadcam terminals to experiment with design. Others choose to herd sheep. There are still people who grow corn and beans, squash and tobacco. The corn that is grown on the Rez does not taste like the corn that is put into cans in Nebraska and Indiana.

''I can see that we will have to expose you to some more local cooking. You have already had frybread. Do you like tortillas?''

''I'm from South Florida,'' Moody reminded him.

Ooljee was nodding to himself. ''Blue corn tortillas with tomatillo salsa. I'll bet you do not have that in South Florida.''

Talk of food was making Moody hungry but he forbore

mentioning it, suspecting that the canyon bottom was not home to a profusion of restaurants. Fastfoodies did not generally locate on dirt roads. Anyway it could not be much farther to their destination, because the side canyon they were traversing was beginning to narrow. It was like driving through a crack in the planet. The air was cool and still. Sunshine was but an occasional, fitful visitor to this place. Moody was very glad he was not claustrophobic.

FIVE MINUTES LATER they rounded a bend in the canyon and Moody saw that which he had been anticipating.

The multisided domed structure was much smaller than the average motor home. It was built of mud or adobe, with a roof that came to a slight point. To the detective it most nearly resembled a Mongolian yurt, which he was familiar with only because he'd seen one on an International Geographic special on the Divit channel one night when the game he'd planned to watch had been pre-empted.

A dog of indeterminate breed lay in a path of sunshine in front of the building.

"Doesn't look like anybody's home."

"Maybe because that is not the home." Ooljee leaned forward, resting both hands on the wheel. "That's an old hogan. You would be surprised how warm it is in winter and how cool in the summer. There is something about sleeping on packed earth that puts you in touch with a whole range of feelings you miss while sleeping on water or foam or air-suspension. You should try it sometime."

"Not in Florida," Moody countered. "Too many creepy-crawlies."

Ooljee drove past the hogan and the indifferent dog,

crossed the lazy stream that looked far too feeble to have
cut the mighty canyon. It flowed quiet and unhurried, in no
rush to find the next inch nearer sea level.

The second hogan looked much like the first except that
it was considerably larger, two stories tall, and constructed
of prefab plastic walls filled and insulated with blownfoam.
Copper-tinted polarized windows regarded their surroundings, while from the central peak of the roof a large satellite
dish pointed southward. Even though the canyon ran north-
south, Moody knew that reception had to be limited.

Much of the roof was lined with tracking, hi-dope solar
panels. A large rectangular building with few windows dominated the yard behind the hogan. A twinge of recognition
went through Moody when he noted that the entrances to
both buildings faced east. He was beginning to feel a little
less like an intruder.

Next to the creek stood a large abstract sculpture that on
closer inspection turned out to have a practical function.
Brightly hued metal poles supported a roof of artificial tree
limbs. They varied in color from deep raw purple to intense
blue to a light rose, shifting subtly within the metal itself.
The poles looked too thin to support their sculpted burden.

"That's a summer shelter," Ooljee explained, "or rather
a modern interpretation of a traditional one whose boughs
would have to be replaced every year. This one is more
practical, but I miss the wood."

He didn't know what the remarkable metal was, though.
They were to find out later that it was anodized titanium.

As Ooljee parked in front of the building two more mutts
materialized to greet them. One might have had some honest
shepherd in him, but Moody wasn't sure. Both were curious
and friendly.

He hung back and let Ooljee ring the bell, hunting in vain
for some visible security device like a scanner or heat sensor.
It was either expensively concealed or nonexistent. Probably
not needed here. This wasn't Metropolitan Tampa. Besides,

anyone trying to steal from a home in this canyon would find himself with but one avenue of escape, easily closed off.

Not that the man who opened the door looked like he'd need any help subduing an intruder. He was taller than Moody and just as heavy, though his weight was far more aesthetically distributed on his bones. He looked like one of the Bucs' better linebackers. In point of fact he had played football, though only on the college level.

He chatted with Ooljee for a bit, then stepped out and favored Moody with the kind of big, down-home country smile the detective hadn't encountered much since leaving Mississippi. He felt immediately at home.

"*Yinishye* Bill Laughter." He looked to be in his early or mid-thirties. His handshake was as solid as the rest of him, though Moody was quick to note that unusual pressure of the index finger along the back of the hand.

"Vernon Moody. I'm—"

"Paul has told me." He beckoned for them to follow. "Come on around back. I'd take you through the house, but Marilee's shopping and my dad's watching the game."

They walked around the building, with its views of creek and towering canyon walls. All three dogs accompanied them, one sniffing at the detective's heels, the other two scouting ahead.

The big, barnlike structure behind the house turned out to be an industrial workshop. Moody had expected cars or trucks, perhaps even a gyrocopter, maybe farm equipment; not an artistic assembly-line. Acrylic bins overflowing with colored sand lined one wall. Long benches and tables occupied the middle of the floor, flanked by stacks of flat boards cut from high-quality hardwood, sheets of metal, rolls of flexifan.

There was a section set aside for welding, with its own scrapmetal yard and anodizing equipment, as well as a potter's corner with clay, electronically controlled wheel, and flash kiln. A big commercial-grade laser cutter dominated a back table like a lost piece of army ordnance.

Finished sandpaintings were stacked neatly in sorting racks, next to framing equipment. Laughter even had his own seal-wrapping machine and shipping materials. The paintings themselves varied considerably in size, from miniatures a few inches square to a pair of eight-by-ten foot monsters leaning against the near wall. Ooljee asked about them before Moody could.

"They are for the new terminal going in at Casa Grande International Airport." Laughter was obviously proud of his work. "They'll be viewed from a distance, hence the outlandish proportions. As you can see, all the designs and *yeis* are rendered oversized."

"What's a yei?" Moody inquired.

"A spirit. A god. A person. It depends. *Yei-bei-chei*. Yei for short."

The two young men working near the back of the shop paid little attention to the newly arrived visitors.

"Apprentices. My assistants," Laughter explained.

Moody watched as one of them prepared to apply an adhesive base to a foot-square piece of thin metal. His companion finished adjusting a protective mask, then turned to his left and picked up a hose-and-nozzle arrangement. It hissed like a snake giving warning as he sprayed transparent fixative over a quartet of finished sandpaintings.

"They do a lot of the drudge work." Laughter studied the pieces with a critical eye. "It frees me to concentrate on painting and design."

Moody was still a bit taken aback by the sheer scale and mass production aspects of the operation. To him it didn't look much like art. But then what did he know?

"You don't paint. You use sand."

"Paint is just a medium. Sand is another." Laughter indicated a custom industrial easel that held a half-finished sandpainting.

"In the old days you had to lay sand fast because your adhesive would set up. That made for some sloppy work. This is much better. I use a debondable elastomeric transparent adhesive. You can cover a whole board with it and work on any section you want without worrying about the rest drying out in the meantime. The next day you just spray the area you want to work on with the debonder and it becomes malleable again. None of it sets up hard until you apply the fixative. As for a paintbrush—" He reached behind a nearby workbench.

Moody flinched instinctively when Laughter emerged holding what looked like a gun. In an industrial sense, it was. Instead of emitting a high-powered stream of fine grit to scour away old paint and varnish, Laughter's sandblaster had been modified to *apply* sand. The width and impact of the stream could both be manipulated electronically. A built-in switch allowed the attached vacuum hose to select from any of the nearby bins of colored sand. The whole contraption was no bigger than an automatic pistol. One hose connected it to its air supply, a second to the sand distributor. The custom device was a compact cross between a sandblaster and an airbrush.

Laughter slipped on protective goggles and demonstrated how it all worked by adding to the sandpainting in progress. Three eagle feathers, white tipped with black, appeared in the lower right-hand corner of the board as he played the nozzle back and forth over the treated surface.

"You can go pretty fast with the setup we have here," he said as he shut off the unit and picked up another self-contained device. While they looked on, he carefully applied fixative to the feathers he'd just drawn, securing them to the board.

Moody found the technique more intriguing than the technology. "There's nothing on there; no tracings, no outlines. Don't you sketch in your designs before you start?"

Laughter slid the goggles up onto his head. "Don't need

to. I started learning from my father when I was eight. The designs we use are sketched in permanently up here.'' He tapped his forehead. ''That's where a good hatathli keeps his. But I'm not a hatathli, of course. I'm just a painter. Though I know what not to paint.''

Moody kept pace with him as they exited the workshop. ''Paul's told me about that.''

Laughter smiled softly. ''Then you know that no commercial, fixed, permanent sandpainting, no matter how accurate it looks, is a precise reproduction of a medicine painting. If it was an exact replication it might adversely affect the painter, or the purchaser, or universal harmony. If I made such a reproduction and harm befell the purchaser, I could be sued. Maybe not in a Florida court, but things can be different here on the Rez.

''No commercial sandpainter would do such a thing anyway, because the misfortune might befall him instead of a customer.''

Moody found himself wondering about the Kettrick painting. Could it be the unfortunate exception, the exact reproduction Laughter seemed so confident no sandpainter would create? Did that have something to do with the obsession of their killer? Misfortune had certainly befallen Elroy Kettrick.

Been out in the sun too long, he told himself. *Need to spend more time inside.*

That was exactly where Laughter was taking them. They turned right and entered the main house, emerging into a high-ceilinged kitchen. Wide, tinted windows looked out over the indifferent creek. The appliances were modern, though designed to run straight off DC. That made sense to Moody. Solar electric production was always more efficient when it could be used directly, instead of having to be run through a converter first.

The painter waved some coffee for them. When it was ready, he and Ooljee resumed talking.

Left to himself, Moody studied his surroundings. There were fewer of the homey, traditional touches that distinguished his partner's condo, perhaps because the awesome setting in which this house stood would detract from the finest art.

Ooljee brought out the fax for Laughter's inspection. He frowned at it in disbelief. "Somebody killed somebody, over *this*?"

"For a copy of it, we assume. Or maybe just for the chance to look at it. We do not know for a fact that a copy was made. We do know that the original was destroyed."

Laughter was studying it closely but without especial interest, like a lepidopterist examining a brilliantly colored but not unique specimen.

"We were told in Ganado that this painting or one similar to it might have been painted here." Ooljee was watching the artist closely.

"Not by me." Laughter shook his head. "I sure as hell have never seen anything like it."

Mentally Moody was already back in the truck. It was the same answer they'd received from a hundred different people back in town.

Laughter, however, wasn't through. "Let's ask my dad. He won't yell too loud if we break in on him."

"You said you learned from him. Does he still paint?" Moody asked.

Laughter led them through the house. "Sometimes when he's in the mood, or just when he gets bored. He leaves most of it to me. He prefers to handle the financial end of the business."

The den was a cool, sunken oval dominated by a huge fireplace. A six-foot square top-of-the-line zenat color monitor occupied a recess in the curving wall. The oversized couches and peeled-wood furniture were covered with the familiar earthtone upholstery. San Idelefonso black pottery shone side-by-side with intricate titanium sculptures.

Clearly there was money in sandpainting as well as in art and tradition.

The man who rose from the couch in front of the screen was as tall as Bill Laughter but much slimmer. He looked as if time had worn the bulk off him much as the wind had sculpted the wild sandstone monuments of the canyon.

Moody glanced at the zenat, which the elder Laughter had thoughtfully muted at their entrance. Tucson was playing Dallas in the Columbia Dome, ahead 49 to 6. Good. He had nothing on the game and the boring spread would allow him to concentrate wholly on the discussion at hand.

Once more Ooljee repeated the reason for the visit, waiting while both Laughters studied the fax and conferenced. The younger asked questions while the older man nodded and ventured comments in Navaho. His first words in English drove all thoughts of football from the detective's mind.

"Yes, I think I have seen this before. Or something very much like it."

"Where?" Ooljee asked quickly, as though the response might slip away if he didn't inquire rapidly enough.

"I think it might be one of my father's pieces. Of course, I could be wrong."

In the excitement of the moment Moody spoke without thinking, a fault he was not usually prone to. "Where is he? Can we ask him about it?"

"My father's been dead for many years." Courteously, the elder Laughter did not allow Moody time in which to apologize. "He taught me, just as I have taught Bill."

"Then that's it."

"Not necessarily." The elder Laughter smiled softly. "I had to prepare for the day when he would no longer be here to help me. So I put everything he could teach me on file. Come into the office and we'll see what we can find. That is, if I'm not completely mistaken and there is actually something to be found."

The room located just off the den was long and narrow, the zenat on the far wall a strictly utilitarian model from Zenith T&T's industrial division. Red Laughter palmed a well-used tactile 3.4 Black Widow spinner from a desktop and aimed it at the mollybox squatting beneath the window.

Images washed across the zenat, the outside windows automatically dimming as the mollybox was activated. The elder Laughter's fingers played with the Widow. A succession of sandpaintings appeared on the monitor. Some were badly positioned for recording purposes, others were frozen in primitive, uncorrectable out-of-focus.

"A lot of these were taken when I was just a kid, with an old hand-held two-D camera, and transferred to my file much later. When I was learning and helping my father we couldn't afford fancy stuff like mollystorage, and I didn't know anything about holomaging. This was the best I could do."

"You deserve credit for thinking so far ahead," Ooljee told him.

"I can't take credit. It was my grandmother's idea. Preserving these designs and techniques didn't strike me as important until I was a lot older. Only then did I realize the debt I owed to her. She was very proud of my father's work and didn't want it to be lost. I can still remember the two of them arguing about it. My father didn't want to spend the money for film and developing. He said I should learn everything by rote, the way he had learned from my grandfather. He wanted me to be a hatathli, like him." Red Laughter's gaze shifted to Moody, who stood listening respectfully.

"My father was a *real* hatathli; one of the very best. He believed the paintings should only be used to make medicine. That was how he supported himself; by doing traditional medicine. Not by making paintings to sell in the stores." Laughter froze the screen on a particularly complex piece of work.

"Look at this; at the detail, the fine edges and the straight lines. All done from memory, right on the ground on the floor of an old hogan. Depending on the Way, something like this could take many days to complete. When it was finished and the ceremony completed, Father and his assistants would destroy the entire work, end to beginning. For another client he would have to start all over again with the same painting, or a completely different one. From scratch. A terrible waste, but that is the way it was done. Done still, by the few men with the skill or gall to call themselves true hatathlis." He resumed searching.

"So y'all don't make any medicine paintings?" Moody was surprised how naturally the question came to mind.

Laughter looked at him as if he were crazy. "Are you kidding? Even if I knew how, I wouldn't have time for it. Bill and I sell our work all over the world. I don't mean to imply that we're not respectful of it, but sandpainting can be art in the pure sense as well as the basis for traditional medicine. We develop and incorporate many of our own ideas into each painting, though it's nice to have the original designs to use as a starting point." Abruptly he hesitated, staring at the monitor.

"Wait a minute."

Carefully he backtrawled until he found the image he wanted. It was difficult to make out details because the sandpainting was so large. Using the Widow, he focused on specific sections, enlarging them for a better view.

Moody grabbed the fax and held it out in front of him, placing it tangent to the monitor visually if not physically. Ooljee didn't need to see the copy.

"That's it, or if it's not, then it's something awfully damn similar." Moody eyed Red Laughter. "You said your father only did paintings for medicine."

"And for my file, because my mother insisted on it. He was very reluctant to do it. He always grumbled."

"He never made anything for commercial sale?"

"Not intentionally. But"—Laughter thought hard—"he did render a few of the more complicated ones on wood, so I could be sure to make a good copy for the records."

"What happened to those?"

"I still have some of them."

"Some?"

Red Laughter looked out the darkened window. "There was a time when we needed money badly. That's when I think my mother sold one or two of the paintings. I remember there was yelling about it. You must understand, my father was a hatathli. But people offered her a lot of money." He turned back to the monitor. "This might have been one of those." He enlarged the edge. "See, it's done on wood, not on earth. A very uncommon design. Let's see what the accompanying text has to say. I always tried to make a record of what my father said about each painting."

He thumbed the Widow, and a text window appeared in the lower left quadrant of the monitor. It was in English, for which Moody was grateful.

"This sandpainting," it informed them in obsolete two-D font, "is from a Way which has been forgotten. I remember only that it was an important Way. It was taught to me by my father, who learned it from his father, who learned it from one whose true name I do not know and which can only be guessed at. Like many of the Ways which the young people have forgotten, it is a very old Way. I put it down here so it will not join the forgotten, even though it seems to be of no use in medicine, since no one knows what ceremony it is a part of."

"My grandfather's words." Bill Laughter was solemn.

"None of the museum specialists or academics I showed this to has any idea what Way it is from," Ooljee informed their hosts.

"Then it is truly from a forgotten one." Bill Laughter looked at Moody. "The simplest of the traditional Ways is unbelievably complicated. Elements and devices are swapped between them whenever the resident hatathli thinks it expedient."

"Not all is forgotten." The elder Laughter generated a pointer within the Widow, used it to circle a substantial portion of the center-right section of the painting. "This whole piece here; it I know. The colors are strange and so is some of the design, but it is still recognizable."

Moody tried and failed to make any sense of what the father had isolated. "What is it?" he finally asked exasperatedly.

"A painting within a painting, called 'Scavenger Being Carried Through the Skyhole by Eagles and Hawks Assisted by Snakes with Bird Power.'"

"I can see the bird shapes," Moody conceded.

Bill Laughter took control of the spinner, isolating a long, impossibly attenuated human figure within the painting. "That's Scavenger in the middle. The figures on either side of him are snakes. See the feathers they've been given, here and here? Bird power. As for the birds themselves, there are many kinds represented: big black hawks; black and white eagles; white hawks; big blue hawks; yellow-tailed, bald eagles. Even the guardians are snakes with bird power.

"These eagles on either side of the Scavenger figure, see how they're linked by ropes of rainbow and lightning?" The pointer moved. "But these lines here I don't recognize, or these small shapes. They shouldn't be in this painting. And these designs just outside, that link it to the rest of the overall, larger work, I don't recognize them at all. They could all be personal embellishments, but an old hatathli like Grandfather, I don't know how much he'd go in for that kind of thing."

"Maybe he was in an unusually artistic mood the day he made this one," the detective blithely suggested.

"Embellishing was not unknown in my father's time, or even before it. Hatathlis can be as individual as their medicine." Red Laughter rubbed his chin. "It is just that it was not like him. I do not remember him doing this particular sandpainting, but it is here in the files, so that means he must have done it. Grandmother probably put it here. She's the one who taught me the importance of keeping good records.''

"The Scavenger portion," the younger Laughter explained, "is from the Bead Chant, but the rest of it is a total blank to me.''

Moody was squinting at the monitor, trying to will himself to make sense of it. "How do you tell the snakes and the lightning apart?''

"Sometimes you don't. In our mythology they can be one and the same.''

"What about this business of a 'skyhole'?''

Red Laughter sighed. "I do not want to go into the whole Way. It's very complicated and uses many paintings. There used to be a fire dance involved, but—" He shrugged. "Today young people go to different kinds of dances.''

"At least we found it." There was satisfaction in Ooljee's voice.

"Let's go back to the kitchen." Bill Laughter switched off the zenat and mollybox, put the spinner back on the crowded desk.

Ooljee wanted to talk sandpainting, while Moody was much more interested in finding out if there might be a way to trace the original sale. He found himself talking to the younger Laughter while Ooljee engaged the elder at the kitchen table.

"What about that old building we saw coming in?" he asked, by way of making casual conversation.

"My grandfather's. We maintain it for tradition's sake. Also it's nice just to go inside sometimes and sit on the floor and do nothing. Some of Grandfather's things are still there and, well, it takes you back.''

Moody remembered the house he'd been raised in, back in Mississippi. Tin roof, wooden screen door always in need of repair, a porch slowly subsiding toward the Gulf. He understood.

"How come," he wondered, studying the fax and sipping coffee, "you and your father haven't reproduced this design? It's sure enough attractive."

"And much too complex to be a cost-effective proposition." Laughter traced the intricate patterns with a finger. "Besides, it doesn't come with a convenient, easy to understand explanation. Tourists need that sort of thing. They like plenty of yeis, rainbows, the four sacred plants. Not complex interconnected abstracts. We're doing fine. No reason to make something too complicated to earn back the time and effort spent on it. Not when you can do corn, beans, squash, and tobacco over and over again and come out way ahead.

"Oh, every once in a while Dad and I will do something different, but it's usually of our own invention, and to fill a prepaid order. Remember, sand is just the medium, not the art. In any case, we'd never do anything this big on spec."

Moody glanced around the kitchen. "Seems to me you could afford the time."

"Sure we could. We just don't want to. Dad's got a forty-foot twin GE Craft catamaran docked down at Puerto Peñasco. You have any idea what the upkeep is on a sucker like that? Come to think of it, you're from Florida, so you probably do. Doesn't leave him a lot of time to play at being an artist. We run a business here.

"Not that we don't have respect for tradition; we do. You don't see us turning out any of the pornographic sand-paintings that show up in downtown Ganado or Gallup. Then there are the computer games based on the stories of the Holy People. We wouldn't have anything to do with stuff like that. So we feel pretty good about what we do." His attitude had turned almost belligerent. Moody hastened to calm him.

"I understand. I was just asking. We're trying to find a motive in all this and we're not having a lot of luck so far. So sometimes you've got to ask some awkward questions. For example, if the Kettrick design was the only one of its kind, maybe one of your people felt the need to have it all to himself."

Bill Laughter chuckled and waved the fax. "A Navaho collector would laugh at this because it makes no sense. A rich Brazilliana, now, or an Asian, they'd put a light on it and stick it up on their wall and be happy with it. But not a Navaho collector."

"So he'd shy away from it because it isn't traditional? How do you know it isn't? Maybe your grandfather was wrong. Maybe the Way described in this painting is still known to someone."

"So what? It's of no use to anybody."

"What if it's an exact reproduction, laid down without any of the little changes necessary to render it harmless?" *Ooljee should be asking these questions*, he thought.

"Hey, my grandfather wouldn't have done that." Up to now Laughter had been brash and confident. Suddenly he looked uncomfortable.

"You just said you don't believe in this stuff."

"I know that." Laughter leaned forward, lowering his voice. "Look, if you asked me straight out do I believe in any of the old ways, I'd say no. But it never hurts to play it safe. There's a whole history of funny things that have happened on the Rez.

"Maybe your guy is another artist. Maybe he's working for someone else who wants something really unique. Except that it's a lot simpler to create your own designs than to kill to acquire somebody else's.

"There's also the possibility that this guy *is* a hatathli, or a would-be hatathli, or some nut who thinks he can be a hatathli and that he really can work miracles by muttering ancient baloney over a pile of colored sand and dirt."

"People who believe what they want to believe are capable of anything," Moody informed him coldly. "I know that from experience."

"That's what I'm saying. Me, I believe in positive cash flow. My dad, he maybe believes in this stuff a little. My grandfather believed a lot, and he wasn't an isolated case in his day. If this guy you're after thinks using this painting will make a real hatathli out of him . . .

"Me, I wouldn't kill for a sandpainting if it was made out of gemstones. We've actually done a couple like that. Ruby dust for red color, amethyst for purple, emerald for green and so on. Strictly for tourists, of course.

"The whole point being that while this is real interesting"—and he tapped the fax—"I don't see anything here worth killing for."

"How do you think I feel?" Moody finished his coffee. "Y'all have no way of telling if it's a true medicine painting or if it's been altered?"

Laughter shook his head. "We don't know the design, so how could we tell if it's been changed or not? Like I said, it makes no difference anyway."

"People keep pointing that out to me a lot."

Laughter eyed him uncertainly, unable to tell if his visitor was making a joke or not. It made Moody feel good to be able to turn the tables a little.

The younger man rose. "I've got to get back to work."

The detective watched him leave, then ambled over to rejoin his partner. The elder Laughter was speaking earnestly.

"Have you considered the possibility that your murder might have nothing to do with the sandpainting?"

Ooljee looked startled.

Moody sympathized. "How do you mean?" he asked.

"Whoever destroyed the painting might have been fulfilling a promise made many years, perhaps even generations, ago. Among the Navaho there are many old feuds, though few end in bloodshed. This might not have anything to do with your Mr. Kettrick. It might be between your murderer and whoever hired him and someone else entirely. An old argument, an ancient dispute. This Kettrick might simply have been in the wrong place at the wrong time.''

"No," said Ooljee with assurance. "The man who killed spoke too often of the painting. I still believe it is central to understanding our case. If only there was a way to interpret its meaning."

"I wish you luck." Red Laughter rose. The visit was over.

He tried to console his guests as he escorted them to the door. "I hope my son and I have been of some help."

"At least now we know where the painting came from." Ooljee paused at the entrance. "We may need to access your records again."

Laughter fumbled in his pockets until he found a business card. "Call any time. I will open a modem for you." He extended a hand. "It was nice to meet you, Mr. Moody. I hope you have not come so far for nothing."

"Thanks," said Moody, adding with careful enunciation, "*Doo ahashyaa da.*"

The painter's eyebrows narrowed and he glanced sharply at Ooljee, who smiled back. "I see you have been getting some lessons in Navaho. I admire you for making the effort. It is not an easy language to learn."

"What now?" Moody asked his colleague as the truck bounced back along the dirt track that paralleled the main creek. Ancient cliffs towered above them, silent and unhelpful, the edges of the wound in the Earth that was Canyon de Chelley.

"Now that we know where the painting came from originally, maybe we can trace the original owners. I'm going to do some more cross-checking. The hands it has passed through over the years may lead us to the hands that slew. Something might turn up."

"I hope so, 'cause I'm getting damn sick of talking about sand and painting and Ways when we're supposed to be trying to catch a real person. You sure you got composites out all over this place?"

For the first time since they'd met, Ooljee tensed. "Do not try to tell me my job, detective."

"Just thinkin' out loud. Something else."

"What?"

"I think you ought to run a background check on the Laughters. They were real friendly and real helpful, but I'm not sure I buy the old man's story about not remembering that particular painting. He said himself how unique and different it was from anything else he'd ever seen. If that's the case, why would he forget it? If this involves some old dispute, maybe it involves his family as well. That'd be a good reason for forgetting."

"But he found the painting for us in his files," Ooljee pointed out.

"That's so."

"Still, you are right. It will not hurt to run a check. What are you going to do while I am mollydiving?"

"Well, I'm sure as hell not gonna sit around and stare over your shoulder. Maybe I'll take a stroll through town. I don't want to impose on you and your missus's privacy any more than I have to. And I'd like to see some more of the city."

"Suit yourself." Ooljee shrugged. "I will drop you off centrally downtown. If you get lost . . ."

"I remember your number. And the address. And I can always walk into the nearest station."

"That's right." The sergeant was relieved. Moody was his responsibility.

"I've got a copy of the composite." Moody tapped the spinner attached to his belt. "Maybe I'll just flash a few street people, since I'm not familiar with your regular sources."

"A good idea, since my 'regular sources' do not seem to be helping us any."

Moody leaned back against the seat, relaxing against the high-acceleration padding. "Could be I'll get lucky. It's a dumb fisherman who sits in the same spot without catching fish and never moves on."

"I wish you luck." Ooljee negotiated a low river dune. "But it would be better if we knew what to use for bait."

CHAPTER 9

OOLJEE DROPPED HIM outside the downtown Intercontinental Hotel. Moody followed the police pickup until it was swallowed by the traffic. Then he turned a slow circle, alone for the first time in an alien environment.

He felt more at home than he'd expected. The stream of well-dressed tourists and white-collar workers flowing past him was little different from what he would have encountered in a cosmopolitan eastern city, except for the invigorating racial diversity. He rubbed the back of his neck. It didn't itch as bad as it had on the day of his arrival. Maybe he was getting acclimated a little.

It was late and the holasers and neons and airborne electrophosphorescents were emerging from electronic hibernation, flaring to luminescent life in search of consumer prey. More of them would appear as twilight gave way to night, their messages insistent, visually and aurally demanding your attention.

Hands jammed in the pockets of his jacket, he chose a direction at random and began to walk, trying to recall what he could of blocks and street names but more or less just letting his legs and his curiosity carry him along.

Most of the shops were long and narrow, their limited

frontage a sure indication of high rents. They sold jewelry, paintings, souvenirs classy and cheap, sculpture, electronic gadgets; designer clothing from China, Russia, Japan, Paris; high-quality furniture from Brazil and the South American Union; antiques, Oriental specialties, and fine pastries. Moody was especially careful to avoid the latter.

Amerindian artifacts he could not judge, but he suspected what he was seeing on the street was not the most authentic available. Ganado was a commercial, not a cultural, center. Ethnologists would find better hunting in Kayenta or Window Rock.

However, the materials, if not the designs, were the finest. One store displayed a magnificent watchband fashioned from platinum, turquoise, and blue sapphires. That these were not traditional materials would not deter wealthy businessmen from Hakana, Shanghai, or Frankfurt. The absence of tradition did not in any way detract from the fine craftsmanship or the beauty of the final product.

He had been doing his best to avoid the many tempting window displays of the various food emporiums, but now as he crossed the street he was attracted to an open establishment from which issued halfway listenable music and the robust aroma of exotic coffees. Stepping through the air curtain, he ordered a double cup of the best Arusha blend from the counter, along with a cleverly woven little Indian basket piled high with scones and an accompanying pot of clotted cream.

An empty table by the window allowed him to indulge in his high caloric purchase while observing the steady flow of pedestrian traffic outside. He remained thus, sipping the pungent dark brew and noshing, until the last vestige of sunlight was but a recent memory, and existing illumination was supplied solely by electrons which had been bent to the will of determined advertisers, much as toy poodles had been bred for the delight of elderly women suffering from emotional deficiencies.

With the lateness of the hour the composition of the crowd began to change, growing perceptibly younger as he watched. Businessfolk had retired to their homes and zenats and laptops. The people out and about now were dressed for excitement, for fun. Some were intent on specific destinations, while others simply wandered in hopes of encountering stimuli, or at the very least something to interrupt the monotony of their lives.

He downed the last of his coffee, the final chunk of scone, and debated ordering another cup, finally deciding that he was going to have enough trouble sleeping tonight. The air door *whooshed* softly as he exited.

Out on the boulevard he was surrounded by flashing lights and insistent whisperers proffering suggestions and invitations in a dozen different languages. The crowd pressed close around him as he headed down a side street, seeking enlightenment along with relief from the crush. He was tracing a whiff of Tandoori when something slim and shiny flashed in an alcove on his right and a voice snapped, "Demobilate right there, fatso."

The voice he ignored, but the object gave him pause. As his eyes acclimated to shadow he made out three figures standing in the shuttered entrance of a shop. One aimed a device at his chest. It might have been a knife, it could have been a gun. The stocky figure standing next to the weapon-wielder beckoned. A cerebromassage red-and-yellow headband pulsed softly against his forehead like a somnolent snake.

"In here, *bilagaanna*. Quick, unless you want to die."

A glance showed Moody that he was alone on this side of the street. This bunch had been waiting for someone just like him, which was to say, stupid and preoccupied. Without justification, he'd allowed himself to relax. Just because this wasn't Tampa.

Behind the speaker and the one with the weapon stood a last, larger mugger. He wasn't quite Moody's size and like his companions he was disappointingly youthful. At least none of them were wildeyes. Just a trio of anxious kids. Potentially murderous kids, but unscrammed. Good. It meant he might be able to reason with them.

Acutely aware of the gleaming metal lance focused on his sternum, he obediently edged into the shadows while keeping as close to the street as possible. The big kid nervously scanned the pavement while his companions inspected their quarry. Meanwhile Moody had time to identify the weapon, which was neither gun nor knife. He noted the supercooled lithium power cell on top and the crudely fashioned trigger on which the shooter kept a taut finger.

The homemade device could pass for an innocent-looking decorative baton or cane, until the cell was activated. Then the uninsulated tip would probably deliver enough of a charge to knock any one human being flat on his back. It was a convenient way of avoiding weapons regulations. Moody knew from experience that one thing bureaucrats never gave street punks sufficient credit for was inventiveness when it came to creating devices capable of inflicting severe bodily harm. In this instance it was the power cell that bestowed lethality, not the wand itself.

The speaker was gesturing anxiously. "C'mon, *bilagaanna*. You can start with the watch, then the wallet."

"This won't do you any good." Moody's fingers slipped slowly toward his inside jacket pocket. These kids were not only nervous, they were also dangerous and dumb, he decided.

Well, maybe not so dumb. The speaker snapped at him.

"Pause it right there. I just wanted directions. *I'll* do the digging. Put your hands on top of your head and lock your fat fingers."

Moody obliged, standing motionless as the kid began roughly rifling his pockets. The detective's wallet he found almost immediately.

When he came to the police ID, he and his buddies would

react in one of two ways: either they'd run like hell or else they'd fry him on the spot. Probably there wasn't enough of a charge in the lith cell to do any real damage, but neither did he relish acting as temporary home for a few thousand volts with nothing better to do.

"Hey, I told you you're wasting your time. I don't carry our credit cards. My wife does." Abruptly he looked street-ward and shouted at the top of his lungs, "Run, Millie!"

The big kid in back made a strangled sound and glanced across the road. For an instant, so did his companions. In that instant Moody, who was much quicker than any man his size not employed in professional sports had a right to be, reached out and grabbed the shockwand just above the uninsulated tip, simultaneously bringing his left leg up in a straight front kick. The punk wielding the device let go of it with alacrity, choosing to grab hold of something else instead.

Yelling, the big kid lunged, a real knife clutched in his right hand. Moody blocked the wild stab and brought the butt end of the shockwand down on his assailant's head, busting the device all to hell and not doing the punk's skull any good either. It began to bleed profusely, as head wounds are wont to do. He stumbled away, uttering scattershot obscenities as blood filled his eyes.

The one who'd done all the talking had drawn his own knife and adopted a combative pose. Moody was already relaxing. Unless he'd badly misjudged their cortexal con-dition, the fight was already over.

"I'm going to cut you, *bilagaanna*!"

Moody put a foot on his wallet, which had been dropped in the fighting, and advanced the other. "You might. On the other hand, if you'd had time to look through that"—and he nodded down at his wallet—"you'd see that I'm from out of town but that it doesn't matter, because police from different departments always cooperate with each other."

From nearby, the big kid cursed in Japanese. "He's a goddamn cop, Ree! You would pick a cop to jump."

"Skeel up, man! Don't you know better than to use names?"

Moody's attention was on the one he'd kicked, who was concluding a brief period of concentrated retching without having paid any attention whatsoever to the preceding conversation.

"Take your woman and get out of here. Y'all better look into another line of work. You're not real good at this."

The speaker and his companion warily helped the third member of the unlucky trio to his feet. Moody tracked them with his eyes as they lurched up the street. Curious pedestrians gave him the eye as they strolled by, looking away fast when he glanced in their direction.

He checked and repocketed his wallet, making sure the pickpocket seal was intact, while chiding himself for taking it too easy. Ganado might be a lot smaller than Tampa, but it still had its share of mean streets. Usually his size was enough to discourage punks like these, but this part of the country seemed to be chock full of contradictions and sudden surprises.

Back on the main avenue he located a public phone, intending to call a cab. Then he remembered the number Ooljee had provided and punched it in instead. He didn't want the sergeant worrying and waiting up for him.

It was Lisa Ooljee's face which appeared on the screen above the speaker. The detective thought she looked not worried, but concerned.

"Hello, Ms. Ooljee."

"Mr. Moody." She was trying to see behind him. "Paul's not with you?"

"No." Moody frowned. "He's not back yet? He dropped me off downtown. I thought he was going straight home from here."

"He must have gone to the office. He'll do that sometimes. Just for a few minutes, to check on some little detail, he says.'' Her tone was tired, as if she'd been through this many times before.

''So call him there.''

''I've already tried. His phone doesn't respond and nobody's seen him. When he's working really hard he'll shut himself away someplace with his research, so he won't be interrupted. But I would like to know. Maybe I should run down and look for him. That always upsets him, though.'' She looked into Moody's eyes. ''He's become so absorbed with this case the two of you are working on. I'd just like to know that he's busy at the station and not out wandering the streets somewhere. He's been known to do that when he's preoccupied.''

Like me, Moody mused. It was hard for him to envision the ever-alert sergeant stumbling through back alleys, wandering blindly down dark lanes.

''Don't worry, Ms. Ooljee. I was going to head back there, but I'll go by the station and have a look for him myself. No reason for you to leave the kids. If he's locked himself away somewhere, I'll kick the door in and tell him to get his self-indulgent butt to the nearest phone.''

She smiled gratefully. ''That is very good of you, Mr. Moody. I appreciate it.'' She moved to disconnect and he hurried to ask her a final question.

''Ms. Ooljee, what does *bilagaanna* mean? Is it Navaho?''

Lisa Ooljee hesitated. ''Could you say it again, please?'' Moody complied, trying to repronounce the word exactly as he'd heard it. ''It means 'white person.' Why?''

''Just trying to enlarge my vocabulary. *Doo ahashyaa da*, right?''

She looked as if she might want to say something else, but he figured on doing her more good by hustling over to Ooljee's station and hunting him down for her. Let him do any requisite reassuring.

He plugged his spinner into the phone, called a cab on a local frequency, and waited the necessary minutes until it homed in on his signal. The driver grunted acknowledgment of the address and slid away from the curb. Moody could have made use of police transport, but he didn't want to pull some cop off duty just to run him to the station.

As it was, the operator of the cab displayed a distinct lack of urgency in taking him across town.

CHAPTER
10

THERE WERE FEW people on the street by the time he reached the station. It was late, cold, and moonless; not the best night for a casual stroll in a sometimes dangerous city. Only the glittering, strobing, relentless ads were unchanged from downtown.

His police ident card admitted him, utilizing the visitor's code he'd been authorized. Tired night-shift personnel didn't spare him a second look. The station was spacious and busy.

Ooljee's office was locked and empty. Inquiries as to the sergeant's whereabouts met with blank stares or negatives, though that wasn't so surprising: Ooljee was day shift. Moody wondered if he ought to try his home again. Maybe he'd already returned. But if he hadn't, then a call would only worry his wife further. So he kept asking around, and was soon glad he had.

"He's downstairs." The young Hispanic woman deftly juggled an armful of folders. "Playin' around, probably. I've seen him come in other times and do that, sometimes all night. I think Paul shoulda been a programmer or nexus jammer instead of a street cop. But he claims he'd rather work with people."

"How do I get there?"

Her directions led him to an elevator which descended to a level twenty feet below the street. It was a strange sensation to someone coming from greater Tampa, where there was a distinct dearth of basements due to the fact that the water level lay only an inch or two below one's feet. Here it made sense to locate the department's most sensitive electronics and communications equipment underground, where electronic interference could be minimized and climate control made easier.

The lighting was subdued, the overhead fluorescents brightening automatically ahead of him as they sensed his oncoming presence. Finding the door his guide had described, he thumbed a nearby buzzer.

At first there was no response, but the third try brought forth a familiar voice from the inset speaker.

"Go away. I'm busy."

Moody leaned toward the vocup. "The whole world's busy, Paul. You hibernating or what?"

There was a pause, then a click as the door was unlatched from inside. "Come on in, if you must."

Entering, the detective advanced far enough to allow the security barrier to close behind him.

Ooljee sat in a swivel casket chair on the far side of the room, surrounded by banks of glowing lights, softouch zenat screens of varying size, and digital readouts. Some displayed text, others figures. A few boasted simple diagrammatics. His attention was focused on the single small monitor directly in front of him. Moody ambled over.

"Look, friend, I don't give a hog's rear end where y'all spend your time, but your woman's concerned."

"Lisa's a worrier." Ooljee didn't look up from the screen. "It is one reason why we get along so well. I do not worry enough."

"Okay, but just as a favor to me, give her a call so she knows you're not lying dead in a gutter somewhere."

"She knows that. She just likes to keep tabs on me." He stole a quick glance at his watch. "But I admit I should have called in by now."

"How come your desk phone didn't relay her calls to your spinner?"

"Turned it off," murmured the preoccupied officer.

"Yeah, she said you might do that." Curious now, Moody leaned close for a better view of the monitor.

It was a foot and a half square, the half-inch thick LCD board protruding from the console on a short, flexible stem. Ooljee had his pocket spinner, a standard police Scorpion model, plugged into the main board. One hand worked its keyboard while the other toyed with a ratpad.

"What are you into so intently?" Moody finally asked him. "X-rated mollyware?"

"I got curious about the origin of the sands used in the Kettrick painting. I thought that if all the sand came from one place it might give us a clue to the feud angle. Sadly, there is nothing remarkable about where the sand is from. Black from the San Francisco Peaks region. Red from Monument Valley.

"It is the yellow sand itself that is interesting. It's radioactive."

Moody blinked. "Come again?"

"Weakly but distinctively so. Oh, that in itself is not unusual. Uranium has been mined on the Rez for more than a century. In fact at one time houses were constructed using the mine tailings, until people understood the danger and had them torn down. Uranium-rich sand provided a nice yellow color for use in sandpainting. It is not used anymore, of course, but there are still some old paintings around which are slightly radioactive. Museums keep them shielded.

"I told the mollysphere to eliminate every color in the painting except red. Then black, and so on. Nothing of interest resulted from my playing around—until I got to the yellow. This is the result."

Moody found himself holding his breath as the image of the painting gave way to—a mass of patternless dull yellow blotches.

"Am I supposed to react to that?"

"Not very impressive, is it?" There was a gleam in the sergeant's eye. "That was my initial reaction. Just for the hell of it I asked the mollysphere to regenerate the original pattern, utilizing one color at a time. I expected it to reproduce the painting each time. That is what it did—until it came to the yellow. Then it asked me a question."

Feeling put upon, the detective mumbled, "A question?"

"Yes. It asked me, 'which pattern?' If I had entered the query differently, it would not have responded in that manner and we would be no wiser."

"And are we wiser?"

"I replied by asking it to generate all the patterns it could, using only the yellow markings as a basis. This is the first image it produced." A perfect reproduction of the Kettrick painting appeared on the monitor.

"This is the second." He fingered the ratpad.

A dazzling display filled the screen to its edges; an overpowering melange of swirls and lines, of diagrammed explosions and crystalline constructs, of bubbles with barbed skins and of reticulated transparencies.

"What the hell is that?" Moody blurted.

"Watch what happens when I enlarge a portion of it."

The molly-eye zoomed in on the upper right quarter of the crazed image, which changed without losing any of its complexity. Again the sergeant enlarged, this time by a factor of four. Alteration and enlargement in no way reduced the amount of detail on the screen.

Moody had to swallow. "I'll be damned. Fractals."

"Yes. Julia Sets within a Mandlebrot Set, the likes of which nobody's ever seen before. All extrapolated from the yellow grains in the Kettrick painting. The radioactive yellow."

"The fact that the sand that was used happened to be radioactive has nothing to do with this."

"Perhaps not, but it makes for an interesting coincidence, don't you think? I instructed the web to repeat the exercise again, utilizing each individual color from the painting: red, black, all of them. They generated random garbage. The yellow generates this." He indicated the monitor.

"The work was so delicate that only a molly could find the underlying fractal pattern. Which leads one to a question: if you need the use of spinner and molly to uncover the pattern in the yellow, how was Grandfather Laughter able to insert it there in the first place? Never mind how did he do it; how did he know what he was doing? Fractals were known in his time, but why put them into a sandpainting, in disguise no less?"

Moody had no comment. He was trying to catch up.

"What is most interesting to me, my friend, what is most interesting to consider is this: if Grandfather Laughter, a real hatathli, was only reproducing a design which had been taught to him by his own father, then where and when did this fascinating little pattern originate?"

Moody glanced up from the monitor. "Accident."

"An accident in radioactive yellow that is not repeated with any other color. How accidental indeed. The proportions are astonishing, as are the relationships between the sets. Even a non-mathematician like me can see that, because the mollysphere says it is so.

"Before you got here I was programming the molly to run some relationships to see how they interrelate."

The detective was still trying to grasp what he'd been told, what he was seeing. "What do you expect to get from that? More sandpaintings?"

"I do not expect to get anything. But since we are dealing with impossible coincidences, I thought it only sensible to go ahead and see if we can find any more. I won't let it run all night. This is a metropolitan municipal-level molly.

It ought to be able to run through several billion resolution levels for us. If nothing else, we'll get to see some pretty pictures."

"Go ahead and run it, then." Moody was feeling simultaneously excited by the discovery of something wonderful that made absolutely no sense and exhausted from his nocturnal sojourn. "And then, for God's sake, call your wife and tell her you're okay."

"Just five or ten minutes." Ooljee was reassuring. "If all we get are changes in the basic schematic, I'll pack it in and we can go home."

Moody looked on as the sergeant's fingers worked the spinner and ratpad. Figures flooded the two monitors to his immediate left, digital dopplegangers of the rapidly sequencing succession of fractal images that filled the main screen. He stood staring until the schematic blur made him turn away, slightly dizzy.

He had a pretty good idea of what was going to happen. The mollysphere would obediently try to reduce the fractal pattern to a finite level, which was impossible. Ooljee would eventually get bored and shut it off. Which was fine with Moody. How an old Indian had managed to install a hidden fractal pattern in a hundred-year-old sandpainting was sufficient mystery for one night.

"Y'all had enough?" he finally asked his colleague half an hour later, "or you gonna wait until you run out of storage?"

"If things get too hot, it will shut itself off." Ooljee was staring at the blur of images on the monitor. "Something here is not right."

"Y'all are right about that, and it's got nothing to do with what the molly says," the detective muttered.

"It should be running sequential patterns. It is not. It's bouncing all over the place." Ooljee worked his spinner. "This does not look right. It is not just searching to expand resolution: it's lining up specific Julia Sets from the Mandlebrot.'' He glanced back and up at his colleague. ''*I* did not tell it to do that.''

''How do y'all know for sure it's not just processing your request in its own way?''

Ooljee gestured at one of the smaller screens off to the side. ''Because the corollary figures are not emerging sequentially. Numbers are lining up, but in what looks like random order.''

''Nothing's random in a Mandlebrot.'' Moody stared hard at the monitor. ''Damn if it don't look like it's building something. Pulling a whole new pattern out of the existing series.'' He was having a hard time believing what his eyes and mind were telling him. ''If I didn't know any better, I'd say that the yellow schematic from the Kettrick painting was acting like a template.''

Ooljee stared unblinkingly at the monitor. ''The deeper the resolution goes into the basal pattern, the more extensive the simulation becomes. One is like a distorted mirror image of the other.'' He sat back. ''Well, this is all very fascinating, but not what I had hoped to find. And if we keep letting it expand and eat up mollystorage like this, pretty soon we will start triggering alarms in the departmental database.'' He tapped a sequence of keys on his Scorpion.

Nothing happened. Numbers continued to speed across the two subsidiary screens. The blur of images on the central monitor continued their rush toward infinity.

''Must have entered the wrong sequence.'' Ooljee repeated the spinner entry, slowly this time, only to be rewarded with an identical lack of results. He leaned forward in the chair.

''This is very interesting.'' He spoke calmly, quietly. ''I don't seem to be able to interrupt the sequence.''

''Shut down the input.''

''What do you think I just tried to do?''

''All right then, shut down your sphere reader.''

"I tried that too." He indicated a readout. "It shut off just the way it is supposed to."

The detective studied the console. There was nothing exotic about it, nothing radical in the design or setup. It was much the same as the molly he was used to working with every day in Tampa. But if Ooljee had ceased inputting and had also shut down the read-enter laser which read the concentric molecular layers of the mollysphere the way a good paring knife peels an onion, then why was the resolution-search sequence still running?

"Procedural error," he finally suggested.

Ooljee made a face. "Shutting down is not a very complicated procedure. It's not one any fool is likely to mess up."

"Okay, granted. Then the problem's got to be mechanical."

"That is what I was thinking." He sighed, straightening in the chair. "I will have to bring maintenance into this. There will be harsh words."

As he reached for the phone, two screens on the far side of the room sprang to life. Each was attached to a spinner. But no one was seated before them.

"I did not turn those on." Ooljee was staring stupidly at the precessing images.

Moody was no longer tired, no longer bored. "I think we'd better find a way to shut this thing down. Fast." As he finished, another pair of screens high up on a wall became active. Ooljee grimly worked his spinner, the ratpad, and nearby input keys, until he was literally stabbing at them.

"No good. No damn good. *Y adil.*"

"I can see that." Moody was trying to make some sense, any kind of sense, out of the millions of images and figures that were avalanching across the multiple screens.

"It's still resolving and still expanding." Ooljee was just sitting now, his gaze flicking in dumbfounded amazement from one monitor to the next. "And whatever it is doing is affecting the hardware. We are getting active response as well as analysis. What is that damn sandpainting a template for?'' He gestured at the no longer quite so innocent-appearing fax of the Kettrick painting where it lay on the console next to his Scorpion. ''If this is some kind of virus, we may be causing a lot of damage.''

''C'mon, man,'' said Moody. ''From what the Laughters told us, that design is at least a couple of hundred years old. They didn't have computers then, or viruses to affect them, much less mollysphere storage.''

Ooljee was rising. ''I am going to have to ask the building engineer to cut the power. For all I know, we are already on course to crash every opdisk and molly in the department.'' He eyed the detective resignedly. ''You had no part in this. I will bear the consequences. It is now unavoidable that there will be consequences. And all I thought to do was to play a few picture games with the painting.''

The lights went out, flickering once before silently expiring. Not the screens. Every monitor glowed with diagrams or numbers as the mutating program continued to build upon itself, utilizing more and more of the station's mollystorage. A wall phone began to jangle insistently. Without taking his eyes from the first monitor he'd activated, Ooljee lifted the receiver. The voice on the other end was loud and frantic enough for Moody to make out some of the words.

''Who's down there? Everything's going nuts upstairs! Who are you people? What's your authorization? I demand to know your—!''

The sergeant calmly replaced the receiver on its hook, effectively silencing the unidentified interrogator. ''Someone is very upset. I think we should try to think of an explanation.''

''How're y'all gonna do that when you don't even know

what's happening?'' Moody spoke without looking at his colleague. He could not help but ignore him in favor of the dazzling displays that now filled every corner of the room.

Every screen, every telltale, every readout and monitor, was alive and glowing, bombarding them with information they could make no sense of, and chromatic schematics as bright and ever-changing as an exhibition of kinetic art. All that was missing was deafening popular music, Moody thought, preferably by a group like Molten Scalpel or the Raucoids, and they could sell admission.

In place of music there was a persistent, electronic hum that rose and fell in a pattern that, while not recognizable, was self-evidently anything but random. An eerie, fuzzy whisper that tittered in the background, emanating from an unidentified source like rats running the conduits.

Ooljee disconnected his spinner. It had no effect whatsoever on the now self-sustaining program. Both men began backwalking toward the door. Moody's imagination was beginning to run away with him. While whatever was happening here might not be easily or readily explained, he reminded himself, it wasn't an excerpt from a horrorvid either. Ooljee's fiddling with a Mandlebrot Set derived from the Kettrick sandpainting had inexplicably generated some kind of reproduction program within the police mollysphere. That was physics, not phantasy.

Still, he was measurably relieved when the door did not resist Ooljee's touch. Behind them the room was filled with a booming *whu-whu-whu* sound, a deep-throated electronic pounding. It was interrupted frequently by the first sharp cracklings and snapping noises of overloaded circuits. Above it all echoed the plaintive wail of the wall phone.

Suddenly Ooljee pointed to the original monitor. While the rest of the screens were awash in incomprehensible psychedelic babble, it had turned a calm cool green, a verdant field on which throbbed a single flickering word:

WORKING

Working, Moody mused wonderingly. *Working at what?*

He would not be spooked. There was a reasonable explanation for whatever was happening. As soon as they could shut everything down, recovery specialists would run a trawl on the mollysphere web and figure out exactly what had occurred.

The *whu-whu-whu* sound in the room was now accompanied by a faint rush of air that sounded like *hahowa hahowa*. It was a most peculiar electronic counterpoint.

Ooljee thought so too. "You hear that?" The detective nodded. "That is really strange."

"Why? We've got a room full of visual garbage. Why not aural as well?"

"It is strange because I do not think it is garbage. I think I know what it is. At least, I remember hearing something like it when I was a kid."

Moody turned on him, more uneasy than he would have cared to admit. The pounding, pulsing sounds that filled the room meant nothing to him. He began to wonder if his colleague was starting to extrapolate upon reality, or to put it another way, crack under the strain of what he'd inadvertently committed.

"We've been in this hole long enough. The weavers will work it out. That's what they're paid for." He put a big hand on the sergeant's shoulder, pushing him toward the elevator. "Let's get some air."

Explosive cracklings drowned out Ooljee's mysterious electronic mumbling. Moody glanced back over his shoulder. Wisps of smoke were beginning to appear in the room.

"Shit. That's all we need."

They reached the elevator, had to wait impatiently for it to descend from the main floor. A small screen set in the wall to one side of the lift-controls was flashing figures and diagrams at them. Abruptly and without any warning they were replaced by words. Ooljee stared dumbly at the screen on his spinner. The words were repeated there, and for all they knew, on every screen and monitor back in the room. All around them the first smoke alarms were beginning to howl.

**With the far darkness made of the He-rain over
your head
Come to us Soaring**

**With the far darkness made of the She-rain over
your head
Come to us Soaring**

**With the zig-zag lightning flung out on high over
your head
Come to us Soaring**

**With the rainbow hanging high over your head
Come to us Soaring**.

It flickered on the wall monitor, blinked back at him from Ooljee's screen. It made sense in and of itself, but not to him. As they entered the elevator their ears were assaulted by a rising electronic thunder, rumbling and spitting ominously. It pursued them up the shaft.

The doors parted, letting them out on the main floor. Smoke alarms were wailing everywhere. People were gathering up mollysphere backup cubes and printouts and personal effects as they raced for the exits.

Ooljee allowed himself to be led, his expression dazed. Moody got directions from an officer hurrying past them. His arms were piled high with cubes and boxes of holomages.

The sergeant finally looked at the man dragging him along. "You read it too, didn't you?"

"Yeah, I read it. What is it? Something from the local Top Forty?"

"It's from the Nightway. Part of a long chant addressed to the Thunderbird. You have heard of the Thunderbird?"

"Yeah, sure." Moody plunged into a crowded corridor. There was a lot of smoke in the air now, acrid and eye-stinging. People were starting to cough. Down below, something was burning.

The external security doors had been flung aside. No one was checking idents now. Moody stumbled down the stairs leading to the street, nearly fell as a percussive blast rocked the station behind them. A thin tongue of orange flame licked through a window flanking the doorway. Sweat poured down his back. For an instant he thought he heard that strange electronic pulsing, *whu-whu-whu*, hammering away in counterpoint to *hahowa hahowa*. Then he realized they were only echoes of what he heard earlier, down below.

Except for the flames vomiting from the station windows and the indifferently drifting advertising holasers shrieking the virtues of cigarettes, deodorants, autos and vidshows, restaurants and hotels, it was pitch dark outside. Night-shift personnel and a few late-roaming curious civilians were gathering in groups, trying to assist each other, trying to help, trying to make sense of what was happening. A few stood alone or in twos, gawping dumbly at the building.

Moody pushed through the swelling crowd. He was not in the mood to talk to anyone, in any language. Right now he was more concerned with protecting his partner and assessing his mental state. No one confronted them. Probably no more than one or two people knew that Ooljee had been direct-accessing the system's mollyweb. No one shouted at them to stop.

He did not see the bolt strike the uplink dish atop the precinct house, but was sure that he heard it above the screams of those who did. It melted the upper two-thirds of the big antenna and left the remainder smoking like fried fish bones. The thunder of its passing was replaced by the mournful song of approaching fire engines as one city department raced to the aid of another. Later, much later, a few witnesses would insist that the lightning had been full of color, like a shard of jagged rainbow, instead of simply a normal bright white.

Ooljee had been staring past his friend and had seen it hit. The color of it lingered on his retinas. Thunder and lightning continued to torment the night sky, but the building was not struck again.

THE FIRE DEPARTMENT arrived just as the rain began; steady, hard, and cold as an iceman's tattoo. An exhausted Moody slumped to the sidewalk. The droplets chilled his neck and back. He pulled his jacket up to protect his head.

His partner sat beside him; legs crossed, hands resting on his thighs. Together they observed the flaming, smoking scene as men in uniforms very different from those of the late-night refugees scattered to their work.

Aware he was breathing too fast and that his heart was working too hard, Moody struggled to slow both by concentrating on something else. He glanced uncertainly at his colleague.

"I don't suppose you can explain this?"

It took the sergeant a moment to react. Only then did he regard his paler, larger companion through the falling rain.

"If it is a step-by-step reconstruction of events that you want, I can't help you. I cannot help myself. We know that the departmental web built some kind of program based on a fractal template derived from a portion of the Kettrick painting. We know that after it reached a certain point, it began running itself, because we were unable to shut it down. Some kind of mutation took place within the mollysphere. It went on autoplait, or whatever you want to call it.''

Moody nodded slowly. ''All of which is patently impossible, because the work Grandpa Laughter created dates from a time when nobody knew about such things.''

''Quite so.'' Ooljee continued to stare at the burning building. ''Then there is the matter of the sounds we heard.''

''Yeah. You said you recognized some of it. It was just noise to me.''

The sergeant nodded. ''Noise like this.'' He repeated what they'd heard as they'd fled the room. The hair on the back of Moody's neck stiffened slightly.

Sheets of water and suppressant poured into the precinct house as the men in yellow slickers beat the flames down.

''I have not seen many ceremonies,'' Ooljee was saying, ''but those few I remember. When I was ten, eleven, my father took me to see one that was being performed over in Tuba City. There is a spirit called Talking God. He is, they say, in charge of the eastern dawn and also of the chase. That is of course no more than coincidence.'' Ooljee mustered a tired, soaked smile.

''He is said to function as a spiritual *deus ex machina*, materializing with useful suggestions whenever a hero is at an impasse.'' He stared at the station. ''If a suggestion was given, I missed it.''

''So what's the connection?''

Ooljee looked back at him, water dripping down his face, his black hair slicked tight against his forehead. ''The *whu-whu* noise we heard? That is the sound the hatathli makes. It is supposed to be the voice of Talking God.''

''It was an electronic hum, a byproduct of whatever the hell it was you set off.''

''Of course. But don't you think it interesting that the chant used in an ancient ceremony closely duplicates an electronic hum?''

''I think you're nuts.''

"Yes. But it is still intriguing, don't you think? One might well ask if my judgment is weak and I am simply willing what we heard in there to resemble the chant of the hatathli I remember from childhood."

"What about the other sound?" Moody pressed him.

"*Hahowa, hahowa?* Just a different frequency, wasn't it? What if it does sound like the voice of xactce'oyan, who is Talking God's twin?"

"What the hell does that mean?"

"It cannot be translated." He rubbed his legs and sighed tiredly. "It is said that Talking God is very compassionate."

Moody indicated the station. "If that's compassion, give me sirloin."

"I am not foolish enough to say that Talking God and xactce'oyan are responsible for what has happened here tonight. What I am saying is that if—" He hesitated.

"Go on," Moody urged him. "Nobody here but us madmen."

Ooljee spoke carefully, measuring his reply. "If there is anything to the ancient ways, then perhaps something somewhere, if only part of an inexplicable program, was trying to warn us."

"Warn us? Warn us about what?"

The sergeant shrugged. "Trying to make use of the template. Who knows?"

"If something was trying to warn us, to help us," Moody asked him, "then what was responsible for *that*?" He gestured in the direction of the burned-out station.

"Big Thunder," said Ooljee simply.

"Right, sure." Moody rose, kicked at an empty plastic container lying in the street. "That's just fine. It all makes sense, except that it's all impossible." He turned sharply on his partner. "You're not really asking me to buy a bunch of crap about 'talking gods' and their twin brothers?"

"I am not asking you to believe anything. I am hardly sure what to believe myself. I am just telling you what I know about what seems to fit. I am not saying that it makes any sense.''

''For a duty cop, y'all sure know an awful lot about your mythology.''

''We are still raised with it,'' Ooljee replied simply. ''A child grows up hearing many of the old stories. In a highly homogenized, internationalized world we have done well to preserve a little of our original culture. It is good that the planet shrinks daily and brings people together, if only in quest of financial success. But when it happens too quickly, the little cultures get squeezed between the big ones. Sometimes they get squeezed right out of existence. When high-tech came to the Rez and my forebears started making money they were determined that the Dineh would not be squeezed out of the world.

''Even so, much has been forgotten by many. That is one reason why I was assigned to this case. Because of certain of my school studies, I know more about sandpainting than any of my colleagues. Otherwise you would now be talking to someone else. But most of them wouldn't know Bat from Big Fly.''

''What are those?'' Moody frowned.

''Sandpainting guardians.''

The detective grunted, wiped rain from his forehead. ''So we're back to that again.''

''You make it sound simple. It is not, *bilagaanna*.''

''*Bilagaanna*, yeah. Your wife told me. Hey, you'd better call her. If she's still trying to reach you and gets a recording saying that communications are down, she's first gonna be worried.''

''You're right, I should do that. But I do not think I will tell her about the fire just yet. Vernon Moody, my friend, we have tapped into something very peculiar. Perhaps we cannot give it name or rationale, but neither can we deny its existence. You were there. You saw what happened.''

''I saw a police molly going crazy. That's all.''

Rising, Ooljee brushed his hair off his face. "I see I have spoken too much about Talking God and old legends. Maybe you are right. Maybe I have. If we could access the department's AI molly we could ask its opinion, but somehow I feel it may not be operational at this time.

"Believe what you will, but the fractal pattern derived from the Kettrick painting is the key to all this, whatever *this* turns out to be."

Moody stood next to him. Together they watched the firemen work. "We could try sticking the molly with an AI search and recovery program."

"If there is anything left to recover and the molly itself is not damaged. Don't get me wrong, my friend. I have not stepped over the edge on you. What we saw was physics at work, not spirits. But it involves something we do not yet understand, and it involves that sandpainting."

"Okay, okay. Just go easy on the spirit talk."

"We prefer the term Holy People," Ooljee told him. "The *Deginneh* are not necessarily spirits, not necessarily gods. They are simply those who were here before us. Before the Dineh, the Navaho."

Suddenly Moody found himself wishing he was away from there; away from the dark street with its mob of surging, querulous pedestrians and outgrabers and drunks, away from the evicted police and cursing firemen. Back in Florida, throwing a line into the Bay in search of bonefish or perch. Back where life was warm and moist and alive. Not stuck in this high, dry, half-dead place where the buildings seemed to merge with mountains and the alien voices of black-eyed street punks mocked him everywhere he looked. Back where he didn't have to deal with a partner who talked of spirits and chants and Ways, of Holy People and fractal sands.

But while his heart might choose to deny it, his mind knew that something more than passing strange had taken possession of a police department's mollyweb, peeling its sphere and replacing it with a shape other than orthodox.

It ought not to have happened. A police mollysphere was supposed to be invulnerable, protected from any external intrusion, impervious to virus or peeling. Only a military sphere would be harder to penetrate.

He'd been there when the template had begun to mutate, had seen it expand to overwhelm the station's security system as though it didn't exist. What would have happened had the fires not stopped it? Would it have spread via linking fiber optics to the rest of the city's police web? Or perhaps farther than that, into financial and commercial and administrative mollyspheres, growing and changing as it wiped out records and programs to satisfy a voracious need for more and more web space?

"I'm sorry," he said at last. "I know what I saw, and I know what you did, but I don't know what happened back there and I just can't buy the idea that something in a hundred-years-old piece of folk art is sophisticated enough to infect a modern high-security molly. Y'all ain't gonna insist that's what happened, are you? Y'all ain't gonna sit there and tell me you think old Grandpa Laughter was web-literate?"

Ooljee regarded him thoughtfully. "Let me suggest to you two possible explanations for what happened here tonight. The first involves Nayenezgani."

Moody rolled his eyes.

"The Dineh had no way to record the knowledge that the Holy People had given them. So Nayenezgani told them how to use powered rock to make sandpaintings. The Holy People did not use sandpaintings themselves. They drew on sheets of sky. Do you know anything about helical molecular masking?"

Moody blinked.

"It is the first stage in the manufacture of custom microprocessors. I could describe the process but it is enough to know that it might be described by someone with an imaginative flair for words as drawing on sheets of sky. Very tiny sheets, it is true.''

"I don't much care for that explanation. I hope I like your other one better.''

The sergeant steepled his fingers. "Ignoring for the moment the question of how it got there, we must assume that something very unusual is present in the sandpainting, an inserted fractally coded program which affects the mollysphere much as any modern viral program might. Grandfather Laughter might have added it in his old age when computers were first becoming common, or it might have been put there by someone else, either when the painting was originally done or at some later date. We can't check on that, because the original has been destroyed, but I think it a not invalid hypothesis.''

Moody was nodding approvingly. "That I can relate to.''

Gratified, Ooljee took the concept and ran with it. "It gives us a new motive for our murderer. Whatever the template's primary purpose, there is no denying its power to infect a supposedly shielded web. Something like that might have military applications. Easy to understand why someone might wish to possess the only copy.''

"So we've finally got something worth killing for. Sure beats the crazed collector theory to a pulp. For the first time, that part of the case makes sense.'' Moody was slapping his right fist into his open left palm. "It means our suspect's probably not nuts. That changes a lot.''

"Indeed it does,'' Ooljee agreed. "We now have a killer who knows exactly what he is about, instead of an unpredictable maniac. He may or may not be a hatathli, but I think we can assume that he is a trained weaver.''

"We can check this.'' Moody was enthusiastic, hopeful. "We can see if anything similar to this has happened recently anywhere else in the country. If it has, I may be leaving.''

"And what if our experience here tonight proves to have been unique, an isolated incident?"

"Then I'd say that whoever we're after either doesn't know yet what he's got ahold of, or else he's still waiting to make use of it." Side by side the two men started walking toward a cab stop.

"Possible military applications aside," the sergeant continued, "this template program would make a very interesting instrument of blackmail. Envision it: 'Deposit so many millions into this numbered Swiss account or I will turn your irreplaceable database to photic slag.'"

"That's possible," Moody agreed, "or maybe our boy has something else in mind."

As they reached the cab stop Ooljee reached for his pocket spinner. "First I need to let Lisa know that everything's okay." He glanced back at the precinct house. The flames had been knocked down but thick smoke continued to pour from several ground-floor windows. "I don't think we need to tell her about the excitement just yet. It will only make her worry."

"As long as you're gonna call in, how about we find some coffee before we do anything else? I've got a lot of ideas racing around inside my head and not many of 'em make sense. I'm not used to that. I'd like to try and do something with 'em."

Ooljee checked his watch. In an hour the sun would be up. It hardly seemed worth going all the way across town to disturb Lisa and the kids. She would not be upset by his absence, so long as he gave her an explanation. He'd worked double shifts before. The thought of coffee was a good one; coffee; *ahehee*, yes, and something more substantial. Inexplicable chaos stimulated the appetite.

"You talk," he said to the big Southerner, "and I will eat."

Moody didn't wonder why his friend chose to call a cab instead of a police vehicle. A request for the latter might arrive in tandem with questions neither of them wanted to try answering just yet. Homing in on the sergeant's spinner, the cab arrived in a few minutes.

The rain had let up for a while, but by the time they entered the all-night café Ooljee had selected, it was coming down like fractured icicles. Moody followed his partner inside. The sun might be rising but you wouldn't be able to tell it in this country. When it rose back home, you anticipated warmth and mist and comfort, a tactile as well as visual greeting. The sunlight here was possessed of a penetrating harshness that was as much to be avoided as sought after.

The café was nearly deserted. Ganado's nocturnal life forms were retreating to their burrows and it was too early for the rest of humanity to be stirring. They chose a booth in back, upholstered in faux leather designed to resemble red cedar. Twisting gods and arching yeis had been engraved on the sides of the booth with a sculpting laser. All the yeis were similar. The artist who had done the work had opted for speed over imagination.

Not everyone hanging out was Amerind. There were a few Anglos and a couple of Thais: service techs lingering after work, web spinners arguing in their obscure languages, maybe security cops longing for bed.

The wall dispenser offered a surprising variety of coffees, and the live waitress, when she finally appeared with their order, produced a cinnamon roll the size of a small two-layer cake. Moody hadn't thought long about ordering it and he didn't hesitate to dig in. Hard thinking made him hungry.

The Colombian was hot and fulfilling. Friends often asked how he could differentiate between brews. The younger ones thought coffee came from restaurant wall-dispensers or pre-mix servings instead of beans. There were no gourmets left, he mused, and in any event you weren't likely to encounter one in the police department of a large eastern metropolis.

"I suppose the fax got smoked along with everything else downstairs."

"Probably," said Ooljee, "but I have copies in my desk, which is fireproof, and at home. As for the template, it is in here." He tapped the spinner holstered at his belt, nibbled at the corn-lingonberry muffin he'd ordered. "I wonder exactly what we did."

"Just don't do it again real soon," Moody advised him.

"Not me. Precinct houses are expensive."

They were silent for a while then, each man busy with his own thoughts. Moody looked up from the skeleton of his cinnamon roll.

"The Laughters identified part of the Kettrick painting. Something about a scavenger?"

Ooljee nodded. "He figures prominently in the Bead Chant and is also called One-Who-Goes-About-Picking-Up-Discarded-Things. He was the one carried up through the Skyhole. You would need to check with a real hatathli, but as I remember the story, he got in trouble with the Pueblo people. Then the hawks and eagles, assisted by snakes, helped him to flee through a hole in the sky. Forty-eight birds are generally shown aiding him, though sometimes twenty-four are used. In our culture, multiples of four and twelve have much power.

"The birds wrapped him in a black cloud to conceal him and carried him up into the sky, boosted by three rainbows and three bands of lightning. It was very dark inside the cloud, and the birds provided Scavenger with a yellow tube to breathe through and a large crystal to furnish light. Interesting, isn't it? A legend thousands of years old that mentions breathing tubes and light-generating crystals?"

"Don't get me started," the detective muttered.

A grinning Ooljee continued. "It is said that Talking God helped also. He is in many of the Ways."

"That's it? That's the whole story?"

"Oh, no. There is a lot more, but that was the portion

that was illustrated in the sandpainting. Many times individual components of one sandpainting will be used in another, just as similar electronic components are featured in many different devices. Though it is unusual to have so elaborate a painting incorporated bodily into a larger one.''

"You keep talking about a 'chant'?" Moody spoke absently, distracted by a young couple who'd just come in out of the rain, laughing and giggling and shaking water from their slickers.

"The chant is not just a sandpainting," Ooljee explained. "It is a complex combination of the painting and singing and other things. The song sequence for a single chant, for example, may contain several hundred songs intoned as a litany. A hatathli will sing over his patient while also building the sandpainting. As for the paintings themselves, there are probably many like the Kettrick that have gone unrecorded. Even so, over five hundred distinct and different sandpaintings are known. At least, that was the last figure I remember seeing.

"There is no telling how many were lost before a couple of hatathlis were finally convinced to allow their work to be recorded in permanent form." He hesitated. "I think I can tell you what happened tonight, if not how."

Moody finished the last of his coffee, ordered a refill. "Tell me. I could do with some enlightenment."

"We disturbed *hozho*."

"Beg pardon?"

Ooljee leaned back in his seat. "The Navaho imagine the universe to be a delicately balanced place, alive with powerful forces that have potential for good or evil. If you upset that balance, called *hozho*, terrible and strange things can happen. We believe that only mankind can upset the balance, but perhaps that is wrong. Certainly we upset some kind of balance tonight."

Moody tried hard not to smile. "Let's say that we did. How do you fix your *hozho*?"

"By performing the correct Way."

"I see. So what you're telling me is that we ought to go find ourselves a compliant hatathli to chant over what's left of your office?"

"That would not be a bad idea." Seeing the look that came over his partner's face, the sergeant hastened to add, "Of course, nobody believes in such things anymore. The only people who are going to restore balance to the precinct are contractors and accountants. They have their own chants and ways. Though sometimes I think of accountants as masters of the Red Ant Way."

"What does that make us masters of?" Moody was feeling lightheaded from the exhaustion brought on by the night's events and from lack of sleep. "The Shooting Way? That's one you mentioned, I remember."

"I don't know, but the moment you think you understand the Ways, they will surprise you. You might be interested to know that there is a Prostitution Way, though it is connected not with what you think but with witchcraft."

"Yeah, I can see where that might disturb your *hozho*, all right."

"At least now we may have a motive that makes sense."

"What's this?" Moody feigned astonishment. "Police talk?"

"Be as sarcastic as you like. But forget for a moment where the Kettrick painting comes from, how old it is, or how Grandfather Laughter came to make it." There was impatience in Ooljee's voice. "*Something* derived from its design penetrated and altered a police molly. Anything that can do that is worth money to certain people."

"You think that's motive enough?"

Ooljee shrugged. "*Daats'i*. Perhaps, maybe, possibly. We will find out."

He paid for the coffee and pastry, waiting for the wall dispenser to process his card. As soon as it was returned they rose to depart.

"Have you heard of the Anasazi?" Ooljee asked his colleague. "They were here before the Navaho. We don't know if they did sandpaintings or not, but they made drawings on sheer canyon walls. Nearly all of what they knew has been forgotten."

"Just when you were starting to sound sensible," Moody replied in disgust.

"It was just a thought. Since I am talking so much nonsense, what is *your* explanation for what happened here tonight?"

"I'm easier than you. I don't have one, and I'm not going to lose any sleep over lack of it. We'll do our best to rerun your procedure and that way we'll figure out what took place inside the web. Since we're big on stories tonight, do you remember the one about Pandora's box? This time we'll make sure the proper safeguards are in place when you run that expansion."

"Then you do not deny that the sandpainting triggered a mutation within the web?"

"I know that your departmental molly went nuts. Until we know for sure why, I withhold judgment."

"I will use a much smaller molly next time." Ooljee was thinking aloud as they exited the café. The rain had finally stopped. "We'll try it on my home spinner. It is not linked to anything substantial. I wonder what would have happened if the system had not broken down?"

"Isn't it obvious? We'd have ended up with the world's first Anasazi spreadsheet."

Ooljee made a face at him. "If our murderer has something more specific than that in mind, it will behoove us to locate him before he figures out how to implement it. Lisa has been wanting to visit her parents in Albuquerque and I've kept asking her to hold off. If I can get her to go and take the kids with her, we can work on this quietly at my place, see what we can find out, before Personnel recovers

its wits enough to find me and assign me to something else.''
He tapped his spinner.

"We'll plug the template into my home unit, clear a space
in the kitchen in which to work. This time we will be
employing far less storage capacity. I do not see us doing
any serious damage to anything except my own equipment,
though I will have to make certain Lisa's household files
are backed up. God help me if I wipe her grandmother's
recipes.

"This time if I burn anything it is only a few dollars out
of the family budget. We won't be using enough power to
damage the building.''

"Y'all are sure about that.''

"No, but I don't know what else to do.'' He looked to
his left. "Besides, until they reassign me to another precinct
or make my old office functional I have nowhere to report
to. So we might as well work at home.''

CHAPTER
12

LISA OOLJEE WAS somewhat taken aback by her husband's abrupt change of heart as far as visits to his in-laws were concerned, but her suspicions weren't strong enough to override the children's enthusiasm. By midday Ooljee had bundled them off via tube to New Mexico.

There was then the matter of the previous night's lost sleep, which the two men gratefully accounted for. By evening they were ready to proceed.

Moody could only watch while Ooljee made preparations, conscious of the suddenly incongruous domesticity of his surroundings. The relics and reproductions of the crafts of an earlier era—the pots and paintings and rugs—loomed large in his thoughts as well as in the condo's decor.

There was much less spiritual baggage to deal with in the modern kitchen. He waited while his host connected the home molly mounted on the counter to the police spinner on the table. The home unit would supply just enough web for their needs.

After rechecking his connections, Ooljee activated the small zenat which hung on the far wall next to the refrigerator and ran an autobraid through the portable's entry-board. Colorful abstract patterns flashed across the monitor.

The sergeant gestured toward the home molly. "I have installed an autointerrupt box between the unit and my spinner. If either approaches overload, everything will shut down automatically."

"You hope."

"Is Florida populated exclusively by optimists these days?"

Moody forbore from pointing out that the safeguards at the station were infinitely more sensitive and effective than the discount-store special Ooljee was relying on. On the other hand, their little kitchen experiment had the virtue of simplicity. There was only a single cable to worry about, and no potentially troublesome optic connections.

The sergeant sat down next to his spinner like an old-time projectionist preparing to unspool cinematic magic. He muttered an order and the household fluorescents obediently darkened in response. Moody found himself staring not at the zenat but at the nearby refrigerator. It was wallpapered with childish scribblings lovingly carried home from school, awkwardly posed holomages, cheap decorative magnets, and gaudy plastic flowers. It reminded him powerfully of the family he did not have. Irritated, he returned his attention to the monitor.

Ooljee's fingers danced over the spinner board. The zenat cleared, its surface a bright, cheerful green.

"I think this will be okay, now that we have some idea of what to expect."

"Do we?" Moody was standing behind him, looking over his shoulder.

"We have the example of the previous night. I am going to make essentially the same requests of the home web that I made of the bigger one at the station, only I am going to run it at one-twentieth the speed congruent with an interrupt program, which I hope will react at the critical moment and bring everything to a halt so that we will have time to note exactly what is taking place."

"What if the template program ignores all your instructions and we get a straight-up replay?"

Ooljee gestured at the kitchen counter. "There is a large, wood-handled meat cleaver in the first drawer to the left of the sink. If both my programmed and on-line interrupts fail, take a good swing at the cable. That will be just as efficient at halting the flow of mutational information, if a little more expensive." He grinned. "One never forgets how to make use of low-tech on the Rez."

Moody tensed as he stared at the zenat. The spinner had commenced the same inexplicable fractal sequencing which had taken control of the police station mollyweb. The monitor was alive with the fractal flow, colors and patterns racing past too rapidly to comprehend. Ooljee's preparations and precautions notwithstanding, the sequence appeared to be running as fast as before. He couldn't be certain, though. When reproduced at high speed, even the simplest fractal patterns could be disarmingly mesmerizing.

There were no additional screens in the kitchen to come to life, however; no high-density readouts to belch forth incomprehensible figures, no tattle-telltales to warn of impending web failure. Just as there were no heavy-duty backup devices to come on line if the web they were using suddenly tried to expand beyond its proscribed boundaries.

As the sequencing progressed in the absence of smoke, flame, and spark, he relaxed a little. Behind him, uninvolved kitchen appliances hummed quiescently.

"It is replicating," declared Ooljee tersely. "It's mutating again. But this time we have it under control. Sometimes less is more."

"We can't be sure of that. What about this building's maintenance-and-service molly? Are you sure it's isolated?" If that began to smoke and blaze, Moody mused, they could look forward to an interesting time trying to deal with it from their position near the top of the tower.

"We'd hear an alarm. At least we know we are on the

right track, that what happened last night was not a fluke. The yellow sand in the Kettrick painting generates a reproducible template. It is working just as well, maybe better, on this system as it did on a much larger one. What I do not understand is why it works and what it is supposed to do. If we knew that, we might be able to make use of it, to direct it. Surely it was not designed to keep expanding until it self-destructs.''

The kitchen molly whirred softly, the zenat was bright and silent, and Ooljee's fingers occasionally fiddled the board of his spinner. It was motionless in the room except for the unending transformation the program was working on the surface of the zenat. Perhaps because it was so scaled down everything seemed less frantic, less out of control than it had at the station. Whatever changes Ooljee had made prior to and concurrent with entering the program appeared to have had the desired effect. They had tamed the template.

The last thing Moody expected was for the seemingly ceaseless rush of images to slow down. However, that was exactly what was happening. As they watched in fascination, the runaway fractal forms began to mutate less and less rapidly, taking on the aspect of recognizable shapes and symbols, until the schematic that took final possession of the monitor shone calm and unchanging back at them from the far wall.

It was determinedly Euclidian. It was quite attractive.

It was a sandpainting.

Not the Kettrick. Something different, figures and shapes organized around a black circle flanked by four curving colored bars. Outside the bars, angular silhouettes clutched a profusion of unidentified objects. The figures were surrounded by additional symbols and devices. If any of it had been created using colored sand, Moody decided, it had to have been very fine sand indeed. The painting displayed no granular texture whatsoever.

A jagged border stuck through with arrowheadlike points surrounded and enclosed the design on three sides. The open end faced the refrigerator. Faced east.

"Pretty," he commented. "What's it supposed to represent?"

"Who can say? We need a hatathli here, or somebody from the museum. All I know is what I remember from when I was a kid and what I have picked up while working on this case. That is not a lot."

"Why'd you call it up instead of the Kettrick painting?"

Ooljee glanced back and up at him, his face lit only by the glow from the monitor. "I didn't bring it up. The template program generated it."

"Y'all telling me that it did all that processing just to show us another sandpainting that we also don't know nothing about? Shee-it, my friend, I'm a patient man, but I have my limits too."

Ooljee hardly heard him. He was entranced by the image on the screen. "Some kind of semi-Möbius program. Begins with a painting and ends with one. Look at it this way, Vernon: it is better than smoke and flames." He glanced uneasily at the interrupt box he'd spliced into the cable linking his spinner to the kitchen unit. The single warning LED glowed a comforting, steady green.

The frustrated detective relented a little. "I suppose so. What do we do now? Go find ourselves a medicine man? Or an art catalog?"

Ooljee rose and approached the monitor. With a finger he traced the jagged border. "This is a lightning guardian. I doubt it has anything to do with what we witnessed earlier, but it is kind of nice to see it here." His finger spiraled inward. "I do not recognize any of these yei figures. The feather designs are all wrong. So are the heads. They should be rectangular for female yeis, round for male. Not like this. Perhaps whoever originally drew them was trying to be funny."

"Yeah. I can hardly restrain myself," Moody murmured sardonically.

"They are holding many things I also do not recognize." Ooljee tapped the monitor's plastic surface. "This might be a medicine pouch, or it might be something completely different. I do not have any idea what the central pattern represents, because of the strange shapes it contains. These," he indicated the colored bars, "could almost be whirling rainbows, except the colors and proportions are all wrong. But these two additional guardian figures up here"—and his hand moved up toward the top of the monitor—"look very much like Gila monsters."

"Very instructive." Moody belched. "Anthropology 101. What does it get us?"

"Very little, on the face of it." Frowning, Ooljee walked back to the kitchen table and turned to study the complex image anew. "But there is a relevant ritual."

Moody sat down tiredly. "Not another ritual."

Ooljee was unrepentant. "It is called the Hand-Trembling Ritual. By it you specifically invoke Gila Monster, a deity who sees and keeps track of everything that occurs. So the legends say."

"What about it?"

"Ever hear a better description of an all-inclusive database?"

"I've heard better names. So there's a database called Gila Monster. Do you access it, or feed it?"

"You do not believe me. I am not sure *I* believe me. But there is *something* there." He studied the softly humming screen appraisingly. "When working with Gila Monster, you do the Hand-Trembling ceremony. If it works, it leads to what you are looking for. That, or . . ."

"Or?" Moody prompted him.

"You hear the voice of Gila Monster."

Though he'd never been outside the South, Moody knew what a Gila monster looked like from watching nature programs on the vid. He was not sure he wanted to speak with one.

Ooljee continued. "The Navaho name for the ceremony means 'to look for something without looking.' You could not pronounce it."

"Do you have a vitamin ceremony? My enthusiasm level is way down."

"And I am running out of ideas." The sergeant pursed his lips as he eyed the monitor. His spinner sat on the table, active and alert. The telltale on the interrupt box leading to the home unit shone bright green, giving no indication of behaving in anything other than an accepted, dignified electronic manner.

"I have told you before that I am no hatathli: just a cop with an interest in the old Ways. As I remember it, the Hand-Trembling ceremony is comparatively simple and straightforward. Not like Blessingway or Shooting Way. Wait here a minute." He turned and exited the kitchen.

Moody looked after him. "Where are you going?"

"To look up some details."

"How many domestic mollys do y'all have in this place, anyway?"

"Just two. The one on the counter, and one in the boys' room for their schoolwork. It won't interface with the tower molly, but I can access the educational library system with it. That should be sufficient."

While waiting for his host to return, Moody busied himself with raiding the refrigerator and examining the image frozen on the zenat. The twisting humanlike figures and accompanying symbols, though unfamiliar, were arrayed against the neutral background in symmetrical, orderly fashion. Nor did one have to be an expert to identify the two shapes at the open east end of the sandpainting as lizardlike. East was the direction from which spirits entered, he remembered Ooljee telling him.

The sergeant returned, studying some paper printouts.

His lips moved as he read, as if he were rehearsing.

"I probably will not do this right."

"It probably won't matter," Moody argued. "Look, why don't we just call it an evening and go get some supper? If you're that into continuing this we can come back to it in the morning."

"They may call me to report to work in the morning. I want to work on it *now*."

Moody shrugged. "It's your kitchen. I'm just taking up space here. It's just that I thought you told me you didn't believe in any of this spirit stuff."

"Not in spirits. In reason and logical progression. Even coincidence has its break point, my friend. Anyhow, it won't take very long." He wasn't exactly pleading, but the detective could see that his colleague was going to have to get this out of his system. Well, it would be worth a few minutes of silliness to accomplish that.

"There is just one thing: you are going to have to help."

"What, me?" Moody sat up straight. "Look, Paul, I'm just a good ol' boy from the Sip. You may want me to concentrate on sandpaintings full of funny shapes and people with different-shaped heads, but all I can think of is steak and yams and red beans and rice. And iced tea, about one part sugar to ten parts tea. I don't fry my bread, neither. What could I do that would help?"

"I do not have a drum."

Oh, mama, Moody thought. "A drum?"

"I just need someone to help me maintain a rhythm."

"You mean, something like this?" Moody extended a big hand and softly tapped the upholstery of the chair next to his.

"A little slower, please."

"That's all? Shoot, I can handle this much. So long as I don't think about how stupid it looks."

"There is no one here to see you."

"You don't need for me to emphasize any beats?"

"No. A steady, unvarying rhythm will be best."

"You got it. Okay if I switch hands once in a while?"

"That will not matter." Ooljee had already turned around to face the screen.

Even though he had some idea of what to expect, Moody was surprised when his partner began to sing. The voice was still that of Paul Ooljee, Sergeant, NDPS, but the intonation was archaic, like something out of an old two-D vid or ethnographic recording. It was not difficult or incomprehensible—just different. Moody thought that with a little practice and instruction he could do it himself. There was much that was basal and primitive in it, a simple monotonal chant that was probably common to all primitive cultures including his own, irrespective of origin. It grew easier instead of more difficult to maintain his drumming on the chair as he listened to his partner.

Ooljee stretched his left hand out toward the monitor. His right still held the papers he'd brought. There were only a couple of pages. The left hand had begun to tremble like that of a man afflicted with Parkinson's and Moody mentally complimented his colleague on his accomplished amateur theatrics. He was on the second page of his notes now. In a minute or so this would all be over with. Then they could get something to eat.

The police spinner on the table was equipped with a vocup for recording reports and the confessions of suspects, so presumably it was picking up its owner's chanting as well. Certainly Ooljee wasn't prolonging this nonsense for his friend's benefit.

Something alerted Moody's nostrils. He sniffed, his gaze shooting to the gall-like growth on the linking cable that was the interrupt box.

"Okay, Paul, that's enough." He stopped drumming, but his partner continued the chant, glancing briefly in his direction to indicate that he'd heard but that it didn't matter. "Hey, that's enough!"

Smoke was rising from the corners of the interrupt box. Something in its vicinity vented a loud *pop*.

Moody shoved his chair away from the table and lunged at the cable which connected the home spinner to its wall jack. He let out a yelp of pain and surprise, letting go of the cable as quickly as he'd grabbed it: it was hot enough to burn.

Tiny flames spurted from one corner of the interrupt box, which started to melt. Oblivious, Ooljee kept chanting, his left hand still vibrating madly. The image on the zenat was unchanged.

His host had said something about—Moody yanked open a drawer and fumbled in the semi-darkness until his hand closed around the handle of the cleaver. He'd pay for the cable: cables were cheap. He could not allow whatever was happening in the condo to work its way into the tower mollysphere. For one thing, he was far too afraid of heights.

A single stroke would suffice to sever the thin connection. He raised the cleaver over his head, brought it down swiftly. When it was within six inches of the cable something that felt like hard air took hold of the utensil, wrenched it out of his hand, and flung it into the wooden cutting board on the other side of the sink, missing Moody's ribs by about a foot.

Gaping, he backed away from the smoking, sizzling, slowly imploding interrupt box. His eyes were very wide and not a smidgen of sarcasm hung from his lips.

In the interim Ooljee had ceased chanting. He put the papers aside and lowered his left hand, which was no longer shaking. The image on the monitor remained. The kitchen was unchanged save for the melting, stinking interrupt box.

No, Moody thought, that wasn't quite true. There was the matter of the meat cleaver which had somehow leapt free of his clenched fist, flown through the air, and buried its blade half an inch deep in the cutting block. He nodded at the police spinner.

"Turn that damn thing off," he said tightly. Ooljee regarded him calmly.

"Let's give it another minute. Maybe something will happen."

"Whatta you think, something hasn't happened already?" He tried to divide his attention between his host and the now motionless but previously ambulatory blade.

Something had yanked it out of his hand. He had not gone nuts for a few seconds and slammed it into the block himself. Or had he? Right then reality was a state of mind dearly to be desired. It was something he'd never previously had reason to doubt. Vernon Moody didn't believe in poltergeists and ghosts. But then, he didn't believe in flying knives either.

" Just a minute or two more," Ooljee insisted.

"For what? So it can set the whole building on fire?"

"It is not burning anymore." This was true: smoke no longer rose from the lump of slag that had been the interrupt box. For some reason Moody was not comforted.

"We are doing something wrong." Ooljee's gaze shifted from his papers to the monitor. "Or we are not doing something right."

"I'll go along with that," Moody agreed tensely.

Maybe a spark had struck him, startled him, and he *had* lost control for a moment, just long enough to slam the cleaver into the cutting board. It made some sense, which was more than he could say for what he imagined had happened.

"C'mon, let's go eat," he suggested anxiously. "I'll even drum on the restaurant floor if you want."

Ooljee was ignoring him. "Missing something. Not making a connection somewhere." He remembered his colleague.

"In the old days when a hatathli did a sandpainting, it was to help cure someone of a disease or a problem. In order for the chant to work, the supplicant was required to actually sit on the painting and in that way to become part of it. It was a way of achieving temporary union with outside forces. There was a definite path of action: from the original source of power to the Holy People to the sacred vehicle of the sandpainting and then to the patient.''

"We don't have a patient," Moody pointed out in what he hoped was the voice of reason. "Just you and I."

"And we do not have a hatathli either. Just me."

"What do you want to do? Sit on the monitor?"

"No." Ooljee walked toward the zenat. "I believe the idea is to make contact with the design. Think of it as accessing the database. In this instance I am the supplicant, if not properly a patient."

"Don't sell yourself short." Moody hesitated, uncertain whether to restrain his partner or not. It all seemed so silly, all of it. Except for the meat cleaver. "What are you gonna do?"

"Just touch the monitor. There cannot be any harm in that. It is only a projection."

"Maybe it's nonconducting Lexan, but it's still drawing current from the wall jack. Keep that in mind."

"I am not going to stick my fingers in any sockets," Ooljee assured him. He was very close to the monitor now. The colors of the sandpainting illuminated his smooth skin, bleeding across his face: red and blue, yellow and black, white and green.

"You can rip it off the wall for all I care." Moody told him, "but let's get this over with, okay?" He fought hard to avoid looking at the cleaver.

Ooljee was muttering to himself again. "If the Kettrick painting was true, if no changes had been made . . .''

Gingerly he extended a hand and touched the flat, cool surface of the screen. Whether by coincidence or design (Moody could not tell) he put his open palm over the dark circle in the center. The instant that contact was made, the painting changed.

It was a very small change, one that neither man would have noticed had they not been concentrating all their attention on the monitor. What happened was that the pair of lizardlike shapes guarding the opening pivoted slightly, until their heads were facing the center of the design. At that instant Moody wouldn't have been surprised if they'd jumped right off the screen to clamp their tiny teeth into the sergeant's flesh, at which point he'd surely scream.

They didn't do anything of the sort and he was spared any such embarrassment. It was nothing more, he decided, than a brief moment of unexpected animation, crudely rendered at that.

He expected Ooljee to reach the same conclusion and return to the table. Instead the sergeant spoke softly.

"Interesting. All of a sudden it feels flexible, almost as if . . ."

Gently exerting pressure, he watched in disbelief as his hand entered the screen, pushing beyond the dark center of the sandpainting, past the edge of reality. The angular yei figures of the painting looked on. Their straight-line mouths did not comment. Their unfathomable dark eyes did not mock.

CHAPTER 13

BEYOND THE SYMBOLS and figures was a holomage of infinite dimensions, aswarm with glowing shapes and lines and rainbows, unidentifiable solid objects and geometric forms. Nor was it static. Everything was in constant if lugubrious motion; objects bouncing off one another, rainbows twisting and writhing, tiny explosions of light making the two men blink reflexively.

The striking, undistorted light illumined every pore on Ooljee's face as he stood there fascinated, his arm extended fully beyond the plane of the screen. The colors were an *in vivo* physicality, washing away the dullness of his life, cleansing, invigorating, life-affirming. The brilliance beckoned, drawing him onward, rife with a richness of experience he'd never known. With his right hand he reached out to draw it all to him, into him, leaning forward into the screen.

A much less mesmerized Moody let out a yell. ''Paul!'' Ooljee didn't appear to hear him. Cursing, the detective charged around the table, not caring if spinner and home molly were knocked to the floor in the process.

Ooljee was two-thirds into the monitor when Moody threw a bear hug around his thighs and dragged him back.

There was no resistance and it took only a moment. He was much bigger than the sergeant.

The younger man stood dazed, surrounded by the familiar accouterments of his kitchen, arms hanging limply at his sides. Slowly he came around, finding solidity in the blocky, unyielding outlines of the refrigerator, sink, cabinets, cooker, in the decorations made by his wife and children, in the wall phone and the spinner lying on the table.

Then there was the monitor, where infinity lay just behind the now transparent diagram of the sandpainting. A mysterious, boiling, animate infinity ablaze with an inexplicable reality accessible via a drawing of unknown origin. Was it another reality or just a hole in this one? Moody wondered. Whatever, it was capacious enough to accommodate most of his partner's body. Ooljee sensed that the big pale detective from Florida was watching him intently, alert to anything he might do. Suddenly he was thankful for having been blessed with such an unimaginative partner.

"I'm okay. It is all right." Moody cautiously backed away. Together they turned to examine the view through the window that the sandpainting had become.

"It is not a projection, not a holomage." Ooljee spoke with new assurance. "It is an opening into somewhere else. Or something else." He looked around the room and for the first time noticed the meat cleaver stuck in its chopping board. Moody noted the direction of his gaze.

"When your interrupt box started smoking I tried to cut the cable, like you suggested."

Ooljee nodded slowly. "I think I remember that. What happened?"

"Something didn't take kindly to the idea. It took the cleaver out of my hand, right out of my damn fingers, and plonked it in the board. Didn't miss me enough by half. I thought maybe all that homemade country shine I'd sucked in my youth had finally caught up with me, like my momma said it would, but after watching you start for a hike inside

that zenat, I decided that maybe it was happening after all.''
He nodded in the direction of the screen. ''Whatever this
is, it don't want to be shut down.''

''You probably tried an invalid procedure.''

''Okay. You tell me what the correct procedure is and
I'll implement it.''

''I have no idea. I do not even know what we are onto
here. I made contact with the image and it reacted. Then I
tried to become one with it, exactly as one would with a
traditional medicine painting. I guess I sort of lost myself.
It was not exactly like I was being hypnotized. More like
I was being—invited.''

''What'd it feel like? Inside, I mean.''

''Pleasant. Cushiony and warm. It tingles the way your
foot does when it goes to sleep, only it was not in any way
irritating or painful. I wonder. If you hadn't stopped me,
if you had cut the cable after I had entered fully, would I
have been trapped in there, wherever *there* is? Or would I
have ended up on the other side of the wall when the connection was broken? That would have been awkward.'' He
nodded at the monitor. ''That's an exterior wall. The only
thing on the other side is a thirty-story drop.''

''Well, if it don't want to be shut down, maybe we can
figure it out some. Anyone can see that it's real pretty, and
it's fun to stick your hand in. What else is it good for?''

''To search for something without looking,'' Ooljee murmured. ''That is what the Hand-Trembling ceremony is
about. That's exactly what we did.''

''Lay off the superstition,'' Moody snapped. He was
frightened but not intimidated. Vernon Moody hadn't been
intimidated since he was eleven years old. ''We've got
ourselves an extranormal spatial manifestation generated by
the Kettrick template. It's an outgrowth of a standard mollyweb and it can be terminated the same way. The chant
you used, the hand trembling? Aural and visual stimuli.
Nothing mystical about that. There are plenty of contem-

porary programs that rely on those for activation.'' He concentrated on the zenat and on what he knew of suggestion-intensive webwork, refusing to think about Holy People or old gods.

"Forget for now how the template originated, how old it is or how it came to be. Let's deal with what we have. You say this hand-trembling ritual of yours is designed to help search for something without looking. Well, we've found something. You thought it might be some kind of database. Maybe it is. It just has a little more depth than what we're used to.

"If you don't find what you're looking for, you're supposed to hear this Gila Monster's voice. Okay. Ask it something. Try accessing verbally. If it was set up in Navaho, then I imagine that's what it'll respond to.''

Ooljee hesitated, showing that he had yet to contemplate this line of thinking. "How do I know what to ask it?''

"Ask it anything. Say hello, curse it, insult its origins. Either nothing will happen or something will.''

"Sure. It responded to the chant, didn't it?''

The chant he'd borrowed from the library, via a child's spinner. It would be all right, he was sure. He had to be sure or he couldn't do it. What did they have to lose, so long as he didn't put his arm back through the painting? Though the sensation had not been unpleasant. It had almost been . . .

Moody's tone was sharp. "You're drifting, my friend.''

Ooljee started to argue, then nodded slowly. He stared at the hole in the wall, the hole into elsewhere. The detective was right. It was a physical manifestation of the real world. It had to be, else he would not have been able to interact with it.

Knowing that, he could deal with it.

He addressed it in the language of his grandparents, the difficult rasps and gutturals as natural to him as English. A peculiar language, Navaho. Devoid of many words for specific things, but rich in suggestion. A difficult language in which to do science. It had evolved to serve other needs.

He did not know what to expect, but somehow he was not shocked when a voice responded from the speaker set in the base of the zenat. The Navaho was heavily accented and it was a struggle to grasp the meaning of each phrase. But he understood.

Moody heard too. "That's no reptile. That's an electronic vocomposite if I've ever heard one."

"Don't jump to conclusions," Ooljee warned him. "Spoken Navaho is not like spoken Shakespeare."

"I don't care if it's kin to street slang. That's a synthesized voice. What'd it say, anyhow?"

Ooljee was a little surprised at how calm he was. "It said that it was functional."

"Good." Moody was feeling much better. "I like programs that aren't evasive." He wondered what would happen if he picked up the cleaver and flung it at the monitor. Would it freeze in midair, reverse course, or sail on forever? Better to keep asking questions instead of thinking such thoughts.

"The trouble is we don't know what it means by that. Whatthehell, ask it what the score of last week's Steelers-Wasps game was."

"Wasps I can manage, but Steelers is not directly translatable into Navaho."

"Improvise. Go on, try it. Let's see if the damn boojum's as smart as it is pretty."

Ooljee spoke, listened to the reply, turned to his partner. "Steelers forty-two, Wasps thirty. Is that right?"

"How the hell should I know? I'm a cop, not a bookie. What matters is that you asked, and it answered." He approached the monitor, squinting into the crystalline clear light that emanated from beyond. He discovered that he could turn his head and look up, down, or sideways into the screen without experiencing any diminution of scale, without seeing any suggestion of a border or horizon. Writing threads of rainbow swam like lambent worms through a sea of electrified blackness, avoiding fluorescent geometric shapes and unpredictable small explosions of gold and silver.

Before Ooljee could do or say anything, the detective extended his own hand toward the hard, flat surface of the zenat. It passed through, penetrating an unresisting yei figure clutching unidentifiable symbols.

His hand and forearm floated unrestrained, free to drift among the rainbows and silent explosions. He twisted it to the left, then to the right, wiggling his fingers, feeling the light tingling sensation Ooljee had described, experiencing the same gentle warmth. With the latter came a slight dizziness. He sensed himself starting to falllll. . . .

He jerked his hand clear, glanced down at it. There were no visible changes, no marks, nothing to indicate it had momentarily drifted beyond reality.

"Ask it." he suggested to his partner, "where it is."

Ooljee addressed the monitor in soft Navaho, translated the reply.

"It says it is right here."

"Somehow I expected something like that. It's functional, it's right here, and it knows last week's football scores. Cute." He rejoined his colleague, still examining his hand, slowly wriggling all five fingers. The tingle was fading from his skin.

Whatthehell again, he thought wildly. "Ask it if faster-than-light travel is possible."

Ooljee did so. Moody awaited the reply with interest. "It says no," the sergeant told him.

"Then ask it if there's another way to travel between the stars."

This time Ooljee's reply came as one long exhalation. "It says yes, but without faster-than-light travel."

"I wonder how you travel between stars without going faster than light?"

"This is not helping us locate our murderer," Ooljee pointed out.

"Nope, but it sure is fun. Ask it how."

Ooljee had more trouble phrasing the query in Navaho than he did translating the response. "It says you travel other than light."

The detective nodded slowly, as if some long-held personal theory had just been confirmed. "That's what I was afraid of. We can ask the right questions; we just don't possess the necessary referents to understand the replies." He sat down at the table, staring at the zenat's revealed wonders. "You're right: it's a computer, or database, or library of some kind. It answers questions."

"I wonder how big it is?" Ooljee murmured.

Moody pursed his lips. "Ask it."

Ooljee did so. The reply was at once imposing and disappointing. "It says, 'big enough.' "

"Big enough for what?" Moody was determined to extract at least one specific answer from the device if they had to spend the whole night trying.

This time he jumped slightly at the reply. Not because of its content but because the response was formed in ordinary, if obviously artificial, English:

"Big enough for any request."

"How did you do that?" the detective asked his partner.

Ooljee shrugged. "I asked it to speak in English, if it could. It was such an obvious thing, I did not think of it earlier. I would be surprised if it does not know other languages as well."

"How do you know that?"

"Just a guess. If it is familiar with methods of interstellar travel I would not think it ignorant, say, of French. Do you want me to query it further on that subject?"

"Shoot, no. English is enough for me."

Ooljee regarded the monitor and its panorama of tantalizing beauty. "I am glad you pulled me back, Vernon my friend. But don't you wonder what we might find if we entered that field fully?"

The detective snorted. "A couple zillion miles of rainbow threads and pretty sparklies. That could get old after a while. You could also get hungry. What really interests me is where the hell this thing comes from. Not withered old Navaho hatathlis playing in a colored sandpile, I'll bet. The Kettrick painting provides a way to get in. It doesn't tell us anything about origins."

"I suspect it has been here for a long time," Ooljee theorized. "It is just that until now no one had figured out how to access it."

Moody shook his head. "I can't buy that. I can't accept that it's been here for very long. Not without more proof than we have so far. Like the whore, we have some idea of what it is. We just don't know the relevant parameters." He remembered the cleaver.

"Speaking of parameters, maybe we better hold off asking it any more tricky questions until we're sure we know how to turn it off."

"Why not," suggested Ooljee with stunning simplicity, "just ask it?"

"Too easy. That'd be too easy. So, why don't you?"

"Why don't *you*? It understands English."

Moody considered. Why didn't he? Wasn't it just a big computer of as yet unknown type, a molly in rainbow drag? Where was the harm?

Funny; he'd never actually *touched* a database before, if that's what all those bright lights and shapes were.

"Ask it," Ooljee was urging him. "Ask it to turn itself off. Ask it *specifically* how large it is, where it comes from. Ask it . . ."

"All in good time. First I'd like to be sure it's not gonna

suck us in there''—he gestured at the monitor—''if we happen to ask the wrong question, or ask the right question the wrong way.''

The corners of the sergeant's mouth turned up slightly. ''Maybe you just have to be sure you ask it nice. Remember what I told you. The correct way to conclude a sandpainting ceremony is to destroy the painting being used in the reverse order of its creation. Generally meat cleavers are not employed for this purpose.''

''Very funny.''

''I should use the Gila Monster chant again, try to do exactly what we did backwards. If one does not exit a computer properly, the database can be damaged. If that is what we are dealing with here, it would be shocking if it did not contain a number of built-in safeguards to prevent such damage.'' He reached for the spinner.

''Not yet, man.'' Moody restrained his partner. ''Lemme ask it one more question.'' Ooljee paused, then nodded.

The detective addressed the monitor. ''You understand English?''

''I understand all acquired languages,'' the unisex disembodied voice replied.

''Glad to hear it, but English will do just fine for right now.'' He hesitated. Would his next question set off some kind of built-in alarm? No way of knowing save to ask. But go slowly, he reminded himself. Slowly.

''Are you,'' he asked, ''accessed frequently? Relate your response to local values.''

''No.''

''When exactly was the last time you were accessed prior to this past year?''

''Hey—'' Ooljee said worriedly. Moody shrugged him off.

The reply was harmless enough. On reflection, perhaps it was not.

"Eight oh-four on the morning of June the twenty-third in the year eleven sixty-two anno Domini—relating response to local values."

"Really?" It was all Moody could say. Ooljee said nothing at all, but he was pondering just as hard.

Of course, the device might have misunderstood his request. It might be misinterpreting values. It might be an absurd, complex joke of unknown origin. There might be a thousand other possibilities.

One of which was that the reply was accurate.

Well, he decided, that was certainly an interesting thought. But it was not the question of the moment. Right now they had to forgo the awesome in favor of tracking the prosaic.

"When was the last time you were accessed within the past year?"

The voice replied. Ooljee checked his watch. "Sixteen minutes ago. That would have been us."

The detective considered, trying to frame his queries as if he were conversing with the familiar police web back home instead of some gargantuan construct out of an as yet unidentified time and space.

"Prior to that, how many times within the past year have you been accessed?"

Again the mechanical response. "Thrice." It proceeded to elaborate. Once the previous morning. That would have been the little episode at Ooljee's station, Moody reflected. The second time was a number of months ago. Atlanta, perhaps. The third and last was far more recent.

"Only a week ago." Ooljee muttered a silent thank you. "It seems that our friend has not yet learned how to make extensive use of this. For which, without even knowing its capabilities, I think we can be thankful."

Moody was thinking hard. It seemed too easy but, nothing ventured, nothing gained. "Can you identify by name the individual who accessed you the last two times?'' Moody asked.

"Yistin Gaggii."

A great peace washed through the detective. "At last: we've got ourselves a damn name."

"Navaho," said Ooljee. "It translates as 'frozen raven.'"

"Can't wait to meet him. But hey, why stop now?" He looked back at the monitor. Suddenly it seemed innocuous, even helpful. After all, no matter how bizarre or alien in design, it was no more than a machine, right?

"What can you tell us about the individual Yistin Gaggii?" *There*, he thought. *If we're gonna trigger any implanted alarms that ought to do it.*

Nothing of the sort happened. Instead, the voice proceeded to give them a full description of the man portrayed in the police composites, complete to a reproduction of his voice and notable facial mannerisms.

And as if that wasn't enough, it calmly provided an address.

"Out in the country," Ooljee commented. "Somewhere up the hill between Ganado and Window Rock. He's been right here all this time, just outside of town. If he has been keeping to himself, it explains why no one has seen him to call him in."

Moody leaned back in the kitchen chair, very pleased with himself. "Shoot, that was easy enough. We were just trawlin' in the wrong molly, that's all." He remembered an earlier query. "Eleven sixty-two A.D. That when your stories say these 'Holy People' showed up in the neighborhood?"

The sergeant was studying the monitor, unable to take his eyes from the ever-changing scene. "Specific dates are not given. The gods created First Man and First Woman. There were four worlds of which ours is the fifth. Our Creation Myth is not so simple as you might think. There are many legends, and then there are legends about legends.

"There is so much yet to be learned. Modern archaeology has barely scratched the history of the People. You can walk around Mesa Verde or Betatkin or White House or any of a thousand ruins on the Rez and still find potsherds and pieces of basketry and old corn, though I have yet to hear of anyone digging optical disks or mollyspheres out of the floor of a cliff dwelling. And if the Anasazi were into computers, it is news to me.

"The ancient ones must have had friends, if our voice is to be believed. Very skilled friends, very advanced. I do not think they were Aztecs from Mexico. They must have come from elsewhere." He gestured at the screen.

"This *thing* is an artifact, just like the bits of pots and the beads and the arrowheads people find every week on different parts of the Reservation."

"It's a database," Moody countered. "I wonder where its storage facility is located, its molly-equivalent? Every database needs storage. . . .

"Or maybe it's everywhere," he went on, unsure whether he was being philosophical or predictive. "In the air around us, in the Earth itself. Maybe it encompasses the whole world. I'm just bullshitting, but this is a good time for it, don't you think? Perhaps we're all components of a big database somebody set up and forgot about when they finished their own work here. An Earth-mollysphere, a chunk of database backup not worth a second glance.

"Maybe we're all just little pieces of ROM: you, me, your kids, everybody else. Pieces that this Scavenger character fussed with before shooting up through his skyhole, or whatever. Maybe it or something else decided to make a joke and give the ROM a way to access their own storage. So they provided a method the local ROM could understand."

"Sandpainting," Ooljee whispered thoughtfully.

"Yeah, sandpainting, and maybe the chants too. Not

necessarily the specific words, but the sequence of tones and sounds. I dunno. What's the chance of somebody accidentally hitting the right combination of sandpainting and aural accompaniment? You've been telling me all along nothing sounds quite like Navaho. Maybe there's a reason for that, one that has nothing to do with linguistics."

"Forgotten," said the sergeant. "One of the dozens of old Ways that have been forgotten. Except in this case one line of hatathlis remembered, without even knowing the importance of what they were remembering. Grandfather Laughter knew the painting but not what it was for. Because in his time it would have made no sense." He looked sharply at his partner.

"But it makes sense to Gaggii. The second time it was accessed, in Atlanta, people died. Gaggii may know how to utilize at least a small part of this to serve his purposes."

"Let's see him utilize it fast enough to stop a slug from a twenty-eight Sledge." Moody's expression was grim. "You remember that address?" The sergeant nodded. "Then what are we sitting here in the dark for? Let's go get the bastard." He rose from his chair—and thought again of Atlanta, of crumpled bodies and bloodless holes in cold flesh. Bravado was all very well and good, but the department's honor rolls were filled with the names of cops who'd died flashily and too young.

"Think we should request backup?"

"As much as I would like that," the sergeant replied, "we would have to explain too much. No one would believe us. I go in and tell this story to the duty lieutenant, you know what he will say. He will want proof, he will want to know— Let's just bring Gaggii in. He will not be expecting us. We will surprise him, and there should be no problem. I have my concerns, but I think at this point it would be best to keep things simple."

Moody nodded. "Okay, then. Simple it is."

"But not yet," Ooljee pleaded. "I want to talk to Lisa before we go after him, and I am tired."

"All right." Moody was tired, too. "First thing tomorrow. Like you say, he's not gonna be expecting us."

"And we get some real rest. But first we turn this thing off. Maybe you can go to sleep with it active, but not me."

"Afraid of something coming out and painting dirty drawings on your belly while you sleep?" Ooljee taunted him.

Moody made a face. "How about it decides to vacuum us out of bed and into wherever *it* is? Or something we can't even imagine. I just don't want to leave it running. You leave it running long enough, maybe it gets clever ideas of its own. We don't know enough about it to trust it."

"Very well." Ooljee rose and walked over to the refrigerator. "Then *you* turn it off."

The two men locked stares for a long moment. Then Moody turned in his seat and deliberately reached for the power switch on the police spinner. His finger made it to within half an inch of the tiny sliding control. Moving it slowly over the hard plastic case, he found it would approach no closer.

"Like sliding over oiled rubber," he informed his partner, "except that there's nothing there."

"Oh, there is something present, for sure, my friend." Ooljee came over to watch. "A field of some kind. I doubt even a good physicist could tell us exactly what is happening here."

Moody sat back. "That's the extent of my ideas. Now we have to go with your chanting."

Ooljee took a deep breath, assumed a position next to the table facing the monitor, and began. Moody listened, trying to make some sense of what was being said, failing utterly.

As the last phrase faded away and the sergeant lowered his trembling hand, the impossible vista which had occupied the zenat vanished, leaving in its wake the image of a flat, familiar sandpainting devoid of any depth.

Ooljee cleared his throat, reached past Moody toward the power switch on his spinner. "That's it, then."

"Not quite. Remember the sandpainting."

Ooljee looked at the monitor. "I remember it. So?"

"The two lizard drawings. They're still head-down. When the fractal sequence gave birth to the painting, they were heads-up."

"Guarding the entrance." The sergeant nodded. "I'd forgotten." He walked over to the monitor and put his hand directly over the dark circle in the center of the image, just as he had previously. To his very great relief it remained there, his palm hard against the unyielding glass of the zenat. The pair of guardians obediently pivoted slightly, resuming their original positions.

Ooljee stepped back, keeping his eyes on the screen. "Try it now."

This time no unseen barrier prevented the detective from flicking the spinner's power switch to the OFF position. The sandpainting vanished, leaving behind only a softly glowing green screen.

The sergeant slumped into a chair opposite Moody, suddenly bone-tired. He shook a couple of times, a reaction that had nothing to do with the Hand-Trembling ceremony. Moody dropped his face into his hands, rubbed at his eyes. Tension was draining out of him all at once, thick and heavy, like oil from an old car.

"What was that all about?" The sergeant repeated it several times, a querulous mantra that fully expressed the way he was feeling. "Or as my father might have said: *shash l 'y' adi*." He managed a slight grin. "What in the bear happened?"

Moody responded with the deep, reassuring chuckle he employed every year when he played Santa during the department's seasonal visits to local hospitals.

"I think we can make a few good guesses. What we got here, ol' buddy, is an accessible interstitial alien database or library or question-answering whatsis that dates to about a thousand years ago." He shook his head at the wonderment of it all.

"I feel like a goddamn five-year-old trying to drive his dad's car. We have only the vaguest notion of what we're getting into, we don't know how it works or even for sure what it's capable of. All we know is that you activate the ignition and away you go."

Ooljee was staring at the blank, quiescent monitor. Only moments ago it had been a window into infinity, or perhaps somewhere even less comprehensible.

"I would not be so concerned if all it did was reply to questions and allow you to reach into itself, but it has shown it can also affect immediate reality in the form of the meat cleaver and the spinner power switch. That leads me to wonder what else it could do, if it became so inclined. Perhaps it could seal off this room from the rest of the building, or this building from the rest of the world."

"Shoot, why think small? Maybe it could seal off the whole planet. We haven't a roach in shitpile's idea of how big this thing is."

"Surely it was placed here for a reason," Ooljee said.

Moody pushed his chair away from the table. "Let's leave that question alone for a while, okay? Right now I'm interested in a shower, something to eat, and a good night's sleep. Tomorrow we're gonna get our boy. Business before metaphysics."

"I will go along with that." Ooljee rose slowly from his chair. He was intensely curious, but also very tired. "You want to shower first?"

"Naw, you go ahead. I'll have a look in the pantry."

As his host left for the bathroom, Moody cracked the pantry seal and began poking through the neat stacks of cans and boxes and plastic containers. Feeling conservative, he chose a big box of French bread strips and cheese, inserted it in the cooker. As he waited for the bread to cook and the cheese to melt over it, he walked over to the monitor for one last close look prior to retiring.

Putting his huge hand against the flat surface, he pushed gently. There was no give, only smooth resistance. He tried to peer behind the monitor, which hung nearly flush against the wall. The receive-activate unit attached to the back of the screen was little more than an inch thick. He tapped the monitor a couple of times, ran his fingers around the protruding edges. The cooker beeped its readiness.

With a last shrug of contemplation which no one was present to observe, he turned to devote his full attention to his habitual nightly quota of calories.

CHAPTER 14

THE FOLLOWING MORNING the kitchen showed no evidence of nightly excursions into other worlds or dimensions. Nothing prevented Ooljee from casually disconnecting his spinner from the interrupt box, or the interrupt box from the kitchen molly. The experiences of the night before seemed as unreal to both men as memories of childhood.

The address the web had given them was real enough. Ooljee checked it out before calling his wife. Though enjoying her parents' company and the delights of Albuquerque, she was still wary of the speed with which her husband had changed his mind and boosted her and the kids on their way. Ooljee reassured her in a calm voice, his expression neutral, his words betraying nothing of the remarkable events which had transpired so recently in her kitchen. Only when he'd convinced her all was well did he hang up and prepare to depart.

The pickup took them out of the city on a route designed to avoid both rush hour and the city center. Soon they were cruising at high speed through Ganado's eastern suburbs, where expensive residences chipped away at tree-shrouded hillsides and people paid fortunes for unobstructed views of the offices and factories they couldn't wait to abandon during the day.

Gradually the last homes gave way to National Forest. Altitude markers tracked their steady climb. Once, a fox darted across the two-lane highway in front of the pickup. Moody was at peace with himself. The morning was cool, crisp, clear, the contrails of hypersonic shuttles wild white etchings on the cerulean chalkboard of the sky. Cedar and scrub oak gave way to tall conifers. Patches of shade offered refuge to the last, stubborn clumps of winter. The snowpiles sagged in on themselves, pockmarked with bites inflicted by the heat of early spring.

It was late afternoon when they finally turned off the highway. Ooljee shut down the pickup's scanner and took manual control of the vehicle. The road they'd entered was narrow but paved. Dirt tracks extended through gaps in a fence line on either side, like fingers from a hand.

Though Moody had managed to exert himself in Ganado without much difficulty, he was having some trouble catching his breath now. Not surprising when one realized that the little paved road was winding its way northward at over eight thousand feet. All he could think of was how lucky he'd been not to have had to come here first, straight from sea level.

"This ain't gonna work," he said without warning.

Ooljee eyed him questioningly. "Why not?"

"Too easy. It's too damn easy. All those months of searching and theorizing and querying sources, then we just ask a strange machine a question and that's all there is to it."

"Leading up to the question was not easy," the sergeant reminded him. "I do not feel like we fell into this without having to work for it."

"Maybe so." Moody was inhaling the rich perfume of the pines, trying to relax a little. "How much do you think he knows about this web?"

"It told us that someone, probably the man we are after, has accessed it twice—once probably from here, once probably while in Atlanta. That is not much. I think he is unlikely to be an expert."

The locator on the dash beeped and Ooljee slowed to make a right turn onto a dirt track. They drove about a mile before crossing a small wooden bridge hand-built of huge old wooden timbers. The creek beneath was running loud and wild, snapping with spring strength and fresh snowmelt.

They climbed out of the shallow creek bed and saw the house. Though the entrance faced eastward, no attempt had been made to make it look like a traditional home. It was rectangular in shape, with a sharply raked roof lined with high-efficiency solar panels. A separate garage was attached to the back. An impressive array of non-domestic antennae protruded from the north side of the structure, clustered around a huge satellite dish whose bowl was aimed southward, just clearing the crest of the roof. The pines standing in its way had been professionally topped.

No one emerged to confront them, despite the fact that their approach had to have been both visible and audible to anyone inside. They parked and stood together in front of the truck. The metallic lump under Moody's arm felt larger than usual.

"What do you think? I've spent so much time behind a desk I've gotten rusty at making collars."

"No guns. As we discussed, there is no reason for him to be expecting us."

"I'd go along with that okay, except for the fact that if this is our boy, he's killed two people already." His gaze swept the empty, cool woods, so different from the forests back home. The animals hereabouts were skittish, hard to see. Probably as cold as I am, he thought.

They'd passed the last house a couple of miles back down the paved road, though the sound of gunshots would travel farther than that in this high mountain air. Not that anyone was likely to call the police if they heard anything. Not in this kind of country.

Then he recalled that Kettrick and his housekeeper hadn't been slain with traditional weapons.

Well, there was nothing traditional about this whole business, and if anyone inside harboring hostile intent wanted to cut them down without warning, they could do so just as easily from a window as in the parlor.

The front entrance was made of wood-grain metal, solid and secure. Ooljee thumbed the intercom switch. After a short delay, a voice issued from the tiny door speaker.

"Yes?"

"Am I speaking to Mr. Yistin Gaggii?"

"Yes," again, without hesitation or any attempt at guile.

"I am Sergeant Paul Ooljee, with the NDPS office in Ganado? If you don't mind, Mr. Gaggii, my friend and I would like to talk to you for a minute."

"Talk to me?" Just the slightest pause this time, Moody thought. "About what?"

Ooljee glanced briefly at his partner before again directing his voice to the door.

"We're having a little communications problem with our field spinner. We heard that you knew communications and we thought maybe you could give us a hand."

"Really? Who told you that?"

"Does it matter? Is it true or isn't it?"

A long pause ensued. The two officers waited tensely, did not relax when an internal lock popped to grant them entrance.

"It is too cold to discuss this outside, my friends," the voice declared. "Summer is still a month away. Please come in."

Ooljee took a deep breath, exchanged a look with Moody, then entered.

They found themselves in a den, or living area, that was startlingly clean. There was nothing to suggest that Gaggii was married, but even allowing for the presence and use of modern housekeeping devices, the place was cleaner than was natural.

The sterility was muted somewhat by the pretense of traditional artwork and the by-now-familiar earthtone furniture, all pinks, reds, and yellows. The center of the room was occupied by one of the most astonishing holomages Moody had ever seen. It was a medicine yei: seven feet tall, bristling with feathers, elaborate attire, war club and axe and medicine pouch. Unlike the angular abstracts of the sandpaintings, this was a full-figured human form, a life-sculpture of unsurpassed craftsmanship.

The detective admired it as it twisted and danced for them while Ooljee searched for their host. The room was all straight lines and angles, nothing round or curved. There was no softness in it, a feeling that the profusion of sand-paintings on the walls only enhanced. They were impossible to miss, impossible to ignore despite the dominating presence of the holomaged yei. Tiny works a few inches square clustered together as if to ward off the power of larger pieces whose borders could be measured in feet.

"It's not here," Ooljee announced after scanning the walls carefully. Moody did not have to ask what his partner was referring to: the Kettrick painting or a copy thereof was not among the dozens that occupied the walls of the room.

Yet despite the presence of the paintings and the powerful holomage and the comfortable furniture, there was nothing in the room to suggest that a distinctive personality lived there. Everything had been laid out and arranged with near-mathematical precision, as precise as a holomask used for cutting molecular chips. It might not look like a hospital room, but it felt like one.

This wasn't a real room in a real house, Moody abruptly decided. It was a sham, a set for a vid, designed to fool eye and mind.

They had no more time to contemplate the emotional

overtones of the decor, because Gaggii emerged from a back room. Ooljee shook hands as he introduced himself, politely and with programmed professional enthusiasm.

Moody thought he detected an air of chronic impatience in their suspect. Though Gaggii looked straight at them as he spoke, the detective had the feeling that the man's thoughts were always several steps ahead of the subject at hand, as though he were devoting only a part of his mind to the conversation. Though he tried to fake it, it was clear that he wasn't really interested in what was being said. It was just something that had to be dealt with and disposed of, like a leaky faucet or the buying of groceries. The rest of his brain was always otherwise occupied.

It made Moody feel inadequate. He didn't like that. But then, he didn't much like Gaggii either. The man smiled frequently, but it was about as honest as the wood-grain in the front door. It was not a genuine smile but rather a conscious manipulation of skin and facial muscles to achieve a desired effect, much as the room had been designed and decorated to appear warm, homey, and accommodating. Like its owner, it was none of those things.

As he listened to his partner engage the suspect in casual conversation it was clear to Moody that Gaggii wanted only for them to leave. Moody did not feel slighted. That would be Gaggii's reaction, he decided, to any visitor. And yet he sensed no hatred in the man, no outright dislike for other human beings. It was just indifference, he decided finally, as if visitors took up space and time which might otherwise be put to better use.

Moody helped himself to an unvolunteered seat, enjoying the brief look of distaste which slipped past Gaggii's carefully crafted veneer of hospitality. His gun lay against his chest, unsecured and ready. Still Gaggii displayed neither panic nor concern. That did not induce Moody to relax. The soft-spoken, self-assured ones were the most dangerous because they offered no clue as to what they might do next.

"Actually, Mr. Gaggii, as you may have guessed by now, we are not here because we are having a problem with our communications."

"Ah," said Gaggii softly, regarding the sergeant as casually as he might a perambulating bee.

Moody rested his right hand casually on his sternum, close to the butt of his gun, while his partner related some of the events which had brought them to this particular house. Ooljee concluded by declaring that while the evidence they had gathered was not conclusive, it was sufficient to arouse more than a little suspicion, and if he, Gaggii, had nothing to hide, he should be more than willing to accompany them down into Ganado to clear himself by answering a few simple, detailed questions. It would not take much time and it would be of great assistance to the department.

Gaggii listened silently to Ooljee's words, standing quite still and relaxed except, Moody noted, for his hands. All of his fingers curled back and upwards, so that he appeared to have a fleshy hook attached to each wrist. When the sergeant had finished, Gaggii responded, displaying more interest than at any time since their arrival.

"I think I can answer most of your questions right here, my friends. How did you finally find me?"

Ooljee glanced at his partner. Moody's fingers slipped inside his jacket to close around his pistol. But Gaggii gave no indication that he knew, made no sudden moves, just stood and waited.

"We used the Kettrick template, got into the web or whatever it is, and asked it," Ooljee told him.

It had to be a shock, but remarkably, Gaggii's expression didn't change. "I had not thought of that, because I didn't imagine anyone, least of all the police, could figure out what this was about, much less find their way in. For nonspecialists, my friends, you have done astonishingly well. I have only myself to blame. But then, the web was designed to be used by nonspecialists, so I suppose I shouldn't compliment you too highly. Its simplicity of operation is exceeded only by its capabilities, of which I am every day in awe. How did you happen upon the secret of the template? I thought that when I destroyed the original and the insurance company's archival copies, I had left nothing behind."

"Kettrick had his own file." Moody spoke from his seat on the couch, watching every twitch of Gaggii's eyes and fingers. "His wife showed us. That's where we got our copy."

"Of course." Evidently Gaggii was not one to indulge in self-recrimination. "I thought of that possibility, but had only enough time for a rapid, unrevealing search. One can only do so many things so fast. It is when things are rushed that people get hurt." He moved and Moody started to reach for his gun, stopped himself when he saw that Gaggii was only taking a chair opposite the couch. Ooljee remained standing, alert.

"All I wanted was the sandpainting, or a copy thereof. It took me a long time to track it down. Even then, all was still supposition."

"You are saying that you didn't know if there was anything to it, and still you killed the two people?"

"He would not let me have a copy of the painting." Gaggii spoke quietly, as if that explained everything. "When every other method failed, I tried to get it without disturbing anyone, but burglary was not something at which I was experienced. Mr. Kettrick was in a place where I did not think he would be, as was his servant. I tried to discuss the situation with him but he became abusive and irrational. When he started to call the police, I was forced to react.

"Understand that I would not have minded going to jail for breaking and entering. I tried to explain this to him. But he would have forced me to give up the holomage of the sandpainting, which I was making at the time he interrupted me. Like so many wealthy people, he kept confusing arrogance with power. I regret the death of the servant more.

"Much of my life has been spent seeking this sandpainting." He was watching Ooljee as he spoke. "You have no idea how seminal it is to the history and culture of the People."

"I'm starting to get the idea," the sergeant told him brusquely.

"Then you have progressed. That is gratifying."

"Boom the oil," Moody snapped. "What exactly is the damn thing, and where'd it come from?"

"What is it . . . ?" Gaggii smiled, an unexpected inner contentment radiating from his lanky form. "I think it is a database of extraterrestrial origin, which can be accessed with remarkable ease. As to where it is from, I believe it was put here by the Holy People."

"I don't think I've seen that name advertised under Databases in the usual catalogs," Moody replied.

"I use it for lack of a better local reference." Gaggii crossed one leg over the other, at ease, enjoying himself. *He's playing a damn game with us*, Moody thought suddenly. *Well, let him. He and his partner would have the last move.*

"That is the reference our ancestors employed. If I had a better name I would use it, but I have been unable to find out anything about them. It is a subject for future study."

"We got some idea of what it's like." Moody's fingers caressed the butt of his pistol. "One thing's for sure: it's dangerous. People a lot more knowledgeable about this sort of thing than you or I need to be studying it.

"Ah, but there are no people knowledgeable about 'this sort of thing,' my friend. So why should I not be the one to study it, or you? True, it may be capable of actions our feeble imaginations cannot grasp, but we will not know that until we reach out to it. As for myself, I have a good imagination. It has already given me one idea worth further examination. As you have discovered for yourselves, once accessed it can be activated by simple voice command.''

"Anything that can override a police department security system and burn down the building it's housed in isn't simple, *or* safe," Moody argued.

"I do make time for the news," Gaggii replied with interest. "I heard about the fire in Ganado, but of course had no reason to connect it to my own work. So that was you two toying with the template. You are lucky all you lost was the building. A system simple to direct is also easy to misdirect. One must progress carefully, in modest increments."

"We won't make that mistake again," Moody assured him. "Nor will you. Maybe you have some idea of what it is, but you still don't have the vaguest notion of what it's for."

Gaggii waxed philosophical. "Perhaps it was emplaced to help the Anasazi and later the Navaho, only the Way was forgotten or deliberately obscured by superstitious medicine men. Or maybe the Anasazi did make use of it. Sometime around 1300 A.D. they simply disappeared. Nobody knows why. Nobody knows where they went. Maybe they used the Way to go someplace where the soil and climate were better. Maybe they went into the web. I do not believe that myself, but when one considers the implications of this discovery, many things suddenly become possible."

"If you do not think that, what do you think it was put here for?" Ooljee asked him, caught up in contemplation of the mystery.

"I do not think it was put here for any purpose at all. It is just a tool, a device. Like any good tool, it waits to be instructed, to be told what to do." His smile widened slightly. "Unless information to the contrary presents itself, I see no reason not to assume that the beings who built it just left it here."

Moody frowned. "Nobody would just 'leave' something of this magnitude."

Gaggii turned to face him. "You apply your values to the immense unknown." He laughed softly, full of self-contained amusement. "Perhaps they were just passing through and paused only long enough to, say, change a flat tire. We cannot imagine what they came for any more than we can imagine them. It is said that one cannot envision a real alien because a truly *alien* alien would by its very definition be incomprehensible to us. So might it be with their devices, their tools.

"I think the template design is a tool, the web it accesses a greater one. There may be others lying about whose existence we do not even suspect, devices we cannot see or sense.

"Picture it, my friends. You are traveling in your truck through the high desert. You have a flat and stop to change the tire. In your rush to depart you forget some of your tools; the power jack, the lug seal, perhaps some paper clips and an empty beer can. Accelerating to eighty, you vanish rapidly from the scene without anyone witness to your activities.

"A little time passes. Can you imagine what happens then?"

"Enlighten me." Moody strove to sound bored, knew his obvious interest belied the attempt.

"The ants come out, my friends. The ants come out for a look around.

"They clamber all over and around the forgotten tools, not realizing what they are because of their own ignorance and the sheer size of the devices. But one ant acquires a key. Perhaps he stumbles across a diagram rendered somehow ant-comprehensible. Or possibly he is present when the tools are being used. Perhaps he is even given instruction, much as children playing by a creek will offer ants leaves and twigs so they can make a tiny bridge with which to cross a rivulet. They do this because they find it amusing to watch the ants at work. Ants that do not understand the concept of a bridge will still make effective use of one. So it might have been with whoever painted that first template.

"Somehow this one perceptive insect learns how to activate the previously invisible tools, only the tools were not invisible: they were simply too massive for the ants to comprehend. They seemed a part of the natural order, of the everyday terrain.

"The hard part is not making use of the tools, my friends. It is recognizing that they exist at all. The sandpainting holds the diagram recognized by the ant who preceded the rest of us, a thousand years ago. No, gentlemen, if the web was placed here for a defined purpose it would have announced itself long ago. It is just something that was left behind, forgotten.

"I am only just beginning to learn how it might be used. The possibilities are impressive. After all, if a colony of ants discovered a power jack next to their anthill and found a way to activate it, consider what they might accomplish. Lizards eat ants. A power jack would smash a hungry lizard to pulp. It could crush huge pebbles to provide easier access to food, or for building stronger shelter. It might even offer a way for ants to advance themselves mentally. I know my analogy is weak but—"

Moody cut him off. "So basically what y'all are saying is that this web is somebody else's garbage?"

"Only that it is one possibility among many," Gaggii replied reprovingly. "It may in fact be of value to its original owners, but not of sufficient value to be worth the cost of recovery over time and distances we cannot imagine. You might, for example, leave an expensive holomager in Paris. While you would regret its loss, you would not travel all the way back to France to recover it."

If it had not been evident before, it was clear enough now that whatever else he might be, Yistin Gaggii was no madman. He had yet to raise his voice. While unusual, the ability to maintain control of one's emotions under abnormally tense conditions was not generally an indication of mental instability. Now that he'd been found out, he actually appeared to be enjoying the sharing of his discoveries with someone else.

"What's your interest in this?" Moody found himself asking. "I mean, what do y'all want with it, personally?"

"Goodness." Gaggii eyed him with mock surprise. "A really perceptive question that deviates from the strict guidelines of police procedure." His sarcasm did not affect Moody, who'd suffered it a thousand times before. It was standard prisoner modus for trying to reassert rapidly disappearing independence.

"Let's just say that I have my own desires, as do all of us. Recall the analogy of the power jack. Suppose that instead of that, our imaginary travelers leave behind among their debris a can of bug spray. What might the ants make of that?"

"I liked the power jack analogy better," Moody snapped.

"Such a device could be devastatingly employed against enemy ants."

"Or against its discoverers, if they did not properly understand how to use it," Ooljee pointed out meaningfully.

Gaggii nodded agreement. "In any event it would be of no use to those who had departed."

"We asked it how big it was," Moody said. "It replied, 'big enough.'"

"Yes. It can be responsive without being specific. I do not think there is a deliberate intent to be evasive. I suspect instead that we simply do not possess the terminology necessary to ask the right questions. So it provides answers in the form it thinks our simple brains can most easily comprehend."

"One last thing." Gaggii waited patiently while Moody framed his question, as though he had all the time in the world. "You say you have your own desires, your own idea how to make use of this whatever it is. What might that be?''

Gaggii looked straight at the detective and pursed his lips. ''I am sorry, my friend, but that is none of your business.''

Moody sniffed. It was no more than he'd expected. He started to rise from the couch. ''Well, we're real sorry to have to put a crimp in y'all's hobby, but there's still this lousy business of you killing two people in cold blood.''

''I am very close to answering my own questions.'' Gaggii made no attempt to rise.

If he's trying to put us off guard, Moody thought, *he's damn sure taking his time about it.*

''I don't suppose I could appeal to your higher senses, though it is clear that you are both unusually intelligent individuals—for policemen.''

''Sorry,'' Moody replied. ''I'm afraid my higher sense tells me it ain't a good idea to let murderers run around unpunished.''

''I see your point of view.''

Gaggii rose. Both officers tensed, but still their prisoner made no move toward hidden switches or concealed devices. Instead he extended both arms out in front of him.

''Do you wish to cuff me?''

Ooljee glanced at his partner, who shrugged. ''I do not think that will be necessary. The back seat of my truck is equipped with a restraining mesh. That will be sufficient. Cuffs can chafe and it is a long ride down to Ganado. I would not want injured wrists or hands to delay your arraignment.''

''I appreciate your concern. Bearing that in mind, may I get a coat? It is quite cold outside.''

''What coat?'' Moody asked warily.

Gaggii smiled at him. ''The one with the explosives sewn into the lining, of course.'' He pointed. ''In the closet over there.''

Moody nodded tersely, went to the closet and looked inside. "Which one?"

"The false wolf, with the low collar."

Moody checked the coat over minutely. Gaggii's composure troubled him more than anything he expected to find. But the coat was clean. After patting him down, he handed it to the prisoner, who chatted easily as he put it on.

"I guess I have to go with you, my friends."

"I guess you do." Moody opened the door while Ooljee remained behind. Now that the moment of departure had arrived, neither officer was taking any chances, no matter how cooperative their man seemed to be. They both had their guns out. "And do us a favor, will you?"

"If I can," said Gaggii graciously.

"Don't call us your friends."

Gaggii's only visible reaction took the form of still another tight-lipped, impenetrable smile.

Moody was relieved to be outside again, in the cool evening air, away from the sterile mask that was Gaggii's house. It was as devoid of genuine human warmth as a tomb, the furnishings frozen skeletons pinned to the walls and floor like specimen moths.

He wanted to see Gaggii's workshop. Plenty of time for that once the prisoner was safely incarcerated in Ganado. Ample time to return for a leisurely examination of his notes and files.

"I have to admire you, gentlemen." Gaggii had to turn sideways to fit into the truck's narrow back seat. Ooljee locked the restraint net in place. The carbon composite mesh would prevent anyone in the back from reaching through to the front.

"Thanks," Moody replied flatly as he climbed in on the passenger side. "We're doin' the best we can."

Ooljee started up, turned and headed for the dirt track that led to the little bridge. They'd acquired a lot of information at the expense of the rest of the afternoon. Twilight was creeping through the pine trees as the truck bounced down the slope, over the bridge, and climbed into the woods on the other side.

"No, honestly. I did not think anyone would ever find out. Certainly not so soon. And to think you have even accessed the web."

"Everybody thinks cops are dumb." Moody settled himself deeper into the seat. "It's the shows. Cops on the vid are always overlooking the obvious and then they have to compensate by shooting all their suspects. That's not police work any more than trials are lawyers making big speeches in court all the time. It's mostly legwork, dull and plodding. Me, I'm weird. I happen to like research. That's how you really catch people."

"But not how you keep them," Gaggii responded. "You realize that you cannot tie me to Kettrick's death. I know that you were not recording any of our conversation in the house. I would have been warned if you had been and would have comported myself accordingly. Since you were not, I felt free to talk. I enjoy talking."

Ooljee shook his head sadly. "You may know a lot about mollys and webs, but you do not know shit about legal procedure. At least one secretary and two security guards witnessed you arguing with Kettrick in his Tampa office. Also, as an important businessman, Kettrick recorded all *his* conversations. Voiceprinting will identify you easily."

"Arguments supply a possible motive, but they are not grounds for a murder conviction." Gaggii was confident. "Nor can you connect me to the wiping of the insurance company files in Atlanta."

"We'll see," said Moody, adding offhandedly, "then there's our eyewitness, the one who saw you enter Kettrick's house the night of the killings."

This time it took their prisoner a while to reply. Moody

was pleased at having finally gotten under his skin, however minutely.

"You are bluffing," Gaggii said finally. "You may be a good card player, detective, but I know I entered unobserved. There is no such witness."

"Oh, good." Moody shrugged indifferently. "Then you've got nothing to worry about, right? Shoot, I'm just a big ol' fat liar from the sticks. There's no witness, so you can just relax in your holding cell until the time comes for you to appear before a magistrate. Be tough for the local D.A. to prove anything because there's no such witness. See, I just made it all up, just to bug you."

Out of the corner of his eye Moody could see that his partner was fighting to keep from smiling. When Gaggii spoke again there was a hint of uncertainty in his voice. He was trying hard to maintain his former aplomb.

"It will not work, this bluff. You can prove nothing. Search my house all you wish. You'll find nothing to confirm your suspicions. If you attempt to access my molly, the database will self-destruct."

"Hell, why would we bother with your work?" Moody was enjoying himself now, knowing that he shouldn't be. "It don't mean shit. All we want to do is tie you to Kettrick's murder. Don't y'all worry none about that. We'll manage."

"I see. Then, if I'm to be put away you don't mind if I amuse myself while I have the time?" He began to sing, softly and liltingly, to himself.

They were coming up on the main road. Moody looked back over his shoulder. "Amuse yourself another way. I don't want to have to listen to that all the way back to Ganado."

Gaggii paused momentarily. "Why, detective, it is only a song. A little something to pass the time. As you point out, it is a long drive down the mountain." He resumed singing.

"It would not be so bad if you could carry a tune."

Ooljee was concentrating on the track ahead. "So do as my friend says and—" He broke off abruptly, staring into the rearview mirror.

Moody tensed. "What is it?" Gaggii ignored them both, concentrating on his song.

"Bracelet. Left wrist."

Moody whirled, the seat complaining beneath him. His gaze went straight to the specified piece of jewelry, a thick band of traditional turquoise and silver. Except that the turquoise wasn't copper ore and the silver was an alloy of something else.

There was more than enough metal in the bracelet to form a strong receiver-transmitter, just as the chunks of blue which Gaggii was toying with moved too freely in their bezels for stones that should have been firmly epoxied in place. Several of them shone with a faint inner light.

Moody drew his service pistol and aimed it through the mesh. "Put a clamp on it right now, Jack, or you won't have to worry about a trial."

"Easy now, detective." Gaggii cautiously moved his right hand away from the bracelet. "What are you worried about? That I might be signaling friends? I have no friends. That I might be calling up the gods? That is superstition, suitable only for troubling the sleep of children." The bracelet continued to glow.

"I don't care if you're trying to pick up local radio," said Moody threateningly. "Stop it."

"Ah, it doesn't matter, does it? You have your witness, sergeant. So I think it only fair that I invoke mine."

Ooljee uttered a violent curse. The pickup swerved wildly as something immense filled the windshield. Its surface was as yellow as the sun and its eyes boiled crimson.

CHAPTER
15

THE TRUCK SWUNG off the dirt road and went bouncing and squealing through the forest. Ooljee wrestled wheel and suspension, somehow avoiding the army of trees that loomed dangerously in front of them.

A vast pulsating shape struck repeatedly at the careening pickup. Sparks flew from the composite frame every time contact was made. Lowering his window, Moody tried to get a better look at the impossible manifestation.

It had to have come from the alien web, the web that was all around them. They walked through it, breathed it. It imperceptibly thickened the fabric of existence. Now something denser had coalesced out of that region of rainbow threads and animate explosions, some kind of program sucked up by Gaggii's manipulations to harass and frighten them. At which it was succeeding admirably.

Moody flinched as the glowing head twisted toward him. He fired reflexively, suspecting even as he did so that his shells were unlikely to have any effect on the force field or database or whatever the hell it was. But he'd been trained to return fire during an attack. Besides which, it was the only response at his disposal.

He remembered how Kettrick and the housekeeper had

died. Here before him, twisting and contorting madly in midair, was the instrument of their death immensely enlarged. The tinier version Gaggii had invoked that night on Steel Key had killed two people. Its monstrous relative was trying to destroy their truck.

He recalled what Ooljee had told him about a hatathli being able to utilize one portion of a sandpainting. Gaggii was using a small part of the alien web. It was a device an ancient Anasazi might have found useful in dealing with an enemy, something formulated in familiar terms—if one could call a fifty-foot-long yellow and red serpent familiar. It continued to strike at the hood and sides of the fleeing pickup, trying to smash its way in.

Moody fired again. It was impossible to miss the gigantic writhing shape. The shot had about as much effect as he expected. It was like trying to kill a breeze. The snake was more concept than creature, a tenebrous serpentine program dredged from the depths of some hatathli's thousand-year-dead imagination, a realized representation of old legends.

Meanwhile Ooljee was cursing in an extraordinary mix of English, Navaho, and Japanese as he struggled to keep them from compacting against the nearest ponderosa pine. This he succeeded in doing for a commendable length of time.

Forward motion ceased abruptly and without warning, accompanied by a tremendous metallic *clang*. Moody felt like the clapper inside a gigantic bell. His head swung forward to smack the dash.

Providentially cushioned by the restraint mesh, Gaggii escaped a similar concussion. The impact cracked the rear window, allowing the prisoner to kick out the rest of the glass. There was just enough clearance for him to crawl through to the bed of the pickup.

A dazed, groggy Moody tried to aim his pistol in that direction but he was having a hard time just hanging onto the suddenly heavy weapon. His head and vision cleared fast, but by that time Gaggii had vanished into the woods.

"He's getting away!" Ooljee yelled unnecessarily.

"I can see that!" Moody forced open the damaged door and started to climb out, quickly withdrew his legs as the yellow vastness struck at them. Glistening yard-long fangs sent dirt and rock chips flying.

As his partner tried to get a bead on the violently twisting shape, Ooljee struggled with the truck, alternating curses with prayers. One of them must have worked, because the engine hummed to life. Slamming into reverse, the pickup bounced away from the tree, then rolled awkwardly forward once more.

The snakeshape struck at the front windshield, spidering safety glass tough enough to turn bullets and darts but not fangs the size of pickaxes. Moody threw up his arms to protect his face, but the glass held. It would not withstand a second such assault.

Ooljee swung around, did something to the wheel, and yelled at his partner, "Jump!"

Moody eyed the hard, rough ground outside. They weren't going very fast, but still . . .

No time to argue. He popped his own door, tried to will into existence a depression filled to the brim with a hundred years worth of pine needles and leaves, and jumped.

Any local accumulations of vegetable matter had already been spoken for. They lined fox dens and squirrel nests, not the ground beneath the careening pickup. He hit hard, pain splintering his right shoulder. It felt like some crazyboy had taken a good whack at him with an iron bar. He rolled over a few times before coming to rest.

Struggling to hands and knees, he watched as the driverless pickup, headlights gleaming, rumbled away into the night with its brilliantly glowing yellow and red nemesis twisting and coiling above it. The snake thing struck repeatedly at the truck's cab, attacking effortlessly, a mad manic mass of pulsating serpentine energy.

Let it expend itself against the unfortunate vehicle, he thought. *Save your shots in case it comes looking for you.*

"You okay?" An anxious, exhausted query.

Grimacing, Moody rose while clutching his injured shoulder, his useless gun dangling from his right hand. He'd hung onto it when he'd jumped from the truck, and he was damned fortunate not to have blown his guts out when he'd hit the ground.

His eyes tried to penetrate the blackness between the trees. "Any sign of our boy?" he muttered, ignoring his partner's concern. Somewhere behind them the truck was rattling down a slope, still pursued by the malevolent yellow snake-shape.

Ooljee shook his head tiredly. "This is his backyard, not ours. He knows it, we do not."

"Bet he ran back to his place."

"If so, he will not stay there. And I do not think we should go after him. I do not think that a second reception would be either as indifferent or polite as the first."

Moody grunted agreement as he stared into the woods. His shoulder throbbed and he was mad—at himself more than their former prisoner. They should've stripped him bare-ass and slapped sealant tape over his mouth, though his chanting probably had far less to do with generating the snakeshape than did the cleverly disguised transmitter on his wrist. For all they knew, the tiny device was capable of running every molly in his house.

Ooljee was right: it would be stupid to try and take Gaggii again tonight. Having conjured up one lethal tactile program, he could probably conjure another, and they no longer had the hard shell of the pickup cab to protect them. They would need backup after all, enough to handle Gaggii no matter what he called up.

Their police spinners, built to military-level specifications, were undamaged. If they could just get to a phone, any kind of phone, they could fill the woods around Gaggii's house with riot squads. It meant a long walk back to the road, and at this time of night, probably an additional hike all the way to the main highway.

Meanwhile Gaggii would be busy at his place—doing what? Barricading himself in, emplacing defenses, or preparing to flee? Or maybe he was so sure his fanged tactile had taken care of the two intruders that he would relax? Moody knew better. Someone as smart as Gaggii wouldn't take that chance. Arrogant he was, but not stupid.

No, he wouldn't be accommodating enough to linger in the vicinity. He'd run. If they could get to a phone in time they might be able to throw a cordon around the county, if not the state.

"That is how Kettrick and his housekeeper were slain," Ooljee was saying.

"Yeah. With a smaller version. Forensics wouldn't have figured it out in a million years." Moody didn't have the faintest idea which way they were going. Much simpler just to follow his friend.

They descended into a shallow arroyo, jumped a foot-wide creek, clambered up the far side and immediately dropped into defensive crouches.

Smoke drifted capriciously through the trees, but there was no sign of the monstrous glowing serpent-shape. Either the program had run down or Gaggii had called it off. They advanced warily on the pickup.

Moody yanked open the door and started to reach inside. He stopped as soon as he saw that they would not be able to use the truck phone to call for assistance, because it was no longer there. Nor was the front half of the truck. In its place was a cooling lump of metal and composite about four feet high. The pickup's bed was still intact, but the cab and engine compartment had melted like a chunk of pork fat in a pot of greens.

Moody tried to imagine the snake-thing clamping tight to the truck and expiring in a burst of incredible energy. It must have been quick; a single violent spark lighting up the night, completely overloading the electric engine's surge suppressors. In addition to the body itself, the intense heat had melted all four tires.

Gaggii had called it up to rescue him, but he hadn't had time to program it selectively, Ooljee was thinking.

"He directed it to attack the truck, but not us. So when we jumped out it ignored us. That is what I prayed would happen."

"What if you'd been wrong?"

Ooljee shrugged. "Then we would have had to rely on your shooting. I thought flight the better option."

"Too bad it didn't start a fire." Moody glanced at the surrounding trees and brush. "Might've brought a ranger out to check on it. I don't think what's left of the truck is putting out enough smoke to be noticed from a distance."

"Doesn't matter. We must get back to the main road."

"He's used the web to kill twice, and he tried to kill us with it." Moody spoke as they strode through the trees. "He's learning how to handle the infernal thing."

"He still needs a mechanical interface to access it," Ooljee pointed out. "The bracelet was only a link to whatever setup he has constructed in his house. Take that away from him and he is harmless." He considered aloud. "He must have used it to make contact with his home molly via a cableless modem at Kettrick's house. I wonder what he intends to do with it besides defend himself?"

"You heard him." Moody felt like he was carrying a fifty-pound pack on his back. In a sense he was, except that he had the location reversed. "He's the ant who's figured out how to use the garbage. Or if this web was set up with a purpose in mind, he's trying to figure out what that is."

"No one will believe what happened to us here." Ooljee

squinted into the night, changed direction. "We will have to say he had a gun, or that the truck sprung a wheel. If we go into a station and say we lost our prisoner because he was rescued by *Klish-do-nuhti'i* they will lock us up instead of Gaggii."

"Say again?"

"*Klish-do-nuthti'i*. Endless Snake. It appears in many of the Ways." He nodded back over his shoulder. "Or maybe it was only *Ah-yah-neh*, Big Snake."

"Got a lot of snakes in your religion, do you?" Moody was in no mood to be understanding.

"All kinds," the sergeant admitted readily. "Crooked snakes, water snakes, arrow snakes: they are as common to us as fleas are to you in Florida. It is not surprising that the spirit a hatathli would call up to protect him would take that form."

"He's not a hatathli, dammit!" Moody was good and frustrated by their failure to bring Gaggii in, after all the time and effort that had been expended in tracking him down. He felt angry and helpless. He was not going to let reality slip away from him too.

"He's just a good weaver who's stumbled across the web to end all webs. He hit back at us with technology, Paul. Not metaphysics or spiritualism."

"I did not mean to suggest otherwise." Ooljee started up yet another slope. Moody followed, sucking air. "But he clearly understands sandpaintings, and probably the Ways as well. There is nothing that says a weaver cannot also be a trained hatathli.

"If the term metaphysics bothers you, perhaps we should call them *muta*physics. Mysticism is just a name, my friend, for a different level of reality that we haven't learned how to tap into yet. Try going back eight hundred years and telling one of my ancestors that the spinner on my belt or the watch on your arm is not powered by magic. Tell me that the cutting edge of modern science does not sound more like something out of a sandpainting than a textbook. Take particle physics, for example.''

''You take it,'' Moody said with a snort. ''I'll have pastrami on rye.''

Ooljee was not dissuaded. ''Particles that have names like smart, and lazy. Forces called weak, up, down. Colors. Is that physics? Or the chant of hatathlis? Take modern recombinant metallurgy. Nothing more than alchemy without the pointy hats. Even a couple of hundred years ago who could have imagined metallic glass, or carbon-alloy shuttle bodies, or all-ceramic engines? Not to mention mollysphere storage.

''Where lies the line between sorcery and science? It is only a matter of terminology, my friend. This web is another place we are just finding out how to visit, the way people decades ago learned how to make photons line up to lase. One more step. Primitive peoples did not understand radio or television because they could not see the signals in the air. That does not make the vid magic. We can't see this alien web, but we know it is there.''

''There's the road. Let's access *it*.'' Moody nodded ahead, where the welcome strip of pavement slashed through the forest. ''One thing I promise you, *my friend*. Whether weaver or hatathli, if Gaggii so much as sneezes the wrong way when we get our hands on him again, I'm going to blow his head off.''

''Is that standard Greater Tampa departmental procedure?''

''Naw. That's Vernon Moody procedure.'' The detective wheezed his way up the embankment.

''You are angry. I am angry too. It will not help our situation to give way to anger.''

''Maybe not, but it sure feels good. Want to go back to his place?'' He bent over and rested his hands on his knees, breathing hard in the center of the empty two-lane road. The east-west laser pickup strips shone softly in the faint light, waiting to guide the next vehicle that came this way.

"No. He will surely be ready for us if we try anything so foolhardy."

"How're we gonna fight something like that—what'd you call it? Endless Snake?" He gestured with his gun. "Might as well have thrown dirt clods at it."

"It is some kind of tactile program. We must either get to him before he can access it, or else assemble enough firepower to convince him that no matter how much damage he does, he won't be able to escape."

Moody nodded, straightening and stretching. He eyed his partner quizzically. "You scared?"

"You bet I am scared, Vernon Moody. Gaggii is learning how to use the sandpainting's web. Maybe it is no more than alien garbage, but that is enough. I consider myself good with a spinner, but this is beyond me. I am a practical weaver, not a theorist. We need the help of someone who can deal with Gaggii on his own level. We need some heavyweight advice." He looked past his colleague. There was a light in the distance, coming up the road.

Ooljee fumbled with his service belt. "I am scared because Endless Snake may not be the only program Gaggii has learned how to invoke." He held up a compact road flasher, began to wave it over his head. The oncoming lights slowed.

Moody turned to regard the woods. Somewhere back there was the turnoff they'd taken earlier, the dirt track and bridge that led to Gaggii's home. He hated the idea of abandoning a suspect this close at hand. It went against his every professional instinct.

Instinct and experience counted for nothing now, he told himself. This was not a case where standard police procedure applied. Hell, this wasn't a case where standard reality applied. Besides, there was no guarantee Gaggii had gone back to his place. Maybe he'd kept a car hidden in the woods for a fast getaway. It was gratifying to think they'd upset him, maybe panicked him.

They knew who he was now, exactly what he looked like. They'd bottle up the escape routes. Gaggii wouldn't be able to cross a border, board a shuttle, buy a tube ticket without being recognized. He was free, sure, but within an area soon to be severely circumscribed. When they located him again, they'd jump him so fast he wouldn't have time to say boo, much less utter any elaborate chants or threats.

Regrettably, the driver did not have a carphone. He didn't even have a road scanner. But he did drive them, rattling and banging all the way in his ancient pickup, to the outskirts of Window Rock.

They stopped at the first public phone, Ooljee leaping out to slap his spinner against the emergency terminal while Moody waited nearby—cold, tired, and hurting. Little yeis were excavating his shoulder, hacking away with arrows and medicine knives. It was a relief to see the phone screen light up with the image of another officer sitting calm and relaxed in a warm station.

Ooljee spoke rapidly in a mix of Navaho and English. When he was finished he clicked off, removed his spinner, and walked back to stand next to his partner. Together they watched the road, busy with tourists and commercial travelers.

"Official word is: pick him up *now*. You want to get some rest and talk to him when they bring him in?"

Moody hugged himself, half-jogging in place to keep warm. He was nearly unconscious from the unaccustomed exertion and lack of food. He knew they could check into a hotel, have something to eat, or borrow a cruiser for a quick ride back to Ganado.

"What do you want to do?"

''My friend, you know me a little by now. Do you think I am crazy?''

''That's what I thought.'' From the depths of his exhaustion Moody dredged up a grim smile.

CHAPTER 16

SWALLOWING THEIR EXHAUSTION, they followed close on the heels of the heavily armed infiltration team as it violated the integrity of Gaggii's house four hours later. Procedural caution was misplaced. The owner had long since fled.

The converted garage back of the main house yielded as impressive an array of electronics as Moody had ever encountered outside a university lab or Greater Tampa Operations HQ, all of it state-of-the-art and expensive. Every square inch of wall was boarded with storage flats, zenats, Fordmatsu holomagers, spinner jacks, and I-2 Septimus sequencers, all of it sandwiched around a Cribm mollysphere big enough to store the annotated Library of Congress, more storage than even a modest-sized company would need.

Buried somewhere within that rare earth-doped fiber-optic mass were the answers to his questions. Somehow he doubted it would be safe to plug in his spinner and try calling them up. Gaggii had warned them that the merest kiss of an unauthorized probe would unravel his molly. Moody didn't delude himself into thinking he was weaver enough to braid between the seams. They needed an orber here; the best in the country.

Ooljee had reached the same conclusion. "We go back to Ganado and make out a report that includes the details I didn't have time to phone in. An APB goes out on Yistin Gaggii. We particularly want to alert regional dealers in heavy-duty mollys and spinners. We do not want him reassembling anything like this in a rented house somewhere in Hope or Page Springs. He can only do so much with that wrist unit."

"What about a little preventative medicine?" Moody asked tersely.

"I have already had the power to the house shut off." Ooljee gestured at the overhead lights. "Our own equipment is running off a truck generator. Same for the phone, so he can't access by radio link, and the roof dish, so he cannot use an orbital relay. This house is now isolated, my friend. There is no way he can reach his database. He's isolated, too, wherever he is.

"The next time we run into him it will go better. Let him try to call up snakes without a molly."

"Unless he's got a backup stashed out in the woods someplace." Ooljee eyed him sharply. "Another building, an apartment somewhere: we don't know one way or the other. If he did lay in a backup, it's probably not this elaborate. But it's liable to be enough to let him get on with his work."

The sergeant nodded slowly. "It depends how vulnerable he thought himself, despite what he told us."

"From what we saw of him, he struck me as a pretty careful sort of guy. I'd be surprised if he didn't have *something* to fall back on."

"In the end it will not matter." Ooljee was optimistic. "His features are distinctive. We will find him quickly."

"Hope so." Forensics personnel bustled around the garage while men wearing puzzled expressions and heavy sidearms griped about the lateness of the hour. "What do y'all think he'll do now?"

Ooljee considered. "If he is as dedicated as he seemed, he will continue with his work. Otherwise he will try to flee the country."

"That's the way I figure it. I imagine he's trying to get deeper into the web. Wonder what else he can call up besides serpentine-shaped electromagnetic fields? What other cute li'l critters do you find in sandpaintings? No, never mind: I don't want to know. I've had enough of your mutaphysics for one night. Let's get some rest. Somebody else can scan reports for a while."

"Rest, yes," agreed Ooljee readily, "and some help. Specialist help."

Ooljee's lieutenant spent five minutes listening to their story before he cut them off and passed them up to the assistant chief, who escorted them to the Chief's office and departed in haste. Chief Yazzie tolerated their story of weaver hatathlis and alien webs and thousand-year-old data-bases of unknown dimensions. Being a sensible, reasonable man with thirty years police experience, he bought little if any of it.

On the other hand, he was compelled by the reality of two people murdered by mysterious means in Florida, a house in the woods filled with more equipment than your average forward-listening military outpost, and most damn-ingly, one half-melted departmental pickup truck. He was willing to allow that something odd was going on within his jurisdiction, something illegal and dangerous if not im-mediately explicable. That much he was willing to acknowl-edge. Endless Snake he was not.

All in all, he decided, it would be a good thing to accept the recommendations of the two earnest officers that they find one Yistin Gaggii as quickly as possible and subject him to some serious questioning.

Of that much sought-after individual there was as yet no report, but Yazzie was as confident as his men that they would find him. He had not had sufficient time to get far, and controls had been placed on all roads and forms of public transportation. The Arizona Department of Public Safety was cooperating fully with Reservation forces. Mobile radar units would ensure that no off-road vehicle exited Reservation boundaries without first being challenged. Tonight Gaggii's face would appear on one of the vid's most popular criminal-cache programs. After that there would not be a place in the country where he could go without a chance of being recognized.

The department had moved fast. There was a good chance they could restrict their quarry to the Rez, the Four Corners area at worst. With every law-enforcement agency in the region giving him top priority, Yistin Gaggii was going to have a hard time buying breakfast without being spotted.

Samantha Grayhills agreed. It was she who took the form, if not the shape, of the help Ooljee had requested.

Moody found himself being introduced to a short, voluptuous, dark-haired woman with a broad smile and trenchant gaze. She didn't eye him like a cop.

She smiled even when she talked, no matter how serious the subject matter. Her skin was the color of oiled oak. She had a man's handshake, not some flighty caress-and-pass like a pair of railroad cars uncoupling. He wondered if she lifted weights, though he could detect no evidence of any unusual musculature beneath her clothing.

Her hair clip was traditional silver and turquoise, her attire anything but. The pleated beige jumpsuit boasted enough zippers and pockets to equip a closet full of uniforms. The pockets bulged with mysterious lumps and knots which distorted more familiar curves.

Unlike most of the other Navaho women he's seen, she wore no jewelry save for the hair clip. Not that she was either poor or unfashionable; he guessed that she didn't wear a lot of metal because it might affect the readings of some of the instruments she carried with her.

"What agency are you with?" Moody asked her.

That unwavering smile illumined the room where they had gathered. "I am not with an agency, Mr. Moody."

"Vernon. Not with an agency?"

She sounded sympathetic. "I am the principal orber for Noronco International. That will have to do for credentials. Perhaps you have seen one of our commercials?"

Moody turned on his partner. "What the hell is this?"

"The department pulled some strings." Ooljee tried to allay his friend's discomfort. "Flew her up from Phoenix just a little while ago. I have barely had time to brief her."

"I still don't see why—"

"Because you apparently need my services, detective. Noronco is a Thai-American combine whose North American operations are based in Phoenix. We specialize in the manufacture of mollyspheres; everything from kids' games to military mollyware. My particular area of expertise happens to be syndetic security. I would not be surprised if you used one or two of my inserts in your own office."

"Oh." Moody looked at her differently.

"When the department put in for assistance," Ooljee explained helpfully, "they requested the most qualified individual in the area. The request did not go out with occupational restrictions."

"From what I was told on the way up from the airport," Grayhills said, "you two are either candidates for therapy or else you've stumbled across one of the secrets of the ages. The story is so fantastic, I find myself hoping there is something to it."

"That's funny," Moody told her, "because we keep hoping there isn't."

"I know that you're looking for a murderer. That's not my department. Show me something impossible."

So they did, back at Ooljee's apartment, well away from the prying eyes of the press and possible leaks. She looked on silently as the sergeant accessed the sandpainting and the enlightened darkness beyond.

"I've never seen anything like that in all my work." She was enthralled by the image in the zenat. "This exceeds the boundaries of theory."

"There is more to it than meets the eye," Ooljee informed her. "Go and dip your hand in it."

She eyed him sharply. "*Into* it?" He nodded.

Moody was standing next to the screen, waiting. Her smile was as thin as it got. "Is this dangerous?" she asked.

"I've done it. Paul's done it. We're still here. But this is all new. We can't make any promises."

"I see." She gazed into the swirling, sparkling depths of the zenat. Then she reached out. In contrast to the rest of her, Moody noted, her fingers were slim and delicate. As Ooljee would say, a fine woman.

He heard her intake of breath as her hand passed beyond the monitor's surface and into the warm, tingling *otherness* beyond. She rotated her hand from side to side, slowly, before withdrawing it.

"How deep does it go?"

"We were hoping y'all might be able to tell us. Paul kind of pushed the limits until I pulled him back. For all we know, you can jump in and go swimming or running around, or whatever, until you're out of sight. There might be gravity in there, or there might not. There might be up or only down." He turned to study the mesmerizing view. "We kinda thought all-out experimentation on the physical level might be a tad premature."

"Good thought." The experience left her breathing faster. "I think I'd do a lot of long-term study before bodily committing myself to a place whose physical reality has yet to be defined."

"Kinda like marriage," he ventured. That brought back the full smile.

Utilizing the procedure they had developed earlier, Ooljee shut down the web. He poured tea and coffee as they took seats at the table. Every so often, Grayhills would glance uneasily at the flat gray rectangle of the zenat.

"How do you get it to answer questions? I hardly had a chance to skim the written report, and it wasn't overflowing with detail."

"Plain language; verbal queries." Ooljee dumped sugar in his cup. "It responds readily in Navaho and English. It would probably do so in Urdu if requested."

She nodded. "First time I ever entered a database bodily—if it is a database and not some other state of matter we don't have a name for. But until we learn otherwise, that's how I'm going to treat it." She turned to Ooljee. "I don't know shit about sandpaintings, but I can unstick a gummed-up ten-molly parallel processing web inside twenty-four hours. My family traditions don't originate on the Rez. They're the six years I spent at Tucson Polytechnic and Caltech."

"Understanding this can come later." Moody struggled with his impatience. "What we need right now is to find this Yistin Gaggii again before he can do any real damage."

"What makes you think he wants to do damage? Maybe he's just an eclectic seeker after knowledge?"

"Call it a gut instinct based on two decades of police work." He spoke more sharply than he intended. "That and the fact that he's already committed two murders."

"Besides which, you hate him because he made you look bad. I read the report."

Moody was taken aback. "He's just a suspect we want back. I don't have any feelings about the guy one way or the other."

"I do not believe you. I think you have developed a personal dislike for him."

"Get off my case, lady. I never let my emotions interfere with my work."

Sure you don't, he told himself. Truth to tell, he'd taken an instant dislike to the guy. Gaggii's attitude of superiority was one that a poor fat kid from the backwoods of Mississippi had been forced to deal with much of his life. He'd encountered plenty of it in high school and lots more in college, even though he'd slimmed down enough to make his size something of an athletic advantage. But people still made fun of his back-country manners and cultural rusticity. What was natural and charming back home city kids found cloddish and laughable. His innate good nature had enabled him to hide the hurt, but not to eliminate it.

Not until he'd been promoted to sergeant in Tampa had people stopped making fun of him. That was understandable within a police department, where the individual you gibed at one day might be guarding your back the next.

"All right," he admitted grudgingly, "so I don't like the guy. So what? It doesn't affect my judgment."

"I did not mean to imply that it did." He had a good nature, and she had that smile, he mused.

"Look, this guy's no hobbyist, and he's no cracker trying to steal a few corporate secrets for resale on the open market. He's got something a lot stronger in mind and we'd damn well better get to him before he can put it into effect."

"For example?" she asked him. Moody noticed that his partner was looking at him, too.

"Well, he's already figured out how to use it to kill people who don't cooperate with him, by accessing something unpleasant within the database. Since he made it clear to us that that wasn't enough to satisfy his curiosity, I imagine he'll try to access something more. I wouldn't care to lay odds on its being of a benign nature." He glanced at his partner.

Paul Ooljee drained the last of his coffee. "There are worse entities in the old stories than Big Thunder and Endless Snake."

"I understand that you've isolated the facilities he was using. Does he have access to any others?"

"We do not know." Ooljee fidgeted with his cup. "He'd built himself a city-sized web in his home. It is hard to imagine him mustering the resources to duplicate it elsewhere.''

"He wouldn't need to replicate all the analytical hardware.'' She sipped hot tea. ''All he'd need is a tight molly and a fast transfer program. Or he may have transferred everything as he learned it, if only to make sure of a quality backup. Depriving him of his hardware, though, may keep him from making any new discoveries, which would mean we would only have to deal with what he already knows.'' She looked at the zenat again. ''I'm still having a hard time accepting all this.''

"Any time you find yourself feeling particularly doubtful,'' Moody told her, ''all you have to do is access that little sucker and stick your hand into it. Kind of removes it from the realm of the abstract right quick.''

Yistin Gaggii pulled off the dirt track and parked near the edge of the little mesa. A broad, flat plain spotted with low scrub stretched out below him, rising abruptly and with the uncanny precision of geometric geologic forces to a much larger mesa beyond. To the north a gigantic dormant volcano stood sentinel over this part of the sacred land, its summit sugared with snow. The sky here was big and bright enough to swallow a man's worst fears. It was the blue roof of the world. He began removing equipment from the motor home, his boots kicking up dirt and gravel. Dust flowered briefly around his legs before settling softly back to the ground. It was red and clinging, for this was the land where the earth rusted.

The nearest paved road did not have a pickup guide embedded in its surface. Few people came this way for the simple reason that there was nothing here. The porous rocks held no water for wells, the barren ramparts no cliff dwellings for study or pillage. There were not enough weeds and scrub on the surrounding acres to support half a dozen steers. Even the creatures that eked out a miserable living here resented the niche to which ecology had condemned them.

He would have chosen an even more remote spot save for the fact that even a four-by-four had its limits and his motor home was not designed for extended off-road travel. It was top-heavy and unwieldy; not the vehicle of choice for bounding through washes and up steep grades. But it had carried him comfortably clear of prying eyes, both human and electronic, and had allowed him to make his way westward in peace.

It also held a great deal of expensive equipment, some of which he was now piecing together beneath a fold-down sunshade on the vehicle's port side. As long as he did not exceed the capacity of the portable generator, he would be able to continue his work.

After the first frantic half-hour's driving he had stopped worrying about pursuit. Worry was a waste of time anyway. It broke down proteins in the body. Once he was able to leave the highway and go off-road he felt relatively secure. His motor home was indistinguishable from a thousand similar tourist vehicles in the Four Corners area and was not registered in his name. There was no reason for a passing police vehicle to challenge it.

They had no idea which way he'd gone. The last place they would look for him was here, in the middle of the Reservation. No doubt they expected him to rush to Klagetoh in hopes of fleeing via plane, or to drive like mad for Mexico. He had no intention of doing any such thing. He had been readying the next stage of his research when the two policemen had surprised him. All they had done was hurry his planned embarkation. He regretted the loss of his house and all it contained, but he could manage with field equipment. Improvisation had been important from the start.

Time was important now. The police could not be allowed to interfere. He had come too far, drawn too close. If he succeeded, it would not matter what they or anyone else tried to do.

He adjusted the contrast on the zenat attached to the exterior wall of the motor home, then carefully checked the cables that connected it to his spinner and to the molly inside. At home he used infrared and UHF, but cables were more secure when working outside. They were shielded and would not broadcast his activities to potential eavesdroppers. Depending upon the nature of the job, a pick and shovel might be more practical than a mechanical excavator.

Hard driving had brought him to this place. He was pleased with it. High overhead the sky was filling up with wild cirrus clouds, spray kicked up by the bow of an advancing high-pressure system. Soon he could begin. He needed information and help, and planned to call for both simultaneously.

By now the ceremony was as familiar to him as a mother's lullaby, the chant and fine-tuning second nature. He could have built an audio-visual macro and installed it in his wrist transmitter, but there was an aesthetic to accessing the web manually which he deeply enjoyed.

The activated zenat revealed a dimension formulated by Einstein, with decor by Lewis Carroll. As always he did nothing for long moments but savor the image of writhing rainbows and darting, glowing shapes. Then he recited the new program.

Actually it was not new; it was very old. It simply had not been thought of as anything other than one of many hundreds of chants. Without access to the web it was useful only as an aid in the performance of traditional medicine ceremonies. When access to the alien web was added, it became something very different.

The words were symbolic and descriptive rather than overtly active in the web matrix. They helped the singer to remember the correct phrasing, the proper tones. It was the pitch that mattered, the duration of each vowel, the aural vibrations which actually reacted with the web. Not the words themselves. The chant functioned as a weaver's chiastic mnemonic.

"I am the frivolous coyote.

I wander about.

I have seen Hasjesh-jin's fire.

I wander about.

I stole his fire from him.

I wander about.

I have it! I have it!"

Gaggii patiently repeated the chant time and again, singing tirelessly, striving to better his rendition with each successive repetition. The words came from the Creation Chant, but were active in a way no modern Navaho had ever dreamed of. It had been composed, or adapted from unimaginable sources, by some ancient Anasazi hatathli, passed on down to his descendants, and thence to the Navaho who had inherited this land in their turn. The words and music had endured. Only the original purpose had been forgotten.

Like anyone else who had ever taken time to contemplate the mystery of their disappearance, Yistin Gaggii wondered where the Anasazi had gone. They had simply disappeared, leaving behind the beginnings of a culture that in time might have rivaled that of the Maya or Inca. Instead they had vanished, leaving behind only their marvelous cliff dwellings to show that they had ever been.

Had they made the jump into the web? Or had they been removed elsewhere by its makers? Or had bad weather and failed crops simply forced them to disperse throughout the Southwest? Was their abrupt disappearance the result of natural causes, or unnatural ones? One day he would have

the answer to that question, as he would have the answer
to everything else.

Each time he repeated the chant the sky grew a little
darker around him, as though a bubble of evening had begun
to grow atop the mesa, enveloping chanter and motor home,
boulders and brush. Seen through the dry fog of that unnatural darkness, the sky shone dull purple. Nor were these
the only visible changes in his immediate environment.

As he chanted, a few of the migrating sparks and points
of light within the zenat began to dilate—twisting and flaring. They began to move not in the lazy, meandering fashion
of the rainbow threads but with direction and purpose,
breaking free of the fractal patterns in which they had here-
tofore been embedded. They expanded steadily, tumescent
with energy, until they filled the screen from edge to edge.

Then they emerged, drifting out of the zenat into the soft
false night which had engulfed the mesa top, hovering above
the dry red soil and wild grasses.

Gaggii kept chanting until he was surrounded by a half
circle of bobbing, corposant shapes, each yellow or red-
orange, each an individually expressive nimbus. Despite the
fact that it was chilly, even cold atop the mesa, he was
sweating profusely. When he felt the time was just right he
shifted from the Creation Chant to the web shutdown sequence. Instantly the zenat became again only a blank sheet
of photoluminescent composite hanging on the wall of the
motor home.

Immediately, several of the cold, refulgent orbs darted
toward it. They bumped up against the monitor, curled
around its edges, tested it like moths tempting a lamp. They
gave off no heat.

Finally they retreated and resumed their places in the
semicircle surrounding Gaggii. He picked up the chant
again, singing slower and softer now, soothing them to
Earth.

The dancing spheres began to extrude projections, expanding riotously as they searched for definition. Heads emerged, followed by legs and tails, smiling jaws, and fine sharp teeth. When the last of the emancipated energy had become *mah-ih*, one of them sat back on its newly acquired haunches and cocked its head quizzically to one side as it studied the chanter.

"You Who Reach: why do you strand us?"

"I have need of you." Knowing what he was dealing with, Gaggii tried to watch all of them at once. His fingers did not stray from the controls of his spinner. If they tried to sneak around behind him, he might yet be able to do something. For now, their curiosity outweighed their discontent. But that could change.

Another stopped licking itself long enough to speak. "This is not our place. Let us go back. Though familiar to us from memory, these shapes are uncomfortable. Reopen for us what you have closed."

Gaggii relaxed just a little. "Are you Holy People?"

Several of them exchanged glances, enjoying the novelty of eyes. One laughed softly.

"We hate the ones you call Holy People. To them we are less than nothing."

"We exist because of what they have defined," said another. "Without their definitions we have no existence."

Gaggii nodded to himself. The ants might aspire to utilization of the garbage, but the fleas could never do more than exist in it.

"Why do you take these shapes?"

"In this place these are the shapes that fit," explained the first speaker, as if restating the unavoidably obvious.

"The place within a place," said another.

"No," interjected a third, "a place without a place."

Quite unexpectedly they fell to arguing among themselves, emanating loud, disturbing, immature noises.

"This shape is less uncongenial than others," declared

the second speaker. "It was the first shape we encountered in this place."

"In and out," chanted another, "in and out."

"Why assume it now?" Gaggii inquired.

"A shape once assumed is a shape learned. Make us an opening."

"In time." *Templates*, Gaggii mused. *So much of this is about templates. These shapes they take are no more than that. Are we no less? What else is my DNA but a template?*

"I will tell you what I intend."

They listened silently to him; some with apparent indifference, others with casual interest, though he suspected that all heard.

"Is it dangerous?" he asked when he'd finished.

"The concept is meaningless. Only existence has meaning."

"Good. Then you have no reason not to help me. If you refuse, I won't make an opening for you. This I know you cannot do for yourselves, or you would have done it already instead of sitting and listening to me."

"We could hurt you," one insisted in a flat, emotionless voice.

"You cannot hurt me enough to make me do what you want, and if you hurt me too much then I will die and leave you trapped here forever in these forms. If you help me, I will make a good opening for you."

Again several of them exchanged glances. "You have told us what you intend. Can you imagine what it involves?"

"I have studied it and have some idea." Gaggii tried not to seem overly eager. "I suspect I will need to make use of Hasjesh-jin's fire. Do you still have it?"

All of them laughed then, an eerie yet familiar collective amusement that echoed across the mesa and down into the side canyons.

"You pass on long memories," one finally declared.

"Then you no longer have it?" Gaggii was crestfallen.

"No," said another, "but something akin is near here. You are right to say that you will need to make use of it to do what you intend."

"Can you help me make use of it?"

"Once before we stole it," announced a member of the semicircle. "Why should we not steal it again?"

"This could be of interest," said the one next in line.

Gaggii looked at it. "You told me only existence has meaning. Why should you care about this?"

"As your words say, we are frivolous. This is a fortunate thing for you." The first speaker smiled at him, showing many teeth. "We will help you steal Hasjesh-jin's fire, though this time not from Hasjesh-jin. Be aware that though danger is meaningless to us, it is not to you. This thing you intend could threaten your existence, which is far more transitory than ours."

"My existence is my concern. You simply exist. I, on the other hand, have purpose. I exist to learn. I believe that knowledge can transform existence."

"Knowledge is camouflage," he was told. "It merely disguises what lies beneath."

"I want what lies beneath," Gaggii declared flatly.

"As you say, that is your concern." The first speaker shifted his position on the hard ground. "Ours is an opening."

"Where will we find Hasjesh-jin's fire?"

One of them turned and pointed. "That way, not far."

"By whose standards?" Gaggii gazed through the harlequin twilight toward the far horizon.

"Not far, by your standards."

Gaggii frowned as he considered what lay in the indicated direction. Then he understood, and was able to smile.

"We will lead you," said the speaker, turning to leave.

"No. This is a place we cannot go to all together. I will meet you slightly to the north of it. I will describe the exact spot where we can gather."

"This is a strange reality," one of them murmured as he gazed at the dark sky and shadowy mesas. "I will be glad to leave it."

Gaggii wound cable as he spoke, still careful to keep his spinner close at hand. Around such as these one could never relax vigilance.

"I want to move quickly. I have reasons." He stowed the last of his equipment and climbed into the motor home. Making sure it was still in all-wheel drive, he flicked on the engine, backed up, and began to edge down the dirt track that cut into the flank of the mesa like a brand on an old horse.

Behind him the coyotes dispersed, each taking a different route but all inclining northwest. There were almost a hundred of them. They were coyote from their wet black noses to the tips of their bushy tails, but they were not of pure coyote lineage. This was not their plane of existence. An ancient template imprisoned them in their present form. They would remain thus until Gaggii made them an opening and allowed them to return to the place where they existed.

They remembered only a little of where they were, but they had correctly sensed the nearest source of Hasjesh-jin's fire. Playfully they moved toward it, anxious to do whatever was necessary to flee a reality they found unpleasantly constricting.

CHAPTER 17

THE DETECTIVE LUMBERED into the conference chamber. Ooljee was setting up his spinner while Samantha Grayhills looked on. Moody eyed her thoughtfully. Having little natural aptitude for academia, he was uncomfortable with those who did. Higher education was a tradition which was alien to his family. Everything he'd learned since leaving home he'd acquired through long hours of hard work and arduous study, poring over disks and through mollys, learning through drill what swifter minds seemed to absorb with nary a glance.

None of that, however, qualified one for promotion to the rank of detective. So he'd plowed relentlessly through every manual and text available until he'd mastered enough information to pass the requisite tests through sheer force of will, trying not to watch while college-educated candidates flipped through the questions faster than he could read them.

But Grayhills was different. She was proof one could be academically inclined without being narrow-minded. It helped that she wasn't a cop. He could discuss weaving with her without having to bring up relevant police technique. Practical applications gave them common ground for conversation.

He was conscious of her greater intellect, but because she was patient and understanding it didn't bother him. Whenever the conversation grew too technical for him or his partner she would back up, slow down, and explain—without being in the least patronizing. And always there was that radiant smile; the smile of one who understood, the smile of instant sympathy. The smile of someone who didn't need coffee first thing in the morning.

Ooljee looked up tiredly as his friend approached. "Lisa'll be back tonight, so I have to play husband again as well as cop."

"Just so long," Moody quipped as he shut the security door behind him, "as your kids don't figure out how to access that web."

"That is not funny." Ooljee's sense of humor had been strained by the disappearance of Yistin Gaggii. Though no one could have foreseen the hatathli's escape, the sergeant still took it personally. As time passed without word of their quarry's whereabouts, he had grown irritable and snappish.

The rumors circulating around the station didn't stop until they ran a demonstration for the department's upper echelon and a couple of government specialists. As soon as it was over and the initial shock had begun to fade, everyone was sworn to absolute secrecy under pain of penalties too numerous to mention, and all records pertaining to the discovery were sealed as if they were the lost jewels of King Solomon, before being carted off in a military molly by a team from the National Security Institute. Given the number of people Moody and Ooljee had talked to already, it was probably too late to satisfy Security, but the government representatives insisted on following procedure.

In fact, the only reason they hadn't used the web right away to locate Gaggii a second time was the reluctance on the part of their superiors to allow them to do so. That was

Security for you. They had been compelled to demonstrate the existence of the web in order to prove its dangerous potential, and now that they'd done so they were forbidden to use it to try and prevent its possible misuse.

The longer the authorities bickered, the more time Gaggii gained to perfect his technique. Ooljee and Moody pointed out that it was vital they find him as quickly as possible, by whatever means necessary. They yelled and screamed, until finally it was allowed that they might be right. Reported sightings of their quarry had all proven false. There was no sign of him anywhere. It was as if he'd dropped off the face of the Earth.

Even if that turned out to be the case, Moody and Ooljee argued, they could still locate him using the web. As more time passed, even the people from Washington began to grow nervous. Permission was finally granted to the two officers to utilize the device they had discovered.

So it was that they found themselves admitted to a quiet, sealed room on the first sublevel of police headquarters. Stores had issued them a brand-new five-by-five zenat, a full-sized Plessevetti desk spinner, and a request to please try not to overwhelm the entire NDPS molly system in their search for one suspect.

"If we blow this one," Ooljee muttered as he checked his spinner connections, "we are likely to wipe the database for the entire department." The wall monitor opposite was three times the size of the one in his kitchen.

"We won't blow it." Moody did his best to shore up his partner's confidence. "We know how to handle it now. We're damn-well experienced."

"Are we? Do we know as much about this as we think we do?"

"I hope so. I'd sure hate to know less than we think we do."

Ooljee grinned weakly, turned to face the screen, and activated the spinner. He began the chant almost reluctantly.

Moody kept a wary eye on his friend. Samantha Grayhills stood nearby and watched silently. She was trying to divide her time between the zenat and her own spinner as she frenziedly took notes.

On strict orders from the NSI they were alone in the room. It had been hell obtaining the agency's permission to proceed. Ooljee had convinced them by insisting that if they were not allowed to proceed, Gaggii was sure to find a way to use the web in some unimaginable but highly damaging fashion that was certain to compromise national security. His claim was more speculation than certainty, but like any other government agency, the NSI thrived on speculation. Its worried representatives gave the two officers the go-ahead.

Out of deference to departmental concerns, the room had been smothered in interrupts and fail-safes so that in the event of another program runaway the web could be isolated from the rest of the building. Hopefully. It was one thing to have a precinct station burn, another to watch Reservation HQ go up in flames.

No, there could be no mistakes, Moody knew. He wasn't worried. Hadn't they successfully accessed the web several times since that incident? They knew what they were about.

As the strains of the chant echoed around the room, Grayhills beckoned Moody close and whispered in his ear.

"I was just thinking. We might be overlooking a potential problem. If this Gaggii has learned how to manipulate the web, and he knows that you located him before by using it, he might plant something to ensure that it doesn't happen again."

"Fine time to bring that up." Moody joked to cover his unease. "Y'all are assuming he's learned enough to pretty much do what he wants with it. I don't buy that. If that was the case, we'd have heard something by now, because he as much as told us that he's got it in his mind to do something noticeable."

"You don't call the conjuring up of Endless Snake noticeable?"

"He did that to deal with a real threat in real time. Maybe he's learned enough to use the web a little bit, but I don't think he's had time enough to learn how to prevent others from doing the same. Until Paul and I dropped in on him, he didn't even suspect anyone else knew of its existence."

She considered, still watching Ooljee at work. "I hope you are right."

Moody straightened, watching his partner carefully. "Well, we'll know in a couple of minutes, won't we?"

The access sandpainting appeared on the zenat. Ooljee approached, made the necessary adjustment with his right hand, and stepped back as the image gave way to the coruscating infinity that was the web. Nothing leaped out of it to attack him. Nothing suggested that access was now in any way restricted or forbidden.

Ooljee didn't hesitate. "Have you recently been accessed by the individual Yistin Gaggii?"

"Yes," came the prompt reply.

The sergeant glanced with relief at his companions, addressed the zenat again. "Where did this occur?"

"Near the place Shungopavi."

Samantha Grayhills was puzzled. "That's on Hopi lands. What's he doing there?" Seeing the confusion on Moody's face, she explained, "The Hopi lands sit in the middle of the Navaho territories, like a square hole in a square doughnut."

Ooljee queried the web anew. "Does he have a destination?"

"He is going to the place Cameron."

Grayhills' confusion deepened. "I wonder why Cameron? As I remember it, there is nothing there except a few tourist facilities and a Northern Arizona University science extension."

But Moody saw the possibilities immediately. "Mollys!

Webwork. He's looking to replace the equipment we've denied him.''

She sounded dubious. ''Not unless he's easily satisfied. There's nothing fancy up there. It's all typical university facilities. Pure research stuff, no heavy-duty analytic equipment.''

Moody looked disappointed. ''Nothing else?''

''Just administrative offices and labs. Mostly geology and high-energy physics. Not my department, really. I saw a short vidpiece on NAU last year. It mentioned the extension.''

''But no intense mollyware?''

''Sorry. Nothing more than they need for local support. Cameron itself is a tiny town, an academic outpost.''

''Maybe that's not his final destination.'' Moody regarded the compliant zenat. ''Maybe he's just going to be passing through. What else is in the area?''

''There's the main NAU campus down in Flagstaff. It's home to the biggest network between L.A. and Albuquerque.''

''Now, that makes sense. We need to alert the security people there, and get the local police to organize a cordon.''

''Maybe we can find out what he is up to.'' Ooljee looked back at the screen.

''Do you know what Yistin Gaggii is going to do in Cameron? Is that his final destination or only a stop on his journey to somewhere else?''

''I do not know,'' replied the vocomposite, ''because he does not know himself.''

''That makes no sense,'' said Moody. ''Ask it again.''

Ooljee complied, the web replied. ''I cannot divine purpose.''

''Well, that's real helpful.''

''Unless one of you can think of a better question, I am going to turn it off,'' Ooljee told them.

Moody had no new ideas. He watched while his partner

ran through the shutdown procedure, relaxed when the screen was once more dominated by the familiar harmless lines of the Kettrick sandpainting.

The security door was unsealed and a lieutenant stuck his head through the opening. He did not look especially happy. Moody sensed other bodies crowding close behind, trying to see inside.

"Everything okay in here?"

"Everything is fine," Ooljee assured him.

"The lights and work stations upstairs have been going nuts. What are you working with, anyway?"

"This." Ooljee picked up his machine. "Department spinner. Mine, as a matter of fact. You can see that."

"Yeah, I can see that. I just do not want to see the department's electric bill for the month." He backed out. As he shut the door behind him, Moody could hear him arguing with unseen people out in the hall.

Ooljee moved to cut the power, paused at Grayhills' gesture. "Leave it on. It's pretty, and it's nice to be able to study it on a big screen. You can see the details better." The sergeant shrugged, clipped his spinner to his belt.

"I don't know much about sandpaintings." She stared at the monitor. "Just what every kid on the Rez grows up hearing, along with whatever other traditional lore your parents decide you should know about."

"That's more than me," Moody reminded her.

"I know more about them than I want to." Ooljee took a seat with his back to the monitor.

"What's that part there, left of center?" She pointed at the painting. "The part with all the birds."

Ooljee gave his partner a look, turned resignedly.

"That is one portion we have been able to identify. Its full name is 'Scavenger Being Carried Through the Skyhole by Eagles and Hawks Assisted by Snakes with Bird Power.' As you can see, it is very complex even for a sandpainting. It comes from the Bead Chant.

"Now over there," he said, pointing, "you might expect to find something related, but as near as I have been able to determine, that has something to do with the Red Ant Way. Up near the top of the painting is an excerpt from the House of Moving Points. It is as if a painter decided to take bits and pieces of different Ways and slap them all together in one place, linked by devices of his own design, without rhyme or reason. Except that in this case the use of yellow sand is just such a hidden device."

Grayhills rose and approached the monitor. Moody followed, curious; watched as she traced a portion of the image with a finger.

"What is this House of Moving Points?"

Ooljee scratched the back of his head. "Remember, I am a cop, not an academic. This is just a hobby of mine. As I recall, within the chant it is used to invoke the aid of Nayenezgani, or Monster Slayer, in relation to . . ."

"It makes me think of Cameron," she said, interrupting him.

"You think there's some guy named Nayenez Gani working in Cameron?" Moody asked sharply.

"No, no." Her irritation could not completely subdue her smile. "I thought of Cameron because of the high-energy physics research facility there. According to the vid-piece I saw, the university had just finished installing a Möebial toroid particle accelerator on the north end of the campus. The piece talked about what an ideal location it was, since the entire installation had to be underground and the rock around Cameron is totally devoid of moisture."

Moody thought hard. Particle accelerator? House of Moving Points?

"C'mon, not you too. It's bad enough part of this damn painting tells you how to access some kind of alien web-work. Now you're trying to tell me another part describes a *particle accelerator*?"

"I didn't say that," she told him. "But maybe your man Gaggii believes that it does."

"It is something. It makes sense. Perhaps he is after information he cannot get from the web." Ooljee oozed optimism. "He won't get there quickly. The roads between Shungopavi and Cameron are not the best, and there is good reason to believe he is keeping to the back country."

I thought this whole part of the state was back country, Moody thought to himself. "Even so, he's got one helluva start on us."

Again Grayhills directed their attention to the image on the monitor. "And this part here is Scavenger being lifted through a skyhole?"

"Assisted by eagles and snakes with bird power, yes." Ooljee traced the image with a finger. "Sometimes twenty-four eagles and hawks, usually forty-eight. I've never seen a sandpainting this complicated. Maybe that was what attracted Mr. Kettrick to it. Notice the lightning guardian, here." He pointed.

"And over there," she continued, "is the House of Moving Points. A particle accelerator? Or something else?" She took a deep breath. "Tell me about Scavenger."

"Legend says he goes around picking up discarded things."

Moody looked sharply at his partner, recalling Gaggii's alien garbage analogy.

Grayhills was drawing metaphors and analogies like an artist, all of them rife with impossibilities. What kind of scenario was she trying to sketch in their imaginations? He stared at the sandpainting, striving to comprehend its mysteries. Each grain of sand was a dot that had to be connected to another dot to form a complete picture. They only had bits and pieces to work with. It was akin to building a plane without the engines. It looked like something, but when it was finished it just sat there and wouldn't go.

Ooljee went for the phone. "I am calling a cutter. We

will get to Cameron before Gaggii. As to what he is after, we'll ask him—as soon as we take him into custody.''

"What," Moody wondered aloud, "would this guy want with a particle accelerator? It ain't like he's after a plane or a free-state mollyblank.''

Grayhills looked thoughtful. "Maybe it has something to do with this Skyhole legend.''

"You can't shoot holes in anything with a particle accelerator.'' Moody hesitated. "At least I don't think you can. I don't know kudzu about physics, but I follow the news. All an accelerator does is throw particles you can't see against other particles you can't see, to make more particles you can't see half as well as the original ones, right?''

"I'm no physicist, either. But then, what you usually do with a sandpainting is look at it, not use an extract from it to access some incomprehensible alien web. If you can do something out of the ordinary with one device, why not with another?''

Moody found himself hoping that Gaggii was simply insane. If he was working with real purpose, with a specific goal in mind, it raised a specter far more chilling than that of an ordinary madman running amok.

Ooljee hung up, looking satisfied. "Skycutter is on its way. It's a Flex, the fastest transportation I could wheedle out of the department. They balked at first, but gave in when I invoked the NSI's good name on our behalf.''

"We taking backup this time?''

Ooljee shook his head impatiently. "No room on the Flex and we want to get there well before Gaggii. Any help we need we can recruit in Cameron. There is an NDPS office there and the university's own security people can help. Gaggii's description will be all over the town and campus in ten minutes.''

Grayhills was apologizing as they entered the elevator that would carry them to the VTOL pad on the roof. "I should know more about my own heritage, but when you're trying to keep pace with the latest advances in interfacing spherical database security, it's hard to find time to study what you learned as a kid. Is there anything else you can tell us about this Skyhole legend, or the House of Moving Points? Anything that might give us a hint about Gaggii's plans?''

The sergeant muttered a mix of English and Navaho as the lift ascended. "If I think of anything, you will be the first to know. I keep trying to tell you I am no expert in these matters. It's only a hobby with me.''

"Don't keep selling yourself short," said Moody reprovingly. "I don't think there are any hatathlis running around with degrees in criminology, either. Thanks to you, we've made some connections. We'll make more.''

I'm just not sure I want to, he thought worriedly. He felt as if he'd stepped off a hyperatmospheric shuttle into a deep, dark well. Now he'd been falling for so long, he was afraid of what would happen when he finally hit bottom.

He glanced surreptitiously at his partner. *It must be a lot harder on him*, the detective mused. *Assisting on a murder investigation, only to end up haunted by his own heritage. At least I don't relate to a lot of this. So it doesn't scare me.*

Then he remembered the mutaphysical projection Ooljee had called Endless Snake and decided it was all right to be scared.

CHAPTER 18

MOMENTS AFTER THE elevator deposited them on the roof next to the landing pad, the skycutter arrived, its rotors sending red dust flying. There hadn't been time to brief the pilot. Ooljee filled him in as the streamlined craft ascended and turned westward.

Despite their speed, it would take them a while to reach Cameron, which lay on the opposite side of the Reservation, more than a hundred miles from Ganado. It would take Gaggii a lot longer.

Ooljee was on the cutter's radio as soon as they were airborne, lighting a fire under the NDPS office in Cameron and the security department at the university. Both would plug Gaggii's description and vitals into their dayboards. Without volunteering specifics, the sergeant requested that security around the accelerator facility be enhanced. Anyone demanding an explanation was told to go through Ganado channels.

He did not request that added roadblocks be set up between Shungopavi and Cameron, for fear of alerting Gaggii and scaring him off. The last thing they wanted was for their quarry to bolt the Rez. This time there would be no slip-ups, no mistakes, no underestimating their man. The instant they had him back in custody, he would be stripped naked and conducted to a holding facility where he wouldn't have access to anything more electronically sophisticated than a wall socket.

Once safely clear of the towering artificial canyons and buttes of the city, the pilot configured the skycutter for high-speed flight. The rotor blades retracted to a third of their former length, while the engine slid down its guide slot until it was facing backwards between the two rear-wing supports. It roared with full power, driving the craft forward instead of providing lift. Their speed doubled despite a substantial headwind.

There was no commercial traffic to slow them. Transcontinental flights stuck to higher altitudes, allowing Klagetoh Control to vector them straight to Cameron. The cutter could bypass the town's VTOL port and land right on the university grounds, saving time and worry.

Moody peered down through the glass at a land dominated by immense table-top mesas and sloping canyons. Scrub and individual trees staked out individual plots of soil, each competing warily with its neighbors. God had spent so much time preparing the ground here, he mused, that He'd grown tired and left without finishing the landscaping.

Grayhills was gazing at the back of the pilot's seat, seeking inspiration in bruised vinyl. "The answer's in the sand-painting somewhere," she was mumbling to no one in particular. "Maybe he's not interested in the accelerator. Maybe House of Moving Points refers to chemistry instead of physics." She leaned forward. Ooljee sat opposite the pilot.

"Isn't there anything else you can tell us about the Scavenger story?"

"You've seen the painting." Ooljee turned in his seat to look back at them. "Scavenger was supposed to live at a place called Whirling Mountain. It was one of the gates between Earth and the home of the Holy People." He looked at his partner. "A sandpainting itself is called *ikah*, which means 'the place where gods come and go,' referring to their spiritual abodes.

"Such gates are common to many cultures. In Tibet they think the city of Lhasa is such a place. In Italy I suppose many believers would point to the Vatican. Geography that is spiritually as well as temporally tangent. Such concepts are not easy for some people to understand."

"Imagine where that leaves me," Moody murmured.

Ooljee continued. "The eagles gave the snakes bird power so they could help raise Scavenger, who ascended through the skyhole wrapped in a black cloud to shield him from his enemies. Lightning and rainbows, which signify power, guard the design."

"Rainbows." Grayhills traced lazy designs on the back of the pilot's seat. "Jagged lightning. Black clouds. Does that suggest anything to either of you? I mean, you two have been studying this sandpainting for weeks, solely with an eye toward catching a murderer. Stand back a little and try to view it from a different perspective."

Moody's expression knotted as he realized what she was driving at. "I've crossed the peninsula a few times to visit the Kennedy Center and watch a couple of launches. Nothing major; just weekly orbital station resupply flights. But even the small ones make an impression." He stared at her. "Lightning. Black clouds ascending. Bursts of multicolored light. Birds flying every which way. Maybe not all hawks and eagles, but birds. That's not a bad description of the scene at a liftoff. Is that what you're trying to get me to say?"

She didn't reply, simply met his gaze evenly.

Ooljee looked back at him, wincing as the skycutter impacted a pocket of inconsiderate air. Moody didn't think his friend liked flying.

"The Anasazi made good pots. They built substantial dwellings. They wove baskets. But to the best of my knowledge no launch facilities have ever been discovered at Keet Seel or Awatobi.''

"That might also be true of whoever left this web behind," Moody pointed out, "so maybe they used something else instead. Something different."

"One hatathli's rainbow is another's stream of photons," Grayhills suggested. "Jagged lightning as force field, black cloud as exhaust. The sandpainting we're discussing isn't about frogs and the four sacred plants. Analogies can be drawn here, gentlemen, that are no more farfetched than what we know to be real. The eagles and hawks could be suggestive of something else, or they might actually be representative of birds disturbed by a liftoff. Or a landing."

Moody's thoughts were racing now, and try as he might, he couldn't rein them in. "How do the snakes fit in?"

Grayhills sagged a little. "I admit they don't make any sense to me, and they're central to the design."

"They may be descriptive of something we have not yet imagined." Ooljee stared at his partner, his fingers tightening on the back of his seat as the skycutter bounced through a cloud. "We are in over our heads again, my friend. We need more help." His eyes darted to Grayhills. "No offense."

"None taken, but you could call in the entire advisory staff of the National Academy of Sciences and it wouldn't do any good. By the time you could assemble and brief them, this Gaggii will likely have accomplished whatever it is he has set out to do. I haven't been here very long, but you two already have me thinking like a cop. Let's catch him first. Then we can turn the business of interpreting the sandpainting over to a properly accredited committee so I can go back to debugging mollys and you can go back to catching ordinary rapists and crazyboys.

"Until then we are faced with the reality of this web, so why should we not also be willing to allow the possibility of ancient visitation by spaceship? If you grant that, you can also envision a few surviving Anasazi turning whatever knowledge they may have acquired from such visitors, either by intent or accident, into sandpaintings and chants. Ways that have almost but not quite been forgotten.''

''I wonder what else our hypothetical visitors left lying around?'' Moody tried to see past the pilot. ''Paul's told me that more than five hundred distinct sandpainting designs have survived. No telling how many have been forgotten. I wonder how many others contain templates?'' He swallowed hard.

''I'm with Samantha on one thing, though. I still don't see how the snakes fit in. If we're envisioning some kind of craft taking off, everything else makes sense. But not the snakes.''

''Maybe they were the passengers,'' she suggested.

Moody found the image thus sparked unpleasant to contemplate, coming as he did from the tropical South, where snakes of any kind were automatically treated with caution.

''Unlikely,'' said Ooljee. ''The Way is clear on that much. The snakes helped Scavenger to rise through the Skyhole. He was the passenger, not them. Still, who is to say how accurate even a hatathli's interpretation is? For example, there are many words in the chants which cannot be translated. Words whose meaning has been forgotten. Interesting to imagine what some of them might really be describing: webs, visitors, strange machines.'' He was silent for several moments. ''So much of our tradition is oral; so little written down.

''Our legends say that this world is only one of five. Other religions mention but a single world. Why do the stories of our forefathers describe four others? They are real places in legend. Might they also be real places in space?

''The People traditionally regard space as unbounded. We allow room for growth, adaptation, reinterpretation of ideas old and new. Just what you might expect of people whose ancestors were forced to cope with the appearance of strange beings from another world.'' He tapped the spinner clipped to his service belt.

"It is traditional to combine new powers with the old. Why not sandpaintings and chants and computer webs? What troubles me are those legends which speak of the universe as a very delicately balanced place, full of immensely powerful forces for good or evil. You would say beneficent or malign. If this balance is upset, even unintentionally, all kinds of terrible things can happen.

"You recall that I spoke of *hozho*.'' Moody nodded. "It is interesting that tradition insists only man can upset that balance.''

Moody mulled it over. "That could be the warning the visitors left behind with their garbage. Like the skull and crossbones on a can of poison.''

"Or it might refer to something entirely different,'' Ooljee argued.

"How do you fix the universe if somebody like Gaggii knocks it out of kilter?''

"I'd think you would know the answer to that by now, my friend. You restore *hozho*, balance, by performing the right Way.''

"Wonderful.'' Moody leaned back in his seat and crossed his arms over his chest. "Hey, I got it. Gaggii's committed two murders. By catching him and putting him away where he can't bother anything ever again, don't we restore balance? The DA's office will think so, anyway.''

"You grasp the concept, my friend.'' Ooljee was amused. "I hope that is all it will take.'' His smile faded. "Something else: if certain conditions and behavior are repeated with precision, prior events can recur accordingly. Say a sick deer wanders down a certain path in ancient times. Today another deer takes the same path, at the same pace. Traditionalists believe that the first deer's sick confusion can enter the mind of the contemporary one and it will become ill or disoriented in the manner of the first.''

"What are you driving at?" Grayhills asked him.

"Nothing." The sergeant loosened his death-grip on the back of his seat. "Only that if Gaggii uses the web to reiterate some kind of ancient alien schematic, a traditionalist would expect any occurrence relevant to that schematic to also repeat itself. Tradition insists that a precisely determined set of conditions should always produce precisely the same effects at a later time."

Grayhills pursed her lips. "Sounds like causality to me. I thought we were discussing traditional Navaho medicine, not quantum mechanics."

Ooljee shrugged. "A rose by any other name."

"What kind of 'relevant event' should we be on the lookout for?"

"I have no idea. But it might be a good idea to keep an eye on the sky."

Moody involuntarily glanced upward, only to note when his gaze fell that his partner was grinning at him. That Navaho sense of humor again.

"If we run into any large black clouds descending on bolts of lightning and rainbow pillars, you'll be laughing out of the other side of your face."

"I do not expect that to happen." Ooljee repressed his grin. "I am just telling you what the old legends say. As we have seen already, some of them have turned out to be true in ways not previously imagined. We cannot rule any possibilities out.

"Keep in mind that the Universe is affected by what is good, which in Navaho means that which is under control, and that which is evil, which is anything out of control. Right now it is Gaggii who is out of control, not the web, not something we have yet to put a name to. Perhaps you are righter than you think, my friend. Maybe we catch Gaggii, maybe we do restore *hozho*. Not to mention complying with contemporary criminal procedure. I don't have any trouble with that."

"Hang on!" the pilot called out to them. "Might be a little choppy coming into Cameron. I'm starting down."

Moody had plenty of time to think as he checked his harness. The flight from Ganado had left him more uneasy and confused than he'd been before. His mind swarmed with unbidden images of strange craft inhabited by alien creatures, of refuse dumped just outside reality, waiting to be gathered up by a garbage truck that was a thousand years behind schedule.

Someone had watched and waited while that garbage was being dumped, the way a cat waits for its chance. Or maybe that nameless Anasazi or Navaho had been instructed by a visitor with unknown motives on how to sift through the pile. By one means or another, the knowledge had been handed down and passed along for a thousand years, its purpose forgotten, until Yistin Gaggii had learned how to interpret the symbols, had rediscovered how to access that which had been left behind.

Moody found that he was furious with the long departed visitors. Leaving behind something as awesome as the web without proper instructions or warnings was akin to dropping a pocket nuclear device in a schoolyard. If Ooljee's traditions were to be believed, they might be blindly poking and prodding at something just as lethal.

They might never know *exactly* what it was, he thought nervously, unless it went off.

What if Gaggii banged on it hard enough, or shook it violently enough, or in some other way upset its *hozho*? He almost preferred to think of giant snakes wriggling their loathsome way out of attenuated starships. Were those sinuous shapes simple embellishments which had been added down through the centuries by imaginative hatathlis? Or did they somehow really relate to the sandpainting's greater purpose?

Snakes. What else was unto a serpent?

If the web *was* equipped with a warning, how would they

recognize it if they did encounter it? They might have missed it several times already. *"This is what we have left behind and this is what it does—but don't do it or it will remove your face."*

If Gaggii was similarly concerned, he'd chosen not to say so to his visitors. That was another reason why they had to catch him before he could proceed with whatever it was he had planned: no fool is so dangerous as a fearless one.

What bothered Moody more than anything else, he decided suddenly, was not whether the visitors had left the web behind on purpose or out of forgetfulness, but that they might have done so indifferently, not caring one way or the other how it might impact on a miserable bunch of primitive bipeds. The one thing Moody hated more than anything else was to be ignored.

"It is funny to think of it now," Ooljee murmured as the skycutter bounced through an airstream, "but the chants and sandpaintings described to us as children were *always* designed to deal with powers beyond human control. I never thought that one day I might have to consider that proposition literally.

"We must not just think of this web as dangerous. The hatathlis like to say that what can harm a man can also cure him. Bad things can be controlled and put to good use, just as the good can be turned to evil."

"The precision of it appeals to me," said Grayhills. "The idea of using specific sandpaintings and repeated chanting to achieve a desired result. But I still don't see how chanting and touching the image allows one to access the web."

Moody was the first one out when the skycutter touched down. A small multiwheeled vehicle started toward them from the edge of the landing pad.

Ooljee was right behind him. "Consider this," he said to Grayhills. "A number of studies make the claim that sandpainting images are really interpsychic symbols. Some academics think that the reason sandpaintings allowed the old hatathlis to cure diseases was because they literally created a pattern in the patient's psyche—whatever that means."

Moody didn't try to understand what it meant, now that they were out of the skycutter and back on solid ground. He did find it interesting, though not surprising, that the entrance to the accelerator facility faced the east.

Not only did the chief of campus security operations doubt anyone could break into the installation, he wondered why anyone would want to.

"Even if they could sneak inside," he explained as he parked outside the three-story structure, "they could not do anything. You do not operate a particle accelerator by pushing an 'On' button. It takes the skills of a number of highly trained technicians just to set up an experiment, much less run one."

"We're not arguing with you." Grayhills exited the little electric bus. "We just want you to understand that we're dealing with someone who is responsible for a number of unexplainable incidents, and we don't want him doing unexplainable things to your accelerator."

That got his attention. "The only other Möebial toroid accelerator in the country is at North Carolina," he announced importantly. "We don't want anybody monkeying with ours any more than you do. And you claim that your suspect is not a mental case."

"Not insofar as we have been able to determine." Ooljee flanked the security chief as they walked toward the entrance. "He may not be able to make use of your facilities here, but we want to make sure he doesn't do any damage, either."

"Don't worry. There aren't many entrances, our alarm system is as up to date as the accelerator itself, I've put extra people on because of your warning, and most of the really sensitive machinery is located below ground level anyway. Every access point not personally supervised by one of my people is scanned by closed-circuit vid.'' He smiled confidently.

"Every once in a while we have to deal with students who think slipping inside and draping toilet paper or something over the equipment is outrageously funny. They always get caught, and we have some clever students at this outpost. Our security approaches military specifications. I think that if your Mr. Gaggii comes anywhere near our installation, not only will we be able to detect his presence, we will be able to catch and hold him for you.''

Moody wished he could be as confident as the security chief. But then, he reminded himself, the man had not seen what Yistin Gaggii could do with the alien web.

The above-ground portion of the facility housed administrative offices, labs, supply rooms, and monitoring equipment. The inwardly sloping spraystone walls were painted brownish-pink to blend in with the surrounding terrain, while the windows were copper-tinted glass. As they'd been told, there were few entrances.

Moody was gratified to observe that the one they used was covered by both monitoring vids and live security personnel. Everything was calm and normal, as they'd requested. Obvious precautions like partial evacuation of the campus, for example, might frighten off their man.

Administrators, graduate students, and techies were coming and going, actively discussing subjects incomprehensible to the detective. Navaho, Hopi, Apache, Hualapai, Havasupai; Anglo and Asian; Hispanic and Black, none of them aware of the existence of the alien web all around them, through which they passed as smoothly as sharks through saltwater.

Once the right people had time to study it properly, he mused, the existence of the web might explain a lot of things. Ghosts and poltergeists, all sorts of supernatural phenomena might be related to accidental or partial accessing of the webwork.

The ghosts in the machine. He tried to remember where he'd encountered the phrase. What might they not find when they went fishing in those warm alien depths?

As Gaggii was doing, he reminded himself. What was their murderer after? What did he hope to find there? He'd told them he had something specific in mind, but had neglected to fill in the blank. Did he want to shake hands with a ghost? Or was he after a discovery that would make him rich?

Any of those ends could be gained by working out in the open, without the need for secrecy and murder.

He knows more than he told us, Moody decided. Twenty years of police mollywork insisted on it. *We should have pressed him on his goals when we had him, should have demanded to know what he was after. More than just knowledge, surely. Knowledge is an abstraction, and people no longer kill for abstractions. Only nations do that.*

His partner's tales of Holy People and gods kept creeping into his thoughts. Could Gaggii be doing the bidding of something inside the web?

Abruptly aware that he was letting his imagination run riot, he forced himself to admire the spacious lobby, with its impressively realistic artificial rain forest and soapstone sculptures of relevant fauna. He was quite content to let his partner do the talking to the cluster of security people and NDPS uniforms who were waiting to greet them. The latter would patrol a designated perimeter, while the locals would see to the security of the facility itself.

The accelerator occupied a circular tunnel large enough to also include a narrow underground roadway. Electric carts transported scientists and security personnel along the same path down which the accelerator propelled selected bits of matter, allowing quick and easy access to every part of the machine. There was no reason to post people in the tunnel, the security chief explained, because the above-ground access ports were tightly locked and watched over by CC vid.

Anyone talented and stupid enough to actually make their way inside would find themselves trapped underground.

All duty personnel had been provided with holomages of the suspect. There was no way he could hope to approach the facility unchallenged, much less get inside. The security chief was very positive. Ooljee and Moody allowed themselves to feel hopeful, if not assured.

Building Security became their base of operations. One entire wall of the room was lined with monitors, one for each vid installed in the facility. Moody alternated his attention between the multiple screens and the nearby snack vending room, while Ooljee hovered near Grayhills and tried to pick up a few orber's tricks as she wove with her elaborate Noronco spinner.

Nightfall found them tired and irritable. Of Gaggii there was no sign. Moody wondered if he had fooled them utterly by instructing the web to respond with false information to any inquiries concerning his whereabouts. In which case he might be halfway to Salt Lake City or Denver by now, while they squatted here relying for information on a mendacious alien vocomposite. It was possible. Gaggii was far more familiar with the web than they and had demonstrated that he could make use of it. What kind of relationship had he established by now with that mysterious melange of mutating Mandlebrot patterns and rainbow threads and incorporeal coronas?

And who was Vernon Moody, late of Pushkatawny, Mississippi, that it should fall to him to have to try and figure it all out? How did a good cop stake out the impossible?

They waited and watched and grumbled until the clock came round to the cold black dawn of early tomorrow, and still there was no sign of their suspect.

He should've shown by now, Moody knew. *Unless he's stalled somewhere out in the mesas, or had a breakdown, or changed his mind, or been laughing at us all along, while he went east, or north, or south instead of this way.*

Initial anticipation had been dissipated by the uneventful night. Day staff had made way for the night-watchers, who had already passed enough time in front of their multitudinous monitors to grow bored.

The visitors from Ganado did not allow themselves that luxury. They hung around Building Security, making themselves obnoxious by their continuing presence while sustaining a wary consciousness with coffee by the liter.

"We blew it." Moody gazed bleary-eyed at his friend and colleague. Nearby chairs displayed the debris of late-night snacks. Security personnel sat at their stations, ignoring the suspect visitors in their midst. Grayhills napped on one of several cots which had been set up against the back wall.

"Not necessarily." Ooljee rubbed his face. "It might be a matter of timing."

"What kind of timing?"

The sergeant scrutinized the flotsam on the chair next to his, extracted something yellowish from the center of the pile, and began to munch on it.

"A chant is usually performed in two parts over a period of two, five, or nine nights. The first part involves purification and the exorcism of evil. In the second, supernatural powers are attracted and *hozho* is restored."

"Or disrupted," said Moody.

His friend nodded. "The final night's vigil lasts from ten o'clock until the dawn of the concluding day."

"What happens then?"

"The one who is being treated supposedly breathes in the dawn, at which point he or she becomes one with the gods and shares their power."

"I get it. What happens if the god doesn't feel like showing up?"

"They have no choice. If the chant and sandpainting are done right, the deity is compelled to attend."

A sleepy feminine voice chimed in. "You don't really

believe that timing has anything to do with accessing the alien web?''

''I do not know what to *really* believe anymore.'' Ooljee stuffed the rest of the yellow mass into his mouth, chewed reflectively. ''Until this, I thought I knew what police work consisted of. I thought I knew what a computer web did and how a database was structured. I thought I had a pretty good idea of the world and my place in it.

''Now I am no longer sure of much of anything. Nor do I understand how either of you can be otherwise. These past several days we have seen things to give a man pause. So who is to say whether timing is or is not important in these matters?''

His partner was not only tired, Moody decided; he was clearly on edge. Sandpaintings and hatathlis and chants were part of his heritage, his environment. He'd grown up with them. Now the world of his childhood was being turned inside-out in front of his eyes.

It is always hard when reality intrudes on belief.

Nevertheless he couldn't keep himself from asking, ''Paul, you don't think this guy's trying to call up some kind of alien deity or something?''

Ooljee was silent for a long time. When he replied it was slowly and carefully. ''Be they purposeful, careless, or indifferent, it seems to me possible if not likely that there are others besides humans involved in this business. Whoever created the web and left it here, whether for reasons unknown or for no reason at all. Whether we choose to call them deities or aliens or yeis or Martians or whatever, they existed. We know they existed because the sandpainting exists, because the web exists. They were here a thousand years ago. We know that they *were*. We do not know if they *are*.

''What Gaggii works with the web I do not know.''

''A long time to wait between calls.'' Grayhills sipped hot tea. She did not drink coffee, Moody had noted. No

basis for a relationship there. He was startled to discover
that he had been contemplating one.

"Truly," the sergeant agreed. "Yet the web has endured
all that time, waiting for someone to rediscover the secrets
of the sandpainting, waiting for someone to again use the
right Way. It is still active and functioning. Why should
we assume those who created it are not also active and
functioning somewhere?"

"If it's garbage it won't be much good for making long
distance calls," Moody pointed out tiredly. "You know, if
Gaggii hadn't killed two people I wouldn't give a frog fart
what he does with the web. Maybe he's just after some
peer-group recognition. Wants to win the Nobel."

"I do not know what he wants, my friend. Like anyone
else, I can only guess. All I know is that the more I contemplate my own mythology, the more frightened I become."

Dawn brought light but no sign of Yistin Gaggii. The
rest of the long day was equally unrevealing. Evening found
Ooljee and Moody swapping catnaps while Samantha Grayhills stuck to her routine of alternating sleep with periods
of observation and study.

Their suspect had effectively vanished.

Moody suggested to Ooljee that they query the web again
as to their quarry's whereabouts. Ooljee declined, pleading
exhaustion. Tomorrow. He would try again tomorrow.
Maybe Gaggii would show before then, or perhaps an NDPS
patrol would stumble into him and save them the trouble.

As the second night spent in the accelerator facility ticked
away uneventfully, both men retired early in hopes of soak-
ing up some extended sleep. The cot Moody had been al-
lotted was barely wide enough to accommodate his bulk.
He tossed and turned fitfully, conscious of the fact that his
partner was resting soundly nearby. Conscious of that, and
something the sergeant had mentioned earlier.

Consider sandpainting drawings as intrapsychic symbols.

Lighting up inside a person's mind. If that were true, a trained patient could just as easily visualize the necessary symbology as a trained hatathli. Do away with the painting altogether. Do away with the chant. Do away even with a spinner.

Think it. Visualize it. Activate the web by thought alone. Was that how its makers did it? If the web offered a possible explanation for sightings of ghosts and poltergeists, then why not for other fractures of the mind as well? What about certain kinds of mental illness? Had those sufferers unknowingly and accidentally accessed the web? Wouldn't finding oneself confronted by, or perhaps even immersed in, an endless void inhabited by only twisting, writhing shapes and forms be enough to drive anyone mad?

True that such accidental accession was unlikely. But impossible? Was anything impossible anymore? As any country kid knew, there were all kinds of ways to get into a garbage dump. Even dumps that were posted and guarded. If the web was everywhere, then it stood to reason it could be accessed from any place.

His thoughts raced onward, out of control.

What if we're all, billions and billions of us—man, woman, and child—just tiny bits of walking, talking, thinking RAM? Components of the web. We're not accessing something separate and distinct; we're accessing ourselves. All you needed was the proper pattern, the right timbre in your voice. Call it metaorganic parallel processing: human and web, web and human. Side by side, working together. I, the Web. For what? The same questions applied to man that applied to the web. Was there a purpose involved, or was it all just garbage?

And in the center of the web, manipulating the Mandlebrot patterns of the universe and electrotactile Endless Snakes and me and thee and your Uncle Charlie, what? Something vast and unconcerned, cosmically indifferent? And why not? Since when does an operator worry about his bytes? He doesn't empathize with his database; he just switches it on and off.

He woke up drenched in sweat, the cot creaking beneath him.

CHAPTER
19

ON A HILL north of Cameron, Yistin Gaggii greeted the sun as it sucked the chill from the morning air on the Moenkopi Plateau. Four-legged shapes watched him emerge from the motor home. They had not slept because they did not need sleep. They had difficulty merely comprehending the idea.

Gaggii had not slept either. The night had been spent in preparation. He stretched and inhaled deeply, feeling no different save for a tingle of anticipation.

The track that led down into the little valley was narrow and treacherous, but the motor home would make it. He had come this way before. Without a word to the unblinking canine faces surrounding him, he turned and reentered his vehicle. The engine started smoothly.

Moody woke from a dream not of vast emptinesses between the stars or rainbow threads and tentacles of unfathomable purpose, but of fishing from the back of a flat-bottomed boat moored to the mucky basement of a cypress tree. The sun was warm and damp on Florida Bay and the solar cooler in the bow was stuffed with sandwiches and cold beer. It was the best of all possible worlds.

When wakefulness came, he resented it deeply.

The room was full of talk. Ooljee was sitting on the edge
of his cot, trying to rub the sleep from his eyes. He saw
his partner eyeing him.

"You have not missed anything. Yet."

Moody nodded, rose, and checked the location of his fly
and his pistol. A partition had been erected to separate the
temporary sleeping quarters from the rest of the room. Inspection introduced them to a dozen newcomers; a couple
of techies, university security people, NDPS officers. He
looked for Grayhills, didn't see her.

People were clustering around an elderly guard. He was
leaning against a wall for support. Someone thrust a cup of
coffee into his hands and he drank gratefully. His hands
were shaking and some of the brown liquid slopped over
the sides, staining his uniform.

Moody fought his way forward, undiplomatically nudging
people aside, and spoke to the NDPS officer nearest the
trembling guard. The corporal looked alert and competent.

"What happened?"

The younger man nodded at the senior. "This guy just
came in. He was patrolling the tunnel when he was attacked.
He *says*." There was doubt in the young man's voice.

Ooljee confronted the elderly paladin. "Was it by any
chance a tall, hatchet-faced man about my age?"

The guard was too shaken to speak, so the corporal replied
for him. "He claims it was *mah-ih*."

Ooljee stared at the trembling oldster. "He says he was
attacked by a *coyote*?"

The corporal nodded. "Says it went right for him and he
had to shoot it. Three shots and it kept coming, but his taser
put it down."

"Coyotes keep their distance from people." Ooljee was
studying the elderly guard's face. "They'll come right up
to a house looking for a dog or cat to snatch, but they avoid
human beings. Unless this one was rabid."

"Oh, it was rabid, all right." Everyone looked at the

guard. "Crazy for sure." He drained the last of the coffee.

"Did you check for that?" Ooljee asked him.

The man straightened, not trembling as badly now. "I was a cop in a Flag for thirty years. I've worked security here for the last four. I know ninlocos and sneak thieves and purse snatchers. I'm not a veterinarian."

"I thought all the entrances to the tunnel were sealed," Moody said.

One of the onlookers spoke up. "A coyote might find a way in that a human would overlook."

"That's right," commented a techie. "No matter how often we spray, we still have trouble with rodents in the conduits. A coyote that managed to find a way in could make a living in that tunnel."

This wasn't what they'd been expecting. Moody thought furiously. If it was just a burrowing coyote . . .

"Somebody find Samantha Grayhills, the lady who came with us, and get her down here. If she's sleeping somewhere, wake her up." A guard tech swiveled in his seat and picked up a phone.

"Maybe someone ought to have a look at this coyote," the corporal suggested.

"Maybe we ought to stay right here." Ooljee was staring intently at the wall of monitors. "If our friend Gaggii had a diversion in mind, this might be it."

"You think maybe he shoved that coyote in there?" Moody mulled the idea over. "How could he do that without showing up on vid or setting off an alarm?"

"I do not know."

"None of the alarms were tripped," said one of the monitor operators. "Not one. Anyone entering the tunnel would have been seen."

There were three operators, two men and a woman, seated at the monitor bank. Moody regarded each in turn.

"Nobody went out for a sandwich or anything?" If anyone had, he didn't expect the guilty party to confess to it.

He'd been through this sort of thing before, in Tampa. Leaving one's post while on duty could result in swift termination of one's job.

The corporal wouldn't give up. "You don't think we should go and check the carcass?"

"Leave it," snapped Moody. "If it's just a dead coyote it's a matter for the custodial staff, not us. If it's something else, you don't want to go running after it." His eyes narrowed as he studied the guard. "You said you fired three rounds at it before you used your taser?"

The guard looked up at him. "That's right."

"Any of them hit?"

"Couldn't say. I didn't take the time to find out. I had three shells in my gun and I used them all. I might've hit it, maybe not. But the taser stopped it cold. It ought to, as many volts as that thing puts out, and it was set to deliver full charge."

That was when the graduate student came running in. She rested one palm on her sternum as though it could somehow pump extra air to her lungs. Her expression was wild.

"I think—I think somebody better come with me."

The corporal tried to calm her. "What's the matter, miss?"

She was trying to speak and swallow at the same time.

"I—found a man near where I was working. I think he's dead."

The corporal glanced at Moody. "Want to check *this* out?"

Moody ignored the sarcasm. "Be right behind you. Oh, and can my friend and I get a couple of those tasers?"

The tiny armory was opened and weapons removed from their chargers. Thus additionally armed, the three officers followed the student to an elevator.

"You sure he's dead?" the NDPS man asked the girl as they descended.

"I think so. I'm pretty sure."

Moody thought she was handling herself well. Where the devil was Grayhills?

They found the corpse of the security guard outside a maintenance alcove on the lowest level of the complex. As the graduate student simultaneously hung back and tried to see, the three officers clustered around the body. Moody was "pretty sure" he was dead, too. His head lay bent at an unnatural angle and his throat had been torn out. Ooljee bent to examine the wound, cursing softly in Navaho, while Moody held tight to the taser. He didn't like tight places and he didn't like being below ground.

Ooljee carefully pried the gun from the dead man's fingers and removed the clip. He held it up so everyone could see. "Empty. Barrel's still hot." He eyed the shadows and the dark places between pipes and tubes uneasily. "This didn't do him any good."

"Any ideas?" Moody asked the corporal.

"The guard said he was attacked by a coyote. What do you think?"

"I don't know what to think." The detective looked over at his partner. "How in hades do coyotes fit into this?"

"Who can say?" Ooljee straightened. "According to legend, all things, all creatures, have some power and can be controlled with the right chant. If this was done by a coyote, then something new has been added to the equation."

"Are you trying to tell me," Moody sputtered, "that our buddy Gaggii has learned how to hypnotize a bunch of coyotes into doing his dirty work for him?"

"We do not yet know for certain that Gaggii is involved in this." Ooljee gestured at the body. "But I believe I can be excused for thinking of him whenever anything unnatural happens, and this is certainly unnatural. Draw your own suppositions from what you see, my friend. All I am saying is that someone who can produce a manifestation of Endless

Snake''—the corporal looked at him sharply— ''might not find it impossible to manipulate a few animals.''

''Yeah. But that snake-thing wasn't a real animal. It was a manifestation, like you said. Something from out of the web. Maybe our 'coyotes' are more closely related to it than to Lassie. And if that's the case, maybe it's why this works on them''—he held up the taser—''and bullets don't.''

Ooljee considered. ''Our guns were useless against the snake-thing. Shells passed right through it.'' He drew his own taser, eyed it thoughtfully.

''This delivers a violent electric charge. Enough to kill a real coyote—or disrupt a circumscribed electromagnetic field?'' He looked at the corporal. ''I think it would be a good idea to issue tasers to all your people.''

At that moment the howling began, a single high-pitched, mournful wail ending in laughter. It sounded like a human trying to imitate a coyote, which is just what a coyote sounds like.

The song was picked up by another throat, then another, and another, until the depths of the complex resounded with the diabolic chorus. The four humans drew together for protection, the terrified graduate student huddling close to Moody's protective bulk.

''He's inside the building,'' Moody insisted, trying to see everywhere at once. ''I don't give a hound's dump what anybody says about monitors and alarms, he's in here somewhere.''

''Who is?'' The corporal studiously avoided looking at the body at their feet.

''The guy we're after. Gaggii.'' He glanced at his partner. ''The web was right. This was where he was headed all along. He just took his time getting here.'' The awful howling echoed around them. ''That's a helluva noise for a 'circumscribed electrical field' to make.''

"Maybe it is not him." The corporal sounded more hopeful than convinced.

"Sure," said Moody tersely as they moved in a body toward the elevator. "A pack of rabid coyotes having nothing better to do just decided to invade the only particle accelerator in Northern Arizona and rip out the throats of the people working there. Or maybe they want to enroll."

"Coyotes," Ooljee pointed out, "are very unpredictable."

Moody shot him a look. "So is Navaho humor." He was greatly relieved when they finally reached the elevator.

The door slid aside. The girl moved to enter, stopped and screamed. There followed a mad moment of intense confusion, panic, and firing. But the guard had told the truth. The tasers worked. When hit with them, the canine shapes vanished in showers of coruscating sparks.

The howling reverberated throughout the complex, wild and unabated.

Ooljee looked at his partner as the four humans crowded into the elevator. "Did you see their eyes?"

Moody studied the ceiling. He was breathing hard. "Man, all I saw were their teeth."

"They were not natural. They glowed. There was something there besides coyote life."

"What is it?" The poor graduate student held her fingers steepled below her lips. "What's going on?"

"A bad dream," Moody told her.

The howling was as loud at ground level as it had been below. Security was beset by confusion if not outright panic as techies and officers bustled about, wondering what to do.

The arrivals from the basement tried to fill them in. Tasers were issued to as many people as possible, with explanations being put off for another time. Nonessential personnel were evacuated from the building.

Samantha Grayhills was there to greet them. While Ooljee tried to explain what was happening, Moody stalked over to the monitor wall and addressed the operator in charge.

"Anybody sees our man, they shoot him on sight, understand? That's the order. We've got another murder victim downstairs and we can't play games, no matter how much I'd like to question him."

The operator was a solid, prosaic woman in her forties, but she looked shaken. "Can you tell us what is going on? Has every coyote on the plateau gone crazy?"

"I don't think these coyotes are from around here." Moody left her more confused than ever.

Ooljee had overheard. As Moody rejoined him he said, "You may be more right than you realize. They are *yei-tsos*. Evil beings. They do not even die like coyotes."

Moody gazed at the corridor. People were rushing to and fro, some of them to take up assigned positions, others hurrying to get out of the building.

"Whatever they are, he's controlling them somehow. We're not gonna find out how until we find him."

"*Yei-tsos.*" Samantha Grayhills said the word several times, as if repetition might add reality, might make it a part of the real world.

Behind them the monitor operations supervisor uttered an exclamation of disbelief. Moody rushed to lean over her shoulder.

"What now?"

"Look at this! This is crazy." Techies and security personnel crowded around.

The accelerator was coming on line.

One of the techs mirrored her astonishment. "There aren't any experiments scheduled until next week."

Moody ignored him. "Can you shut it down from up here? Can you turn it off?"

"This is Security, not Engineering, but—"

Moody, Ooljee and Grayhills were already on their way out the door. Central Engineering was a short sprint down a side corridor. The skeleton operations crew on duty there was careening toward panic.

Telltales and readouts glowed like ornaments at Christmas time. Every screen in the room was brazen with stats that refused to be ignored. Techies fumbled with spinners and boards like clumsy children suddenly handed complex puzzles.

A tall woman in her fifties fluttered from one station to the next, waving her arms wildly like a sandhill crane in the throes of its mating dance.

"Don't give me that," she was shouting at a harried member of her staff. "You *can't* power that up without going through here!" Turning, she noted the arrivals from Security. "Do you people have any idea what is happening to my accelerator?" Moody recognized her tone, familiar to him from endless wiretap transcriptions.

"Just an idea," Ooljee told her.

"Well, you have to stop it. Now. Immediately."

"You can't?" Moody asked her.

She started to snap at him, then caught herself. Maybe it was his attitude, maybe his size. "What do you think we've been trying to do?" A hand flailed in the direction of the nearest console and its baffled operator. "Everything is powering up, nothing is shutting off, and our backups and fail-safes might as well be out for repair. And what is that noise outside?" Even within the room the invaders' eerie chorus made itself known, though it was in danger of being drowned out by the rising whine of machinery coming on line.

"He is using the web." Ooljee glanced through the window at the corridor beyond. "That must be how he is bypassing this place."

"So we can't stop him?"

Grayhills stepped forward. "Apparently not from running the accelerator, but I don't see anything to keep us from pulling the plug."

The chief engineer glanced sharply at her. "Don't you think we've tried that?"

Grayhills stood her ground. "Sometimes a switch isn't the best way to deactivate a recalcitrant device."

Moody and Ooljee left in a hurry, gathering up the NDPS corporal and two plainclothes on the way. Grayhills eyed the engineer.

"What's your current study setup?"

The woman hesitated, then replied laconically, "We've been working with Z-particle collisions, but that was two weeks ago." She forced herself to look back at the screens. "Why would anyone want to take control of the unit? There's nothing on line, no experiment to run."

"Maybe the man we suspect of causing this has another use for some runaway protons."

The engineer shook her head violently. "A Möebial toroid accelerator doesn't work like that. You don't just fire it up and dispense protons like candy!" Her nails dug into her palms. "All this can do is ruin some very expensive machinery."

"I don't think that's what he has in mind." Grayhills studied a readout.

"Then what *does* he have in mind?"

"I wish I knew. I wish I knew," she muttered.

"Outside, by the south end of employee parking!" The corporal led the way as they exited the building. One of his men jogged anxiously alongside.

"Sir, if we're gonna disconnect lines, we ought to have somebody from APS do it. They'll have a truck and authorization."

Moody glared back at him. "Son, we can't wait for the local utility company to show. Our job *right now* is to keep the man we're after from making use of this facility." He looked at the corporal. "I'll take full responsibility."

"You can't," the younger man declared. "You're from out of state."

"When your boss wakes up, tell him I insisted. Tell him I threatened you, if you want. It'll get y'all off the hook."

The corporal nodded somberly. They could worry about it later. He'd seen too much already to argue with the two cops who'd flown in from Ganado. If they thought it necessary to shut down the power to the accelerator facility, he'd damn well help them to shut it down.

The column of heavy-duty concrete power poles ran from a corner of the main building along the southern curb of a large parking lot. Like a spider clinging to its nest, the transformer attached to the last pole spun a net of heavy-gauge wires into the facility.

"What now?" The corporal looked at Moody.

The detective reached into his coat and removed his pistol. Bracing himself, he took careful aim at the transformer. The NDPS plainclothes who moments ago had voiced reservations as to this course of action backed away.

"Oh, no. I am not taking any part in this."

"No one is asking you to." Ooljee drew his own weapon, pointed the barrel at the transformer.

"This is unauthorized destruction of university property," the man added weakly. He glanced at his superior, who shrugged.

"Tell it to the dead guy in the basement." Moody jerked his head at the building. As he did so, something caught his eye and he lowered his gun. "Jesus Mary." His companions turned with him.

The entire structure was enveloped in a pale, nacreous effulgence redolent of St. Elmo's fire.

Clouds were gathering overhead, much more rapidly than clouds had a right to, even in this part of the world where sudden, violent thunderstorms were commonplace. As they stood watching numbly, rain began to fall; a steely, freezing mist. The temperature in the parking lot was not falling: it was fleeing.

"Too much time talking." Ooljee grunted, whirling to take aim with his gun.

His first shot missed, the second struck one of the insulators atop the pole. Moody stood next to his partner, firing steadily and methodically. One insulator after another exploded under the impact of the high-power shells. Spitting sparks, lines began falling to the pavement.

"That should do it," Moody murmured as the last cable fell from the smoking, crackling transformer. He turned.

The installation still blazed as if it had been doused with phosphorescent paint. If anything, the diffuse, boreal light was brighter than before.

More significantly, the internal lights had not gone out.

Moody eyed the corporal accusingly. "There's an in-house generator, comes on in emergencies!" He had to raise his voice to make himself understood above the brisk wind which had sprung up around them. It drove the cold mist sideways into their eyes and mouths.

The officer shook his head, using one hand to keep his cap steady.

"Goddamn him!" Moody glared at the building as if it were personally responsible for the present situation. "He's getting power from *somewhere*!"

"The web." Ooljee turned and started back toward the building. "This is no good: we have to find *him*."

CHAPTER 20

LIGHTNING FRACTURED THE sky. Thunderstorms were common in Florida, but Moody had never seen one of this intensity coalesce so fast. He did his best to keep up with Ooljee and the others.

The corridor that led to Engineering was deserted. All nonessential personnel had long since fled the structure or been evacuated. Lights gleamed everywhere, though they flickered with each flash of lightning. Machinery hummed smoothly, defiantly. Moody felt like a puppet, and didn't like it.

Gaggii was here somewhere. They would find him, he thought grimly. An instant later he was reminded that their man hadn't come alone.

There were three of them, loping up the ramp from the first subterranean level. Big, fast, and snarling all the way, their eyes burning like shards of a bad dream. One managed a good snap at Moody's face before the pins from Ooljee's taser decussated its field, sending it flaring into oblivion. The detective had time to note that their attackers had no odor.

They stumbled into Engineering. Moody concentrated on

catching his breath while his partner and the harried corporal did all the talking.

"We shot out the lines. There shouldn't be any power to this building," Ooljee declared, "much less to the accelerator. We do not know where it is coming from."

The chief engineer gestured. "It's sure as hell coming from somewhere. Emergency generator read's off."

Grayhills joined Moody. "So Gaggii is having his way in spite of us."

"It is more than just this installation." Ooljee looked over at her. "I think whatever he is doing is also affecting the weather. The storm outside came up too fast. What really scares me is that he may not know what he is doing."

Moody lumbered forward, his eyes roving the banks of readouts and monitors. "There's got to be a way to shut this thing down. Some critical components we can disable."

"You don't know what you are suggesting," said the engineer. "You don't have any idea what a facility like this costs."

"You tell us where to start," Moody replied emotionlessly, "or we'll pick a spot and begin disassembling at random. The result will be the same. Only not as neat."

She met his gaze briefly, then dropped her eyes and let out a resigned sigh. "Come with me."

On the way they were attacked twice by intruding *mah-ih*. One plainclothesman suffered a bite on the arm before the corporal blew his assailant to oblivion with a blast from his taser.

They descended two levels via open stairways, not trusting the elevators. Not with Gaggii in control of the building's power supply. While the others stood guard, the project's chief engineer set to work with an assistant in the bowels of the machine. As they removed a protective panel, exposing circuitry and delicate processor cubes, the unearthly howling rose in pitch around them.

The flickering lights made it difficult to see. Moody

squinted at shadows, searching for low, loping shapes, his taser clutched tightly in one hand. He muttered urgently at his companions.

"Hurry it up!"

Already furious at what she was being forced to do, the chief engineer yelled back at him. "This isn't a bathtub, young man. You don't drain it by pulling a plug."

The detective tried to put a rein on his impatience. Gaggii might already have gotten what he was after anyway. Whatever the hell that was. Ooljee's remarks about the universe being a delicately balanced, easily upset place kept haunting him. Was Gaggii playing around with that somehow? And if so, why? If they had learned one thing about Yistin Gaggii's character, it was that he liked, even needed, to be in control. It followed that he would do everything to keep from losing it.

Somehow that was small consolation.

In a moment of candor he'd confessed to them that he had a specific goal in mind. Did he know how to achieve it? Or was he simply seeing how far he could push what he'd learned?

The whine that reverberated through the lower level of the facility reminded him of a shuttle just lifting off, of a wave rolling in from Africa, which, finding no beach to break upon, kept crashing and tumbling in upon itself, the very picture of kinetic frustration.

Ozone tickled his nostrils, burned his eyes. Strobing lights distorted his vision. He thought he could see shapes advancing. Not coyotes. Coils and loops of light, violent neon, gaping auroras with sparks for teeth. The plainclothesman on his left cursed and fired, struck nothing. You couldn't shock a reflection, a trick of the eye. No dragons roamed the service corridor, no demons occupied the depths of the machine. Blurred images of vast tentacular shapes and ambulatory geometrics were no more than the hallucinatory offspring of tired minds. The toroid accelerated heavy particles, not dreams.

Here there be nonsense, he whispered silently. *Get ahold of yourself. All lawbreakers thrive on confusion. Gaggii's no different. Don't give him that.*

The two engineers worked silently, applying their tiny and insignificant tools to the vaster instrument that was the accelerator. From their position they were unable to see the howling phalanx of buff-colored shapes that came snarling up the corridor. One of the cops turned to flee. Moody grabbed him by the arm and yanked him back. "Hold your ground!" he roared. "Use your taser!"

Then everyone was firing madly at the onrushing *mah-ih*. Coyote bodies exploded in fountaining sparks and blinding light. Moody found himself ducking and whirling as he tried to avoid teeth and claws, cursing the several seconds the taser's battery needed to recharge. Nor did it matter how many he and his companions obliterated. The survivors pressed on relentlessly, as if delighting in their own destruction.

"Got it!" The triumphant shout came from behind him, not from the battle line.

Almost immediately the whine of the toroidal accelerator began to fade. The chief engineer emerged from the service bay, cradling a rutilant cylinder of metallic glass. The lights in the corridor ceased to flicker as emergency power came on line. Their comforting steady glow banished the *mah-ih* and companion nightmares from sight.

Moody rose from his crouching position, the taser hot in his palm. Officers and techs eyed one another uncertainly. The chief engineer handed the cylinder to her assistant as carefully as an obstetrician passing a newborn to its nurse.

The howling was a memory, the only noise in the corridor the hiss of the lights and the automatic space heaters.

Moody pocketed his weapon. "That's it, then. We stopped him."

"I wonder." Ooljee tilted his head back to gaze groundward, two flights above them. "We have seen some things down here. I wonder what Grayhills has seen up there."

They used the elevators this time. As Moody emerged he happened to glance through a corridor window. It was now sleeting outside. Lightning twisted and cracked through boiling black clouds, millions of volts with no place to go. He was reminded of sandpainting patterns.

Grayhills was not waiting for them. She was seated at an engineering station, weaving in tandem with the young tech next to her. Moody observed the performance, admiring their technique much as one would that of duo pianists.

She sensed his presence and paused long enough to look up.

"We stopped it," he told her.

"I know." She indicated her companion, who grinned shyly at the detective. "Little Bear and I have been trying to determine what happened. There was heavy particle acceleration to near light-speed within the toroid, but no result we can measure because no target was emplaced."

"So what happened to the particles?" Moody asked.

"We do not know." The young tech blinked. "They went someplace. We do not know where. Since they did not collide with a preset target, they must have collided with particles somewhere else. Unless they were aimed at something located outside the toroid." He blinked again.

"Is that possible?" Grayhills' gaze narrowed.

"Theoretically. It is never done, because it would be impossible to monitor the results properly. And there is no guarantee the particles would not strike others before reaching an external target, thus invalidating the experiment. I cannot imagine why anyone would want to do such a thing."

"Unless they want the result of the experiment to remain a secret," Ooljee pointed out.

The chief engineer had been silent long enough. "This is madness! You don't throw heavy particles around like cookie crumbs. If they escape the confines of the accelerator, there's no way to track their paths.''

"There's something else," said Grayhills. "It's this storm. We've been in touch with the National Weather Service office in Flagstaff. A low-pressure system just materialized, right here. No front, no occluded lows. The bottom just fell out of the barometer over Cameron.''

"Gaggii," said the sergeant. "Whatever he is doing is affecting the climate. We have stopped the accelerator, but the storm continues. He is doing something, wherever he is.''

"All I know is that the NWS says this is an abnormal weather system, that its effects are highly localized, and that it's not moving. It's just sitting here on top of us.'' Tired, she leaned back in the swivel seat and closed her eyes.

"I don't know why he activated the accelerator, or how he managed to enlist those coyote-things to help him. I don't know if this crazy storm is related to his activities or not. Accelerator, coyotes, storm: I can't put those three together any more than I can pull a rabbit out of a hat. But that doesn't mean Gaggii can't.''

A phone clanged, dissonant in the charged atmosphere of the room. The tech who answered nodded slowly as he listened, then passed the handset to the corporal. Moody watched his expression change from one of frustration to one of confusion. He hung up and stood staring off into space for a long moment, then turned to face the detective.

"That was the security kiosk at the eastside parking lot. They need advice. There's something they think should be checked out.''

"We're busy here.''

The young man shook his head slowly. "No, I think we ought to have a look at this. I don't want to, but we probably should.'' His tone was that of the hunter chosen to leave the cave and confront the saber-tooth.

Puzzled, Moody and Ooljee followed him out, leaving Grayhills and the tech to their weaving.

No burning eyes, no fiery otherworldly shapes leapt from dark corners to confront them. Nothing impeded their progress as they hurried toward the back of the building.

They slowed in the hallway that led to the parking lot exit. Outside, sleet continued to whiten the pavement, the half-ice spending itself violently against the wide, tinted windows that looked out on a field of cars and minivans and trucks. Farther to the east, transport traveling the north-south two-lane highway was slowing and pulling off the road. Tugging jackets and shirts tight against the sleet, drivers and passengers were leaving their vehicles to stare at what had materialized in the gravelly soil just beyond the graded shoulder.

It was big. Men in uniform were lined up alongside it to gaze at the people gathering below them. At this distance Moody could not see their expressions, but he doubted they could be any less astonished than his own. He had very good eyesight and was able to see the name on its front, but he could not read it, since it was written in a script unfamiliar to him.

The corporal surprised him by translating. The words meant nothing.

The two men from Ganado left the members of the security staff standing dumbfounded in the blowing sleet. Not a word was spoken until they'd returned to Engineering.

"It is a mistake, an error on Gaggii's part," Ooljee murmured as they entered the busy room.

Moody brushed moisture from his shoulders. "It's getting out of hand. I'm beginning to get some idea of what you meant when you spoke of messing around with incomprehensible forces."

Eyes followed them as they entered. Grayhills came over to them and put a hand on Moody's arm. It was a good thing she did so, or the spellbound detective might have walked right through the back door and out into the next corridor.

"I take it you saw something."

He started to tell her, hesitated. How could he explain? It was not an explainable thing. Instead he said, "Can you patch us through to the university library molly? Not the one here: the main one, in Flagstaff."

She eyed him curiously. "I don't see why not." Her attention shifted to Ooljee, who had slumped in a chair nearby. "Why?"

"We need to check out a name," Moody told her.

"A name? What name?"

"The name of a ship."

She shook her head, her confusion deepening. "I don't understand."

"Y'all have lots of company. Be a good gal and run the patch."

Watching him carefully, she resumed her seat and jacked the request. A moment later he found himself confronting an open library prompt. He entered his request and awaited a response, which appeared within the minute.

Ooljee rose to peer over his shoulder. Several techies left their stations to see what all the fuss was about.

As the library patiently informed them, "the destroyer *Akitsuki*, while escorting the heavy carrier *Zuikaku*, was hit and presumed sunk by American aircraft on the morning of October 25, 1944, during the battle for Leyte Gulf, Philippine campaign, WWII."

"Except it didn't sink." Moody muttered aloud. "It went someplace else. Now it's here, outside. In the high desert."

Grayhills turned to Ooljee. "What is he talking about?"

"Out past the parking lot." The sergeant nodded eastward. "A Japanese destroyer from the Second World War. At least some of the crew is still aboard, no doubt wondering what has happened to them. I imagine the majority of survivors are huddled below, praying to whatever gods they prayed to in those times.''

''That's *crazy*.''

''I have no intention of disputing you.'' His expression narrowed. ''The codetalkers.''

Moody blinked, looked at his partner. ''What?''

''Navaho codetalkers. An important part of tribal history. We all learn about them in school. During the second great war, before mollys, all the governments looked for ways to transmit messages that the enemy would not be able to understand. When Navahos joined the American forces, someone thought to station one at each important position. The codetalkers concocted a goofy, personal version of our language. Strange as it seems, the enemy was the Japanese. They never could figure out what kind of code the Americans were using. It wasn't a real code; just mixed-up Navaho.''

''I don't see how that explains that ship outside.''

''The alien web. Some codetalkers must have hit on the right phrasing. Momentarily and accidentally, but enough to access something in the web. Or maybe,'' he added, his voice dropping, ''Great-grandfather Laughter decided to try and make use of his sandpainting knowledge, and this ship ran into some real hatathli magic which yanked it right out of the Pacific and into . . .''

''Strange seas and shores,'' Moody finished for him, ''until our friend Gaggii started playing with the web. Now they're back home—sort of. Wish I spoke Japanese.''

''It can't have been deliberate on his part,'' Ooljee observed. ''He is just stumbling around in search of his own ends.''

Moody eyed his partner. ''You're gonna have to use the template again, ask the web where he is.''

The sergeant was dubious. ''I'd rather not. Each time we access I get the feeling I am going to do something wrong, or that Gaggii will finally have figured out how to insert a

safeguard to cover his tracks and we will all end up like the
men on that ship. Or the building we are in will materialize
someplace else, or maybe the state of Arizona. I do not
want to have to wait on someone to 'accidentally' bring us
back a hundred years from now.''

It was an image impossible to avoid: the whole state,
with all its rivers and cities and mountains and people,
suddenly extracted from reality as neatly as a child would
cut out a piece of map. And why just Arizona? Moody
thought. Why not all of North America, or if Gaggii wasn't
careful with his parameters, the entire planet? Earth shunted
to an obscure corner of an alien database, just another
insignificant byte of data in a web large enough to include . . .

What? How vast *was* this web they'd stumbled upon?

Maybe that's all it was. Just a big database devised by
whoever *they* were. He could feel himself beginning to lose
it, and Vernon Moody, Detective First, TPD, *never* lost it.
But the scale, the immensity, the apocalyptic indifference
of it all, was starting to get to him.

He could see it clearly: galaxies as directories, subdirec-
tories of individual solar systems. Within one subdirectory,
little files. One of a place called Earth, or however it was
labeled. Tiny subfiles for plants and animals and human
beings. Subfile for individuals: Vernon Moody, Paul Ooljee,
Samantha Grayhills, Yistin Gaggii. Infinitesimally minus-
cule bytes easily accessed by anyone who knew how to use
the web. Garbage files.

What was Gaggii after? Surely not something as incon-
sequential as a means for protecting or enriching himself?
No, Gaggii would want to know how to run the subfile
labeled ''mankind.'' Or perhaps his vision was grander.
Perhaps he hoped to discover how to access an entire file.
Press ENTER here and shift the planet a little nearer the sun
(maybe Gaggii was easily chilled). Or move it next to another sun, for a change of pace. Gravity, the speed of light:

suddenly these little constants no longer meant anything. Not when you could access the web and braid yourself a custom Julia pattern here, a Mandlebrot there, and shift yourself into the subdirectory coded Alpha Centauri.

Moody shivered. How could you go on, with the foundations of your reality become as insubstantial as gossamer? Time, space, speed: meaningless. Qualitatively irrelevant. Who punched in the entries up there? God? The aliens? Navaho Holy People with unpronounceable names?

Pain flicked across his face. He blinked at a worried-looking Samantha Grayhills. It took him a moment to realize he'd been slapped. Ooljee stood nearby, equally concerned.

"You were laughing," she said seriously, "and we couldn't get you to stop. I'm sorry I had to hit you."

"I wouldn't do it," said Ooljee. "Thought you might react instinctively and flatten me. What were you thinking about that made you do that?"

Moody hesitated, finally announced brusquely, "Nothing. Nothing important.

"What we have to do now is concentrate on what we can understand. Because if you look at this thing too hard, you lose your focus real quick. Let's just work on Yistin Gaggii. He's a murderer and we're going to take him into custody. That's all we need to worry about."

"I've been thinking." Both men turned on Grayhills. She didn't back down under their stares. "If he's at the center of everything that's been happening, then he also might be at the center of this impossible storm. Pinpoint the nexus of the low-pressure system and we might find him there. If it's over Vegas or Bullhead City then we can try something else, but if it's as close to here as the National Weather Service suggested . . ."

"Give 'em a call," snapped Moody.

She nodded, resumed her seat at the console. "I'm on it."

Ooljee whispered to his partner while they waited. "I

know what your problem is, my friend. You think too much. Especially for a cop.''

"What if the people who built this web left their own safeguards behind? What if Gaggii accidentally stumbles into one of them? You think it's gonna deal with him selectively?'' He smiled crookedly. "Try 'not' thinking about thinking about *that* for a while.''

"Nothing is intrinsically good or evil,'' the sergeant told him. "It is all in how you use it.''

"That really reassures me,'' Moody replied sarcastically. "I'll remember that when Arizona is sinking in the middle of the Indian Ocean.''

"If such a safeguard exists, it may be clearly labeled.''

"You think that'd stop our boy Gaggii? He's come too far to quit now. He'd try getting around it. No, we've got to get our hands on him before he can make any *serious* mistakes.''

"I do not think,'' Ooljee said quietly, "that Yistin Gaggii wants to move the state of Arizona to the middle of the Indian Ocean.''

"Naw. He just wants to make himself President. Or Emperor of the planet.'' The detective glanced down at his partner. "We're gonna have to kill him to stop him. You know that, don't you? Because of that damn unreal boat outside. If some hatathli codetalkers made that happen over a hundred years ago, it means you don't need a monitor or spinner to access the web. All you need is the right words, the right phrasing. It means you can't stop Gaggii by locking him up. You couldn't put him in a hole deep enough to keep him from making mischief. So we have to kill him.''

Ooljee waited a moment before replying, but not for the reason Moody thought. "I think you are right, but that does not solve the problem.''

"How so?''

"What about me? I know the chant. I know the sandpainting.''

Moody eyed him sharply. "What about you, Paul? You tell me."

"I have a fine woman who loves me. I have two wonderful children. I have a job that I like in a place that I like. I have fulfillment. I do not want to be emperor of anything. More importantly, I want as little to do with this business as possible. That which grants power can also take it away. Let specialists who can watch over one another delve into its depths. Let them stumble across any safeguards that may have been left floating in its innards.

"I am no hatathli. If we destroy the remaining images of the sandpainting it will be a long time before anyone stumbles across its secret again. Perhaps never."

"Never." Moody nodded, pleased. "That sounds like a decent length of time. Never, yeah." The terrifying, indifferent emptiness of the universe receded a little, bearing some of the fear he felt with it.

"Don't you wonder?" Ooljee asked him. "If the code-talkers are responsible for what happened to that ship, don't you wonder what else might be floating around in the web?"

"Make you a deal," the detective said curtly. "I won't think so much if you won't wonder so much."

Grayhills had information. "The center of the low is only forty-five miles north of here. South of the gap at Cedar Ridge, somewhere between the highway and Marble Canyon." She looked back up at them. "It's still fixed, not moving."

"Real close." Ooljee checked his gun. "He did not have to come into town to get what he wanted. Let's go. We have a killer to apprehend and a storm to stop. Among other things."

The two men exchanged grim grins.

CHAPTER
21

THE SKYCUTTER PILOT was reluctant to take them up, did so only because Ooljee pulled rank. Like a cork in a whirlpool they bobbed through the clouds, the flight smoothing out only a little when the pilot dropped the rotor and headed north.

Wind rocked them wildly, while the lightning was frequent and heavy enough to extract prayer from confirmed atheists. Though the wipers battled the driving sleet to a draw, the pilot chose to concentrate on his instruments in lieu of the view ahead. There would be no welcoming landing beacon where they planned to set down.

Grayhills assured the pilot that a visual sighting would not be necessary. All he had to do was follow his falling barometer.

Moody's stomach rose and fell in concert with the Flex. He hung on and tried to think about something besides his heaving guts.

Their pilot was a short, wiry, somber-faced youth in his early twenties. Too small for the street, too tough to be stuck behind a desk. As he studied his console he raised his voice to make himself heard above the brutal wind.

"Been flying four years. I've tracked people according

to standard police reports and civilian call-ins. I've trailed vidwits and run spiral searches. Once I blew a suspect armed with a surface-to-air into a ditch where ground cops could pick him up easy. But this is the first time I ever tracked anyone by barometric pressure.'' He tapped the lens protecting a readout. "Look at this damn thing! Twenty-eight point nine-five and still dropping. I've never seen it so low.''

A blast of wind and rain drove the skycutter sideways. The pilot fought for control, cursing the storm and Ooljee in equal measure. He didn't ask questions, because he couldn't spare the time.

Moody clung to whatever part of the cabin was fastened down. Despite her harness, Samantha Grayhills kept bouncing into him, a sensation he would have enjoyed at any other time. From his seat alongside the pilot, Ooljee leaned forward and tried to see through the horizontal weather.

Maybe while trying to track the barometer, fight the storm, and weather the up- and down-drafts, the pilot took his eyes off his radar for an instant. Or perhaps it was because they seemed to be flying one foot back for every two they advanced. In any event he suddenly let out a yell and wrenched the wheel hard over as the butte loomed in front of them.

The skycutter slued sideways. A coarse grinding groan came from its belly as they struck, bouncing once. The pilot tried to shift the rotor to hover, but it was too late. Wind and pressure finished what the initial impact had begun.

The carbon-fiber composite blades splintered like lengths of frozen carpet. One shattered against the Flex's armor glass inches from Moody's face. Only the fact that they were already on the ground saved them. That, and the skill of their angry pilot. In the vids Moody had seen, aircraft crashes always went on and on, long minutes of metal screeching against pavement or stone. In reality, only seconds elapsed between the first contact with the ground and total cessation of movement.

He slipped free of his harness and helped Grayhills extricate herself from her own. "You okay?"

"No, I am not okay. My neck is killing me and my chest feels like someone's been using it for an anvil. But I don't think anything's broken."

Ooljee was kicking open the door on his side. Moody's gaze shifted to the pilot, who sat slumped in his seat, his head lolling.

"Harness did not keep him from denting the console." The sergeant reached over and put a hand on the pilot's chest, inside his jacket. "He will be okay. But he'll feel otherwise when he wakes up." A weight lifted from Moody's guts. He had a fondness for the young and reckless.

The door banged open to admit a blast of damp, cold air. *This ain't no place for a po' country boy from the South*, Moody told himself dourly as the wind whipped at the bare flesh of his face, licking him like a curious carnivore.

"We must be close," Ooljee announced.

"Why?"

The sergeant turned to face his partner. "Because I was looking at the barometer just before we hit, and I don't think it could have gone any lower. So we must be near the center of the storm."

"We don't gotta be near anything," Moody groused, in no mood to be told how things had to be. "If it was still dropping, then we were heading the right way when we went down, but that doesn't mean we're there yet." He indicated the unconscious pilot. "What about him?"

Ooljee considered. "When he wakes up and sees that we have gone, he will do one of two things. Either he will try and come after us, which would be really stupid, or else he will stay with his craft and wait for the storm to die down and searchers to home in on the emergency beacon."

"Wish we had that choice." Moody leaned toward the doorway, halted when he sensed Grayhills right behind him. "Where d'you think y'all are going?"

She made a face at him. "I haven't got time for any of that I'm-police-and-you're-civilian-so-this-doesn't-con-cern-you kind of thing."

"Give me one good reason why I shouldn't make you stay here?"

Bits of sleet clung to the long black strands of her hair like melting pearls. Bright eyes gazed evenly back into his own.

"Because I'm smarter than you, and that might prove useful."

The detective looked up at his partner. "What do y'all think, Paul? Is she smarter than me?"

"Oh, I do not think there is any doubt about it," the sergeant replied with a straight face. "Though whether that rates her coming with us is another matter. However, I do not want to debate the point. She is probably smarter than me also, so we would end up both losing the argument *and* wasting time."

They exited the downed aircraft, Moody wishing for a goose-down parka instead of the light-duty jacket he was wearing. Ooljee oriented himself and pointed. They headed west.

Moody noted that Grayhills was following close on his heels, using his bulk as a shield against the wind and sleet. "Don't y'all know that it's dangerous to follow a bear into the woods?"

"Not so long as you have a pretty good idea what he's going to do there." She grinned up at him, her cheeks rosy from the cold.

Was it intellectual curiosity that induced her to come along, Moody wondered, or like so many of the scientifically minded was she simply ignorant of the realities of real-life violence? As a percentage of the total population, scientists were the victims of muggings far out of proportion to their numbers.

Notwithstanding the wind and cold, he was glad to be

out of the skycutter. Better to walk. He suspected his opinion might change as the chill penetrated his light clothing. But staying in the downed Flex was an option neither he nor Ooljee had considered. They had to find and stop Gaggii as quickly as possible. That didn't allow for squatting around waiting to be rescued.

"Gonna have a helluva time finding anything in this," he announced to no one in particular as he plowed forward, keeping his head down and blinking moisture from his eyes. At least, he thought with some amusement, Grayhills was having an easier time following him than he was keeping up with Ooljee.

The sergeant called back from just ahead. "I think it is letting up!" The wind did seem to be dying a little, Moody thought. Sleet became rain, then mere drizzle. Maybe the ridiculous storm was moving on.

Abruptly—too abruptly—the drizzle gave way to a light mist. Then even that ceased.

He found himself standing on the edge of a rocky mesa, gazing down into a shallow canyon. A narrow stream meandered through this crack in the Earth's surface, running water over the millennia having etched away a frame larger than itself. The rim on the far side of the canyon was higher than the one on which they stood.

Moody turned a slow circle. Dark fog and rain hung like a curtain behind them, almost within touching distance. A circular rampart of cloud enclosed this piece of plateau, reaching toward the heavens. It was thus everywhere he looked. From within the clouds the wind called ceaselessly, but where they stood it was calm and warm.

"*Haal hoodzaa*?" Ooljee muttered. "What is going on here?"

"Leave it to a Florida boy to explain, though if I'd been offered my druthers I'd have picked something else to remind me of home." Moody kicked a rock over the edge, watched it tumble down the steep slope. "We're in the eye."

Grayhills stared at the towering clouds circulating about them. "Can't be. It's too small. The whole storm is too small."

"So it's small. It's still a damn hurricane."

"You cannot have a damn hurricane here." Ooljee reacted as if his denial might itself be enough to banish the outrageousness. "Hurricanes arise in the tropics. This is Northern Arizona, for God's sake."

"Sorry, but there's not much question about it. Classic form, down-sized. A mini-hurricane." Moody was unperturbed by his partner's objections. The storm was just sitting there, hovering above the little canyon with its seasonal stream, not moving at all, content to spin in place.

"More like a micro-hurricane." An occasional stray breeze ruffled Grayhills' hair. "What a meteorologist wouldn't give to be here to study the dynamics."

"He can have my place," Moody muttered. He felt like a bug stapled to the top of a champagne bottle, waiting for the inevitable explosion to blow him into the firmament.

There was more to the canyon than stream and isolated clumps of vegetation. Steam rose from hot springs near the center, close to a traditional twelve-sided hogan of rough-cut logs. The entrance to the structure faced east. Glass windows had been inserted in the stuccoed walls.

A large motor home was parked nearby, the satellite dish on its roof a miniature of the much bigger one mounted behind the hogan. Next to it stood a pyramid of twelve tracking solar panels. Cables ran from the motor home into the building.

Moody automatically drew his gun and dropped to a crouch, studying vehicle and structure. "He's in one or the other. Wish I had a small shapecharger. I'd put one in the motor home, another in the house, and we'd just walk away from the craters, storm or no storm."

"We cannot rush him," Ooljee whispered. "We do not know what sort of weapons he may have stockpiled in there, or may have brought with him." His eyes scanned the ground around the hogan. "There may be perimeter security, either passive or active. And there is something else." He pointed toward the hot springs.

Moody squinted, shrugged. "So he can take a hot bath if he wants to. So what?"

"There is another sandpainting. It deals with an entity named Big Monster."

"Nothing subtle about your traditions, is there?"

The sergeant looked over at him. "Big Monster lives at a place called Hot Water."

Moody sighed. "I'll bet the northern part of this state is full of hot springs."

"So it is. In fact, the San Francisco peaks near Flagstaff are said to have last erupted as recently as the eleventh century. There is plenty of activity."

"So this one reminds you of a sandpainting. So?"

"I would rather it did not. You see, Big Monster did not like Earth people. He destroyed them as fast as they were made. Until he was taken care of, the world was not a fit place for human beings to live in." He returned his attention to the view below. "I just find it interesting that Gaggii would choose a site close to a hot spring for his final refuge."

"Well I don't see any monsters, big or small," Moody growled. "I see a crummy little shack housing a murderer. I see—"

Grayhills interrupted him. She was staring, not at the hogan below, but across the canyon. Staring and pointing.

"What's that? Oh my, what is that?"

Moody looked up sharply.

It was just a tiny dark spot, a small speck of night against the ruddy talus. Except that it shone with an inner light, hanging in the air hard by the opposite rim of the plateau.

As they sat gaping, it expanded like a droplet of mercury on a sheet of glass, ballooning first a little in one direction, then another. Shining down through the eye of the micro-hurricane, sunlight gleamed on its surface as if it were fashioned of polished black steel. It drifted slightly to the south, then stopped.

When it had swelled to an oval the size of Ooljee's truck, it impacted the edge of the plateau. Sand, gravel, then larger rocks, began slipping from the rim directly above the object. When they reached the oval, they vanished. A small creosote bush was undercut and it, too, disappeared into the vitreous umbra.

"What the hell is that?" Ooljee whispered aloud.

Moody spoke without turning. "How should I know? Y'all are the expert on Navaho legend."

"That is a physical manifestation," the sergeant replied evenly, "not a religious one."

"The sonuvabitch has accessed something." Moody's fingers tightened on his pistol. "He's trawling in that damn web and he's snagged something new. Doesn't he give a shit?"

"He has killed at least two people and he tried to kill us," Ooljee reminded his partner. "I suspect he does not."

The blackness continued to expand. As they watched, a huge section of cliff broke free and tumbled into the disk.

And a wind was rising.

It came rushing down out of the sky, whipping past their faces, straight down into the eye of the swirling micro-hurricane like water dumped in a bucket. It blew by Moody's eyes, whispered in his ears; the sound of dust and pollen and bits of soil being sucked away. The disk was inhaling the Earth.

"Sheets of sky."

"What's that?" Moody spoke without turning, unable to take his eyes from the spectacle.

Ooljee sat in the dirt, his gun hanging loosely from his

fingers. "The gods drew on sheets of sky and traveled in ships that looked like black clouds. Remember the painting? 'Scavenger Being Lifted Through the Skyhole by Eagles and Hawks Assisted by Snakes with Bird Power.' We had an analogy for everything but the snakes, because snakes cannot fly. They burrow."

"Burrow." Grayhills stood staring numbly at the carcinomatous tenebrosity that had taken root on the other side of the plateau. "Rats, moles, gophers, worms. Worms. That's funny."

Once more Moody felt like the dumb fat kid in Mrs. Waterson's tenth grade science class.

"What about worms?"

She ignored him, spoke instead to Ooljee. "Snakes burrow. Worms burrow. Snakes also stand for lightning, don't they?" He nodded. "Lightning that burrows. It's only natural to think of spaceships when we try to envision a method of travel that involves lightning and black clouds. Natural, and wrong. Those old hatathlis weren't trying to describe a ship taking off. They were being much more literal. They were trying to describe burrowing." Leaves and twigs blew past her cheeks as her hair streamed toward the far side of the canyon.

"Will somebody tell me what the hell all this has to do with worms?" Moody pleaded.

There was a funny smile on her face. "The sandpainting shows snakes. Today we might use worms. It's all the same burrowing. I think the skyhole in your sandpainting is meant to be taken literally, not as a metaphor. I think Scavenger, whatever he was, didn't go up into the sky. He went through a real skyhole." Her gaze shifted once more to the steadily expanding ellipsis across the canyon. "Or as we might call it, a wormhole."

The faster he went, the farther behind he got, Moody reflected. "What is a wormhole?"

She shrugged, as if precise descriptions did not matter.

"Twisted spacetime. If you grab a cardboard tube at each end and twist it in opposite directions, and keep on twisting it, what do you end up with?"

"A busted cardboard tube."

"Eventually the ends become congruent. There are scientists who believe that if you could get a good grip on spacetime you could twist it like that, so that the two ends which originally might have been hundreds of parsecs apart would end up occupying the same space. You could step through this end and come out somewhere else, somewhere far away." She indicated the obumbrated disk.

"There's a causal boundary over there, a boundary attached to a spacetime that depends only on the structure Gaggii has generated with the aid of the alien web and the Cameron accelerator. A causal boundary, detective, does not distinguish between boundary points even at infinite distances."

By now the disk had taken a visible bite out of the cliff face opposite. It was no longer expanding as rapidly, but it continued to eat away at sandstone and soil.

"What you're saying," Moody said slowly, "is that whoever came avisiting this part of the world a thousand years or so ago didn't use any ships? They just dropped in through a hole in the sky?"

"What does he want with a wormhole?" Ooljee climbed to his feet, struggling against the wind.

"Maybe he wants to talk to whoever left their junk here. Maybe he just wants to say hello." Moody kicked at the ground. "Or maybe he wants to ask them some questions."

"Grand presumptions often lead to disaster," observed the sergeant moodily. "Ants do not ask questions of people who dump garbage, because if that attention is gained, such people are likely to exclaim 'ants!,' and reach for the bug spray or the swatter." He stepped over the edge of the cliff, began slipping and sliding awkwardly down the crumbling talus.

"Hey!" Moody followed, gallantly trying to aid Samantha Grayhills in staying upright.

The disk, the wormhole, the skyhole—whatever it was— had grown big enough to drive a truck through. Boulders and trees continued to slide into the caliginous void and vanish. Air howled around the three as they scrambled down the slope.

"Wait a minute, wait!" The two men slowed, looking back at Grayhills. They were halfway to the bottom of the canyon. "What if you're right and he has the place secured?"

"We have to stop him." Moody hefted his gun. "We can't just sit around and take in the show. We might not like the ending."

"There are other ways to stop him besides trying to put a bullet in his head."

"Maybe, but I happen to like that way."

"He might feel the same about you." She shifted her attention to Ooljee. "You've learned how to use the web to locate him. Why not use it to interfere with what he's doing?" She indicated the sergeant's spinner, which hung from his duty belt. "All the information you've acquired since this started is still in there, isn't it?"

Ooljee put his free hand on the device, licked his lips. He looked down at the hogan, then across the canyon at the circle of swallowing night. He was silent for a long moment. Then he straightened slightly.

"The built-in monitor's awfully small. Hardly enough to fingerprint on. And it is only a spinner. It's not mollyjacked."

"Mine is." She unclipped the expensive precision instrument slung at her belt, unfolded the top section into a foot-square screen. Moody admired it.

"Pretty fancy."

She grinned tightly. "You two are only public servants, whereas I'm charged with ensuring the security of large companies. Naturally they see to it that I'm supplied with the best equipment on the market.''

Ooljee eyed it uncertainly. ''But does it have enough storage to process the webware template?''

She handed it to him. ''Only one way to find out.''

The three of them knelt on the exposed slope, Moody trying to shield the two spinners as much as he could. Carefully Ooljee jacked the police spinner to Grayhills', watched as the screen came alive.

''What kind of molly you got in there?''

''Ten gigabyte Yellow Orb, military spec suspension, Denon floating molecular lasac. Single read only, but that's all we need. You're the only one going to access.''

''I hope that is enough.'' Ooljee's fingers danced over the board.

A miniature of the Kettrick sandpainting appeared on the unfolded screen, the details so fine that only their familiarity with the design enabled them to recognize individual features. Ooljee sat and chanted, his hand outstretched, while the tormented wind shuddered around them, and across the canyon the glistening black oval continued to gnaw at the earth.

Moody tried to divide his attention between the disk and the interlocked spinners. If the intruder grew much larger, it would engulf the motor home and the hogan. That would not be such a bad thing, he reflected, unless the disk remained behind, a manifestation only a vanished Gaggii could deal with.

Where was it all going, the disappearing rocks and trees and sand? To another world circling another star? Or perhaps another dimension, or a big room chock full of rainbow threads and mysterious sparkling lights? Or was everything simply funneled into the vastness between the stars, to suffer instant desiccation? Moody was scared, real scared, more scared than he'd been on that day ten years ago in Sarasota when a ninloco dealer outgrabed on sizzle had stuck a needler to the back of the detective's head and threatened to fry his brains.

Instead it was the dealer who'd been blown away, by another cop on the stakeout. Vernon Moody straightened and sucked it in. He hadn't survived that moment only to be ingested now by some berserk alien Indian Navaho fairy tale.

The tiny screen was alive with rainbow filaments: rainbow power, Ooljee had called it. Fulgurant lights danced around the threads, darting through the blackness, while incomprehensible patterns whirled and exploded on the fold-out screen.

"It's so small," Grayhills murmured.

Easy enough to check though, Ooljee knew. Shoving his hand into the screen, he let the tingling warmth of the web briefly caress his flesh. He withdrew it confidently.

"We're in." He stared at Grayhills. "But where do we go?"

"Look!"

As Moody's gaze rose from the screen he noted that the wind was no longer blowing across the canyon. Instead it was now blasting toward them, making his own hair and (much more impressively) that of Samantha Grayhills' stream out behind their heads. No longer the fresh, dry air of the high plateau, it carried with it a powerful musky odor he could not identify.

Air from elsewhere, he thought. Air and fine particles that tickled his nostrils and made him want to sneeze. Behind it an intimation of something *huge*. His skin grew cold and the small hairs on the back of his neck bristled.

He saw Grayhills staring in the same direction. "You feel it too?" he asked softly, simultaneously wondering why he was whispering. She nodded. "What is it?"

"I don't know." Her eyes dropped to the linked spinners. "We would have to ask Yistin Gaggii."

"I don't think that crazy bastard knows either," Moody

growled. He was frightened and angry and frustrated. "The ant is playing with the garbage and he doesn't care about the consequences. He just wants to see what it will do." He squinted at the cliff, straining to see deeper into the disk.

"There's something in there. Big Monster, Big Thunder; something out of your collective cultural memory. It's in there and it's trying to get out."

"Come through," Ooljee corrected him. "There: you can see it, a little!"

Immense it was, and amorphous. A slowly solidifying shape. Was that because it was near and gradually taking on a recognizable outline, or very far away and slowly coming closer? Would it stop when it reached the causal boundary that was the disk, or step out into the canyon? Moody could not imagine, because he could not envision it.

What if it was Big Monster, whatever that was, coming back? Called back to Hot Water to again make the world an unfit place for human beings, to once more destroy them as fast as they could be made? How could they stop anything like that, something from beyond time and place?

If the web was responsible for bringing it forth, then to the web they must resort to deal with it. What had Ooljee told him, ages ago? About *Na'a-tse-elit*—no, that was the rainbow guardian. Something or someone called Monster Slayer? He couldn't remember the Navaho name, but wasn't that the entity responsible for the destruction of the terrible monsters of legend, the *yei-tso*? The same one who had told hatathlis that the gods drew on sheets of sky but that man could use powdered rock and sand (and rare-earth masking?). Was that what was responsible for the garbage that was the web?

He unburdened himself of that and more to Ooljee, only to discover that his friend had been suffering similar thoughts.

"The key has to be in the painting somewhere." The

sergeant stared at the monitor as if the sheer intensity of his desire might provoke a response, a suggestion. "The Four Sacred Mountains. The danger you don't know."

He started talking to the spinners, chanting so fast his words were incomprehensible even to Grayhills. The web replied in Navaho; guttural, rhythmic, vocomposite phrases.

Grayhills put her fingers to her lips, her eyes wide as she stared across the canyon. "Hurry. Oh, God, hurry."

The disk had become the color of dried blood. Within that otherworldly circular frame of impossibility something monstrous and swollen was trying to get out. Ooljee's voice rose in pitch.

Suddenly the horrid shape contracted, turning sideways and shrinking abruptly to half its former size. Moody gaped. There was something else in the skyhole, another outline as vast as the first. It flared and pulsed with shattered lightning as it clashed with its titanic counterpart. Brilliant rainbow bursts exploded from the disk, searing the earth black where they struck, instantly carbonizing anything organic they came in contact with.

"Get down!" Moody flattened his bulk against the dirt and his companions did likewise. Burnt air whistled overhead, fleeing the disk, seeking escape from the confines of the canyon.

The alien forms writhed and boiled like antagonistic oils confined to a glass jar. Squinting into flying sand and grit, Moody watched as the perfect orb of the skyhole began to buckle. Concavities took neat bites out of its rim.

"What did you do?" he roared at his partner.

Ooljee lay shielding the conjoined spinners with his body. "What we discussed!" He indicated the unstable disk. "*Nayenezgani!* Son of Changing Woman, Monster Slayer, who wears the flint armor and fights with the crooked lightning. Or maybe it is his brother *Tobaschischin*, Born of Water. Perhaps both of them are fighting Big Monster." He caught his breath. "Or perhaps what we are seeing is disruption in the database. Maybe Big Monster is a virus of some kind, and Nayenezgani a Restore program.''

"It's hard," said Grayhills, "to give a name to something you don't understand."

So enthralled and terrified were they by the scene within the disk, they forgot whence it had originated.

The door to the hogan burst open and a lone figure came running out, turning circles as it shouted at the canyon walls. For the first time, Yistin Gaggii was neither composed nor in control.

"Get out!" he screamed at his unseen tormentors. "Get out of the web!" He ignored the disk as though it didn't exist.

As Gaggii raised something to his shoulder, Moody voiced a choice expletive and dragged Grayhills down. A burst of automatic weapons fire scattered sand in front of them.

"Get away!" Gaggii was running toward them now. They lay exposed on the slope, with no cover nearby.

Raising himself onto his elbows, the detective sighted down the barrel of his pistol and fired off half a clip. A startled Gaggii cut to his right and returned the shots wildly. In the depths of the canyon the gunfire sounded tinny and toylike, masked by the driving wind.

Moody lifted his head again, but Gaggii had disappeared. "Damn! Where'd he go?"

"I think he is down in the creek bed." Ooljee was trying to aim his own weapon while simultaneously shielding the spinners. "We will be lucky to hit him at this range."

"Yeah, but he doesn't know that. What's he got?"

Fresh fire sent gravel skipping over their heads.

"Looks like a Provalis Ruger. Cannot tell for sure."

"Self-seeking shells?"

"I doubt it, or he would have used them by now. We cannot stay here. We are too exposed."

"Tell me something I don't know."

Gaggii's anxious voice filled the pause in the gunfire. "You must go away! You do not know what you are doing!"

Moody raised his head. "Who the hell says you do?" For his trouble he had to duck another burst of automatic fire.

"You are breaking *hozho*, *bilagaanna*! You have upset the balance. You—!"

Moody roared back, interrupting him. "*Who's* disturbed the balance? What the hell do you call *this*?"

Ooljee raised his head, pointed. "Something is changing."

The disk was slipping. No longer stable, it was sliding slowly downslope like glycerin on Teflon. Within the circle the violently clashing outlines were still visible.

The sergeant was on his feet, heedless of however their assailant might choose to react. "Run. Get up and run. Don't you see what's happening?" Moody wasn't sure that he did, but if he had learned anything in the past weeks, it was that it was best to follow his partner's lead in such matters. With a grunt, he stumbled erect.

Independent of wind or storm, stone or guidance, the disk continued its drift down into the canyon, swallowing huge chunks of earth and gravel along the way. When it reached the bottom it halted and began to tip over, falling in extreme slow motion. The gale howling out of the dark maw intensified.

Peering back into the canyon, Moody saw Yistin Gaggii rise from his place of concealment in the creek bed, throw away his gun, and begin to run toward his pursuers. He was looking over his shoulder, back and up at the falling, falling disk. That embattled circle of night was rotating on some unknown, unseen axis, responding to forces beyond ken or control, slicing through reality like a circular blade as it fell. The tops of a pair of big cottonwoods began to vanish into it.

The wormhole turns, Moody thought madly as he sought

to increase his pace. Gravel and sand slipped from beneath his boots, threatening to send him tumbling.

Ooljee and Grayhills reached out to help him up the last few feet. Breathing hard, the three of them looked on in horrified fascination at the drama unfolding below. Gaggii was running for his life, running hard, sand flying from his heels. Panic had replaced anger on his face. The disk was collapsing atop him. He ran harder. He would escape its radii. He would not. Would, would not. Would . . .

With a yelp of despair Yistin Gaggii threw himself forward as the disk came perfectly parallel to the floor of the canyon. Moody saw him vanish beneath the outer edge: not crushed, but silently absorbed, swept up, inhaled along with the hogan, the motor home, the solar pyramid and satellite dish, innumerable bushes, rocks, boulders, and smaller insect and reptilian lives.

Standing on the rim of the canyon they found themselves gazing down into a circular black lake. Nothing moved on its surface. But within, the universe itself was in turmoil. Or the database. Gaggii was gone: gone with his dreams and aspirations, his spinners and mollys, his misplaced self-assurance and homicidal indifference. He didn't matter anymore. All that mattered was the conflict he had left behind, some kind of unimaginable contest for supremacy that might be taking place a few dozen yards below their feet or halfway across the cosmos. Within the disk gods, programs, aliens, or something they could not give a name to, struggled and contested.

The ants stood nearby and watched helplessly.

Grayhills grabbed his arm and pointed excitedly, but she didn't need to point. Moody saw it as soon as she did.

The disk was beginning to shrink.

Soon it occupied less than half the canyon bottom. Where it retreated, the surface was as clean and bare as the lens of a camera. It continued to contract until only a black circle the size of a tire remained. Then it was the size of a dinner plate.

Still inhaling dust and dirt, it irised out to infinity.

Released to confusion, the amazing storm which had led them to this place began to shudder and dissipate. Clouds broke up and evaporated. Wind tore the walls of the hurricane eye to pieces, then sought refuge in arroyos and gullies. Moody clutched at his ears as the barometric pressure rose with astonishing speed.

Below, a section of canyon two hundred yards in diameter had been wiped smooth. No pebble marred its perfect surface, no creosote or mesquite poked its desiccated crown skyward. Flowing down from the north, the lonely little stream spread out in all directions, searching in vain for a course to follow as it sought to reclaim a momentarily forgotten corner of the planet.

Samantha Grayhills gazed at the exposed strata; white Coconino and dark red Kaibab sandstone.

"It looks like the setting in a necklace. It looks like—" she struggled for the right analogy, the right word.

"It looks like *hozho*," said Vernon Moody in his easy southern drawl. "Balance and stability, thank God."

Feeling suddenly very tired, Grayhills sat down on the edge of the slope and wiped at her wild, rain-slicked hair.

"It saved us. Maybe saved everything." She squinted at Ooljee. "Whatever it was you called up saved us."

The sergeant shrugged. He was thinking of his wife, of the warmth of her against him in bed at night. Of his boys, making trouble and smiles.

"*Haal hootiid.* Who knows what happened? Maybe we had nothing to do with it. Maybe something decided it was time to pick up garbage that had started to stink." He put down what he had so diligently shielded against Gaggii's fire.

Moody found himself staring intently at the still active, still glowing monitor of the mated spinners. After a moment's hesitation he rose and raised his foot over them.

"That won't make it go away." Ooljee spoke softly. "I have been thinking. It will only delay things. Maybe the next person to learn the secret will be another Gaggii. One who might proceed more cautiously, without leaving behind dead people to draw attention to himself, but one with similar dangerous ambitions. Or it might be some brilliant kid who would do irreversible damage before anyone had any idea what was happening."

Moody put his foot down—alongside the spinners. *That was the trouble with knowledge*, he mused. *Once acquired, it was so damn difficult to destroy.* The Middle Ages hadn't been able to wipe out science. What made him think he could stomp the web into nonexistence? As physicists delved deeper and deeper into the construction of the cosmos they were bound to stumble into the web eventually, with or without the clues provided by the sandpainting.

Grayhills was gazing thoughtfully at the screen. "I wonder: if you knew how, what else could you access through there? Holy People? *Yei-tsos*, aliens, creatures that live in the web itself? Those drifting patterns and lights: what do they represent? Worlds, living beings, or abstracts?"

Moody snorted, flung a rock into the canyon. It did not travel far enough to mar the unnaturally smooth plain at the bottom.

"Maybe you could access a 'delete' button. Ever think of that? 'Have fun, amuse your friends.' Delete 'em. Or maybe there's a command for deleting something else. Like the Earth." He threw another stone, harder. The pain that shot up his arm was real, reassuring.

She refused to let him discourage her. "If you could make a wormhole do what you wanted it to, if you could control its position, it would make travel between worlds as simple and easy as crossing the street."

"Yeah," grumbled Moody. "Think about that for a minute."

They were distracted by the *whirr* of rotors overhead. Someone had located the downed skycutter's emergency beacon. Soon they would be found. Then they would have to explain themselves, not to mention the perfectly round polished basin below.

"The only problem with having a wormhole to step through," Ooljee observed quietly, "is that something else can step through from the other side."

"Not if we learn how to control it, how to manipulate it." Grayhills came up behind Moody and began kneading his shoulders with her strong fingers. At first he tensed, then allowed himself to relax, letting her work on the stiff muscles. "Something did, once."

"You're not arguing fair," Moody objected mildly, feeling the tension ease out of his shoulders. "Where'd you learn how to do this? Not off a molly."

"You'd be surprised what you have to learn while working Security."

"Who, me? A dumb cop?"

"Why does it please you to describe yourself that way?"

He offered no comment.

"I wonder what we might find if we subjected some other sandpaintings to the kind of analysis we put the Kettrick through?" Ooljee said. Moody looked up sharply. "Some of the paintings that are used in the Shooting Way or Blessing Way. I wonder if Grandfather Laughter worked with them too?"

His partner indicated the still flickering fold-out screen. "Don't you think the offspring of one Way is enough to deal with for a while?"

The sergeant looked over at him. "Other paintings, other clues. Perhaps other universes."

"Something else I don't understand," said Moody. "Why you? I mean, not you personally, but why the Navaho? Why did these aliens or whatever decide to pick on you, whether accidentally or on purpose?"

Ooljee rose, scanned the sky for signs of approaching rescue craft. "Maybe they liked the country. If you were coming in via a ship or wormhole or whatever, wouldn't you choose an interesting part of the planet to study? There are not many planetary features visible from a distance. The Grand Canyon is one of them, and it is right over there." He gestured to the northwest.

"Besides, people have been dumping their garbage on the Reservation for a long time. Why should these visitors have been any different?" He walked over to the lip of the canyon, stared down at the newly planed, perfectly flat bottom. The creek was spreading out to form a shallow pond.

"The ants have found the spray can. Devoutly as I would like to, I am afraid that we cannot just ignore it."

Returning to the mated spinners he moved to separate them, paused. Thoughtfully he inserted his fingers into the monitor to disturb drifting rainbows.

Moody watched him, admiring the play of patterns and colors within the screen. They were beautiful. Not just threatening and inspiring and dangerous, but truly beautiful. Maybe Ooljee was right. Maybe there was much in there worth seeking. Given time and hard work and care, might not the ants aspire to understanding?

A curious Grayhills leaned over his shoulder. "What are you grinning at, mister detective? You look like the coyote who has just made off with the chicken."

"I was thinking about one possibility we've been considering. What if we really are components of this database? If that's the case, won't it be interesting for whoever built it, when we start learning how to manipulate it ourselves?"

She considered. "The revolt of the bytes? Is such a thing possible? Bytes do what they're programmed to do. They can't act of their volition."

"Maybe we've developed beyond what the makers of the

web imagined. Maybe we're the virus in *their* programming.''

''I hope not,'' said Ooljee. ''They may have programs designed to combat viruses.''

Moody was warming to his subject. ''What if we're an unexpected factor, something new?''

''I always thought there was a purpose to mankind's existence,'' Ooljee replied, ''but not as a virus.''

''We'll find out.'' Moody eyed the glowing monitor, excited by the prospect it presented, no longer afraid of what they might find when they went aweaving in its unfathomable depths.

They would learn how to use the alien web, how to bend it to their own needs. And if it turned out that man was merely one component of some immense database, why, he was going to have an impact all out of proportion to his designated size.

''I don't think anything will notice us for a while,'' he murmured. ''After all, we don't count for much on the cosmic scale. But eventually we'll make ourselves known.''

''That might be a good thing,'' Ooljee declared slowly, ''or it might not.''

''*Hozho.*'' Moody grinned at his partner. ''We'll have to proceed cautiously, much more carefully than did Gaggii. But proceed we must. It's the way we're programmed. The curious bytes, that's us. I don't think we'll be excised for exercising our internal programming. We might even surprise some people.''

''What people?''

Moody nodded at the monitor, with its silently twisting rainbow threads and soft explosions and pulsing fractal patterns waiting to be understood.

''Whoever is responsible for that.''

He glanced up and over his shoulder. A pair of skycutters were coming toward them, muttering out of the south. Grayhills scrambled to her feet and started waving while Ooljee stood next to her, resting his hands on his hips.

Moody rose slowly, bending to brush dirt and sand from his pants. While his companions watched the approaching aircraft, he ambled over to the mated spinners and gazed down into the depths of the screen, staring thoughtfully at the foot-square image of infinity. If he raised his foot again and put it down, would he fall in, fall forever? Or would something eventually materialize to halt his plunge?

Kneeling, he sang softly to the monitor, was delighted when the dark display gave way to a picture of a sandpainting. He admired it for a moment, the regularity of it, the neat lines and clean schematics. Then he traced outlines with a finger, nodding with satisfaction when the lizards moved and the painting was replaced by a blank screen.

He turned off the power to Grayhills' spinner, then his partner's. The monitor folded neatly back into place. A quick finger-twist disconnected the units. Hefting one in each hand he rejoined his companions. The purr of the skycutters was loud in his ears now.

Grayhills took her spinner without a word. Moody turned to his friend and handed over the other. The two men exchanged a long look of understanding. Paul Ooljee turned the device over in his fingers, inspecting it, appreciating it anew. A smile spread over his face. It wasn't as broad or open as Grayhills', but it could not be denied.

Standing alongside the big man from Florida as they monitored the descent of the nearest skycutter, the sergeant deftly and matter-of-factly clipped the universe back onto his belt.

Author's Note

WHILE THE SPELLING *Navajo* is most common in the South-west, *Navaho* is also used. I have used the latter, since the correct pronunciation is "Nah-vah-hoh" not "Nah-vah-joe."

Sandpainting is often referred to as "drypainting." The former is a more literal description of this unique Native American artform. For readers who would like to view excellent samplings of sandpainting both modern and traditional accompanied by nontechnical text, the following slim volumes are recommended:

Reichard, Gladys, *Navajo Medicine Man Sand Paintings*. New York, Dover Publications, 1977.

Joe, Eugene Baatsoslanii (with Mark Bahti), *Navajo Sandpainting Art*. Tucson, Ariz., Treasure Chest Publications, 1978.

McCoy, Ronald, "Summoning the Gods." *Plateau* magazine of the Museum of Northern Arizona, Flagstaff, Ariz., Vol. 59.

The Navaho phrase "*doo ahashyaa da*" means "I am stupid."

CLASSIC SCIENCE FICTION
AND FANTASY

__**DUNE Frank Herbert** 0-441-17266-0/$4.95
The bestselling novel of an awesome world where gods and adventurers clash, mile-long sandworms rule the desert, and the ancient dream of immortality comes true.

__**STRANGER IN A STRANGE LAND Robert A. Heinlein**
0-441-79034-8/$4.95
From the *New York Times* bestselling author—the science fiction masterpiece of a man from Mars who teaches humankind the art of grokking, watersharing and love.

__**THE ONCE AND FUTURE KING T.H. White**
0-441-62740-4/$5.50
The world's greatest fantasy classic! A magical epic of King Arthur in Camelot, romance, wizardry and war. By the author of *The Book of Merlyn*.

__**THE LEFT HAND OF DARKNESS Ursula K. LeGuin**
0-441-47812-3/$3.95
Winner of the Hugo and Nebula awards for best science fiction novel of the year. "SF masterpiece!"—*Newsweek* "A Jewel of a story."—Frank Herbert

__**MAN IN A HIGH CASTLE Philip K. Dick** 0-441-51809-5/$3.95
"Philip K. Dick's best novel, a masterfully detailed alternate world peopled by superbly realized characters."
—Harry Harrison

279